THESE
VIOLENT
DELIGHTS

ALSO BY SHARON LINNÉA

FICTION:
Chasing Eden • Beyond Eden • Treasure of Eden

NONFICTION:
Lost Civilizations
Princess Kaiulani: Hope Of A Nation, Heart Of A People
Raoul Wallenberg: The Man Who Stopped Death

THESE
VIOLENT
DELIGHTS

SHARON LINNÉA

Arundel
PUBLISHING

THESE VIOLENT DELIGHTS
Copyright © 2012 by Sharon Linnéa
Book design by Christian Fuenfhausen
All rights reserved.
For information:
Arundel Publishing,
P.O. Box 377, Warwick, NY 10990
ArundelPublishing.com
ISBN 978-1-933608-60-0
First Edition: May 2012
Printed in the United States of America

10 9 8 7 6 5 4 3 2 1

*For the writers, directors, and actors
who have given us so many hours of entertainment,
and so many characters we feel we know so very well.
Thanks.*

These violent delights have violent ends
And in their triumph die, like fire and powder,
Which as they kiss consume.

—William Shakespeare,
Romeo and Juliet (II.6.9–11)

THESE
VIOLENT
DELIGHTS

FROM The New York Daily News, MARCH 12:

TRISTAN AND ISOLDE *was one of those films that defined a generation. The final masterpiece of acclaimed actor/director Pierce Hall, who directed and played King Mark, it influenced fashions, music, and hairstyles. (Admit it, ladies, who among us didn't have a silk-weave dress with princess lines, and several gold chain belts that rode the hip)? It also propelled the actors who played the lovers, Anastasia Day and Peter Dalton—apparently a major love story themselves—to international stardom.*

A story of passion and political corruption, it held an uncanny mirror up to the "Me Decade" of the '80s, and a social and political system that touted optimism, materialism, and "trickle down" even as the gap widened between rich and poor.

Will it play as well in the new millennium?

*Paramount is betting it will. The film, never available on DVD, will have a major theatrical re-release in honor of its 20*th *anniversary. Oddly enough, princess-line dresses are making a comeback in the fashion world.*

But I refuse to wear them with platform shoes.

—syndicated columnist Cynthia Anderson

3

PROLOGUE

On what was to be the last evening of her life, Jane Whittle left the studio at 7:13 p.m. Traffic was slow going over the hill, and she briefly entertained her daily fantasy of working on a show that taped on location north of L.A., as more and more of them seemed to do. But her specialty had become extraterrestrials, and somehow alien life forms always headed straight for West Hollywood. She snaked along the Ventura Freeway past Coldwater Canyon, edging her Prius into the right-hand lane just after Sepulveda.

Jane was, in fact, content. Work was steady; she had a reputation for being one of the most creative makeup artists in L.A. Earthquakes and fires she could do without, but she reveled in the thought that this was March and her car windows were closed due to smog, not temperature. This time of year in London—she shivered remembering the looming gray skies, the dampness that penetrated your bones. Here, she had gardenias blooming in her backyard.

She made the turnoff onto 405 North, following it briefly to Sherman Way. She smiled as she turned onto a side street, then off into the parking lot of La Tureen, her favorite spot for gourmet takeout. Outrageously pricey, yes, but the soups and homemade specialties were to die for. She was a firm believer in treating herself, especially after a hard day's work.

As she locked the car, she heard her name.

"Why—Jane. It is Jane, isn't it?"

She looked up to see an old acquaintance just exiting La Tureen, carrying two green and white shopping bags laden with gourmet food.

"By the saints," Jane said, squinting to make certain she wasn't imagining things, "what a coincidence to run into you today."

"Coincidence?"

"Yes, I spent the whole day on the lot discussing *Tristan and Isolde*. Everyone read in today's trades about the re-release; it was all they could talk about. When they heard I worked on *T & I*, they wanted to know all about it," she chuckled. "That film made most of them decide to go into the business, to hear them talk. Oh—sorry. Here I am, running on, and you with food getting cold."

"No, no," said her companion. "I'm in no rush. The *foie gras* here's *magnifique*, so I try to pick some up when I can. And when I do—" the bags were lifted, their weight tested, "I'm afraid I go overboard. Dinner for twelve, and it's just me."

"Can't blame you," agreed Jane. "It's delightful. No one uses saffron in quite the same way." She was feeling heady at being recognized after all this time.

"It would make me feel less foolish if I could persuade you to share the bounty with me."

Jane felt herself blush, actually blush, with pleasure. Certainly she felt comfortable working with different types of people, but this was a real overture of friendship, giving her the feeling she was above-the-line, inside the loop.

"Is there anything else I can pick up while we're here?" she asked.

"I think I've emptied their larder already. Do you know of anywhere nearby we could spread out?"

"Why, my place, of course," said Jane, trying to remember if she'd put away the snack tray after last night's television viewing. "I'm a couple of blocks away."

"If it's really no trouble. I'd hate to put you out."

"None a-tall! Really."

"Shall I hop in with you? I'm sure they won't mind if I leave my car here for an hour."

"It would be my pleasure."

Jane was relieved to find she had indeed straightened up before leaving at dawn. The small house was polished and shiny. She hummed through the kitchen, bringing a lavender vase of yellow Devon roses into the small dining room for a centerpiece.

The piquant aromas of basil and ginger emerged as the strong winners as containers were opened.

"Start with the soup, shall we?" asked Jane, folding navy cloth napkins under the heavy silver. "I'll give us appetizer plates for the brioche."

"You're the boss. I was planning paper plates."

"And for the wine?" Jane asked. "I do have a nice Bordeaux."

"Perfect."

"All this talk of *Tristan* has opened a floodgate of memories for me—as I'm sure it has for you." Jane smiled to herself. "Do you hear anything of Lily—Anastasia Day? I keep meaning to write, but I'd hate to bother her." She brought in the wine and sat down, indicating her guest should do the same. Even as she said it, Jane knew the truth was that she was terrified to risk discovering that Anastasia had forgotten her. That would break her heart. She'd rather protect her memories and not know.

"I'm afraid I haven't heard anything—at least, not recently. But how about you? Here's the question you undoubtedly get all the time: are the inhabitants of that Wild West ghost town actually dead, hermaphrodites, or aliens?" her guest asked of Jane's current series.

Jane chuckled. "All I know for sure is they're on HBO." Her companion was polite enough to feign interest in the anecdotes that came with the show's strange assignments for the cast's makeup. But as Jane described the makeup department, of which she was head, she realized in a flash of revelation that her assistants were incompetent. And she needed to order some new forehead moldings, but the producer had prohibited it. That got her goat. Did he want the inhabitants of *Ghosttown* to look like dime-store trick-or-treaters, or the proud race that they were? The thought made her head throb.

"Forgive me," she said with a short laugh. "None of this is your problem. The brioche is thrilling. There must be fennel in the sausage, don't you think?"

A wave of heat pulsed through Jane's body, flushing her face and arms. *Oh dear*, she thought. *Take a sip of wine. Sit and breathe . . .*

But as the hot flashes intensified, the room began to tilt. Candles flickered wildly and went out. Darkness shrouded her. *What on earth?*

Jane stood, knocking her chair over behind her. She tried to lurch away, but the room was tilting and she felt vomit rising in her throat. Was it an earthquake? No—it was a thing, a presence. She knew because when it grabbed her, it had a sour, evil breath . . . and it had hands. Hands that held thick silver steel blades.

Jane couldn't move. It was as if she'd turned to stone. But her flesh was still soft; she could tell because it tore so easily as the monster before her drove the daggers into her abdomen. With each thrust, a blade of pain coursed the length of her body.

"No!" she shrieked. "No, no, no!"

Her last thought was, *I don't want to die like this.*

And then she was dead.

PART ONE:

AWAKENING

CHAPTER 1

HAVE YOU HEARD? *Richard Riley has signed on to host the* Tristan and Isolde *reunion festivities that will coincide with the re-release of the film. As you recall, T & I was the Oscar-winner's first feature. Paramount is undoubtedly thrilled to have the megastar on board. . . .*

Anastasia Huntington, Duchess of Esmonde, glanced at the review of a new action film next to the "Insider" column of *Daily Variety* before continuing to turn the glossy white pages. Evening shadows cast purple fingers across the golden scrolling in the antique Chinese carpet beneath her satin slippers. Ads for post-production houses and full pages of congratulation to actors whose names she didn't recognize for winning awards she didn't know existed, surrounded articles detailing deals done. She'd once had an amused familiarity with the slang and sentiments set forth in the industry paper, but now it seemed like an artifact from some strange, foreign civilization.

And then, in black boldface, she saw a name she knew: Jane Whittle. She scanned the top of the page, and gave a small gasp when she found the heading to be "Obituaries."

"No," she whispered. "Oh, no."

Jane Whittle, veteran makeup artist, died March 26 of a heart attack in Reseda. She was 53.

At the time of her death, she headed the department for the HBO series Ghosttown. *She began her career in theater in London. Her first film was* Tristan and Isolde. *Among her Stateside credits were* Justin Tyme, The Loves of Archie Leghorn, *and* Deadly Delight. *She became well known for creating alien makeup for* Saturn Inset, *and went on to head the teams for several TV series, including* Moons of Mercury *and* Frank.

"Oh, Janie," Anastasia whispered. "Oh, Janie, no!"

A familiar melancholy seized her, a version of that which mourned the loss of afternoon fading to evening or autumn into winter. She stood and paced restlessly across her sitting room to the casement window. Perhaps morose thoughts were to be expected in a five months' widow. But as she tipped her forehead to the cold pane, her thoughts weren't of her late husband.

She traced the word "Jane" with her finger. Another ally gone. Too many . . . gone.

There was a tapping at the heavy oak door: one long knock, two short. "Yes, Bertie," she sighed, "what is it?"

The door swung inward and a tall, stout woman edging toward sixty marched in. When Anastasia had first come to Castle Dunmore, she'd been easily cowed by Mrs. McGowan. The woman was six feet tall, always pristinely dressed—ironing was her specialty—with every dark gray hair pinned tightly in place. The intervening years had shown that Bertie—diminutive for Alberta—was considerably more bark than bite. But she still towered.

Anastasia pushed at her braid of thick strawberry blonde hair, knowing that compared to Bertie's it must be going astray somewhere.

"Good evening, Your Grace. Cook has announced supper in

twenty minutes," she said. "In the meantime, there's a call for you from California." She nodded toward the cordless phone on the desk. "It's Mrs. Demetrius."

"Thank you," Anastasia said. "Tell Cook and Geoff that I'll be down." She picked up the receiver as the housekeeper gave a small bob and closed the door behind her.

"Hello, Celia," she said.

"Interesting news, darling."

"Thanks for the *Daily Variety* you sent. I was just—"

"This is something else altogether. We're not even going to talk *T & I*. I'm existing in a pretend world in which you're not only going to the reunion, but looking forward to it."

"Uh—"

"Later. I got a call from Evan Masterson's office." There followed a brief pause. "Evan Masterson. You have heard of him? I'm going on the assumption you're in England, not dead. There is a difference? Help me out here, Stacy."

"Evan Masterson? Sorry, I—"

"The television mastermind. He's created half the hit series in the last ten years. Quality. Production values. He's batting eight out of ten. Nobody bats eight out of ten."

"TV mastermind. Got it."

"He's got another show on the drawing board. His all-time favorite, he says. He plans to shoot the pilot in three or four months, and he's got a six-episode commitment from the network, certain to go to thirteen."

"Bully for him."

"He wants you. For one of the two leads. Strong, modern woman. Just the sort of part that will get you back in the game. He doesn't even want you to test, only to meet with him."

Anastasia sat heavily back in the brocade chair stationed beside the desk.

Celia went on, "I know Neville's death was hard. Pardon me for saying so, but I think it might help things for you to get back out, into the swing of things."

"I can't just pack up and go to L.A.—"

"You don't have to. Masterson's flying to London as we speak, on another project. He'll be at the Carlisle."

Anastasia felt her heart accelerate. She pictured the blood pulsing through her forehead in a rush. She sat silently until she trusted her voice. "I can't," she said.

"Tell me why."

"It's not a good time."

Her agent's husky voice had a note of irritation. "Stacy, you never leave that darn castle. Why do you even have an agent?"

"Because you won't leave me alone."

"Trust me, darling. You don't meet with Masterson, consider I've finally gotten the message."

Anastasia's grip on the phone turned her knuckles white.

"I'll take your eloquent silence to mean you're thinking about it. Talk to you soon."

And the line went dead.

Anastasia clicked the receiver button to the off position and went limp in the chair. Her head continued to pound, as it always did when she felt compelled to try to explain her hibernation—something for which there *was* no rational explanation.

She didn't know how long she'd sat in the waning daylight before the brassy tinkle of the dinner bell interrupted her reverie. She sighed, knowing it would cause more trouble than it was worth if she decided not to go down.

Anastasia didn't hear the voices jostling in conversation until she had opened the dining room door; she remembered too late that Geoff and Cathy had guests.

They were already seated in the dark-paneled room, awaiting

her. "Duchess," said Cathy, and the men all stood as she walked to the empty chair at Geoff's right hand. She flashed a demur smile at the guests—three men and a woman.

"Good evening," said Geoff, as he pulled her chair and saw her seated.

"We've poured the wine, well, hell, let's dine," intoned the gentleman on Anastasia's left. He held his goblet aloft in toast, and they all joined in. The conversation restarted and the first trolley arrived from the kitchen.

Anastasia was grateful they didn't try to involve her. Something continued to nag at her. Yes, Celia's call had made her anxious, and of course, Jane . . . Jane's death brought on a melancholy. But there was something else, something deeper. A thread that ran back through time that was becoming impossible to ignore.

Her stepson Geoff now sat at the head of the table, his wife Catherine at the foot—which had been Anastasia's place until five months earlier. Both the title and the castle had passed to Geoff on his father's death. Neville's will stipulated that Anastasia had a home and stipend until her death or remarriage, both of which seemed as unwelcome as they were unlikely.

She quietly studied the new Duke of Esmonde where he sat next to her. He was tall with a muscular build, what was called strapping in days not long past. His best feature was his hair: brownish red, thick and curly. His eyes were small and dull brown, and he didn't have much of a chin. Yet Geoff was in good form for thirty-nine. She wondered how much, not if, he resented her. She certainly had never counted on having a stepson near her own age. She was sure she'd been a surprise to him as well.

Anastasia allowed herself to glance into the mirror that hung along the opposite wall. Her face had looked hollow and triangular since the funeral, especially when rimmed by her profusion of red-gold hair. In the dim light, her green eyes appeared larger and darker than they actually were, and her nose, which she always considered too long and pointed, seemed fine from head-on. It was the angle she preferred. Pierce Hall had loved her pointed nose and high forehead. "They're what make you interesting," he'd said.

"What shall we do after dinner?" Cathy asked from her end of the table.

"Billiards, of course," Geoff answered his wife, "although I know one of your favorite films is on the telly."

"*Eclipse*," Cathy said, leaning in to the female guest. "Have you seen it?"

"Of course," the woman replied. "It's a classic. I could watch it over and over," she added quickly.

"Settled then. We'll send you gents off to brandy and billiards, like in the old days."

The film title caught Anastasia's attention. *Eclipse* was a thriller, one of the first written by renowned screenwriter Bruce Amerman. Bruce had been an actor in his youth, before he turned to writing. He, too, had been in *T & I*. She had counted him a friend.

Thinking of Bruce brought Anastasia's mind again to the planned reunion of the cast of *Tristan and Isolde*. The thought of it now made her terribly sad. Jane's obituary only underscored how things had changed in twenty years. Pierce, Garrett, Gray . . . how many people from the original cast and crew were gone.

How many were gone. Anastasia froze, her spoon halfway to her lips.

It was as if her subconscious had worked out some giant puzzle, fitting all the pieces together, and when the picture was done, had presented it to her conscious mind as incontrovertible fact. Her heavy silver spoon clattered as it hit the lip of the soup bowl.

Dear God, she thought. It was as if with her discovery, the oxygen in the room had been halved. Her mind raced. If her terrible conjecture was true, what should she do? To whom should she turn? And now, as she fought to catch her breath, there was a more immediate question.

How could she get out of that room?

There was warm breath on her ear and she jumped.

"Beg pardon." It was Reginald, the butler. "Telephone, Your Grace. A Miss Hall."

"Thank you," Anastasia said. "I'll take it."

Reginald pulled back the carved chair, and she forced herself to walk calmly from the room. Once alone in the chilly front drawing room, however, she raced for the phone.

"Hello?"

"Hello," said the voice on the other end. "I'm doing a piece for *Vanity Fair* called 'Titled and Available.' I was hoping you could give me a quick rundown of any jewels or other holdings?"

"So you've been reduced to personality journalism," Anastasia joked back. "Leah, I'm so sorry!" She breathed a sigh of relief. The banter was exactly what she needed to break the terrible tension.

There was a crystal laugh on the other end as Her Grace walked over and sank onto an eighteenth-century settee.

"Not quite yet. So, Stace, how are you?"

"Still here. How are you? Have you finished post-production on *Eliza and Elroy?*"

"Just about. I'm afraid the critics are going to think this one is really deep, when all it is is really weird. But I've made a living at fooling them thus far."

Anastasia smiled at her friend's assessment of her slightly strange but surprisingly successful directing career. She could picture Pierce Hall's daughter reclining in her Spanish villa in the Malibu Colony, eight time zones away. She wondered if her blue-black hair was still cut short, framing her face. Anastasia felt momentarily young and foolish.

"So, has the Dragon Lady of Hollywood talked you into coming to the reunion?" Leah went on.

"You mean Celia? I don't know."

"What will a *Tristan and Isolde* reunion be without Isolde?"

"The same thing it will be without Tristan, I presume. Or your dad. Sorry, I don't mean to be flip. Will you be very disappointed if I don't go?"

"Stace, I have faith in the fact that Daddy's last film was a masterpiece. What shenanigans the studio comes up with to get press coverage are of little concern to me."

The Duchess of Esmonde breathed a sigh of relief. But Leah Hall was pressing on.

"What I do want you to do is meet with Evan Masterson."

Anastasia hadn't seen this one coming. "What?"

"Meet with the man, for pity's sake. Talk to him about his precious series."

"Did Celia put you up to this?"

"No. I put Evan up to it."

"What?"

"I was sitting next to him on my way back to L.A. last week. I love first class. It's such a club. Anyhow, he was blathering on about his new television series, and truth to tell, it did sound pretty good. He ran down the list of available actresses, all of them predictable. So I told him that the most talented, interesting actress that he could hope to get was you."

Anastasia threw herself dramatically back on the loveseat. "Why did you do that?"

"Because you *are* the most talented, interesting actress he could get. And because you are an actress, Stace, and you need to work before you forget it."

"Oh, brother."

"You're welcome. Jeez. What gratitude! Have tea with the man. He was a big fan of *T & A*." Her grin translated across phone wires as she used the crew's ribald nickname for the film. "I wouldn't be surprised if yours were the first 't's' he saw."

"Leah!"

"Stacy! So a whole generation of men grew up thinking your incredibly pert, perfectly proportioned hooters were the norm. Live with it. The rest of us have to."

"Come on. As a favor to me. Talk to the man. Truth is, I wouldn't mind having you out here. To have lunch with. To call after mudslides. I miss you, Your Grace."

Anastasia sat up. "Here's a question for you. Bruce Amerman. Where does he live?"

"There's a blast from the past. He was in *T & A*, back in his actor days, wasn't he? He rents a place in Topanga Canyon when he's out here, but he lives in London. So. Will you meet with Masterson?"

"I'm sure you'll be among the first to know."

And Anastasia hung up the phone. The thought of talking to practical, levelheaded Bruce brought her comfort. He had been Peter Dalton's best friend during the shoot; Anastasia had counted him a close ally as well. She wasn't sure why she still felt she could confide in him after all this time. But she hoped with all her might that he would be able to quickly and simply set her straight about the upsetting thoughts that were plaguing her. She resolutely turned back toward her apartments, praying she had the courage to do what she needed to do.

SO IT WAS THAT three days later, Anastasia closed her eyes and attempted to press herself farther back into the supple black leather of the back seat of the Huntington's Rolls-Royce. What on earth was wrong with her? She hadn't always been like this. She had been normal once. Well, perhaps "normal" was too extreme, but she had at least been able to go out in public without feeling like a scuba diver with an empty air tank at the bottom of the ocean.

She didn't remember much of the two-hour drive to London early that morning. Or the supposedly important meeting with Evan Masterson at Neville's flat that she'd agreed to in exchange for Celia finding her Bruce Amerman's home address. Masterson had seemed pleasant enough for an American (*Careful!* she warned herself. *You used to be one yourself*), even deferential. She hoped for Celia's sake that she'd seemed interested in what he'd said, not just in hiding the enormous cloud of panic that had followed her from Somerset.

Anastasia figured that she hadn't been in London for over a year, maybe closer to two. She hoped Neville had not retired from his social circle early because she wanted to stay home. He'd been in his late sixties when they'd met through mutual friends one night after her performance in the West End production of *Daily Life*—though they'd been briefly introduced when *T & I* had shot on location at Dunmore Castle.

Surely he'd had time to kick up his heels before she tied him to the castle. In fact, he'd often apologized to her, especially after he became partially bedridden. "Forgive me for taking your youth, Golden One," he'd said.

She wondered if he'd understood that her youth had been stolen many years before they'd ever met.

Anastasia opened her eyes as unfamiliar street signs and pillar-boxes whizzed past. What she was doing now seemed infinitely more dangerous than meeting with some television prodigy: she was going somewhere she'd never been. She frankly didn't remember the last time she'd done it, although she did remember a couple of aborted attempts. The car made a broad turn and came to idle in a driveway. Benton, the driver, took off his cap and wiped his forehead in a gesture she'd seen repeated a hundred times. He half turned. "This is number thirty-two, Your Grace."

They were in front of a detached house, not ostentatious but large and welcoming. Brown stone rose to two and a half stories. The windows were outlined by blue shutters and framed inside by lace curtains. Three rounded, shallow steps led to a door painted in the same shade of Wedgwood blue as the shutters.

There was no way she could climb those stairs.

On the other hand, she was mortified at the thought of Benton driving her here and being told to turn around because Her Grace was unable to get out of the car.

"Jane," she whispered to herself. She closed her eyes once more and constructed a detailed picture of her friend. No matter how terrifying this was, she owed it to Jane.

"Are you ready, Your Grace?"

"Yes, Benton, thank you," she answered. He opened his door and walked around the car to open hers.

"Jane," she intoned again, and she stepped out into the early April air.

Somehow she made it to the door. There was a round white button by the doorframe and she pushed it.

Time was a chasm that suddenly yawned before her; the afternoon air swirled, grasping at her, trying to pull her into the vortex.

Just as she was ready to bolt blindly for the car, the blue door swung inward. Anastasia looked up a step to where an unfamiliar woman stood peering down at her.

"Hello," she said. "I'm looking for Bruce Amerman. Do I have the correct address?"

Say no, she pleaded silently. *Say no and I can retreat, I can leave, knowing I tried.*

The unknown woman reached out and put her hand on Anastasia's shoulder. "Yes, this'll be it. Do come in."

The woman guided her into the front hall and closed the door. Anastasia was unexpectedly surrounded by soft scents, oregano and dill and the yeasty aroma of bread fresh from the oven.

"It smells heavenly." She caught herself and looked at the woman, who, standing side by side with her, was actually a few inches shorter than she. "I'm sorry, I haven't introduced myself. I'm—"

"Oh, I know who you are, Your Grace. It's a pleasure to meet you." Her voice was musical, with a faint Scottish brogue still couching the words. Natural brown curls hung just below her shoulders. She was dressed in blue jeans and a white blouse with a rounded collar and buttons, one pink, one purple, one blue. She wasn't carrying an extra pound, but her face and body were pleasantly rounded.

"I'm Elise. Bruce's wife."

"Is he here?"

Her lips pursed and her eyebrows arched in a look of abject apology. "Well, yes, he is. But he's writin'. And when he's up in his lair, he won't see anyone." She nodded up the flight of steps that rose off the hall to the right, across from a mirror and Oriental umbrella stand. "Not me, not Harvey Weinstein, not the Queen. Important folks ring from California, but if he's ensconced, there's nothing to be done. He won't let me up, even to clean. I'm very sorry—"

"My fault entirely. I should have called first. I don't know what I was thinking."

"Will you come to the kitchen for a bowl of soup? It's homemade, and there's some fresh bread. It's the least I can do."

Before she could answer, there were footfalls on the floor above them, and a pair of black jeans above white socks and black running shoes filled the center of the landing. The upper form folded at the waist, and a tousled head with at least two days' stubble of beard appeared.

"Stace?" it said. "Stace, is that you?"

Anastasia smiled wanly.

"It is," he said, racing down the stairs. His feet stayed planted on the first and second step as his hand encircled her wrist. "Come on up." And he ascended quickly, towing her in his wake like a motor launch. On the next floor he continued apace to an open door, behind which another set of steps rose steeply into what was obviously the attic. He wedged her onto the second step and pulled the old door closed behind them. There was no railing, so Anastasia grasped his wrist with her other hand and gauged the height of each step by looking down wildly at the creaking wooden floor disappearing beneath her feet.

At the top of the stairs, Bruce released her. He whirled to find a huge, boxy old chair, the brown cloth covering worn away in several places on the wide arms. It moaned across the floor as he pulled it over and offered it to her with a sweep of his hand.

"Please excuse the accommodations," he said, his face flushed. "The decoration is, uh, mine."

She laughed. She sat down. The chair was as welcoming as a mother's lap.

Anastasia expelled a long breath and surveyed the room. Cedar flooring and a sloped roof gave warmth to the space. Golden light from a bankers lamp on his battered old desk was enhanced by a standing lamp, its shade covered by a practical, navy-striped fabric. In front of it sat his laptop computer. A bottle of good whisky sat on the desk, a tall glass next to it. Above the desk, hung from a rafter, was a large corkboard, on which index cards jostled in profusion. Everything else seemed covered with papers. "There is a system to it," Bruce said, apologetically.

"I have no doubt," Anastasia answered, a smile playing at the edges of her lips.

Bruce clasped his hands between his knees and leaned forward. She returned his gaze, studying him as unabashedly as he studied her.

She figured Bruce to also be in his late thirties. He had retained much of his boyish look, which had kept him playing naïfs and best friends long after he wished to play leading roles. However, his soft features now had an edge to them; the thoughts behind his gray eyes were quick and appraising. He'd acquired a smart, jaded air. He looked like someone who'd learned to play Hollywood's game, and had learned the hard way.

She'd give anything to know the character description he was writing of her in his head. "What do you think?" she asked. "'Aging ingénue grasping to hold on to the remains of her former beauty'?"

Bruce laughed out loud. "I don't know what mirrors you've been looking into. You look great. You've come into your own . . . more than fulfilling the promise of your youthful beauty."

She tried to keep a straight face. "And you. Before, you only read lines like that off a page. Now you're coining them yourself."

He flung himself back in his chair, his hands covering his face. "Aargh! Attack of the Giant Screenwriting Monster! You've got to save me from myself."

"Well, that would probably necessitate saving you from numerous healthy paychecks," Anastasia said caustically. "Think about it before doing anything rash. What are you working on now?"

"A money job. Script doctoring. A thriller that's going into production next week about a pack of defense attorneys who transform into jackals to mete out justice."

"I think I just read about it in *Daily Variety*. Does it star—"

"Don't even say their names. I'd have to throw up. It's already had three writers. I'm the director's last line of defense. And you're right. There's good money in that last line."

"No wonder Elise doesn't ask too many questions about what goes on up here."

"I didn't think anyone could put up with me before I met her." He rubbed the stubble on his chin self-consciously. "You've got to forgive me. I live in a world unto myself when I'm working. I don't usually present myself . . . that is, most people see me clean-shaven and sober. Although I don't think I've had anything to drink today. Whisky is my last resort. If a problem's really thorny," he lowered his voice confidingly, "I also smoke a cigar."

Anastasia couldn't believe it. Somehow talking to Bruce had made her forget, at least momentarily, what a crashing coward she had become. It felt great.

"I'm honored to be admitted to your lair. I'll take a blood oath not to reveal anything I see or hear."

The self-deprecating crooked grin that she remembered so well crossed his face as he ran a hand through his unruly hair. "How long has it been?" he asked.

"Since we've seen each other? Well . . . you came to see me and Garrett in *Daily Life*, remember?"

"Wow. That long ago? I read about your husband's death. How are you doing?"

Anastasia grimaced. "I'd rather not get into it."

"An honest answer," he replied. "And how is...was it your mother?"

"She's dead, too."

"Oh. Sorry to bring it up."

"No need. We were estranged. She died somewhere in India, I was told."

"On to happier topics, eh? What brings you here? I assume you're not on a house tour of London. Is it the reunion? I have absolutely no idea how I feel about that. It might be entertaining to see everyone again. But making *T & I* was special. It was one of those times I can't help comparing others to, and they never measure up. I don't want to lose the power of those memories with a fifth-rate re-creation."

"I know," she said.

"So much has changed," he said. "So many people are gone."

Anastasia shifted uncomfortably. "I know," she said. "That's why I came."

She reached into her pocket and pulled out the folded page from *Daily Variety* with Jane's obituary on it. Bruce took it from her and read it, his face blank. It was still blank when he looked up. "Yes?" he said. "You remember her?"

Anastasia nodded. "She was a good friend. I got her hired on the picture."

"Then I'm sorry," he said tersely and handed it back.

"The thing is," she said quickly. "It's not only her."

She pulled out a piece of paper torn from her journal and offered it as well. He took it and glanced at it briefly, long enough to see it was a list of names.

"It's people we worked with on *Tristan and Isolde*," he said. "So what's the point?"

"The point is they share an upsetting characteristic," she said. "They're all dead."

The paper in his hand began to tremble. "This is why you came?" he asked.

She nodded. "I know it's not—"

"It's not what?"

"It's not much to base a theory on . . ."

"A theory of what?" His voice, friendly only seconds before, was now cold as ice.

"That something, well, unnatural happened to them. Maybe is still happening to the rest of us. I know nothing I'm saying is based on fact . . ."

"It sure as bloody hell isn't," he said. His voice remained a monotone, but his body was clearly tense.

"I think you'd better go," he said.

Anastasia stared at him.

"*Now.*" There was steel in his eyes. He wasn't kidding.

Mystified, Anastasia stood and fled down the attic stairs, throwing the door quickly closed behind her. Shaking, she continued down to the ground floor, where she picked up her coat off the peg in the hall.

"Are you done, then?" asked Elise, her head popping out from the kitchen door.

"Yes, I'm sorry," she said. "Truly I am."

Without waiting to explain, or for evidence that Bruce might decide to follow, she opened the front door and hurried to the car. As Benton started the motor and reversed out the driveway, Anastasia gripped the inside handle with both hands.

I was right all along. It is safer to stay home, she thought. But it was cold comfort indeed.

CHAPTER 2

From "The Lowdown" column by Jim Jameson, in Hollywood Style:

WHERE ARE THEY NOW? *is the familiar question we've all come to recognize as the lead-in to pieces about has-been actors (1) explaining why it's more fulfilling to work for charities than studios; (2) expounding upon the passel of children they've raised, whom they now support by designing jewelry/doing carpentry work; (3) staging an alleged comeback and claiming that being filmed stuck in a jungle with other D-listers will only enhance their prospects.*

However, Paramount's much heralded re-release of Tristan and Isolde brings this question past the rhetorical as Tinseltown remembers its love affair with the movie's stars and asks: where the hell are they?

Director/actor Pierce Hall, we presume, is still dead. Another bloody British genius (he was given his planned knighthood posthumously), T & I is acknowledged to be the crowning achievement of his career. This triumph, you may recall, was made all the more poignant by the impeccable timing of his sudden death just before the film's release.

Let us then consider the fate of Peter Dalton. Already a working actor, playing Tristan launched him into the international spotlight. Memories are notoriously short in Hollywood, yet even cynics must recall Dalton's stellar decade, in which he earned two Oscar nominations for serious—and very fine—work, while also managing to star in two of the top ten moneymakers of all time. The world was his oyster, and he overate. We all watched as he flirted with fire and did more than flirt with beautiful women and designer drugs. Ten years after his breakthrough role, and just before the release of his final film, Mango Forest, he disappeared. Is he dead? Alive? Eating Whoppers with Elvis? No one seems to know. His rented house in the Hollywood Hills was vacated a month before the lease expired, but there were no signs of foul play, and no one (including his family, friends, and last reported fiancée, actress Blanche Wynters) filed any sort of report with the police. So is this mega-talent with the boyish smile and the buff body still out there somewhere? Or did the high-flying moth finally, and inevitably, hit the flame?

Which leads to the question I've been playing with in my mind with such tortured pleasure that it feels like a sin that needs confessing.

Anastasia, where are you?

Gentlemen—hetero gentlemen—you had a fling with Anastasia Day. So did I. All right, it was in our daydreams, in our (ahem) night dreams, but, God, those haunting green eyes. Do you remember how, as Isolde, she dared you to tumble into those eyes, to fall endlessly into the yearning, the passion, the sadness, the promise of joy that dwelled therein? Somehow those eyes told us she knew too much, she was too wise, she'd known pain—and yet, yet she was willing to hope. We all wanted to be the one to give her that hope, to sink with her into the promised joy. Oh!

Do you remember her full rounded lower lip—and the upper one like soft cursive above it? All right, forget the poetry, do you remember the bod? I mean, of course, the talent. Sorry, the talent. That's what we all fell in love with, of course. The way in T & I, and later, in Firefly, that she could break your heart by simply lifting her eyes. Or make you laugh with that nose-crinkle thing.

Yeah, yeah, Jameson's finally broken down and lost his million-dollar smart-ass, and you were all here to read it. Maybe I'm still in unrequited love because Anastasia, too, disappeared.

Oh, she's not dead or missing. After two more classy if lightweight films, she was in a hit West End play with fellow T & I alum Garrett Clifton. And then, she got married. Yes, married. To somebody else.

Somebody else, that is, unless you were His Grace, Sir Neville Huntington, the lord of the castle where T & I was shot.

Our Anastasia, a duchess.

Well, now she's a widow. And God forbid I tread too soon upon the toes of sorrow. But she is ALIVE, and she is OUT THERE. And she is FREE. So, before anyone else finds you, Anastasia, WILL YOU MARRY ME?

Most film reunions are kind of sad: love handles and Rogaine on parade. But I admit, the re-release of Tristan and Isolde has me on needles and pins. Richard Riley notwithstanding, will they show?

Tristan and Isolde, we are here.

Where are you?

THE NEXT THURSDAY, the Duchess of Esmonde was still in bed at ten o'clock. The six goose-down pillows that ran the width of the large four-poster canopy bed were propped against the carved headboard. Anastasia pulled herself up to sit against them. She seemed to hardly make a ripple in the sea of sheets. She supposed it should seem odd that Neville was gone from their bed forever.

She did miss Neville, of course. After he married Anastasia, he had acquired a fascination with books, spending hour after hour in the castle library, which was crammed with the collected volumes of two hundred years. Holding them, repairing them, reading them, archiving them, had become his greatest pleasure.

Anastasia never minded Neville's silent hours among his books. In fact, she'd often taken a classic herself and settled in front of the fire. They'd spent years in companionable silence. He'd given shape to her days, a pattern to her life. He had been her shield. She might have been insulted that he didn't talk to her about his past, about his family, about the estate and the antiquities therein. But they weren't hers, would never be hers, and she didn't want them. All she wanted was sanctuary.

She supposed that was why Geoff and Cathy objected to her as little as they had. She was not any kind of threat.

But now Neville was gone. In fact, everyone she cared for in her life was gone. She had no loved ones left. And friends? Well, Bruce, perhaps, and Leah. But she didn't kid herself: she was tangential to their lives. How had she come to this? Thirty-eight years old, and completely superfluous.

She forced herself out of bed, then padded barefoot across the room to the standing mirror. She saw a thin, ghostly figure in a straight white gown. Anastasia pulled the elastic from the braid in her hair and dug her fingers into the triple pleat, pulling it out. It was wild and thick and hung almost to her waist, much longer than it had been when she was working. Neville never wanted her to cut it, and she hadn't. She picked up a brush and attacked it with vigor, then stopped, too sad to continue, and let the brush drop.

Soon she would have to give up the master bedroom to the new duke and duchess. She would be given quarters in the west wing, she was sure. She managed another look at her reflection: the sheer gown and the mounds of wavy hair. Yes, it would all fit the part of the crazy dowager, locked away from the world. The madwoman who had once been the Duchess of Esmonde. Who had once been an actress.

Who had once been a person.

Dear God, she thought again, how had she come to this? Absolutely useless. Take for example, this feeling she couldn't shake that something unnatural was happening to the cast and crew of *Tristan and Isolde*. She could feel all she liked, but she was too terrified to do anything about it. Anything other than plead with someone else to do something.

And if something *was* happening, why couldn't it have happened to her? Why did it have to destroy others and leave her ever more alone?

She walked back to the bed and fell face-forward onto it.

What on earth was she going to do with the next fifty years? She couldn't stand the thought of it, of that many more years of hiding, of fear and pain.

God help me. Or just let me die, she whispered. She didn't really know if she meant it or not. But it was not the first time she'd asked.

"Your Grace?" Bertie said, as she tapped on the hall door.

"Just a moment," Anastasia said. She forced herself to rouse, and listlessly pulled on her dressing gown and slippers and sat on the bench of the vanity table. "Come in."

"There's a Mr. Amerman on the line for you. He says important, but I can't think of anything that won't wait."

"No, no. I'll take it."

"Hullo?" Anastasia said cautiously, picking up the receiver as Bertie left the room. Bruce's unexpected rejection still smarted.

"Listen, something's come up. We need to talk."

So much for abject apologies. "Yes? Go ahead."

"I mean, in person."

"Oh," she said. "Come down to Somerset, then. How long will it take you?"

"I think it would be easier if you came here."

"Bruce, I—" She fell back into the pillows, miserable. "I can't."

"Stacy, you must have thought this was serious, or you wouldn't have come to begin with."

"I do," she said. "I do think it's serious."

"Then what's the problem?"

"I hate myself, I really do," she said. There was a long pause, which he took no initiative to fill. "But . . . I . . . can't leave this castle."

"I don't understand."

"I can't talk about it. I just can't go out again, that's all. Can't you come here?"

"Look, I'm trying to understand, I really am." There was a pause. "You don't mean you're one of those people who can't go out of the house because they'll fall apart if they do? An agoraphobic?" Bruce's voice faltered on the other end. "Stace? Are you . . . crying?"

Anastasia pressed her fingers against her eyelids in an attempt to keep back the tears. "Maybe it sounds like a joke to you, but it's ruining my life. Not be able to go anywhere, do anything . . . it's bloody awful."

"I didn't mean . . . you're serious?" Bruce's voice was now earnest. "Rotten thing. I'm sorry. I'll do anything I can to help you. But I need you to help me, too. Someone's made an attempt on my life."

"What? Someone's tried to *kill* you?"

"We've got to talk," he said.

"Then come here. Please."

"I'll call you back," he said, and he hung up.

BRUCE DIDN'T RING BACK. Two hours later, Anastasia realized she was sitting—dressed, at least—in a rounded boudoir chair, staring at the receiver. She was afraid she'd done it now.

Bruce needed her. Someone had tried to kill him, and she'd refused to help. By doing so, she'd managed to scare off one of her two remaining friends. She didn't remember the last time she had admitted to anyone that she was needy. She had learned at a very young age the importance of seeming in control at all times. If you didn't, people would either take advantage of your weakness or distance themselves from it and you.

When the knock finally roused her, the April sky had gone from clear to overcast, and pellets of rain pattered rhythmically against the windows. She stalked into the next room and flung open the door to find Reginald.

"Telephone?" she asked, hopefully.

"No, Your Grace, you have a guest."

Thank God, she thought.

She took the shortcut downstairs, through the back hall, past the dining room. She stopped to catch her breath outside the front parlor. She screwed up her courage and swept into the room.

Bruce Amerman wasn't there.

Instead, studying the collection of small sixteenth-century painted cameos was his wife, Elise. "Your Grace," she said with a small curtsy. "Do pardon me for coming unannounced." She leaned in close. "My husband says you and he'll be having some business which is of an urgent nature, but you don't want to make a spectacle of going back and forth between our residences," she said quietly. "So I've come to collect you."

The dowager duchess sat down heavily on a loveseat.

"We've a lovely room off the back garden where you'll be comfortable for a few days, and if you need to leave, say the word and I'll speed you back here fast as a fox."

Anastasia sat, incapable of embracing or refusing either course of action.

For the first time, Elise seemed nervous as she said, "I hope you don't mind that Bruce told me about your . . . condition. If you don't mind my sayin', I had a cousin who also had panic attacks. With help, she was able to stop them before they became full-blown agoraphobia. All I mean is—it's a good sign that you could come out to our house before. A real good sign. It means you can do it again. Every step is positive. My cousin . . . it was easier for her if someone went with her places, and drove her. So I've come to drive you."

Anastasia was mildly stunned. She had never before told anyone about her "condition," and yet here was someone she hardly knew, nattering on about it. Making a ridiculous prospect sound completely reasonable.

"Bruce said you knew how important this is."

"Yes," replied Anastasia, "I do." *Murdered. People are being murdered.*

"You'll come then?"

She had a thought then, one that hadn't come to her for many decades.

Lily could do this, Anastasia thought. *Lily could get me to the car.*

If she could just make it to Elise's car. Bruce's home was no longer an unknown, it was a familiar haven. If she could get to the car, she could turn her mind off, go underwater for the duration of the drive, and resurface. She thought again of Jane and of the tone in Bruce's voice when he told her someone had tried to kill him. She thought of how few friends she had left.

She thought, with something approaching terror, of spending the next fifty years alone in the west wing.

She stood and rang for Bertie. "Mrs. McGowan," she said, "I've been invited to spend a few days with old friends in London. Would you send Sarah up to help me pack?"

ANASTASIA FOUND THE GARRET as she remembered it, cluttered, askew, and reflecting Bruce in every stack and pile. He had pulled forward a standing chalkboard. Both chairs now faced it.

"I can't wait any longer. What's happened?" she demanded.

"I finished the rewrite of the script I was working on," he said.

"Good." She could have guessed from his fresh clothes and close shave; his thick black hair was neatly combed.

"And I looked at the list you gave me."

"Yes?"

"It's a lot of names."

"Yes."

"Have you shown it to anyone else?"

"No," she replied, straight-faced. "So you can murder me, cover your tracks, and no one else will ever know."

She was taken aback by his stricken look.

"Stacy, listen, I—first, let me say I'm sorry about last week. But I need to ask you something, and I need you to be truthful. Why did you bring this list to me?"

She met his eyes. "Because I was worried about it and needed somebody to talk to. Because I'd thought we were friends."

She could tell that the past tense of the last statement hit its mark. He broke the gaze first. He'd become a man with a sense of himself, but now he was unsure. "Nothing would mean more to me. But there are things . . ."

She leaned forward and put her own hand over his. "Whatever it is, it's usually easiest to simply say it."

He sat still for a moment, as if gathering courage.

"Well, this is it, what I've had a hard time working into the conversation. I was married once before Elise. My wife died. I was accused of killing her."

Anastasia caught her breath. "That does rather grind things to a halt," she finally said. "So, did you do it?"

Bruce sat back and laughed ruefully. "No. But thanks for asking up front. You really hadn't heard?"

Anastasia shook her head. "How long ago was it?"

"Eight years, something like that. I wish I could say time flies, but it doesn't."

"Bruce, I'm so sorry," she said. "I can't imagine how painful that must have been. Losing your wife must have been bad enough without . . ."

"Without my father-in-law making public accusations. He was a doctor, you see, and he didn't like me as it was."

Mild-mannered Bruce, accused of murder. Seemingly mild-mannered Bruce, she corrected herself. So maybe she had missed some points of interest by her self-imposed exile.

"If you don't mind my asking, how did she die?"

"Poison," he said. "It must have been quite awful. Not even Claudine deserved that. As long as I'm coming clean, Stace, I'll admit we weren't getting on very well. We were separated. Oh, out with it. She was a heartless, Class A bitch. But she didn't deserve to die."

Bruce was rallying a bit, and he snorted a chuckle in spite of himself. "She had the bad fortune to die at my house. And her papa—who, as I might have mentioned, hated my guts—put together a purely circumstantial case. There was never enough evidence for Scotland Yard but there was plenty for the *Sun* and the *News of the World*. It was hell. So, you can see why I get testy when it comes to accusations of murder."

She leaned back into her chair, studying the determined lines of his face. "The only papers we received were the *Times* and the *Financial Times*."

"They didn't cover it," he said sardonically.

"So," she said, putting the pieces together, "you thought I came to you with my theories because I thought you might . . . know something about it?"

"Something like that."

"I am sorry. How could anyone think . . . ? I mean, no one really does, do they?"

"I don't know. My guess is that most people don't really believe I would kill anybody, but they do enjoy wondering. One positive thing did come out of it. The three Hollywood studios that had scripts of mine in development hell suddenly greenlighted them. I became hot. My price skyrocketed." He laughed. "I should write a book. Suspicion of murder as career strategy."

"Hollywood has always liked people who were experts in their fields."

"Anyway, Stace, please accept my apology. I overreacted. But, as you can see, I have buttons that are easily pushed. It was so good to see you, and I value our friendship so highly that when I thought . . . I went ballistic."

"I understand. But you said someone tried to kill *you*?"

"Let's start by going back a step," Bruce said. "If you'll bear with me, what I want to do is list the names of the deceased *T & I* alums that we already know about, along with what we know about their manner of death. You with me?"

"All right," she agreed. Anastasia curled up in the oversized armchair. She noted with interest that sitting in Bruce's lair, about to discuss murder, she felt safe and at home.

"I have a friend in France checking the newspapers about Reggie Camden, the historian, and an Academy librarian in L. A. working on the transportation captain. The rest I think we've got." He ran a hand through his hair, and picked up a piece of yellow chalk. "I'll use your list—I didn't see that you'd put them down in any particular order?"

"As I thought of them," Anastasia said.

"All right. See if you notice anything."

Jane Whittle, he wrote. *Makeup*. "Cause of death?"

"The paper said heart attack."

He added that in a third column.

Pierce Hall, he wrote. *Director/actor. Heart attack.*

Frances Selwyn. Set designer.

"Robbery, was it?" she asked.

"Carjacking, to be specific," he said, and wrote it down.

Merlin Meredith. Choreographer. Suicide.

Garrett Clifton. Actor, "Andret." AIDS.

Tyler Magnusson. Screenwriter. Cancer.

Nelson Reese. Transportation captain.

"Any guesses?" Bruce asked.

"Hardening of the arteries?" Anastasia said.

"He did put away those bangers," Bruce admitted, and they both chuckled in spite of themselves. "All right. Let's get a grip. We'll come back to Reese."

Mac Wheaton. Actor, "Frocin the Dwarf." Heart failure.

Reggie Camden. Historian. Cause of death, unknown.

Gray Eddington. Producer.

"He walked in on a robbery in progress in his home in Switzerland."

Robbery, he wrote.

Then he came and stood behind her. "Ten," he said. "In twenty years. Say there were sixty principal players, counting in front of and behind the cameras. The question is, is that mortality rate too high? And if it is, do you see any patterns?"

Anastasia said, "The deaths all look suspicious to me. But I've seen too many Bruce Amerman movies."

"Three heart-related," Bruce said, squinting at the board.

"AIDS and cancer," she said. "Can't count those."

"But look at the other three," her companion pointed out. "All violent deaths."

Anastasia sat staring at the yellow chalk on the blackboard. Why was it that men's handwriting was always so unruly? "Bruce," she said, "it's all in my mind, isn't it? I mean, it's unfortunate to have three people who worked on a film die in a carjacking, a robbery, and as a suicide. Unfortunate, but not a plot."

"Yeah, that's what I thought, too," Bruce said. "Until I checked my email, and got an answer on Reese, the transportation captain."

As if to demonstrate, he went to his laptop and opened his email program. "Look at this—we've got another one." He grabbed a pen and scribbled a copy of what was on the screen.

"Well?"

"The cause of death on Reggie Camden, our historian. He killed himself with a .45 at his home outside Paris." He walked over to the blackboard. "That's four violent deaths."

"This is giving me the creeps," Anastasia said. "So tell me. What about Reese?"

"Reese was murdered," he said. "He died of digitalis poisoning."

"Yes?" she said. Seeing the drawn look on Bruce's face, she suspected this meant more than she was putting together.

Bruce sank into the other chair, his emotions seemingly in check, but his face was grayish white. "That's what Claudine died of," he said.

"Dear God."

He roused himself. "I never wanted to get back into this," he said, in a quiet, hard voice. "But this leads me to several conclusions. Look at the list again." Bruce perched beside her on the wide arm of the chair and exhaled. "Here's where being a screenwriter comes in handy. Put yourself in the mind of a killer. Say you want to off a large number of people without calling attention to yourself. What do you do?"

"Use different modi operandi."

"Exactly. And take your time. What's the easiest way to kill someone?"

She shook her head.

"It's not a trick question. *Raiders of the Lost Ark*. The scene where the guy was coming after Indy with the scimitar."

"He just shot him."

"Exactly. Just shoot 'em. Blow 'em away. Make it look like a robbery, a carjacking, a suicide."

"But that's only three. Or four, now."

"Well, you just can't go around shooting everybody. Someone's bound to notice. So you go to your second choice. Poison."

"But only Reese died of poison. Oh . . . and Claudine."

"Digitalis poisoning kills by causing heart failure. If the doctors don't suspect foul play, they often don't find it."

"Oh." Her voice was heavy.

"Yeah. Luckily for me, my father-in-law was a doctor, and a suspicious one at that. Otherwise I might still be leading a normal life. But look at this. Besides Reese and Claudine, three others are heart-related. That's four violent, three heart, two poison."

"Nine possibly suspicious deaths," Anastasia whispered.

"Yeah, and it also means," he took a deep breath, "that Claudine was in the wrong place at the wrong time. The poison that killed her was meant for me. I was supposed to be number ten."

"Why?" she gasped. "I don't understand! Why would anyone do this, Bruce?" She jumped to her feet and began pacing restlessly. "I don't believe it. I can't. Not Pierce. Not Janie. Dear God!"

When he spoke, his voice was wry. "I feel almost the same way about Claudine."

"How did it happen?" Anastasia asked wildly. "Claudine's death, I mean. What do you know about it?"

He sank into the other chair. "Oh, I hate this," he said. "You don't know how many depositions I had to give. But here it is. I left London on a Thursday, flew Heathrow to New York, New York to L.A. The maid came in on Monday and found Claudine dead as a doornail on the living room floor. At first they thought it was a freak heart attack, but then Daddy Dearest found traces of digitalis poisoning. The thing is, she had been dead so long that they couldn't assign an exact time of death, only a window of opportunity. And she must have come over to the house— we lived in Kensington—just after I left. I don't know if she expected me to be there so she could hiss at me some more, or if she waited for me to leave so she could take some more stuff. Whatever. The window on the time of death did not preclude my killing her before I left for Heathrow."

Bruce crossed his arms tightly across his chest while he perched on the wooden chair next to hers.

"They didn't find any poison in the house, which meant that someone removed the evidence. And since there was no forced entry, the police thought first of people who had keys, or who knew where the spare was kept. Which was a chummy group comprised entirely of Claudine, the housekeeper, and myself. And the housekeeper did not have the information necessary to conclude Claudine was a heartless bitch. So I become Suspect Number One."

"Whoa," Anastasia said. They both sat lost in the horror of their own thoughts.

Finally Anastasia asked, "So what do we do?"

"That's the question, isn't it?" he asked. "I'm not exactly in the mood to run to Scotland Yard and plead with them to reopen Claudine's case."

"The thing I don't get is why. Why would anyone want to kill the cast and crew of *T & I*?"

"That I don't know. I do have a partial theory about who."

"Well? For pity's sake!"

"It's not much. But it occurs to me that a deranged fan would only go for the visible participants."

"You mean the actors."

"Right. I've never heard of fans stalking historians or choreographers or drivers. Doesn't happen. So that leads me to believe—"

"It was someone connected with the production. Someone who knew Gray Eddington as well as Pierce Hall."

"Exactly."

"Well," said Anastasia. "That's a cheerful thought."

"It's not happy," he said. "But it is helpful. Because if he—or she, let's not be sexist—knows us, that means—"

"It means we know a murderer."

"Yeah. Someone who's already had the pleasure of trying to kill me. In my own home."

"Dear God," said Anastasia.

Bruce, inspired, went to the whisky bottle, opened it, and poured two shot glasses. He walked one over to his guest and she took it. He downed his straight, went back and poured another. Then they both stared silently at the chalkboard, putting the names of former friends and acquaintances together with the idea of murder. Even combined with the whisky it was a sobering experience.

"The truly frightening thing . . ." Anastasia started.

"Can't wait to hear," said Bruce.

". . . is that Janie died just a few weeks ago. Which means, if this theory is right, that our killer is still in business."

"To cheer you even more," the writer said, "if you look at the timing of the murders, the pace has picked up. Which leads me to substantial worry—"

"About the next murder?"

"About the reunion. If someone is trying to kill us all, I can't think of anything more convenient than having everyone gathered in the same place."

Anastasia's face now looked as drawn as Bruce's. "The reunion," she breathed. "Speaking of which—"

She reached into her pants pocket and withdrew a letter that had been forwarded from California. She unfolded it and extended it to Bruce.

My dear Anastasia,
There is a big surprise awaiting you at the reunion.
You simply must attend. Take my word for it.
—A friend and admirer

"Stacy darling, I trust you will be attending," Celia had scrawled on the attached Post-it.

"That's all you got?" Bruce asked in frustration. "Why didn't she enclose the original envelope?"

"Perhaps there was no return address, so she thought there was no reason."

"It would have a postmark, at least," Bruce said.

Anastasia read the note over again. "The reunion's only five weeks away. 'A big surprise.' What's that mean? And if it is from an old friend, why didn't he sign his name? Oh, Bruce, this whole thing has me stymied. I can't fathom it. Why would anyone go to the trouble of murdering so many people?"

"I've been trying to think of anyone who could gain financially from doing such a thing. So far no luck."

"There must be a reason besides money. But what?"

"That's the question. My only theory is that this—rage—if that's what it is, must have been triggered during the film shoot. It has to be tied to the production somehow."

"But how? What could so infuriate someone, that none of the rest of us even noticed? And to make someone kill Janie! She never . . . it makes no sense!"

"It makes sense to our killer," Bruce said. "We just have to figure out how."

A knock on the garret door made them each start nervously. The writer descended and opened the door.

"Sorry to interrupt," Elise said quietly. "I didn't know if I should since you aren't actually working, but Alan Gable's rung for you. Should I ask him to ring back?"

"No," answered her husband. "I guess I'd better take it." He took the cell phone from her hand, turned it on, and stalked away, around and down the next flight of stairs.

"Sorry to interrupt," Elise called up.

"No, it was an opportune time," Anastasia said, following Bruce down the stairs. "I could use a break, as well."

The two women continued together to the ground floor.

"Let me make a pot of tea," Elise said, leading her into the kitchen. It was a pleasant, airy room, with an enclosed windowed patio a step down and skylights above, and green hanging plants and potted bushes and trees lining the patio. The radio was on; classic rock gave the space a jaunty air.

"I could use a cup, thank you," Anastasia said.

Elise filled a kettle bordered by a chorus line of pears, apples, and peaches, and put it on the stove. They could hear Bruce's voice fall and rise in the distance.

"He's got a study down here, for when he has to work with the outside world," she explained, then asked gently, "How are you doing?"

With that question, Anastasia became consciously aware of the black cloud of panic that always hovered just above her. But it was a state of being on the verge that she knew well, and as yet the panic remained above, not surrounding, her.

"I'm doing okay," she said, but she knew it wasn't something on which to dwell. She grasped for a safe topic. "How did you meet Bruce?"

"At the premiere of *Sleepless Nights*," answered Elise. "A business acquaintance of my father's invited us to dinner afterwards—a rather large party that included Bruce. We ended up seated next to each other in a very loud restaurant. He and Claudine were newly separated then, and he seemed a bit lost. As I recall, we talked about tea."

"So you knew Claudine?" she asked.

"Met her once," Elise snorted. "Wasn't impressed."

The new song had been playing for five seconds before both women turned toward the radio. It was "Forever Mine," the hit single from the closing credits of *Tristan and Isolde*. It was sung by Peter Dalton. Anastasia's hand flew to her mouth.

"Should I turn it?" Elise said, reaching quickly for the button.

"No," Anastasia said, gulping air, trying to sit back. "It's all right. I wasn't expecting it, that's all." *How can someone be gone,* she thought, *but still come back to haunt me?* Peter had such a rich baritone voice, and the tune hit a perfect mark between melody and driving rhythm. He let his voice get raw on the plaintive repeat: *Forever mine, our love will shine past death past time forever. Life's grand design, our love so fine shall make you mine forever. Forever. My fair one, forever mine.*

"Turn it," Anastasia whispered. "Please turn it."

Elise switched the radio off. "So, were you in love with him? Peter Dalton, I mean."

The question sounded strange now. "Peter Dalton" had become a brand name. Were you in love with Cary Grant, Brad Pitt, George Clooney? Who wasn't?

The Peter she had loved was a different person than the

"Peter Dalton" the world had known. She hadn't known the celebrity, the star. She'd been in love with a young man, once, who had that same name. "Yes," she said.

"Oh, where's my head? You've had a call as well. Reginald, from the castle." Elise tittered, then caught herself. "Don't mind me. I get the chance to say such things so seldom. Reginald said you'd had a call from—here it is, Leah Hall. Miss Hall said it was urgent. Here, use this phone." She handed her the cordless handset from the kitchen.

Anastasia sat on one of the tall wooden stools across the breakfast bar from the stove. "She said it was urgent? I suppose I should, but I'm afraid I don't have any sort of telephone credit card."

"Och, don't be a goose."

"Leah lives in California."

"So do most of Bruce's chief antagonists. Our phone lines reach. I've got to run upstairs. Back in a pip."

Anastasia shook her head. She turned over the message paper a couple of times, then began punching in the long series of numbers to reach Leah in the United States.

"It's good to finally hear from you. I thought you'd never call. Where the hell have you been? What's up? Tell me everything."

Leah's machine beeped, and Anastasia said, "Here I am calling from Brompton because Reginald said there's a fire—"

"Hey, hang on, hang on!" Leah sounded slightly winded as she picked up her phone receiver. "Stace, that you?"

"How many other Reginalds have you left urgent messages with?"

"In the past hour? Oh, four, five. But then I got in the sauna."

"What? No phone in your sauna? And you expect me to visit? So what's up? What's so urgent?"

"I'm dying to know how it went with Evan Masterson."

"Leah, I met with him a week ago. That's urgent?"

"A week and you didn't call me. So if you don't think it's urgent, I guess I have to urge for both of us."

Anastasia sighed and leaned on at the breakfast bar. "It went fine. He talked a lot. I smiled and nodded."

"Were your breasts perky? I seem to recall they'd made an impression on him before."

"Yes, I gave them both a good talking-to before the meeting. In any case, he told Celia he was delighted, and would be in touch as soon as the series was reality."

"That's great! Let me know when to pick you up at LAX."

"You're jumping the gun only the teeniest bit. He hasn't officially offered, I haven't answered," Anastasia said, as the chugging kettle began to boil. She lifted the crown off the teapot and poured the boiling water over the tea.

Then she remembered the afternoon's business and she sat down heavily. "Leah?"

Her friend detected the change in her tone. "Yes?"

"Sorry to ask, but . . ."

"Yes? This sounds interesting."

"Did your father have an autopsy?"

Leah lost only a beat before answering. "Now, there's a good question to spice up a boring conversation—and the great thing is it's not overused. Did my father have an autopsy. I would guess so. We weren't exactly expecting him to drop dead. He was only thirty-nine. Is there a reason you're asking, or is it just a slow news day?"

Leah's casual recounting of Pierce's age at his death brought back the shock that had engulfed Anastasia, indeed, had engulfed everyone twenty years earlier at the news that Pierce Hall was dead. It had seemed especially cruel since he'd been so robust during the shoot. The memory caused a chilling dread to rain through Anastasia's insides. The only consolation the world had back then was that such an early death was Pierce's fate, that his genius had burned brightly but his time had come.

Supposing his time was years off?

Supposing he had been murdered?

"I don't know what to tell you, Leah. Is there. . .might there be a chance that you could come over here for a few days? I've been talking to Bruce Amerman, and, well, I'd like to talk to you, too."

"Something you can't discuss over the phone."

"I'd prefer not to."

"Having to do with whether my father had an autopsy."

"I've gone about this all wrong."

"You do seem to be backing into something."

"There seems to be a pattern of suspicious deaths among the cast and crew of the film."

"Of *Tristan and Isolde?*"

"Yes. Could you please come and explain to us that it's all in our heads?"

"And to think *I* called *you*, thinking I had an interesting question." There was a long intake of breath on the other end. "Any excuse to see you. Let me make some calls."

Anastasia gave her the number at the Amermans' and rang off. The whole idea was again beginning to seem incredible. She leaned against the counter and massaged her temples.

"Done, then?"

"Sorry?" She looked up to find Elise returning.

"Did you reach your friend?"

"Yes, thank you."

"And you poured the teapot. Lovely."

"More trouble on the set," Bruce announced as he tromped into the room. He went to the round kitchen table and pulled out the ladder-back chair, then sprawled into it.

"What time did you say you'd be there?" asked Elise, who could apparently read his body language.

"Seven," he said.

Elise poured her husband a cup of tea, and both she and Anastasia joined him at the table.

"Sorry about the timing," he said. "Stacy and I are discussing something of a bit more urgency than when the fictional protagonist of this film turns into a jackal."

"Go on. What could be more important than that?" Elise asked, managing to coax a smile.

"I have thought of a possible starting place," Anastasia said to Bruce, blowing the steam from her mug at a steep right angle. Then she realized Elise was there with them and sent a hurried grimace of apology to Bruce.

"It's all right," he said. "Elise knows what happens to my wives if they get out of hand."

"I'd only use poison once, luv, if I were you," she answered. "Scotland Yard's not as dense as they used to be."

Bruce sat up straight and fitted his large hand over Elise's smaller one. "It seems the poison was meant for me, not Claudine," he said.

Elise looked into his eyes, deciphering the implications of the remark.

"Well. Good news, bad news, eh?" she said.

He cleared his throat. "It seems someone is not fond of the cast and crew of *Tristan and Isolde*," he said. "In fact, we seem to be dropping like flies."

"How many flies are we discussing?" she asked.

"Nine," he said.

"Jesus, Mary, and Joseph," she whispered.

"I was thinking," Anastasia said, wanting to break the ominous spell, "that we should start by getting a list of everyone involved with the film. See if we can think of anyone who might have any sort of motive."

"We're convinced that the key to the murders is linked to something that happened during the making of the film," he explained to Elise. "There must be something there, something we're looking right past because we're not seeing it in the correct light. Like—the birds."

Anastasia gave a small shudder. "Never did find out who did it, did they?"

"Birds?" asked Elise.

The actress felt her hostess's scrutiny. "We got to the set one day to find that someone had strangled all the doves—the carrier pigeons," she said.

"Ooh, lovely," said Elise.

"You don't think that's related, do you?" asked Anastasia.

"I've read, in portraits of serial killers, that many of them started in their youths, strangling kittens, drowning puppies," offered Elise.

"At any rate," Bruce resumed, "you and I each know a good part of what was going on, if we think hard enough. Maybe if we go back into the past and start digging, start asking questions . . ."

Anastasia coughed as her sip of tea went down the wrong pipe.

"You all right?" Elise asked.

She nodded helplessly, gasping for air. Making a list was one thing. Opening a door long shut was something else altogether.

"We can get most of the names from Internet Movie Database, but it won't be everybody." Bruce looked thoughtful. "Come Monday, I'll put in a call to a friend at the Academy library in L.A. and get a complete cast and crew list."

"Hang on," Elise said. She thrust her chair back and hurried out of the room.

Anastasia and Bruce locked eyes. "So Elise married you, knowing you're an alleged lady-killer."

He shrugged. "Nobody's perfect. And, you know. My secret weapon."

He gave an exaggerated smile, causing deep wells to appear at either side of his mouth.

Anastasia remembered the good use to which those dimples had been put during Bruce's acting days. "How innocent they make you seem!"

"Looks, as we all know—"

"Cruelly deceiving."

Elise returned, carrying an oversized book, which she placed ceremoniously in the middle of the table. It was hardcover, the front jacket a large, full-color head-and-shoulders photograph of Peter Dalton and Anastasia Day. It had been a popular still: Peter stood with his arm around Anastasia, protectively holding her against him under his cloak. They both faced forward; Peter was looking left, Anastasia to the right. Across the bottom of the photo, over Peter's forest green cloak, was the book's title in gold letters: *Love Will Find a Way: The Making of* Tristan and Isolde. *By Leah Hall.*

The blood drained from Anastasia's face, and her fists clenched around her teacup. Seeing a list of names on a piece of paper was one thing. Sitting this close to a deadly Pandora's box crammed full of memories and emotions was something else altogether.

"That's who you were just speaking to," Elise pointed to the name on the cover. "Leah Hall."

In her mind, Anastasia flashed on the image of her acerbic friend as the fresh-faced eighteen-year-old who had written this book.

"Yes, I did just speak to Leah. As a matter of fact, I asked her to come visit if she could. I hope you don't mind. I thought she might be able to help us work through this," Anastasia said, caught off guard by the concern that clouded Bruce's face. "She was in the middle of everything. Certainly she'll know a lot that we don't. Bruce?"

Bruce's glower didn't abate, but he finally said, "Of course she can come. But we've got to play this very close to the chest. You've got to make certain that Leah doesn't tell anyone," he said emphatically. "Not anyone. We don't need the killer reading about himself in *Variety*."

"You're right," Anastasia said. "I didn't tell her much, but I'll swear her to secrecy."

"This isn't a game," Bruce said.

"No," Anastasia agreed. She read in his eyes telling signs of strain at the knowledge that someone had tried to kill him—and had, in fact, killed his wife in his own house.

"It isn't a game," she repeated.

Bruce shook his head, as if dispelling the tension that had gripped him. He picked up the book. "This must have a full listing of cast and crew."

The book fell open to a page where the binding was slightly cracked from frequent use—a full-page black-and-white photo of Bruce as Dinas.

Both Bruce and Anastasia looked up at Elise, who had flushed crimson. "I didn't have any other photos of him while we were courting," she explained, "so I bought the book."

Smile lines crinkled at the edges of Bruce's eyes. "It served me well, then," he said, and flipped back to the index at the back.

"Bingo," he said.

"What about the fire?" asked Elise. "The book doesn't make

it sound suspicious, but that's one thing I do remember reading about."

"The fire's mentioned in the book?" Anastasia asked in surprise.

"Briefly. Thought I'd ask."

"The fire marshal determined it was electrical," Anastasia said.

"It was almost inevitable with all the cables they were running into a castle that old." Bruce added, "It happened at night, so no one was hurt."

"It was Isolde's bedroom that burned?"

"The queen's chamber, yes." Bruce said.

"The book says the fire started somehow on the down mattress."

"I never heard that," replied Anastasia.

"So someone torched your bed, and it didn't worry you?"

"Darling, really, there's no need to torture our guest. As she said, things were resolved satisfactorily at the time," said Bruce, and he looked at his watch.

"Go get your jacket, and I'll see you to the car," said Elise.

Anastasia gave a faint wave as Bruce and Elise left the kitchen. Bruce had left the book open on the table, and the pages had fanned forward to near the beginning. Anastasia averted her eyes, as if not looking at the book would somehow break its power over her. She had never read or even perused this book. It hadn't been published until the release of the film. By then, her world had shattered and she'd had no interest in the myth that had so enthralled the world; neither the ancient myth of Tristan and Isolde, nor the modern-day myth of love and tragedy that had been created around the film's real-life counterparts. But as she stood to clear the teacups from the table, her eyes swept over the exposed text.

"BIOGRAPHIES," it stated in bold black type. And, underneath, in flowing script, *Anastasia Day ("Isolde")*.

As it had been for the mythical Pandora, the temptation proved too great.

Anastasia sat down and opened the box.

PART TWO:

PANDORA'S BOX

CHAPTER 3

BIOGRAPHIES

Anastasia Day ("Isolde")
Newcomer Anastasia Day caused an international stir when she
was cast in the pivotal role of "Isolde the Fair" in Pierce Hall's new
production of **Tristan and Isolde**. Mr. Hall planned to cast an
established actress in the title role, but when he saw Ms. Day, who had
come to audition for the small role of Isolde's maid Camille, he was
immediately taken with her intelligence, beauty, and self-possession.
"It was as if the real Isolde walked in and started chatting. It wrenched
my gut around, and opened new venues of thinking about the story. I
knew she had the role before she left."

Anastasia Day had no idea.

Ms. Day is the daughter of the late Nigel Whitcomb-Day, the
youngest son of a British aristocratic family that dates back to the
mid-sixteenth century, and his American wife, Beverly Harrison
Day. A brilliant student, Anastasia especially loved literature at the
Chester School, where she is still vividly remembered by masters and
students alike. At 13, she left boarding school to live in London with
her mother. It was here she discovered her love for theater, which

she leapt into with fervor, winning leading roles with a local theater company.

Ms. Day had small but memorable parts in the films **Sara Jane, Sparrow,** and **Snow Slaying** as well as a featured role as the prime minister's daughter in the long-running BBC series **Jackson Circle.**

Says Director Hall, "Anastasia became the backbone of the film. She burns with intense emotion that is both pure and wise. She still has that idealistic spirit which all of us long to recover. She is Isolde."

The world will soon see for itself.

"HOTTEST DURN DAY I've ever seen," said Myra Mae Hopkins as the three girls turned down Spivey Lane on their way home from school.

"Chiggers'll be back directly," agreed her friend Louanne, kicking up puffs of dirt from between the tar and the grass with the toe of her sandals. "You ain't been here for the chiggers. They bite like heck."

"And the heat gets so thick your clothes stick right to ya," added Myra Mae.

It was only May and already the girls were in short-sleeved blouses with pastel short skirts and bare legs. They were ten, and nearing the time when the local boys would notice the length of their skirts. But today it was just the three of them, and they each carried their schoolbooks slung carelessly against one hip.

Anastasia wasn't alarmed by their predictions. She liked South Carolina and she had weathered worse than chiggers. She loved how the sweet scent of magnolias colored the air pink and how the ocean salt peppered her blood even miles inland. She even admired the watery-green grasses that grew wild surrounding the small yards of the one-storied houses huddled on Spivey Lane.

"Y'all comin' over?" asked Louanne, their self-appointed activities director.

Anastasia was about to agree when she saw her mother's maroon Datsun in the driveway. "I've got chores," she said, and turned abruptly toward the ecru-colored house, on which the paint was just starting to chip. She didn't know what it meant that her mama was home so early, but none of the possibilities were happy ones. She adjusted her tortoiseshell headband before she pushed through the back screen door.

Her mother was sitting at the gray Formica breakfast table. It was a familiar scene: how Anastasia would paint her mother if she had been Whistler. A kitchen glass clutched in her hand, an open bottle on the table. Mama had an order to her drinking. Ripple meant an irritation, Mateus a conundrum, Jack Daniel's a disaster.

Today was Jack Daniel's.

So Mama had lost her job again. Eight months this time. That was toward the long end of the cycle; Anastasia told herself she should be grateful. Her mother looked up and their eyes locked just long enough that Mama knew she knew. Because she couldn't stand knowing, Anastasia fixed her attention on the saffron-colored curtains flirting with the kitchen breeze. Mama had bought the material for Anastasia to sew those when they'd first arrived, and Anastasia had seen it as a good sign: you only bought curtains when you planned to stay. Mama was not a decorating kind of lady. She would rent her whole life already furnished if she could. Anastasia had seen both the color of and the impulse behind those curtains as extraordinarily hopeful. She suddenly loved them with furious intensity.

"How much have we got?" her mother asked.

"Two hundred and thirty-six dollars. Enough for the rent."

"We won't need the rent, sugar."

"Mama!" she exploded. "School's almost out. I want to finish. I want to graduate the fifth grade. I want to stay!"

"Well, I want to be the Queen of Sheba!" Beverly yelled back. "You think I want to spend my whole damn life smelling ammonia, planting my hands in the grimy heads of no-account tramps that treat me like paid help? This was not my plan! But I'm not free as the breeze, am I? I've got to buy kneesocks and Kleenex for a ten-year-old deadweight that no man can see past to take me to wife.

"It's all his fault, your damn father coming on to me like he was the Duke of Rothschild. Sticking me with a kid and no damn insurance and going and getting hisself hit by a lumber truck so his solicitor can call and tell me he's a wastrel and disinherited years ago and five fingers in debt. Leaving my whole life ruined, ruined, ruined. I would kill myself if there would be anyone to wipe up after you . . . but then, if I didn't have you, I wouldn't be ruined!"

Anastasia hated this part most of all. She didn't mind so much being blamed for her mother's ruined life, but she hated it when her mother talked about her father like that. She adored her father. She remembered his spicy smell and his kindness and the feel of his large hands lifting her high in the sky. She remembered his laugh. At least, she thought she remembered. She remembered remembering. She was beginning to lose touch with what was real and what were the stories she told herself.

"I can't do this anymore," her mother said in a low, throaty voice. Her dishwater blonde hair was teased back from a wide hot-pink band. Her pear-shaped face was flushed, and splotches were starting to appear from the alcohol. Anastasia couldn't even ask her to stop drinking yet again. The game held no hope anymore.

"Where can we go? That bitch Eileen will have lied about me

to Janice at the Cut'n'Curl, too, I bet."

"Chances are," said Anastasia. She sat down in the vinyl chair across from her mother.

Anastasia saw it all fade: the blossoms, the heat, the chiggers. Everything she'd earned, had thought was hers. She'd done it again. She'd believed things would work out. She felt sick to her stomach.

"What did your father leave us? What a bum. What a—"

"Stop it!"

"He said he was some high mucky-muck. A family of lords and ladies. He doesn't mention his own family doesn't want him. Cut off without a cent. Without a cent."

"He didn't lie, Mama. He *was* their son."

"Fat lot of good. Bastard. Bastard!" Her "pink champagne" nails clicked rhythmically against the glass before she upended and drained it. "You would take up for him."

"I'm his flesh and blood," she said defiantly.

"His flesh and blood," Beverly repeated, and then something clicked. She sat up straight. "Where is the Visa card, Anastasia? I know you have it hidden somewhere."

"We can't use it, Mama. We have no money to pay it off."

"This one time, sugar. Get it. And get the bankbook."

Here we go again, thought Anastasia.

"Get it!"

"Can we take the curtains, Mama?"

"The what?"

"The curtains. I'll only get them if we can take the curtains."

"Yes, baby, you can take anything you damn please! This time, we are crossin' to the right side of the tracks and we're never coming back!"

Anastasia returned with the bankbook and the credit card to find her mother re-emerging from her bedroom. She had changed into her favorite two-piece periwinkle suit that cinched at the waist and gave her an hourglass figure. She was even putting on a broad-brimmed matching hat. Something had pulled her to her senses. Her hazel eyes looked clear and she had a sassy turn to her walk; this is how Anastasia imagined she must have sparkled as a waitress at the Twilight Room when she caught the attention of a young British importer who worked with a large American tobacco firm. A young importer who would turn out to be disinherited aristocracy, and more importantly, Anastasia's father. Anastasia's impression was that her father didn't mind being disinherited. In fact, he'd seemed quite content with his freedom. It was indeed a sad day for his wife and daughter when his car had been slammed into head-on by the lumber truck.

But Mama seemed to have forgotten all that again. She began humming as she led Anastasia down the stairs and out to the car, where she rolled down the window and sang "Heartbreak Hotel" at the top of her lungs. She sang pretty well.

They drove into town and parked at the end of Main Street in front of Holiday Travel. Together they went into the one-room office lined with large posters of exotic locales, and took the two chairs in front of the desk of Miss Alva Mabrey. She finished her phone call and asked pleasantly how she could be of help.

Beverly flashed her a confidence-sharing smile. "We have just gotten a registered letter," she said, and Alva leaned forward in curiosity, "from the parents of my late husband, Lord and Lady Whitcomb-Day, of Devon, England. They are in ill health and have asked to see their granddaughter at once. We are to buy tickets to leave as soon as possible, for which they'll reimburse us when we get there." She gave a happy but flustered sigh. "Why, Alva, I've never traveled overseas. I don't know how to start! What do we need?"

"Why, y'all need passports. Have you got those?"

"Dear me, no! How long does that take? Lady Ruth has angina—"

"Once we get your tickets, you can use that to get you an emergency passport. Let's see, you want to fly or sail?"

And the two women were off, conspirators of travel. Anastasia sat back in her chair and tried to keep her mouth from falling open. There were a couple of tense moments when Alva put through the airline tickets on their charge card—Anastasia had no idea what their credit limit was—but the transaction was completed, and Alva put in a call to her friend at the passport office. They'd moved so often and registered Anastasia in so many schools that Beverly always had their papers, including birth certificates, in easy reach. It was Tuesday. They were flying out of Charleston to New York and New York to London on Thursday.

"All the best people are expatriates," Beverly said happily once they were back outside. She repeated the story of their sudden summons from aristocracy to Thelma at the bank, who wished them all good luck as they closed out their account.

"Figure out how much we'll need for gas to get to the airport," her mother instructed, "and leave us a hundred bucks for good luck. The rest we're spending on the best damn dinner in this burg. Wait till Eileen Prendergast hears tell of this!"

The next day, Mama went to Anastasia's school, where her teacher let her take her final tests early. They got their passports and the certificate that said Anastasia Beverly Day had completed the fifth grade with high marks. They went to the five-and-dime and bought the fanciest frame available for the only surviving picture of Beverly and Nigel and then-three-year-old Anastasia. Anastasia packed the curtains.

At the last minute, Travis Sloan bought their old Datsun for two hundred dollars, so he drove them to the Charleston airport.

Thus they left the United States, and a credit card bill that would come to a house with no forwarding address.

As their connecting flight took off from Kennedy airport, Anastasia looked wide-eyed at the skyline of New York City. Her mother had already opened one of those miniature bottles of Scotch and leaned back in her seat.

"Remind me never to think there's no hope," she said.

Somewhere over the Atlantic, Anastasia befriended a Midwestern family with three children who were going to London on vacation. She was able to borrow their guidebook on seeing England for thirty dollars a day. She copied out the names of small hotels that were inexpensive but clean. She also read the part about getting into London from Heathrow.

In London, they checked into the Langham, got a third-floor walk-up room with a bath down the hall. Beverly would hate that, but when $223 was all you had, there had to be sacrifices. Beverly followed Anastasia blindly up the rickety winding stairs and passed out onto the bed, sinking into a deep slumber.

Lost hours and all-night flying also tugged at Anastasia, but she was so incredulous about being in England that she opened the window and leaned out. Even the air smelled different, and cars careened on the wrong side of the road. Next door, men were digging some sort of hole and calling to each other in the most melodious accents. It was thrilling. It was more than an hour later that Anastasia finally allowed herself to stretch out next to her mother and succumb to sleep.

Anastasia stood outside the phone booth the next day while Beverly placed the call. She could see her mother speaking in the animated, confident way she had when she'd convinced herself that yet another reality *was* reality. It seemed she had to do quite a bit of talking before there was a pause, presumably as the answerer went to call the baron or baroness to the telephone.

Inside the cherry red booth, Beverly crossed her fingers and winked at Anastasia.

Anastasia could not bring herself to think about what was happening, because that would necessitate thinking about the consequences if it didn't happen. What if they'd come all the way here and Papa's parents wouldn't see them? They'd be broke and stranded. Anastasia didn't know if England still had workhouses, but it seemed likely they'd find out and pretty quick.

But minutes later Mama came bounding out. "Your grandparents have asked us to tea tomorrow, puddin'. We'd better go find some proper English clothing, befitting our new station in life!" she almost sang, doing a step-shuffle.

Anastasia knew they'd also better find out how to get to Devon. When she said as much, Mama said, "Yes, yes, you're the practical one, I'm the visionary. You'll get us there."

Only barely. After Mama had picked out some "gentry" clothes for them at Harrods—and had their hair done there as well—they had only ten pounds more than train fare.

The train left early from Paddington Station. Anastasia had to admit that her mother looked very impressive in her new tailored suit. "Quite ravishing," as her father used to say. The thought of it made her smile.

The morning had awakened gray and dreary, but as the train pulled into their station, the sun broke through in great bursting shafts of light. Mama took this as a good sign; indeed it seemed to be. The car that awaited them was lovely and large.

As they approached Wilton Glen, her grandparents' home, her mother began drumming her fingers—nails now free of polish—against the leather seat. Anastasia looked out her own window, trying not to be affected by her mother's nerves. And she wasn't. As they pulled off the country road onto the circular drive, Anastasia saw in her imagination her father as a young man on horseback, cantering across the lawns, laughing, confident, and at home. She ached to be able to run up to him, to hug him, to talk to him. She knew he'd make everything all right.

The house was large and rectangular; a square-shaped center section with wings stretched outward on either side. Windows marched over each other in rows, each with twelve panes of glass, their sills painted a crisp white in contrast to the burnished brick of the home. But most impressive were the chimneys—Anastasia counted six. Wilton Glen might not have been a vast estate by English standards, but it sure as hell beat anything on Spivey Lane.

They were shown to a sitting room. The white ceilings were low and elaborately carved, as was the mantelpiece. White pilasters curved from daffodil-yellow walls. Two leather sofas faced each other in front of the fireplace; Beverly and Anastasia sat together on the one to the left of the hearth. They didn't have long to wait.

Her grandfather was six feet tall, her grandmother barely five foot four. But it was she who had the most commanding presence. She was stout but not fat, and they were both dressed in subdued but fashionable attire. They introduced themselves: Ruth and Denys Whitcomb-Day. Ruth sat on the sofa opposite them. Denys stood behind it.

"So very nice to meet you at last," Mama said to them.

"Yes," said Ruth.

"If I may ask, how is Alan?" Mama asked of their other son, Nigel's older brother.

"He is well, thank you, as is his wife."

"I'm glad he and Caroline are well," Beverly said, smiling pleasantly.

"So you are passing through England on your way back to the United States?" asked Denys. He had a starched white collar that seemed to fairly glisten over his black suit coat. His face had the same angular shape her father's had. But this man's had deep lines chiseled into it as well.

"Yes. I hope you don't feel we're intruding. I know there had been some trouble between you and my husband, and I am sorry about that, but I thought it should not prevent you from meeting your granddaughter, should you wish to do so."

"Yes. Well," said Denys.

This brilliant discourse was interrupted by the arrival of tea. There was a teapot, and sandwiches and deviled eggs and scones and thick clotted cream. Her grandmother poured, asking what they each took in their tea—since Beverly said milk, Anastasia did, too—and she prepared it for them in china cups before passing it over. As she poured her husband's, the butler returned and quietly told him he had a telephone call. He excused himself.

After Denys left the room, Ruth set her own teacup down with an unexpected thunk.

"If you do not mind, I would like to speak to the girl in the other room," she said.

"Of course," said Beverly, trying to seem calm.

Anastasia was jolted from her comfortable role of bystander as she stood and followed her grandmother down the hall and into a small study. It had a dainty, polished writing desk, and many of the appointments seemed feminine. She guessed it to be her grandmother's office. Her grandmother shut the heavy door behind them. Anastasia felt her heart accelerate to a million miles an hour.

"Your name is Anastasia," she said.

"Yes. It means 'of the Resurrection.' My father said I was his second chance."

"Do you remember your father?"

"I remember him laughing," she said. "I remember him

throwing me up in the air." But the older woman didn't respond. "If that's what you mean," she said, suddenly unsure. "Or if you mean do I remember who he was—"

"No," said Ruth Whitcomb-Day in a heavy voice. "No one could look at you and question who your father was." She collected herself for a minute, then lifted her jade green eyes to meet the jade eyes of the girl. "I want you to tell me the truth, Anastasia. Are you really on your way home to America from a holiday in Italy?"

"No," Anastasia said. "We came over from South Carolina to meet you."

"What is it your mother wants?"

"My mother is a good woman," Anastasia said defensively.

"I'm certain she is. But if she came all this way, she must want something, mustn't she?"

"She wants a better life for me." Anastasia looked defiantly back at her. "I don't think that's such a crime. Wanting something better for your child."

And Ruth Whitcomb-Day laughed.

"How old are you?" she asked.

"Ten."

"Nigel's had his revenge after all," she said. "My only grandchild talks back just as he did. And with an American accent."

ANASTASIA AND BEVERLY were never accepted into the bosom of the Whitcomb-Day family. Her grandparents agreed to pay Anastasia's way through the Chester School, a boarding school attended by generations of Whitcomb-Day women. They made it clear from the outset they had no intention of supporting Beverly. Their lawyers did help her fill out the necessary papers to be granted a work permit as the widow of a British citizen. She got a small flat in London and a job as a hairdresser at Harrods. If Beverly hadn't joined the upper crust, at least she had arrived at the top of the hairdressing line.

Anastasia's years at Chester provided her with the most stability she'd ever known. She loved her classes, especially literature. One of the masters commented that she inhaled every piece of knowledge as quickly as she could, as if fearful her access to it could disappear at any moment.

On holiday she never visited Wilton Glen, going instead to her mother's dingy flat in London. Beverly lasted an entire year and a half at Harrods before she slipped back into the abyss of alcoholism. After that, the jobs lasted four months, six if she held on tight, then three, then weeks.

Anastasia had entered the Chester School when she was eleven. When she was thirteen she realized her mother was in a tailspin.

At the end of the summer holiday, she knew if she went back to school she might never see her mother again. Instead, she took the money her grandparents had sent for tuition and moved them out of the dark shambles of the flat in which her mother existed into a cleaner one in a respectable neighborhood. Anastasia knew that doing so meant she was permanently severing all ties with the Whitcomb-Days. But there was no choice.

During the two-month cushion provided by the tuition money, Anastasia began taking in sewing. She presented herself to local tailors and dry cleaners, offering free work as her calling card. She soon had as much work as she could do in a twelve-hour day. Even so, her earnings barely covered the rent and the most meager of necessities.

In self-defense against self-pity, Anastasia cut off her imagination. She couldn't afford books, so she didn't let herself dream of any. Nor a stereo, or records. They had to have a telly; without it, her mother would spend all day in the pub. Anastasia made agreements with all the pubs in walking distance; her mother had to pay cash, she was not allowed to run a tab. Anastasia gave her mother a nightly allowance. It kept a semblance of order in their home. If Anastasia had allowed herself any dreams, she would have had to watch them be drunk away every night. So she aborted them.

With one exception. On one quaint lane behind one of her tailors was a row of kitchen shops, their windows cheerfully displaying everything needed in a well-appointed French country kitchen. She loved the large nesting mixing bowls, the hand-painted ceramic roosters and pigs, the frilled curtains the color of a sunburst, which made her handmade saffron panels seem childish. On the rare occasion she let herself wander down that lane, she imagined a time a handsome, kind gentleman would find her and fall in love. In her mind his face was indistinct, but she knew every detail of the kitchen he would let her decorate.

It was not true, however, to say her world was without color. She knew each garden in each park she walked through, and the number of flowering plants in each bed. And every day, on her return trip, she would stop outside the Richmond Theatre a block from her home and study the posters for the plays that were running. She recognized many of them from her reading at Chester. Usually, there were color photos displayed; Anastasia especially enjoyed studying the costumes; the colors and lines and textures. The only part of the posters she never looked at was the ticket prices. Even though there were student discounts, she wasn't a student, and she hadn't an extra shilling.

And then one day the poster went up for the new production.

It was Shakespeare's *Cymbeline*, which she'd always longed to see. As she reread the information, a thought struck her. She mustered her courage, went through the lobby into the theatre.

There were work lights on the stage, and her heart felt alive in a way it hadn't for many months. When a gentleman asked what she wanted, she said she'd come to speak to Kenneth McIntosh. She was told to come back the next day between four and six, he would be taking measurements. Come in the stage door, he said.

The next day, Anastasia made her way down the brick alley to the stage door. She was on her way back from her rounds, and her hands were loaded with piecework, even more than usual. But she was afraid if she stopped at home, she might miss her chance.

"Mr. McIntosh?" she asked a woman rushing past her at the door. The woman cocked her head backwards. Anastasia wound her way through halls, asking whenever she ran out of direction. Finally she found herself at the open doorway to the costume shop. It wasn't a large room, but it was flooded with light. She tried to imagine the joy of sewing with that much light. The room was crammed with racks and piles of costumes, and fabric and material. In the middle of the room was a block, on which a young man now stood. A thin thirty-ish man with a receding hairline and wire-rimmed glasses was running a bright yellow tape measure along his inseam while a generously endowed woman in a white shirt and jeans jotted the numbers on a clipboard.

Anastasia watched in fascination as the measurements were finished and the subject bounded out of the room. The costumer looked up. "Yes? Who are you? Are you next?"

"No. Oh, no. I'm looking for Kenneth McIntosh."

"Well, you found him. Quickly, quickly."

"I was wondering—if you needed someone to help with the sewing."

"Sweetie, I'm over budget and underpaid. Thanks. But. Who's next?"

The clipboard woman gave him a name.

Anastasia struggled to find her voice. "I don't want money," she said. "I was hoping to earn a ticket for the play."

Ken looked up. "That's it. My drinking days are done. I thought I heard—"

"I'm very good," she said quickly. "I do it for a living."

She lifted the huge pile of tailoring in front of her as if he might not have seen it.

"Let me get this straight. You want to help sew costumes in exchange for seeing the production."

She nodded. "You could give me something as a try-out, or you could ask Mr. Jaspers at the Leicester Tailor Shop."

Kenneth looked at his assistant. "I think we may be able to work something out," he said.

Ken did give her a pair of trousers to try out. He was so pleased with the results that she began helping him on a regular basis. He was overworked, as he said, but he was very talented, and a kind man under it all. He found some extra money to pay her a bit for *Cymbeline*, and then got a small sum written into the budget for her for the next production. He even let her use the costume shop for her own work during the times it wasn't in use.

Best of all, Anastasia got to see as many rehearsals and performances as her time allowed. She was captivated by the textures and materials of the costumes, intrigued by the gossip and bitching of actors as they were fitted or met in the halls. She was fascinated by the rehearsal process. For the first time since she left Chester, she sometimes woke up happy.

One evening, during an endless technical rehearsal for a bleak new play by an Irish playwright, Ken and the makeup woman, Jane Whittle, were sitting in the costume shop having a smoke while Anastasia finished shortening the sleeves on a herringbone suit for one of her tailors.

"You work too much," Ken told her as she finished and reached for the next item in her pile. "Take a minute, why don't you?"

Anastasia heard the teasing in his voice and turned around and gave him a grimace, then a smile.

"Law," said Jane Whittle, studying her, "look at that." She locked eyes with Ken. "Come help me. Let's give it a go."

Ken looked interested. "Stacy, before you start something else, I need you for a minute."

"All right," she said, quickly calculating what remained. She was, in fact, on top of things.

Ken and Jane had gone down the hall to the makeup room, and Anastasia followed, curious. Jane Whittle came in for a couple of days before the beginning of each play to help the actors design the makeup for their parts.

"Sit down," Jane said. She was in her thirties, the kind of comfortable-looking woman you'd like for your older sister or aunt.

Anastasia sat in the chair she was motioned to. Jane brushed her hair and swept it up with large bobby pins.

"What are you doing?" Anastasia asked as Jane selected a base makeup for her.

"Having some fun, dearie, something you could use a little more of," she said.

"Let me pick out a dress," Ken said. "What size are you?"

Anastasia told him, and he went humming down the hall. Anastasia didn't have the energy to protest, so she gave herself over to their amusement. It seemed Jane was working for a long time, with base and powders, rouge, eyeliners, mascara, lip glosses. Then Jane turned her chair away from the mirror and began working on her hair.

Ken returned with an evening dress from *Lady Windermere's*

Fan. "Try this," he said. Anastasia took the hanger, wondering where to go to change.

"Don't worry," said Jane. "I've seen it all, and Ken isn't interested. Off with the skirt and sweater."

Anastasia removed them rather sheepishly. Ken pulled the ruby red dress over her head. "Perfect!" he said, and zipped it up.

"All right," Jane said, turning her toward the lighted mirror. Look!"

Anastasia looked.

Then she stood, frozen, in something like terror. A person she didn't even know was staring back at her, standing where she stood. Her hand flew to her mouth.

"None of that," Jane said. "Turn all the way around. Look."

She did turn. Again she was stunned. She was nearly fifteen. She had a figure. And in this dress, she looked like the sophisticated, blasé actresses she fitted, the ones who had the world on a string.

She felt like she could be arrested for impersonating a human being.

"I knew you were a looker, but I didn't realize . . ." said Kenneth.

"I'd swear she was a high-fashion model, if I hadn't just done it myself," chortled Jane.

"You know, you could be a model," Ken said.

"No!" cried Anastasia. "Take it off, now!" She clawed desperately for the zipper behind her.

"Luv. Luv! Now that's enough," said Jane. "Here, I'll help you. You're surprised, is all."

"If my mother sees me," she said, and tears traced tracks down her cheeks.

Jane and Ken exchanged looks. Ken undid her zipper, then excused himself, shutting the door behind him. Anastasia pulled her wool skirt and shapeless sweater back on and sat heavily in the chair. She was crying harder now.

"What would happen if your mother sees you?" asked Jane quietly.

Usually, the hours she was away from Beverly, Anastasia could shut her out; live in a world totally apart from the drunken rages, the cruelty, and the accusations. But this—looking like this, being this person—was outside the bounds of the life she knew how to control. Yet from now on, she would live with the knowledge that this . . . other . . . lurked somewhere. She broke into sobs.

"Here, chin up. Your mother, what would she do?"

"She would be upset," said Anastasia.

Jane handed her a wet towel. Anastasia pulled its rough texture across her face.

"There now," she said. "You know, a bit of liner and a touch of color would—"

"No," said Anastasia.

"All right," she said.

Jane pulled the pins from her hair and undid the French knot.

"I've got to go," the girl said. As she went for the door, she turned back, shyly. "Thank you," she said. "I'm sorry."

Anastasia returned home to discover that her mother had found the hiding place of the next month's rent. It was all gone. She slid down the wall in the corner by her bed. And she wept.

The next afternoon, she went to the theater early. She helped Ken sort the costumes and pull down the ones that needed to be cleaned. After he'd tagged them and sent them out, he turned to her. She never came before evening. He didn't ask. He waited.

"What you said yesterday . . ."

"About what?"

"That I could be a model."

"Yes."

"Did you mean it?"

"Yes."

"It's just that . . . I need to do something else. Tailoring doesn't pay enough."

"Especially when they pay you off the books, I'll wager?"

"Ken, I need you to be serious. Don't lie because you feel sorry for me. A model isn't something I'd like to be. But I need to know if you honestly think I could make money at it."

"Yes."

"You're not—"

"Stacy, listen. I know you support your mother. I know you don't have money to burn, and that putting together a book would take money. So I'm not bullshitting you. You would have a very good chance of making money, yes. And I would help you. So would Jane."

"Honest Injun?"

He laughed at the American expression couched in the soft English lilt. "Honest Injun."

Stacy set about her attaining her new goal with her legendary resolve. She looked at the magazines, studying the models. She saw how skinny they were, and although she was already thin, she lost fifteen pounds.

Her pictures and her book were first rate. Jane had done hair and makeup for the photographer often, and she got him to call one of the best agencies and say he'd just photographed a girl they had to see.

Jane walked with Anastasia to the agency. "Confident," she whispered. "Bold."

Anastasia nodded and walked in. At the reception desk, she said, "Brian Odin sent me."

"Yes," the girl said. "What is your name?"

Her name. Anastasia thought of the brassiest, most beautiful woman she'd heard of. Lillie Langtry came to mind. "Lily," she said. "My professional name is Lily."

"Let me send in your book," the girl said. "Have a seat."

Anastasia was signed to a contract that day, and began working that week. Suddenly, she could pay the rent and buy groceries—the nice cuts of meat. The joke was, she couldn't eat them without gaining back the weight she'd lost. Feeding her mother meant starving herself.

The only way the shy teen could force herself to be in the spotlight was to become "Lily" when she was out, and to return to her true self, Anastasia, when she got home to the nightly verbal abuse from her mother. She tried not to wear makeup or form-fitting clothes at home, but her mother decided she'd become a whore to make money. Before long, Anastasia gave up arguing.

Lily's agency became her passage into the adult world. In one way, literally—they paid court fees for her to be declared an emancipated minor. The agents at Mayfair also decided they could expand her fee base by launching her as an actress. They began sending her up for bit parts in films and instructed her to take acting lessons. With help from Ken, Anastasia won a supporting part in *As You Like It* at the Richmond, and went on to become a working part of the company. She got small parts in several films and even a recurring role as a Prime Minister's teenage daughter in a long-running BBC comedy. But most of her income came from print ads.

One day she got a call from her agency saying that director Pierce Hall was casting his new big-budget feature film of *Tristan and Isolde*. Rumor had it that the provocative and alluring actress Nicola Neve would play Isolde, and the buzz, as on all of Hall's films, was terrific. They'd gotten Lily an appointment to audition for the small part of Camille, Isolde's maid.

"Look, Juniper," Anastasia said. (She couldn't believe the girl's name was Juniper. But who was Lily to talk?) "I've got three shoots that day. Three. One with Wolfman Weston, who eats little girls for lunch. How many other Camilles are they seeing?"

"Dunno. Forty or fifty."

"So they won't miss me. Please. Let's give it a miss."

"Sorry. Melinda's already booked you. It's the end of the day. Just stop by. You—"

"Learn something from every audition," she finished along.

"Later." The line went dead.

———•———

IT WAS CLEAR TO ANASTASIA that Bruce was surprised and not entirely pleased to find Leah Hall in his kitchen when he returned from a mysterious outing the next afternoon. Leah's hair was, in fact, still blue-black and cut in a blunt pageboy that bounced briskly as she spoke. She wore a flowing royal blue pant-suit and dark ruby lipstick. She could have stepped out of a Hollywood movie magazine from the thirties.

"Stacy's told me about this infamous list," Leah said.

"Good to see you, too," Bruce answered, pulling loose the knot in his tie—he had actually been wearing a tie—and opening his top shirt button. "It's been a hell of an afternoon. I need a bourbon."

"Save me. Not another pseudo-Hemingway. Bruce darling, let's depart from the hackneyed for a moment, shall we? I thought we might be a bit more social in our drinking. I've brought all the ingredients for a pitcher of Mad Margaritas. Liesl dear, point me to the blender."

Elise stood, apparently not minding the near-miss on her

name, and headed for a lower kitchen cabinet, Leah slinging a carry-on bag alongside her in such a way that the glass bottles inside gave a low-pitched thunk. "You don't know how hard it is to find good tequila in a duty-free shop," she moaned as her hostess lugged out a heavy steel and chrome industrial-strength blender.

"Splendid!" Leah crowed.

Anastasia saw Bruce glower, and her uneasiness blossomed into full-blown alarm.

Then the air was rent by high-pitched mechanical grinding, and when it stopped, Leah lifted the lid and slid a spoonful of lime-colored liquid onto her spoon.

"Ah, perfection," she said. "Liesl, there's a box just there in my case. Unwrap the contents, will you?"

"Leah, it's Elise," said Anastasia.

"Come again?"

"Not Liesl, Elise."

"Both lovely names. Yes, good, you've got them."

Elise had unwrapped four margarita glasses, their bowls clear, rimmed with green, their stems shaped like cacti.

"And she calls me derivative!" said Bruce.

"Salt?" Leah asked him.

"No. Hemingway liked his cactus straight. I choose to follow his lead."

"Bruce darling, how could I ever have thought you were boring?"

"Could be your manic desire for overstimulation."

"Enough, you two!" Anastasia said, throwing back her chair. "There is an issue of extreme urgency confronting us, and I'd like to get to it!"

"Stace, settle down. Claws retracted. It's so seldom I get a real one to bait, you see," Leah sighed. "Let's sit in—let's see, I'll bet you call it the conservatory, am I right? While we decide if Professor Plum did it with the knife or the candlestick."

The four of them moved down the two steps into the glassed-in garden room. Anastasia took a seat closest to the kitchen, well under the eaves. Elise sat next to her.

"Stacy's right," Bruce said. "This isn't a bleeding game."

"How could I think it was, when it's about my father being murdered?"

"It's not solely about you, Ms. Hall," Bruce countered. "My wife was murdered, and I was found to be the only apparent person to gain by her demise."

"So, did you?" Leah asked, staking out a three-cushioned wrought-iron sofa.

"Did I what?"

"Gain by your wife's demise?"

"Dear God!"

"Just trying to get the picture."

"As a matter of fact, I got the entire proceeds from our house in Kensington instead of having to split them with her. I did not kill her, but at this moment I would not swear that murder would be forever beyond my boundaries."

"I'm an inspiration to you, then, am I?"

Bruce took a single chair, cushioned in a floral outdoor fabric, and propped his feet on a glass coffee table. "So tell us about yourself, Ms. Hall. What did you inherit from your father's unexpected departure?"

"I got a piano, Mr. Amerman. A beautiful baby grand. I lost my meal ticket and my entrée into virtually every studio in Great Britain and Hollywood. I spent the next decade begging for jobs and replenishing salad bars so I could finance my first film with credit cards." Leah took a swig of margarita.

"I do not play the piano," she added.

"Excuse me," said Anastasia, "but my friend Jane just died, and I believe she may have been murdered. Could we perhaps try to figure out what's going on?"

"That's exactly what I've been doing," Bruce said. "Where do you think I've been all afternoon?"

All three women turned to him.

"Scotland Yard," he finally said. "I presented our list of decedents."

"And?" asked Anastasia.

Bruce took a dramatically long dose of his drink. "Inspector Irving listened intently, asked a number of questions, then politely said something to the effect of 'This would be a rather convenient out for you, wouldn't it?' or some such B-movie dialogue."

Elise set her glass down with a thunk. "You don't really think that they really think—"

"No, no, don't worry. I think they don't think, which is a major problem. It's easier for them to find a suspect when he stops round at their office for a chat. There is no credible evidence, darling, since I didn't do it. But the point is we shouldn't be expecting immediate help from that quarter."

Anastasia sighed, letting herself fall back against the vinyl. "So it's back to us," she said, then turned to Leah. "Bruce thinks that something happened during filming to provoke the killer."

"A possible, perhaps even likely, scenario," said Leah. "In one way, our killer—should there be one—is doing us a great favor by narrowing down the possible list of suspects. There are nine we can rule out right away."

"You do have a way of looking at the bright side," said Bruce.

Leah went on. "It occurred to me that it might be of interest, besides those definitely out of the game, to see who among our little group has gone missing. So before I left, I called a friend in the publicity department over at Paramount, implying perhaps I could help locate some of them for the reunion. She gave me a short but interesting list. First, Alan Norton."

"I knew him," said Bruce. "He played Duke Gilain. He's become a chiropractor in Surrey. No great mystery there. Sorry."

"All right, then, I'll move on to someone whom you might find a bit more interesting. Unaccounted for is . . . Nicola Neve."

Bruce let out a low whistle. "Nicola. You're right. *T & I* turned out to be her last picture."

"Nicola Neve is missing?" asked Anastasia. "Why did she quit making movies? She was so successful. The first thing I heard about the film was that she'd already been cast as Isolde."

"She shot herself in the foot there," smiled Leah. "She was among the final contenders, and she let her people leak word she'd already been cast. She'd virtually promised herself to my father as a sex slave, and I guess she thought that was an offer no man could refuse."

"Really?" asked Elise, "How do you know?"

"My father told me. He found it amusing she would be quite so blatant."

"It's not as though your father was known as a monk," Bruce chuckled. "As a matter of fact, I'd say his lineup of famous and wealthy lovers was, well . . . legendary. Certainly this wasn't his first such offer?"

"Excuse me. He was also my father, and a family man. Yes, he went through a period of sowing his oats, shall we say. I must thank you for throwing it in my face."

"Sorry. You don't have to be so thin-skinned," Bruce said. "No one is questioning his genius or even his considerable moral fiber. Not to mention, I thought he was divorced by the time of *T & I*."

"None of this matters anyway," Leah said tersely. "The point is he had no interest in Nicola's offer. He did say her audition was very good, and he considered casting her anyway."

Leah's tension abated slightly and a catlike grin crossed her face. "I heard that when her agent called and told her she'd been offered the role of Isolde of the White Hands instead of Isolde the Fair, she went through the roof."

"So why did she take the smaller part?" asked Anastasia, somewhat aghast.

"She wasn't exactly overbooked at that point," said Leah.

"And it was a showy—if supporting—part in a Pierce Hall film."

"And no one knows what's become of her?" Anastasia mused.

"I'd say she's on the list of potential suspects," said Bruce.

"Or possible corpses," said Leah.

"Dear God," murmured Elise.

"The final missing actor is, of course, Peter Dalton," Leah said, her eyes fixed on Anastasia.

Anastasia shifted, finding both Bruce and Elise watching her as well. "What?" she said.

"So?" asked Leah. "Where is he? Do you know?"

"No. No! How would I know?" Anastasia asked.

"'Forever mine, our love will shine, past death, past time, forever,'" Leah recited with poetic flourish.

"Yes, we all know the lyrics. That doesn't mean I know where he is."

"Ooh, a bit touchy, isn't she?" asked Leah.

"Miss Hall—" objected Elise.

"I wasn't exactly his last great love," continued Anastasia angrily. "He had quite a number of well-publicized affairs after me, I seem to recall."

"His last love? No. His great love? That's another question."

"And it's moot," Anastasia shot at her friend. "You asked if I know where he is, and I don't. End of discussion."

Leah shrugged, holding her palms forward, deflecting Anastasia's wrath. "Okay, you don't know. So which list do we think he belongs on? Suspects? Or corpses?"

Anastasia dramatically covered her face with her hands. Leah smiled quickly at Bruce and then at his wife. "Okay, okay. We'll move on. I still think it's a good question."

Bruce cleared his throat. "You know what I was wondering. Jane Whittle died—end of February, wasn't it?"

"February 26," confirmed Anastasia.

"I wonder how difficult it would be to find out which remaining cast members—and crew members as we can find them— were known to be in Los Angeles then."

"Ah," said Anastasia, "then perhaps we could start cross-referencing the ones we know of with the dates and places of the other possible murders?"

"Exactly."

"Well," said Leah, "it would take some time and some creativity. But it's a place to start. I'll bet Richie—excuse me, I mean Richard—Riley was in L.A."

"That would be almost too much fun," said Bruce. "Richie as a mass murderer would be better than him joining Scientology."

"But he's had a stellar acting career since *T & I*," protested Elise. "Even I've heard of him. He makes more money than anyone in Hollywood."

"Than God," added Leah.

"The article you showed me said he's practically hosting the reunion," finished Elise.

"Gathering us into his clutches, perhaps?" asked Bruce.

"I take it he wasn't a big favorite on the set," said Elise.

"You know who I did run into in February at some big benefit," said Leah, suddenly thoughtful, "was Conan Marcel. He's not usually in L.A."

"Again, we're lacking motive," said Bruce. "His score for *T &
I* was nominated for an Oscar. It sold millions of units worldwide.
What would he have against the movie?"

"Not to mention, he didn't really know the cast and crew,"
said Anastasia.

"Well," said Leah, "two down, forty to go. At the moment,
I'm afraid I myself am being stalked by the Great Jet Lag. If you'll
excuse me I'll head back to my hotel and my inviting bed. I'm
certain Elise will be gracious enough to invite me back tomorrow
to pick up where we've left off."

"Of course," said her hostess, standing politely.

"Stace, walk me to the door, how about it?" As Anastasia
stood to join her friend, Leah nodded to Bruce, who more or less
returned her gesture from his seat.

When they reached the front hall, well out of earshot, Anastasia said, "For pity's sake, Leah, what's with you and Bruce? I
thought we were going to add to the body count here and now."

"Oh, he's probably still pissed that I stole his girlfriend during
the shoot of *T & I.*"

"What? But I thought . . . I mean, I count on you to date the
strangest men . . . his *girl*friend?"

"Don't look so shocked. It was the eighties, okay? We were
woman, hear us roar, et cetera. Don't try to tell me you never
had any sexual misadventures when you were young and foolish.
Actually, that's a conversation I'd love to have. Remind me to
get you drunk sometime."

"Sorry, I'm afraid I'd bore you to tears in that department."

"Somehow I'd bet not. But, if you want to know the truth,
there's probably some serious professional jealousy between
Bruce and me."

"You? Jealous of Bruce? But you're a director. He told me he's
dying to direct."

"You wanna guess the difference between what I pulled in for directing one low-budget indie prod and the obscene amount he gets for scripting those rootin', tootin' shoot-'em-ups? Duh."

Leah put her arm around Anastasia and gave her a friendly shake. "Don't worry about us, okay? The actual truth is that Bruce and I are fighting over you."

"That's ridiculous. Like second grade!"

"Of course. But mildly amusing. See you in the morning." Leah gave her cheek a quick kiss and headed out to her rented car.

That night, as Anastasia settled into her firm double bed in the garden-themed guest room, she couldn't keep her thoughts from returning to the afternoon's discussion. She had to smile at the idea of Richard Riley—Richie, as he had been known when he was the young American upstart on the *T & I* set—the megastar, plotting a grand reunion to gather them together like some Agatha Christie mystery. He was such a straightforward, unimaginative kind of person. He would never have it in him.

And Conan Marcel. Anastasia remembered the day he had come over to Pierce Hall's manor house and sat at the beautiful ebony baby grand that Leah had mentioned, and first played the haunting melody that would become "Isolde's Passion," and an instant classic. Frankly, she had suspected that Conan had been more than a bit tipsy that night. But when he started to play, it hadn't mattered at all. He and the piano were one, and together they wound a spell that enchanted everyone in earshot. Even Pierce.

Pierce Hall, she thought. *How your name and your life are being bandied about.* She was suddenly overcome with curiosity to see what Leah had written about her father in her book on the making of *Tristan and Isolde*. Leah had been young then, but precocious enough to convince a publisher she had the entrée and savvy to handle such a book. Anastasia knew Elise had left the book on one of the kitchen bookshelves, and she sneaked out into the shadowy house to find it. Once it was in her grasp, she hurried back to her room, shut and locked the door, and by the glow of the bedside lamp she opened the large cover and thumbed again to "Biographies."

CHAPTER 4

BIOGRAPHIES

Pierce Hall (Director / "King Mark")

An auteur of the highest rank, Pierce Hall is known for his devotion to excellence in theater, television, and cinema. Being born in the 1950s, he says, allowed him to grow up "when good and evil seemed black and white, when success was for the taking for anyone willing to work hard." Mr. Hall began acting while in his teens, with the then newly formed British New Theatre. He left the boards long enough to take a degree in ancient literature at Oxford. However, upon graduation, he returned to the British New Theatre, where he performed several major roles, including a critically acclaimed Hamlet. He went on to become one of the most prominent theater directors in London. His **Agamemnon,** starring Glenda Jackson, has become legendary.

Pierce Hall's next challenge was cinema, for which he wrote and directed several stylish thrillers, including **Midnight Mass, At Interval,** and **Woman Unknown.** He also acted in films directed by many of the great directors of Britain, Europe, and, eventually, Hollywood.

But his love and loyalty belonged to Great Britain, where he adapted the postwar novels of Sir Adrian Newbridge into stirring television.

At the height of his success, he took a three-year hiatus, living in southern France with his wife, Alana Morton Hall (from whom he is now divorced), and their three children, Leah, Rufus, and Jeremy. There he spent his days "in blessed peace amongst the apple trees, writing, and being father to the children."

He also spent an entire year working with the L'Auberge Theatre Company on a production of **Tristan and Isolde.** "It was the most marvelous thing, to have time for the process," he says. "We were all taken in by the power of the story."

His love for **Tristan and Isolde** drew him back to film. He has gathered top talent from around the world for the cinematic production of the classic story.

"Every so often, a project comes along that reminds you why you chose a life in art to begin with," he says, smiling. "I hope it will remind the audience why they go to the cinema."

ANASTASIA'S DAY HAD BEEN harrowing, so it was with a mixture of consternation and relief that she found she'd arrived at the *Tristan and Isolde* audition too late. She raced up three long flights of gray stairs to the British New Theatre rehearsal studio which was being used for casting. There were no longer any starlets, or members of that group of casting directors, assistants, and production personnel she'd come to recognize. Instead there was one lone casting assistant turning off the lights.

"Banana cakes," she said. "It seems I'm too late."

"Beg pardon?" asked the gentleman.

"I'm too late," she said. "My agency overbooks me, you see."

"I meant the first thing you said."

"Oh. Banana cakes." And she giggled, then sobered. "Say, do you work with them? I mean whoever has the list of the actresses they saw?"

"Yes," he said.

"Would it be asking too great of a favor for you to check my name off?" She set her bag down for a moment, massaging her palm where the strap had worn an indentation, then sighed. "I suppose that wouldn't really be straight on, would it?"

"What is your name?" he asked. He was very tall, six two or three. He made her feel very young and small.

"Lily," she answered, offering her hand. "My name is Lily."

His warm hand easily engulfed hers. "Lily what?"

"Lily, that's all. It'll be on the sheet. I'd appreciate it. But if it's any trouble, or would get you into a thicket, never mind." Still pulling in each breath, she dropped into one of the black metal folding chairs. Twilight was descending outside, and long shadows were filling the square room. Then she looked up at the gentleman, who was looking at her with a bemused expression, and she sat bolt upright. "Sorry," she said. "I'm keeping you. You're closing up." She reached for her satchel.

"No, no, that's all right, I could use a sit-down myself. In fact, I believe someone left a full bottle of Coca-Cola and some cups. May I offer you some?"

She nodded, and he found the bottle and twisted the top off, catching the overflow of fizz by taking a swig.

"Oops, sorry," he said, wiping the mouth of the bottle off with the cuff of his sleeve. "I've no diseases, I promise."

As he handed her a Styrofoam cup, she saw he looked older than the twenty-some-odd she had expected. In fact, he looked old. Thirty-five, at least. She was suddenly seized with apprehension.

"You're not—Mr. Damarask?" She asked. Sheldon Damarask was the top casting agent in London.

He threw back his head and laughed. "No, no," he said. "No one as important as that." He folded himself into a chair, his long legs stretched out far in front of him. He was wearing black trousers and a black turtleneck sweater. His hair was also black, rather long, and parted just off center, so that a long lock of it fell over his forehead. As he hit the chair, he expelled a long breath and let himself relax.

"So, Lily, you're sorrier not to have your name checked than you are to have missed the audition?"

"I really hadn't much of a chance," she explained, grasping a handful of her wheat-colored hair. "I mean, if Isolde of the Golden Hair is blonde—and she rather has to be, given it's part of her name (how do you suppose they'll work that with Nicola Neve, a wig?)—they'll want someone of contrast for both Brangien and Camille. So if they've thirty or forty brunettes to choose from, I haven't a ghost. Not to mention, I'm taller than Nicola Neve, and that wouldn't play, would it?"

"I can see you've got this thought through."

"Not at all. It's a lame attempt at self-justification."

"Where did you hear that Nicola Neve is Isolde? Mr. Damarask will be interested."

"My agency said so. She'd be good, too, certainly. It would be a polar bear of a part for any actress to try. I don't think I could see my way through it."

"Oh," he said, "how so?"

Stacy leaned forward, her forearms on her thighs. Her hair, held back only with two small tortoiseshell combs, swept forward over her shoulders. "The potion business," she answered. "That's the trouble with the story for me. The idea that by drinking some drink, two people are no longer accountable for their actions. I think that's a crime. It's what's wrong with the world today. No one is willing to be grown up, to take responsibility. Life's not a bed of roses, and we don't jolly well always get what we want, do we?" She noticed her voice had been rising, and she gave a small laugh. "We have to do the best with what we've got, is all I mean," she said more quietly. "If you blow up the bridge, you own up and go on."

"And try to get someone to check off your name?" he asked.

She blushed. "You caught me," she said. "You're right. I was late. I'll own up."

"How old are you, Lily?"

Her emerald eyes narrowed. "Sixteen. Why? How old are you?"

He laughed. "Thirty-eight. How do you know *Tristan and Isolde?*"

"I studied it at Chester."

"Ah, a Chester Charmer," he said.

"That's the nicer name," she admitted with a crooked smile. She reached down for her bag. "Thank you for letting me sit," she said. "Forget the list. Really."

"In case I do see it, what's your agency?"

"Mayfair."

"I'll see what I can do," he said, holding the door open for her. And as she swept past, she saw he was really quite good-looking, for his age. He gave her a conspiratorial wink and she headed down the stairs.

Two days later, as she was leaving through the posh pink-and-rose reception room of Mayfair, Juniper flagged her down from her side office. "You don't have enough faith in yourself," Juniper said, waving a message slip. "You got a callback for *Tristan and Isolde.*"

Anastasia stared at her, and then grinned. Her new friend,

the assistant casting director, was having the last laugh.

"Let's see. Someone else took the message. It only says Thursday, doesn't have a time. Let me ring them up right now." And Juniper was dialing. She was nothing if not efficient. Anastasia was only half listening as she spoke to one person, then another, then scribbled something down, thanked the party to whom she was speaking, and rang off. "Camille has already been cast," Juniper said.

"Oh well," said Anastasia, sliding into her Lily attitude, "Easy come, easy go."

"You have a callback for Isolde."

"What?"

"They're sending over pages. The woman said you were to prepare Isolde."

The two women stared at each other until Lily figured it out. "There are two Isoldes," she said. "I must be up for the smaller part—Isolde of the White Hands."

"Ah," said her booker. "You still did better than you thought."

But when the pages came, there were two scenes for Isolde the Fair: one with Tristan when she discovers he is the sworn enemy who killed her uncle, and one with her husband, King Mark, when he takes her back after she has lived with Tristan for a year in the woods. If either Anastasia or her agency had thought she had any chance at all, they would have hired a dramatic coach, and probably a dialect coach, to work with her intensively. But everyone, including Anastasia, saw it more as a curiosity than an actual audition for the lead in a major motion picture.

She did see it as an interesting exercise, and enjoyed reading over the scenes, memorizing and thinking about them. She wasn't nervous at all on Thursday—she had plenty of other appointments to keep her mind occupied—even as her cab pulled up in front of the barnlike studio on the outskirts of the city. It was not a large complex. She'd been there before, when she did her bit part in the film *Sparrow*. She paid her fare and climbed the six cement steps to the steel door that was the entrance to Building C.

She identified herself to the security guard, who found her name on a clipboard, dialed a number, and went back to his Page 3 girls.

Within a few moments, a pert young woman with shoulder-length dirty-blonde hair approached. She wore tight straight-leg jeans, a blouse, and a tapestry waistcoat. "Hi, I'm Nancy," she said. "This way."

Much to Lily's surprise, Nancy was a hair and makeup person, and there was a wardrobe woman, too, who met them in a dressing room, asked her measurements, and dashed off to find something appropriate.

"You've got great cheekbones," said Nancy. "Is this your natural hair color?"

"Yes," said Lily, who was used to the question.

The wardrobe woman came back with two simple robelike gowns, one royal blue, the other a soft green. "Which do you think?" she asked.

"The green," Lily said.

Nancy did a series of small braids that she brought to a single band in the back of Lily's head. They served as a cap, holding down her profusion of hair, which cascaded even more dramatically once it was let loose. She put on the gown, then the wardrobe woman ran a silk rope-belt twice around her waist, letting the ends dangle free.

"Wow! Great!" said Nancy.

So far it was like any other shoot.

"You people are geniuses," said a husky female voice as the presence of another actress filled the room moments before her body did. It was Nicola Neve. As Anastasia had guessed, she was wearing a long, blonde wig. Her eyebrows were still dark, which gave her a striking look. She wore a figure-hugging dress; her generous breasts crowded each other well above the low circular neckline. She was flushed with victory, and her magnanimity slipped only momentarily when she sighted Lily.

"Hello," she said, "Nicola Neve."

"Nice to meet you," said Lily. Secretly she was indeed excited to meet an actress whose name was internationally known. Lily had admired the posters for several of Nicola's films.

Then Nicola was past her. "Do help me out of this, dears," she said to Nancy and the wardrobe woman.

An assistant had followed Nicola into the room, and she motioned Lily to follow her. Lily knew intuitively that Nicola turned to watch her leave.

"Sorry," said the assistant, a stocky woman in her late twenties. "You weren't supposed to meet like that."

The two of them arrived in the darkness at the back of the soundstage unnoticed.

"That's it, then? The choice seems quite obvious," said an unseen man.

"There's one more. Indulge me on this," said another male voice, which Lily thought she recognized as belonging to her casting assistant. Lily's companion apologized again with her eyes, then coughed conspicuously and led her forward into the light.

Lily smiled at those anticipating her arrival. They included the cameraman, boom operator, lighting man, and a row of seated dignitaries. She supposed some of them were casting people, some the producers. She suddenly wondered with a tightening of nerves if Pierce Hall was here. He'd have to be, wouldn't he? But she calmed herself with the knowledge that Nicola Neve had the part sewn up, and if she could just keep from falling on her face, she'd be more than happy with the way things had gone.

Her casting friend stood and came to greet her. He wore black trousers and an open-collared shirt, with a sports jacket over it. This time she noticed that his face was oval, his features strong, his jaw square and peppered with several days' growth of beard. The impudent long lock of hair still fell over his forehead.

"Let me introduce you," he said. "This is Gray Eddington, our producer; Gray, Lily—" She shook hands with a portly, intelligent-looking man who sat uneasily in his canvas chair, obviously preferring solid, tall-backed leather ones.

"Sheldon Damarask—" (*Wow,* she thought as she shook hands with the wiry, energetic casting director, *the man himself!*) "Sheldon's partner, Cassie Withers; Tyler Magnusson, screenwriter . . ." The others then dwindled off into various studio execs and assistants. She tried to mask her disappointment that she wasn't at least going to meet Pierce Hall.

"Okay," said her acquaintance, "let's talk."

As he turned and led her away onto the soundstage, Lily could hear a tide of whispers unleashed behind her. *I hope they like the braids,* she thought.

When they were well out of range of hearing of the others, he said, "You've looked over the pages?"

She nodded, and he beckoned to someone off to the side of the plain blue cyclorama.

"Good. Then what I'd like to do is try the Tristan scene first. Do your best to forget anybody else is here, except you, me, and Stefan. We don't have our real Tristan today, so Stefan will be reading with you."

The young man who approached was skinny and tall, with a shag haircut. He was dressed in a simple navy tunic over black leggings, and he was wearing appropriate camera makeup. Stefan was saying hello, but Lily didn't notice. The steamroller had hit.

Afraid to know the answer, but knowing she must, she looked again, more closely, at her casting acquaintance. He was also wearing makeup. She felt herself go pale. "You're Pierce Hall," she said.

"Yes," he answered.

"Dear God," she said, and she started to shake.

"Get her a glass of water," Pierce Hall instructed Stefan, and Stefan, looking confused, headed off.

"You really didn't know?" the director said, and Lily shook her head. He saw she was in trouble. He took her arm and guided her into the darkness of the side farthest from the spectators.

"Good heavens, Lily, it's just me. Take a deep breath. Forget who I am. It doesn't make any difference."

She shook her head, gulping greedily for air. "Can't."

He leaned one hand on a table and ran the other across his face. "Look," he said. "I appreciate your high esteem. But I need something from you right now. I need you to show these people that I'm not going daft in my old age, that I'm not suckered by a pretty face, that you can speak English. You can speak English?"

She nodded weakly. He assessed the situation and employed a snap change of tactics. "I'm giving you a bloody chance here," he said. "Don't make me look like a fool."

And he stalked back onto the soundstage, meeting Stefan, who'd returned with the water. He calmly picked up the pages and pointed something out to the young man.

Lily took several deep breaths. She pictured Lillie Langtry. She stood up straight and shook out her hair. She walked out to join them. Mr. Hall barely looked up at her.

"Okay," he said, "we'll start with the third line on the first page. Isolde, you've just found the incriminating sword. You've already begun to succumb to Tristan's charms, and now you're not only betrayed by him, you're furious with yourself. . . ."

The three of them talked for a few minutes, and then they walked through the scene without lights or microphones. As they did, Lily made the discovery that saved her: Stefan was a total stiff. What might have spelled disaster actually worked in her favor. She had spent dozens of photo shoots looking absolutely mad about some intellectually impaired, pectorally blessed male bimbo who might as well have been cardboard. She had also spent two seasons working with the well-known, oft-awarded Harvey McMillan, who played her father on *Jackson Circle* and was the most self-involved, boorish middle-aged man to tread the boards. She had spent the first season of the series finding ways to make her acting work even opposite Harvey. She had spent the second amusing herself by discovering ways to make them both look good in their scenes together.

She could handle Stefan.

Her nerves left as she rose to the challenge. He was young Olivier and Brando rolled into one as far as she was concerned. She became subtle but intense. She refused to say her next line until he looked at her. By the time they rolled tape, she was forcing him to pay attention.

Between takes, she discussed the scene thoughtfully and enthusiastically with the director (which was how she forced herself to think of Pierce Hall), making sure she involved Stefan, asking him frequent questions.

She got a kick out of it. By the last take, she suspected Stefan was starting to develop a crush on her. When Pierce dismissed him, he seemed hesitant to go.

"Thank you, Stefan," Pierce Hall said again, a final dismissal. And Stefan left.

Pierce turned Lily around, away from the others. His shirt and sports coat had been replaced by a black tunic stitched with gold. It looked royal. "All right, Isolde," he said, "you charmed the boy. Let's see what you can do with the man."

She caught the dare in his voice; it was the kind of dare Lily would take. "The way I see it," he said, "Isolde has come back to Mark, and although she says all the right things, she wants him to know that she is back as a matter of honor and duty rather than out of love."

They discussed the specifics of the scene briefly and he gave her some simple blocking. He surprised her by turning around. "Let's roll," he said.

"First time through?" she asked.

He looked down at her, his deep brown eyes meeting her own deep green ones. "Show me what you've got," he said. And he stepped over to his mark.

If acting opposite Stefan was climbing stairs, acting opposite Pierce Hall was being launched into orbit. He was the one always there first, demanding her total attention, daring her to be completely in the moment with him. He was incredible. But that's the kind of presence a king would have. And she was a queen. A queen more than worthy of her king. She held his stare defiantly at the end of the scene till he called, "Cut."

"I thought you had it in you," he said under his breath. "Let's take it again. This time—"

And off they went.

After he called cut for the second take, she said, "I'd like to try it a different way."

"Yes?" he asked.

"I think—I think Isolde does love Mark. She can't help her passion for Tristan, but she knows her love for Mark is the pure love to which she should be true. Her passion for Tristan is her curse. It tortures her. It shames her in the presence of her husband. Especially since he's willing to take her back."

"All right," he said. "Let's try it."

This time, she started the scene defiantly, using a cloak of pride to protect her from the pain she'd caused her husband. But by the end of the scene, when he held her gaze, she had to look down. Overcome with gratitude for his forgiveness, knowing he was still staring at her, she made a small gesture, but with it she was reaching out to him, begging him to reaccept her, not the king reaccepting the queen as he had already pledged to do, but Mark, the man, reaccepting Isolde, the woman. And she waited, an agonizing moment, knowing her relationship with him would be sealed forever by this one response. He weighed his public humiliation and his betrayed love against the wordless plea of the girl before him. He turned away.

She dropped her hand, a silent tear coursing her cheek. And then he turned back around, took a long stride to where she stood, gathered her to his chest and kissed her, ravenously.

When he stopped, she looked up, stricken—and kissed him again. She saw that he was crying, too. They clung to each other—both facing the camera, tormented. The moment lasted forever.

"Cut!" said Pierce, straightening up.

The tension on the set broke. The onlookers applauded. Lily grinned, and dried her cheeks with the back of her hands. When she looked up, Pierce Hall had already disappeared into the darkness of the sidelines. The assistant who had guided her to the soundstage was again at her side.

"I'll show you the way back," she said.

"Thanks," Lily said.

Another shoot over. She headed back toward makeup, the first step toward home.

WHEN ANASTASIA GOT BACK to the flat, it was after seven. She was surprised to find her mother sitting on the Chesterfield.

"What are you doing here?" she asked.

"I've been home every night this week," Beverly said. "Where have you been?"

"Ken was in a bind over at the theater—last-minute costume crunch. I've been giving him a hand."

"Oh, yes, I'm sure," her mother said.

Anastasia had put her satchel down in her bedroom, and she re-emerged carefully. Something was different about her mother. Her hair was brushed, and she wore a clean if shapeless gray dress. She was sitting on the sofa, but the television wasn't on. But that alone wasn't it.

She was sober.

"Mama?" Anastasia asked. "Are you all right?"

"I know this ruins your little game," Beverly said.

"What game?"

"The game where you control me by keeping me drunk."

"I control you?"

"Yes," her mother said, jumping to her feet, the wrath of hell furrowing her brow. "Driving me out into the night! Paying pub keepers to keep me plied with alcohol! God sees all. God will surely punish you. The ways of enlightenment are the ways of earthly penitence. Purity through self-denial. You have lost your power over me."

Well, this was a new one.

"Yes, Mama."

"Don't 'yes, Mama' me! It's not too late. You, too, can travel the path of enlightenment."

"What path is this? Just where did you find it?"

"At the Center for Truth. A woman who I met—she actually came into the Crooked Elbow, seeking the lost. When she took me to the Center, the Master himself said he had been expecting me!"

"That's nice," Anastasia said, helplessly.

"Will you walk the path with me?"

"Not now, Mama. I'm really tired," Anastasia said, and she went into her bedroom and closed the door. She wasn't sure, but as she drifted off to sleep, she thought she heard chanting.

———————

ANASTASIA PUT THE BOOK back carefully on the glass top of the chintz-covered circular table by her bed. She found the long-buried memories of those days exhausting. She switched off the lamp and closed her eyes as soft, suburban night light filtered into her room. She was blessedly tired, certain she could drift off. But as she descended willingly into the first level of sleep, the memory of a familiar voice, an angry voice, fought its way into her consciousness.

"It's sloppy. Nothing but sloppy," it said. She remembered it as clearly as if he were still alive, here in the room with her. It was Pierce's voice.

"You don't know anything." Another voice was answering, replaying a scene long forgotten.

"I know you, and I know what you can do. But you're resting on your laurels. You're getting lazy, but you're so damn famous, no one is willing to call you on it," Pierce continued.

"You're so full of it! This is bloody brilliant!"

"It's repetitive. It's also the wrong mood for the scene."

Anastasia was carried back to where she had been that night—in the evening darkness on the balcony off the living room of Pierce Hall's country house. The two men obviously thought they were alone, unheard.

"Are you willing to go back to work on this? To give me something closer to what we discussed, rather than a replay of the same theme?"

"No one talks to Conan Marcel with such disrespect! No one!"

"Are you willing to do it?"

"Who do you think you are?"

"Well," said Pierce, "I'm not drunk, which you obviously are. I'll ask you again. Will you write me suitable music for the scene?"

"I already have!"

"Then you're fired," said Pierce. "Come back when you're willing to work."

In response, Conan's voice shook with emotion. "You'll regret this, Pierce. I promise you you'll live to regret this."

Anastasia sat straight up in bed.

"Oh, damn," she said.

Because, of course, Pierce Hall hadn't ended up living at all.

"YES, I'M SURE that's what I heard," Anastasia said the next morning as Leah and Bruce once again gathered around the kitchen table.

"He fired Conan?" Leah asked once again.

Anastasia nodded.

"But—Conan was the noble figure in the studio, bravely finishing the orchestration after Dad's tragic death. Dedicating his work to Dad, the whole bit. His score was nominated for an Oscar."

"Yes, and the love theme was so lovely and moody," added Elise, and she began humming.

"That is lovely, darling," said Bruce, "but it's 'Lara's Theme' from *Doctor Zhivago*."

"Oh. Sorry."

"Hang on," said Bruce, "Elise, where have we stashed my old record albums? I'm pretty sure I've got a copy of the soundtrack."

"They're all in boxes under the stairs," she said.

Within minutes, they were all seated on the hall carpet, thumbing through the densely packed old record albums.

"Ha!" Leah called in victory, holding the familiar gold and green soundtrack album aloft.

Bruce snatched it from her and turned it over to the back. "Aha!" he said. "I thought I remembered something about this."

"Aha what?" Leah snatched it back. The others moved behind her, studying the jacket closely.

Anastasia remarked, "Conan did score *T & I*. All except for one selection."

"Exactly," said Bruce, sitting back on his haunches.

"'Chantry Leap' was scored by Paul Norman. Since when does Conan Marcel score *with* anybody?"

"That is odd," Leah admitted.

"And could lead one to believe something was going on behind the scenes," Bruce said. "If we want to know the truth about Conan and *T & I*, my guess is that Paul Norman is the man to ask."

"Any idea how to find him?" asked Leah, standing and stretching.

"He's an English composer. Still working. I bet I can get us pretty close," said Bruce.

"You find him, I'll talk to him," said Leah. True to her promise, she did seem to have sheathed her claws.

Anastasia looked thoughtful. "We know Conan was in Los Angeles, site of at least two murders, because Leah saw him there in early March. Pierce died in England, of course—at a time we know Conan was here—but so were at least half the cast and crew."

"Reggie Camden died at his house outside of Paris. And Conan Marcel now lives in France. That one would have been convenient."

"But a lot of people could have easily gotten to France," Anastasia said cautiously. "How about Gray Eddington? He was killed in his home in Switzerland, back in '99. Maybe we could see if Mr. Marcel had any particular projects that took him to the Alps around that time."

"Okay, let's start tracking the time and places of each death," Bruce said.

"First let's find Paul Norman," Leah said. Bruce nodded, and the two of them turned toward Bruce's office.

Elise turned to her remaining guest. "It's a lovely a day. While they're looking for phone numbers, why don't you walk with me to the pillar-box?"

Anastasia stood straight and stared at Elise. Why would she even suggest such a thing? She had been so understanding during the car ride here. Yet it seemed she didn't get it at all. How could Anastasia explain the terror that lurked in even a simple outing?

"It's not a trick, I promise you. The pillar-box is only in the middle of the block. You can see it from the front door. I was thinking—a step at a time, if you know what I mean?"

Anastasia looked out the window to the right of the door, and there, only twenty yards away, sat the box. Could she do it?

It seemed that she was taking baby steps to re-enter the world of the living. Elise was looking at her with kind concern.

"All right," said Anastasia weakly.

A wicked late-April wind blindsided them as soon as they stepped out the door, but because of it the air was sharp and clear, the sky a light lavender-blue.

"You all right?" Elise asked.

"It's the fear that the panic attack is going to happen that's so awful," Anastasia admitted. "But with you here and no one else around, and the goal in sight, it seems safe."

Even as she said it, Anastasia knew without a doubt that they weren't alone. She felt the presence of someone there, someone watching them, so acutely that the back of her neck prickled.

Without breaking stride, she surreptitiously surveyed each side of the street. Nothing. A row of cars lined the suburban curbs—each empty. Nor were there telltale faces at any of the curtained windows, no one on the stoops or in the gardens.

But someone was there. Someone was watching.

As Elise turned back from posting her letters, Anastasia looped her arm through her companion's and continued sweeping the area with her eyes as they chatted. Nothing.

Who was he? Where was he? Anastasia turned one last time before they re-entered the house. Other than a woman, bundled up much more sensibly than they, leaving the house across the way and hauling her toddler into the car, there was no one.

"Luck already," Bruce said on their return. "Paul Norman was listed in the London directory. He's out doing a mix, but his wife provided his mobile number and we've caught him on a break."

"Paul darling, this is Leah Hall," Anastasia heard, walking into Bruce's office and sitting in his chair. "So good to talk to you! Hope you're working on something exciting. . . . Marvelous. Listen, the reason I'm calling is that we're updating materials on T & I for the re-release, and frankly, I always thought you didn't get the attention you deserved first time around. . . ."

After what seemed like hours, Leah hung up, and leaned back in the executive chair, stretching in a languorous, catlike fashion.

"So?" Elise was the first to jump in.

"So . . ." said Leah. She sat forward, her hands folded squarely on the desk. "So Dad hired Paul Norman to complete the score after he and Conan Marcel parted ways because of creative differences. Paul had worked with Dad before on smaller projects, but this was his big break. He guesses he wrote about half the score, six major themes, before Dad died.

"After Dad's death, Conan reportedly went to producer Eddington, stricken. Conan said his solicitor had told him he was legally bound to finish the score. More than that, the death of his best friend, Pierce Hall, made him truly remorseful, the least he could do was finish the score, make it great, et cetera.

"Paul said he was ready to fight to keep his commission, but Conan was a great idol of his, and Conan insisted on coming over and hearing Paul's work, which he claimed to love to the point that Conan kissed him and cried and said he was the next great film scorer, and Conan promised to use at least one of his pieces in the final score, if not all of them. Paul said he was so overwhelmed by all the alleged legal hoo-ha, not to mention the attention from his idol, he felt he had to agree to give the reins back to Marcel.

"And Conan did just what he'd promised—he used one piece of Paul's. Paul never heard from him again."

"While Conan went on to make a bundle from the score," Anastasia said.

"A mega-bundle," added Bruce.

"That's not all," said Leah, leaning forward conspiratorially. "You might remember that Conan Marcel scored that Sam Rinaldi film in '99. Which they worked on together in Gstaad. Less than fifty kilometers from where Gray Eddington died."

This led to a moment of silence as everyone processed the new information.

"Okay," Anastasia finally said. "So he had opportunity. What was his motive? Even if he killed Pierce to take the project back, why continue? He made a skadzillion bucks off the movie. And why kill Gray and try to kill Bruce—but not Paul Norman?"

"Well," said Leah, "I think there's only one thing to do. Conan Marcel was always well known as a gourmet cook. I say we go to France for a nice lunch."

CHAPTER 5

BIOGRAPHIES

Peter Dalton ("Tristan")

A fresh but already proven talent, 18-year-old Peter Dalton was Pierce Hall's first choice for the pivotal role of the magnetic Prince Tristan. "He has a very rare blend of youthful charisma and mature insight," says the director. "Not to mention a rare talent. Once we had Peter on board, I knew I had a good chance of making the film I wanted to make."

The son of Anglican vicar Andrew Dalton and his wife Sarah, Peter had participated in church and school theatricals when a film crew came to shoot parts of the feature **St. Crispin's Day** on location in the North Moors near the senior Dalton's parish. Searching for a local youth to play a small role, the director found then-14-year-old Peter. He was so impressed with the boy that he hired him for a larger part in his next film, **Union Jack.**

From there, Peter went on to receive critical acclaim for his work as the stricken son in **Midnight Sonata.** Before **Tristan,** he had already completed work on two upcoming films: a strong supporting *part in the ensemble-oriented* **Wooden Soldier** *and his first starring role in the thriller* **Domino.**

"It's a special challenge to do a story as well known as **Tristan and Isolde,**" *says Dalton. "Classics endure because they deal with primal feelings and situations that resonate today. Playing such intense emotions can be cleansing. It certainly puts everyday crises in perspective."*

But Peter claims his favorite role is still that of son and brother, and he happily returns home after every film. "It's where I find my center, my sanity," he explains. "Especially coming off a film where my character dies, having made all his choices and fulfilled his destiny, it's intoxicating to find I've still got another chance at life."

All of us will enjoy watching Peter Dalton share the part of his destiny which is Tristan with us as well.

ONE OF THE MOST SURREAL experiences of Anastasia's life was going with the head of the Mayfair Agency to meet with Pierce Hall at the Heather Hill office. Once there, Mr. Hall jauntily announced he was willing to take one of the largest gambles of his career and cast Anastasia as the lead in *Tristan and Isolde*.

There were a few points Pierce wanted to iron out before sending her agent to Gray Eddington to go over the contracts. Those seemed fairly simple: he wanted Anastasia to use her real name, instead of "Lily," so she'd sound more like a serious actor; he wanted her to gain some weight to add curves to her stick-thin model frame and lose her 'pencil legs'; and he wanted her to understand that Tristan and Isolde's first lovemaking would be a major scene. "I think my work speaks for itself in that I have no intention of being pornographic," he said. "But I have no intention of being prissy about it either."

Anastasia said she understood.

So Pierce Hall officially offered her the role of Isolde the Fair, and Anastasia officially accepted.

Once her agent had left Pierce's office to discuss the contract, Pierce brought up one more caveat.

"I don't know if you've heard that Peter Dalton has been hired to play Tristan," he said.

"I had heard, but I'm afraid I don't know him."

"He's an extremely gifted young man. I'm sure the two of you will get on."

"I'm sure we will."

"In fact, it will be helpful if you do. Forgive me for borrowing trouble, Anastasia, but I'd like to ask you not to sleep with him."

"Excuse me?"

"I've found it's far from uncommon when you throw two exceptionally good-looking young people together in a high-pressure situation for hormones to rule the day. Love on the set is classic. So fall in love with him, fine, you have my blessing. But don't bonk him until after the shoot. You see, affairs on the set usually burn brightly and end badly. And if they end badly during the shoot, it makes a pressured situation ever so much more difficult."

"Mr. Hall," she said pointedly, "I do not . . . bonk . . . my coworkers." But in the content of what he'd said, she was not so much perturbed that he assumed she'd succumb to the charms of some young Romeo as she was pleased he had implied that both she and Peter Dalton were good-looking. It was rather a relief after the Pencil Legs speech earlier.

By the day of the first read-through, her nerves were so jittery she sloshed her morning coffee onto her favorite cotton nightdress. She was terrified that everyone else involved with the film knew what they were doing and she'd be immediately spotted as the fraud that she was. Although she knew her mother was wrong calling her a slut, the no-talent, no-account part was harder to disprove. Pierce Hall had made a gigantic mistake. How had things ever gotten this far?

Somehow Anastasia managed to pull on a purple gaucho outfit with a tapestry jacket and completed the look with black suede boots. At the flat's one mirror, she brushed her thick, wavy, below-the-shoulder hair, wishing again it was straight and manageable. As the car arrived to pick her up, she had a sudden fear that she was dressed not like a serious actress, but like a model cloaked in pretense.

She tried to summon Lily to get her to the car, but today even Lily had a severe case of nerves.

As it turned out, serious actors wore blue jeans. Entering the modern, window-lined room rented for the occasion from the Royal Shakespeare Company, Anastasia felt like a peacock amid mud hens. The table that ran the length of the center of the room was huge. Molded plastic chairs marched in symmetry around it, and another line of chairs ran parallel under the windows.

Many of the participants had already arrived. When Pierce Hall saw her, he grinned protectively and led her over to be formally introduced to "the suits," including producer Gray Eddington and the men from Paramount. As Pierce was pulled into a conference with the set designer, he gave her a conspiratorial wink that gave her confidence a small boost.

Which was further bolstered by the appearance of an unnecessarily good-looking young man by her side. His hair, which had probably been carrot orange when he was a child, was now a striking auburn. It was rich and full and fell below his collar.

"Hi," he said, his grin and his accent distinctly American. "Richie Riley. I'm playing Kaherdin. I bring you the jasper ring and the word that Tristan is dying."

"Hi," she said. "I'm Stacy."

"I've always wanted to work with Pierce Hall. And wow. A free trip to Great Britain. I've never really been anywhere besides Iowa and California before."

"Yeah?" said Anastasia. "I'm from South Carolina myself."

"No," he protested, seemingly fascinated.

Anastasia's eyes kept flitting to the back of the room, where a cluster of young men were joshing with each other.

"Those are the Brits," Richie said. "They know each other already."

In other words, they were the in-group, and she and Richie were on the outside. She smiled wanly. But then something amazing happened. One young man in the tight knot of friends looked over and saw Anastasia.

"Blimey, gentlemen, *this* is the difference," he said. "Come on, then."

He quickly took the paces between his group and the girl.

He put one foot forward and did a sweeping bow. "Garrett Clifton, milady," he said, his sharp features already animated. "And this is the rest of the motley crew."

There followed a brief fidget.

"Say hello, ya motley crew," he said, and laughed.

The other young men gathered around, each introducing himself rather shyly. Anastasia introduced herself and Richie, and it wasn't long until the level of conversation resumed, this time swirling around, and including, the current and former Americans.

Much to Anastasia's relief, she found herself next to yet another nicely packaged young man, this one raven-haired and wearing jeans and a white buttoned shirt, both unwrinkled. When he spoke, it was softly, to be heard under rather than over the general din.

"First day," he said. "Are you excited, then?"

She studied his oval face, his thin jawbone descending from chiseled cheeks. He looked trustworthy.

"I'm terrified," she answered.

His grin was relieved and crooked, causing dimples as deep as troughs to appear on either side. "Read-throughs are always nerve-racking," he said. "The only comfort is that we'll each be so tied up in our own performance, no one will notice anybody else's. So don't worry."

"Stacy," she said, holding out her hand.

"Bruce," he said, grasping it warmly.

"All you chaps know each other?"

He nodded. "Most of us worked together on *Wooden Soldier,* which comes out next month. It's set in a boys' school, so every teenage actor in pants in England was in the blasted thing. We haven't seen each other in six months, so it's rather a reunion." He smiled again, this time remembering. "We had a time," he said, "but Pierce Hall will draw the lads up short, and quickly, too, unless I miss my guess."

The door to the hall swung open grandly, a prelude for Nicola Neve to sweep into the room. Talk ceased. She stood just outside the door, waiting. She wore jeans that adhered to her, and her top might as well have been painted on. But why not? She was tall, slender, and curvaceous with long legs, huge eyes, and straight black hair. She was only in her early twenties, but she had the imperious air of one who owned the world. She stood stock still, coolly surveying the room until Pierce disengaged himself and came to pay tribute. She let him take her hand. He kissed it, bowing with a flourish. "Miss Neve. How good to have you with us."

She gave him a look that clearly implied that forgiveness for his terrible slight in casting was hers to give; she weighed the choice for a moment, then sighed and smiled.

"Let's get on with it," she said. "Some of us do have other engagements."

She brushed past Pierce into the room, where she proceeded to hold court among Eddington and the others.

Anastasia was predictably intimidated. "I don't know any-one."

"You know me," said Bruce.

No sooner had he spoken than the door opened again, this time marking the arrival of a young man wearing jeans and a ribbed tan turtleneck. He had eyes so blue you could dive into them from across the room, and his brownish-blond hair was thick with a slight curl.

He stood hesitantly for a moment—and then he grinned. It was as if someone had turned up the lights in the room by three hundred watts.

Unlike Nicola, who stood awaiting recognition, the newcom-er's smile was ebullient and sincere. And he was immediately surrounded by everyone in the room. Including "You Know Me" Bruce.

Everyone, that was, except Anastasia, who found herself abandoned by the radiator. The newcomer greeted "the lads" warmly, slapping backs and punching shoulders. He pumped Pierce's hand enthusiastically and kissed Nicola on the cheek. Anastasia quit watching. She stood, forsaken, looking like a gi-ant grape.

The next five minutes would forever rank amongst the lon-gest and most dreadful of her life. It couldn't have been more clear who the outsider was had there been a neon arrow above her head.

The volume in the room had shifted up a notch. The young man—obviously the picture's star, who had billing over hers, thank you very much—moved through the space greeting everyone.

At one point, he looked up and saw Anastasia. Unexpectedly, her heart raced, and she held herself firmly in grip so that she wouldn't melt like the others if he turned his mega-voltage smile her way. She met his eyes, and held her breath briefly; to be included by him would put her back in the swim of things.

Instead, he purposefully turned away. Turned away as if he'd discovered she was the cleaning woman or a frothing fan. Except she was certain he'd treat the cleaning woman or a fan with more respect. The others turned with him. She continued to stand alone.

And she knew right then that she hated Peter Dalton.

It was bad enough to think you owned the world like Nicola Neve. The only thing worse was to own the world and pretend like you didn't, then choose who was a worthy subject and who wasn't.

Well, Lily was every bit as good as Mr. Wonderful. If no one else was onto his little game, she was. It was a game two could play.

When Pierce called everyone together to begin the reading, she wasn't surprised to find herself sitting next to her new nemesis.

This time, in front of the others, he grinned at her. "Peter Dalton," he said.

"So I gathered," she answered, smiled briefly in her most condescending manner, and turned to greet the woman on her other side, who was playing Brangien.

They sat down.

Anastasia was enthralled by the reading. The story, the script, and the potential of the actors around the table were so great that she ceased caring about the attitude of Tristan. What mattered was that he was a good actor. All of his line readings were interesting, often unexpected, which made her find unexpected meanings in her own responses.

Her distaste for her co-star was overshadowed by her excitement about the project. It was clear at the conclusion of the afternoon that the others had the same enthusiasm.

Pierce stood to give them a final word of dismissal. "Ladies and gentlemen and actors," he began, and grinned. "I think you can all see the promise of the project before us. Gray Eddington and I have gone to great lengths to put together the finest team possible for this project, both before and behind the camera. And, by God, I think it's going to pay off.

"Go. Get some sleep. Say farewell to your loved ones. And we'll see most of you day after tomorrow in the country.

"Let the games begin!"

ANASTASIA LOVED THE REHEARSAL "days in the country," as Pierce had so quaintly referred to them. The production had rented a large manor house an hour south of London. Besides rehearsals—which, for her, started early and ran late— there were riding lessons, dancing lessons, and lessons in court manners of the time.

Her distaste for Peter the Perfect had grown by the day, but she was dedicated to the production and thought she had done a masterful job of working with him when she had to and avoiding him when she didn't.

Until the day Pierce found her at the stables as she finished her riding lesson. The riding master was helping her dismount as Pierce strode down the path from the house.

"Care for a canter with the king?" he asked, as he swung aboard the riding master's stallion, Empire.

"Certainly, sir, I'd be delighted," Anastasia said, butterflies flinging themselves in kamikaze-fashion against her stomach walls. Certainly Pierce didn't have the time for a nice ride to pass the time of day. What did he want to say that required such planned privacy? Was she disappointing him so much already? Was it too late for Nicola to take over her part?

Stacy tried to smile for the sake of her instructor and wished for all the world she wasn't forced to ride sidesaddle. But she'd mastered it well enough to urge her mount into a canter after Empire as he took off down the path into the deer park.

The fragrances of early spring burst all around them as Pierce reined in his steed and dismounted. Pierce put a strong hand on either side of her waist and lifted her easily from the mare.

"You ride like you were born to it," he said, taking the reins of both beasts and looping them over a low branch.

He took a seat on a cement bench beside a pond and indicated the space beside him. Her heart revved and she hoped she could keep from crying when he sacked her.

"I wanted to talk to you about rehearsals," Pierce said, his eyes still on the water.

She swallowed. "Yes?"

"It's about Peter, actually."

"Yes?"

"Lord, Anastasia, I asked you not to sleep with him. I didn't mean you had to loathe his very existence."

She folded her hands. "It's that obvious?"

"You're both good enough actors that it won't totally ruin the picture, but it's not exactly Bastille Day fireworks between you, is it?"

"Not exactly."

"What's the problem? He's talented, charming, funny, doesn't have swamp breath that I've noticed. Everybody likes him."

"And if I don't believe you, I can ask him," Stacy said under her breath.

"So you think young Dalton's conceited."

"Quite the opposite. He's so sure he's perfect, he has the largess to indulge the rest of us with his well-practiced humility."

"Ah. He's such a snob he has the gall to act humble."

"Something like that."

A grouse, surprised by an unseen assailant, streaked out of the trees above their heads.

Pierce rubbed his hands together. "It should come as no surprise that Peter thinks you don't like him. As a matter of fact, he thinks you're a snob. Now, this would all be very amusing if you were teenagers off for a summer holiday. But it won't do at all for a five month shoot."

His voice had turned hard, like an angry father laying down the law. She knew he meant to be intimidating, and he was. She had a sudden, surprising memory of the feel of his warm mouth on hers, the hungry intensity of his kiss during the audition. She understood how beautiful, wealthy women could desire to give themselves over to his commanding presence.

"No, sir," she said.

"You know that on Monday we break from here and reassemble midweek at our first location, in Scotland, to begin principal photography."

"Yes," she said.

"It's quite a long trip from here to there by auto. Fifteen hours, perhaps."

"I'm not surprised."

"Peter is driving up in his very small Daf. Almost room enough for two. You're going with him. By the time you arrive, I expect you'll have worked out your difficulties."

He couldn't have deflated her more quickly with a punch to the solar plexus.

"Pierce, I see your point. And I promise to go out of my way to be nice."

"Too late," he said. "Arrangements have been made."

"Suppose it backfires?" she countered. "Suppose instead of becoming fast friends, Peter and I grow to truly despise each other? Wouldn't polite distaste be safer?"

"Safer, yes. But safe isn't what I need on this film. I need passion. And hate is a passion. I'll take the chance."

Pierce could no longer suppress a grin. "Anastasia, I want you to promise me two things. First, that you'll give him a chance. He really is a fine young man. I have great respect for him, and I'm very sparing with my high opinions."

"All right," she sighed. "And second?"

"That once you've given him a chance, you won't let him into your knickers until after the shoot."

She gave a small shriek and pushed at Pierce with both hands. "You either have too high an opinion of your diplomatic skills," she scolded.

"Or—"

"Or you have a one-track mind!"

He gave a rumbling chuckle. "You're far too easy to tease," he said. "We'll go through hell, certainly. But we'll have some fun."

IF THERE'D EVER BEEN A LONGER, more uncomfortable ride north up the A1, Anastasia had never heard about it. In fact, it seemed like an excellent basis for night terrors: being crammed into a tiny car with someone you hated, and being unable to leave.

Pierce had been right about the comfort level of Peter's car.

It was a rubber-band-powered Dutch Daf, noisy and slow. It had been the thrust of their only conversation.

"Sorry, but I haven't had time to buy my own car yet," Peter had mumbled as they'd pried themselves into the auto in the early morning hours. "I've had to borrow mi mum's."

They'd fortified themselves with a cold breakfast before leaving the safety of the manor house, but by Doncaster, they were so famished they had to stop for lunch, even if it meant having to appear social. They stopped at the first pub they came to, by then emptied of the midday crowd. They each ordered shepherd's pie. Peter ordered a beer, and they hunkered down in the wooden booth to wait.

Peter took a draught from his mug. "I get the feeling you don't like me," he said.

"I don't have feelings about you one way or the other," Anastasia protested.

"Have I done anything to offend you?" he asked, not buying her answer.

Besides having life handed to you on a silver platter, everything coming easily? Besides not knowing what it's like to go hungry, to work till 3 a.m. on the tiniest stitches until your vision blurs, then continuing to work because you knew next month's rent was due?

Besides not immediately and impulsively liking her?

"No," she said. "Do you have a problem with me?"

He took another swig. "I wouldn't say you're easy to talk to," he answered.

Those were the last words spoken until they were back in the car once again and had been heading north for two more hours.

"Rest stop," Peter announced as he made the turn from the motorway into a large petrol station.

Anastasia returned from the W.C. to find the Daf pulled away from the pump, parked beside a telephone kiosk, which Peter was using. He finished one call and placed another. Then they both resignedly sandwiched themselves back into the car.

They'd been driving for almost another hour when Peter said, "Look, there's been a change of plans. I've got to stop by home. But I checked with the production manager, who said that while some of the crew needs to be on location as early as tomorrow, the shoot itself doesn't start until Saturday. As long as we're there by Friday night there shouldn't be a problem."

Anastasia stared at him, aghast. Who did he think he was, shanghaiing her this way? She'd agreed none too happily to ride with him, but this! He thought he could hold her hostage in some godforsaken place for three days of her life simply because it suited him? What kind of thoughtless egomaniac was he?

"So that's what you do?" she asked. "Make plans, then announce them to whoever has the misfortune to be stuck in the car with you? Did it ever occur to you that it might be all right with the production manager, but it might not be all right with me?"

"I said I was sorry," he muttered.

"Sorry doesn't quite do it this time," she said. "You'll have to take me to a train, or find me a ride. Or something!"

"Why?" he exploded. "What makes your life so much more important than everybody else's? What is it that you have to do in Scotland that you can't possibly accomplish in England?"

"Study my lines!" she said. "Rest and . . . and prepare!"

"I promise no one will bother you," he retorted. "Especially not me!"

She was beginning to panic. She didn't want to be stuck at Peter's for three days. She'd go mad. She could see it now: picture-perfect parents in a house filled with Peter's baby relics, his school trophies, stills from all his movies. It made her want to barf. If Pierce wanted them to get to know each other so badly, it would have been much more fitting for Peter to come home with her. She could show him all Mum's favorite pubs, her secret stashes of booze; or, if Mum was still sober, perhaps they could go visit the Swami of the Week.

"Stop the car," she said.

"What?" he asked.

"I said stop the car," she repeated. "I'm getting out."

"But we're kilometers from anywhere!"

"I don't care. I'll hitchhike."

He didn't stop. He did, however, look miserable. That was something. She rode along, staring out the window. Since Pierce Hall had gotten her into this, he could damn well get her out. She'd call him as soon as they arrived and insist that a car be sent.

Peter Dalton drove. And drove.

"Where on earth do you live?"

"Hawnby," he said.

"Where on earth is Hawnby?"

"North Moors," he said.

The North Moors seemed to be at the ends of the earth. As light began to fade, looming to the right was a towering rock that stretched on, until it rose suddenly into a sheer cliff immediately ahead of them, abruptly cutting off the world as they knew it.

The road continued climbing, black-headed gulls circling from the precipitous drop from the cliffs. After Sutton-Under-Whitestone cliff, Peter shifted down into second, expertly making hairpin turns while continuing to head up—and up—and up. Good Lord, they were leaving civilization. Anastasia might never be seen again.

It was in gathering darkness that Peter said, "We're driving along the River Rye. Hawnby is settled on it."

She was in no wise prepared for the simple beauty—or the

feeling of remoteness—of the valley that hid the tiny town. Lamps were coming on in the red-roofed houses, some of which were nestled in the bottom of the dale along the river, others settled halfway up the steep hill to the moors. It was like circling back into the eighteenth century. It was like finding Brigadoon.

It was like being held captive in *The Twilight Zone*.

Lights poured from every window of the old, three-story stone vicarage as they pulled into the drive. No sooner had the motor died than the wooden door with an old rounded top swung inward and two female creatures shouted and took the steps, while a large, masculine frame stayed silhouetted in the doorway.

"Peter, Peter, Pumpkin Eater!" called the first form, obviously the little sister, who flung herself into her brother's arms as he hit the ground from the car.

"Alice Angel-Eyes!" He easily picked her up and twirled her once around.

"Welcome home, son," said the father, who was much taller even than Peter, as he shook his offspring's hand.

She was thinking she really might barf after all when the three of them turned to her en masse.

"This must be Anastasia," said Mrs. Dalton.

"Yes, this is Stacy," Peter said. "Stacy Day."

"We're glad to have you," his mother said with a welcoming smile. "We so seldom get to meet any of Peter's friends."

You'll have to wait a while longer for that, Anastasia thought, but she smiled and said, "It's kind of you to have me." *Peter will die for this. In little ways, every day. It will be my greatest pleasure.*

There was an unexpected small hand in hers and she looked down to see the little sister looking up, studying her carefully.

"You're beautiful," she said matter-of-factly. "Isn't she, Mother? Look."

"Alice, let's not embarrass our guest the first night," said the mother.

"Nice to meet you," said the father. He couldn't shake her hand because the sister still had hold of both of them. "Your things are in the boot?" he asked Peter, and the two of them circled back to get the valises.

As the others moved away, Anastasia looked down in exasperation at the child before her. The girl was petite and fragile looking, with long sandy hair falling below her waist. Her face was oval, her features delicate—with the exception of her eyes, which were large and round as saucers. Anastasia guessed her to be about seven years old.

"I'm very glad you've come," whispered the girl. "We hardly ever get to meet new people."

Anastasia smiled weakly and let the child lead her inside.

Peter certainly had no room for boasting about his looks in this family, Anastasia reflected as she and Peter helped themselves to the roast beef and Yorkshire pudding set before them. Sarah Dalton, Peter's mother, had an adult version of Alice's refined features, but her attractiveness was more than that. The gentle lines of her face were smile rather than frown lines; she seemed a genuinely kind person.

Andrew Dalton, the vicar, was easily six feet. His thick hair and well-shaped beard were black, a color somehow lost on both his children. It was from him, however, that Peter got the curls. His eyes were dark and friendly, his voice bass, a perfect speaking voice, and he had a deep laugh that one couldn't help but join in with. Anastasia wondered why someone with such obvious gifts was stuck at a remote country parish.

As they ate, the kitchen bubbled with laughter. Anastasia did her best to smile from time to time. There was little on her mind besides getting Peter alone and insisting on using the phone.

Finally Sarah Dalton looked at the clock. "Bedtime, young lady," she said to her daughter. "Peter will still be here in the morning. Let's start moving."

"Can Stacy come and tell me good night?" she asked.

Mrs. Dalton glanced quickly at their guest.

"I'd be happy to," Anastasia said without conviction.

"All right then, off with you," said her father, and both adults followed their youngest child from the room.

Peter and Anastasia were left alone, across from each other at the heavy wooden table.

"I suppose it's too late to make other arrangements tonight," Anastasia heard herself saying. "I'll ring Pierce in the morning."

"Fine," he mumbled flatly.

"How old is Alice? Seven?" Anastasia asked.

"She's nine. Nearly ten," answered her brother. "She's small for her age."

He made a decision, and looked up, directly at Anastasia. "She'll ill," he finally said, trying to keep his voice casual. "She has CF. Cystic fibrosis."

"Oh. I'm sorry."

Anastasia had heard of the disease. But she wasn't prepared as she entered the girl's bedroom on the ground floor to see the oxygen tent and medicines mixed among the pictures of rock stars and posters of faraway cities: New York, Paris, and San Francisco. There was a cot against the wall. Alice was sitting up in her bed, taking a pill from her mother's hand, when Anastasia and Peter came in. Looking at the fragile child with eyes of new knowledge, Anastasia saw how small she was beneath the covers, how vulnerable. Anastasia felt uncomfortable and a bit of a fraud as the four of them formed a circle around Alice's bed. She found herself holding Peter's hand on one side and Alice's on the other as the girl said her prayers.

After lights-out for Alice, the Reverend Dalton led Anastasia upstairs to a small bedroom that hugged the front of the house. The walls were cleared, but there was pretty, feminine white wood furniture. She guessed this had been Alice's room in better days.

Anastasia managed to catch Peter with a restraining hand as he headed into his bedroom, next to hers.

"Who sleeps down on the cot in her room?" she asked.

"We take turns," her brother said. And he closed his door.

The next day, Tuesday, before Anastasia could find the privacy to place her call, Alice invited her for a picnic in the churchyard. Anastasia felt, miserably, that there was no way short of being heartless for her not to accept. To make things worse, Alice told her brother he might come along if he behaved himself.

"And if I don't come, who'll drive?" Peter asked. "Neither of you are old enough."

The Church of All Saints stood alone, hidden from sight by an ancient screen of trees. The church building itself was stone, its slanting roof of red tile in keeping with the rest of the town, but slightly askew from the church's Norman origins.

The churchyard was beginning to bud: pink and green blossoming trees swayed over age-old gravestones. This was how the cycle of life had once been, Anastasia thought: you were christened, married, and buried in the church of your forefathers. They were waiting here for you.

As if reading her thoughts, Alice came to a stop before a graceful monument bearing dates from the 1600s. There, carved in its side, was a woman sitting lovingly beside a baby in a cradle. The gentle scene was flanked by a rosebush—and a clock face. The inscription was to Ann Tankard, who died at the age of two.

"Can you imagine?" Alice asked. "Poor thing. She never got to play like I do. She never got to live, like us. It makes me very sad for her mother."

All Anastasia could manage was a nod.

"Come on, then, down to the river." She lowered her voice. "Peter doesn't like me looking at Ann's monument. He thinks it's morbid. He can't stand to think that I'll die. I won't be buried here, in any case. I'll be buried over in Helmsley. It's also very pretty."

They came to a small slope, below which ran the River Rye. If she had been in different company, this would be an achingly perfect spot: May blossoms casting off down the river and an occasional fish nibbling water bugs, leaving concentric circles in his wake.

Peter spread out a blanket and opened the hamper. Alice played Mum. It was almost possible to ignore Peter and have a good time. Alice discussed a wide range of topics with enthusiasm, stopping to tease her older brother as often as he teased her. She insisted on hearing detailed descriptions of the horses they'd ridden at the manor house, and of the costumes they'd been fitted for. She needled Peter about the fact Anastasia was playing a queen while her brother was "only some old prince."

"It sounds like a lovely film," she said. "I do hope I'll be able to see it."

"You will, Angel-Beans," he said.

"Angel-Beans?" asked Anastasia.

"That's what he calls me most of the time," Alice answered. "He says I might be an angel, but I'm full of beans."

"You know you are!" Peter said, wrestling her to the blanket, tickling her sides, but only until she began to cough.

Anastasia reached for her, but she sat up smiling, wiping tears of mirth from her cheeks. "It's all right," she said. "I cough all the time. You get used to it."

Anastasia and Peter seldom conversed, but Alice served to defuse the tension between them. It was a charming picnic.

As they were packing up, Alice looked at the actress and said,

"I like you. You're different than the other girls around here."

"Oh?" Anastasia answered, amused. "How so?"

"For one thing," she said, her voice laden with distaste, "they're all potty about Peter. Whenever he sings a solo in church, you can hear them swooning"—she demonstrated—"and plopping onto the pews like frogs into a pond. It's disgusting."

"That's enough," Peter said irritably.

"I'm only saying I'm happy Anastasia's not like that."

"Yes, a great stroke of luck," her brother answered dryly.

As they got into the car, Alice announced they would all go on another outing the next day. "Whitby, I think," she said.

Anastasia's good humor fled and she glared at Peter, waiting for him to explain they didn't have time for larks about the countryside, but he said nothing.

As they arrived back at the vicarage, however, Peter let his sister go in ahead of them.

"Feel free to use the phone," he said. "But I don't see how they could get you a ride that will get you there much before Friday, when I'll get you there myself."

She glowered, irked to think he was probably right.

"Look," he countered. "I said I was sorry to ruin your plans, and I am."

He turned and hurried ahead of her into the house.

Inside, Anastasia was surprised to find the Reverend Dalton waiting for her. "Peter's got to go out," he said. "I know you've just come from the churchyard, but I wondered if you'd like a tour of the church itself. I usually take Tuesdays off, but I've got to go over and let the organ tuner in. He comes all the way from Newcastle, so we've got to take him when we can get him."

Anastasia unexpectedly enjoyed her time with Andrew Dalton very much. He seemed like a real father, except truthful and open, qualities Anastasia hadn't known to exist in actual parents.

After unlocking the sanctuary for the organ tuner, they strolled the opposite side of the churchyard. She was surprised by his candor as he told her about how his life differed from the dreams of his youth, but how he'd found peace and even much happiness in what he had.

After a while they wandered inside and sat in one of the back pews, listening to the strange atonal concert, and the Reverend Dalton began asking Anastasia about her life.

And she began answering.

It was the first time she'd been fully honest about her mother, her schooling, her work, and her background. Ever. As she spoke, it was as if a cement block, long tied to her chest, gradually lightened, allowing her to breathe easily. It was a feeling both liberating and unfamiliar.

Even after the tuner left, they sat quietly in the refracted colors of late afternoon light sliding gracefully through the stained glass.

"Stacy, I'm sorry," the vicar said. "Things shouldn't be like that."

Anastasia sat for a moment, mildly stunned. No one had ever been sorry about her circumstances before. She'd spent her whole life resolutely forcing herself away from self-pity. Tears stung the sides of her eyes, but she wiped them viciously away. No. She wouldn't start now.

When Anastasia finally began to weep, the tears came for a very long time. Andrew Dalton held her as she cried.

It was twilight by the time they locked up the old church and headed back to the vicarage. The vicar's car was larger than the Daf—it could hardly be otherwise—and he opened the door for Anastasia before getting in himself.

"I'm glad you could come visit," her host said, starting the engine. "We're all enjoying having you; Alice especially."

"I really like her." Anastasia gathered her nerve. "You must be worried about her."

"We've learned to accept her illness," he said. "It's never easy, of course. But I'll tell you a father's secret. I worry as much about my son as I do about my daughter."

"About Peter?"

"Yes. You see, after Alice's condition was diagnosed, we got settled here, in a place she loves—and near a good hospital. But it is rather shut off. And since he was fourteen and that film crew came through, Peter's been dealing with a much larger world— one more complex than either his mother or I have had to deal with. He's a strong boy, a good lad. But he's young yet. And it frightens me." He smiled at her. "Don't ever let him know I said that. Our secret, all right?"

She couldn't help but smile back as they pulled up into the vicarage drive.

Once inside, the day's focus shifted abruptly.

"In here, Andrew," Mrs. Dalton called from the dining room.

They arrived to find the white tablecloth and two place settings had been pushed back, exposing half the dining room table. Alice was lying on her back against the polished dark wood, coughing. Peter was pounding on her chest, hard, in a rhythmic pulse.

"I'll take over," the older man said.

"I'm sorry," Mrs. Dalton said, turning to Anastasia. "I'm afraid supper may be delayed."

Anastasia took the cue and backed out of the room, standing for a long time with her back against the staircase, listening to a child's racking coughs, wondering why life was never fair.

The next day Alice was too ill to travel, but she had it in her head that Anastasia must see Whitby. "You're going today. Peter's taking you. When you come back, you're going to tell me everywhere you went and everything you did."

"But I came home to see you, Beans," Peter protested. "I'm going to be with Stacy for months."

"You must go. Tomorrow when I'm stronger, I'll go with you to the moors."

"It sounds like it's settled," said Sarah.

"But Mum, perhaps—"

"That's enough, Peter. Don't upset your sister," pronounced Alice from her bed.

A smile crept across Sarah's lips and she gave her son a shrug.

"Yes, ma'ams," said Peter, resigned.

For the day's outing, Andrew offered them the larger car, and it didn't take much persuading. As they left, Anastasia decided with grim determination that she would repay Andrew Dalton's kindness by being civil to his son. Even if it killed her. But once alone with him, she could think of nothing civil to say. He was wearing blue jeans and a jeans jacket over a navy turtleneck; his hair was well brushed so it looked full rather than curly. The back of it fell below his collar; he was under strict instructions to let it grow for the picture. Now his sapphire eyes were fixed resolutely on the road.

Anastasia finally broke the silence. "I'm sorry to be ignorant, but what exactly is cystic fibrosis? What causes Alice's cough?"

Peter glanced at her, perhaps trying to ascertain whether the question was sincere. Then he sighed and said, "Cystic fibrosis is a progressive, degenerative disease of the lungs. Simply put, Alice was born with a body that produces abnormally thick mucus. Because the mucus blocks the passages to her digestive track, she has trouble digesting food. But the biggest problem is that, instead of lubricating her lungs, the mucus clogs them, filling the air passages so she can't breathe well."

"Is there any chance she'll grow out of it?"

"No. 'Degenerative' means it's getting worse. For some CF kids, it doesn't start getting bad until they're in their teens. Alice isn't so lucky. It's gotten worse—noticeably worse—this last year. Her lung infections and hospitalizations are much more frequent. Yesterday was a good day for her, but she's having a bad patch. She needs a few days of drug treatment in hospital, but she's determined not to go while we're here."

"So that's why you came home. Because of the bad patch."

"Yes. And because I'm going to be away for so long."

She couldn't bring herself to say it was all right, or even that she understood. But the air between them was a little less tense.

"I am sorry. About Alice," she did say.

"It isn't fair. She's so smart, so curious about the world. She'd love traveling, seeing places, and it's not likely she'll ever get to . . ." His voice trailed off.

There seemed nothing more to be said. Their tribute to Alice was this trip, so take it they would. They hunkered down in the car and pressed on.

Whitby soon unfolded before them like a picture-book fishing village. The harbor, in the river estuary of the Esk, had a humming waterfront. Whitewashed houses and pubs, fisheries and bakeries, held hands in rows on successive terraces up a series of hills. The mighty backdrop, of course, was the ocean.

They hadn't left for Whitby until late morning, which meant it was nearing noon. "Alice will expect to hear we've eaten at the Magpie," said her companion. "Shall we just go now?"

"May as well."

Peter parked and they walked through the salt air to the quay. The somber gray of morning clouds had burned off; the meld of sun and sea gave Anastasia a jolt of intoxication. Gulls and herons swooped and turned; the spray caught her hair and lashes.

At the Magpie Café, they were seated at a table by the long

windows. They both ordered the set lunch, fresh crab with plaice to follow.

When Anastasia tore her gaze from the sand-marred windowpane, it was to find Peter studying her. Some of the profound sadness that had laced his voice when he spoke of his sister was still mirrored in his eyes. She couldn't stand seeing so much naked pain.

Before she knew what she was doing, she heard herself saying, "I'm sorry I've been so cold with you. Pierce said you thought I didn't like you, that I was acting like a snob, and it was true. It's just that . . ."

She spread her hands helplessly, then put them back into her lap. "It's that . . . you know what you're doing. And everyone likes you. And to top it off, you have a real family with a mum and a dad and a sister, and I've wanted those things so badly. When I met you, it seemed you'd gotten your share of good things, and my share as well. You can't blame me for being jealous."

"You . . . were jealous of me?"

She nodded grimly.

And he laughed.

"So what's wrong with your mum and dad? Mine aren't perfect, you know."

"They seem perfect to me. Your mother's so pretty and your father's, well, kind."

"You say that because you haven't been bent over his desk to feel the smart end of the tawse," said Peter.

"I'm certain you never did anything to deserve it."

This time his smile was rueful. "We needn't go into it. But I admit I could have done worse when it came to folks. What's wrong with yours?"

"My father died when I was three," Anastasia said. "My mother . . . well, she's an alcoholic." It was only the second time in her life she'd said it aloud, but she was shocked at how much easier it was to say.

He digested this information. "Who did you live with, then?"

She picked up her napkin and studied it closely. "I left school at thirteen to support my mother. I still do."

"You were modeling by then?"

She shook her head. "I took in sewing. I had to, you see, or they would have sent her away. But I loved school."

A mortifying thought struck her and she looked up at him pleadingly. "Please don't say anything. No one knows. And I don't want them to. There's no reason for it."

"You know I won't," he said gently. Then, as if to cheer her, "The joke is that I was jealous of you."

"Go on."

"It's true. I thought you were some rich blue-blood who tumbled out of bed onto the magazine covers. You did prove you could act—and you're quite amazing at it, by the way—but I was already too knocky to forgive you by the time I found that out."

"So, why didn't you like me? What did I do?" Anastasia asked.

"If you recall, you gave me the cold shoulder from the first time we were introduced. That first day at the reading, we were sitting next to each other, and you wouldn't even look at me!"

"But you'd already left me alone! You saw me standing all by myself and you ignored me."

"Good heavens, is that what you thought?" He expelled a heavy breath. He nervously picked up the vinegar bottle from the table and felt the smooth contours. "I don't remember you being by yourself. What I do remember is that the first time I saw you, it completely knocked the stuffing out of me." His face colored. "I mean all the stuffing. You were the most gorgeous creature I'd ever seen. And me being the shyest twit, I ran for cover."

"Shy? You were working the room like an air conditioner!"

"Oh. It's that . . . I mean, I . . . how can I make you understand? It's this front, this act of being not scared that I put on. And it works well with everything except what really scares me. Which in this case was how you completely bowled me over."

"So," Anastasia reasoned, "I was terrified of everyone in the room. And you were scared of me."

"I guess we have one of your typical fear-based relationships." He gave a crooked smile.

They were interrupted by the arrival of the waitress bearing two steaming orders of crab, which suddenly seemed to merit a great deal of attention.

When they both surreptitiously glanced up at the same time, each burst into laughter.

"This might have been easier when we were terrified of each other," said Peter.

"Could well have been," Anastasia agreed, then shyly asked, "So you think I can act?"

"You're incredible. You're always surprising me."

"I think you're very talented as well."

They retreated into their meals, although the space between them was heavy with discovery. It was an oddly quiet luncheon, after all.

When they finally departed, Peter took her to the Mariner's Church of St. Mary, the interior of which was designed like an eighteenth-century ship's deck. Outside, Anastasia was so engrossed in deciphering the inscriptions on the weathered tombstones that she gave a small shriek when Peter swooped down on her from behind.

"Couldn't resist," he said, exaggerated menace in his voice. "This is the churchyard where, according to Bram Stoker, Count Dracula finally had his way with poor Lucy."

"You should have warned me!"

"Expect your vampires to be well behaved, do you?"

Before heading back, they explored the antique stores near the strand. On their way out of one of them, Anastasia paused by a long jewelry case. "Look at this ring. It's lovely. What is it, do you know?"

"It's jet jewelry," Peter told her. "It was worn as a mourning decoration in Victorian times. It's popular today as antique jewelry. But I could never get past its original meaning."

Anastasia studied the intricately crafted broaches, earrings, rings, and beads in the case before them. "It's beautiful," she said. "But I see what you mean. Still, it's a sweet tradition, don't you think? To wear something lovely in honor of someone you've lost?"

"That's a nice way to think about it."

As they headed back to the car, Peter said, "If you don't mind, I'd like to take a long way home. There's somewhere I'd like you to see."

As they drove, the new electricity in the car painted everything in vibrant colors. Anastasia felt like an urban workhorse who, after many years of traveling the same weary route, suddenly had her harness and blinders removed to discover a land of endless hills and pastures. To her consternation, she realized that she was nervous. It had to do with the unfortunate discovery that the young man beside her was seriously attractive.

Peter parked in a spot far from any sign of humanity. Anastasia felt a surge of current when he reached over and tentatively took her hand in his as they strolled to where the moors curtsied down into the forever-green valley of the Whitby Esk.

"Good Lord," she exhaled. "Where are we?"

"Egton High Moor," he answered.

Anastasia left the safety of Peter's grasp to spin around, trying to comprehend the expanse of earth that rippled in every direction, forever. It was an unending ocean of land, and its vastness filled her with the same intoxication of infinity as had the sea.

"'Everywhere peace, everywhere serenity and a marvelous freedom from the tumult of the world,'" quoted Peter. "Saint Aelred must have seen this same view."

They found a hidden spot near the busy trickle of a beck and settled in.

Instead of irking her, the presence of Peter Dalton now caused her heart rate to fluctuate wildly. One brown curl tumbled over his forehead; she was chagrined to find she wanted more than anything in the world to touch it, simply because it was Peter's hair. She reached over and pushed it from his face, knowing it would fall back immediately, which it did.

Fleeing these new feelings, she said, "Peter, is there a chance Alice will die young? Is that what you're afraid of?"

When he answered, his voice was quiet. "I know she will, Stace, and she does, too. Last night when she couldn't breathe and I was helping her do her exercises, she looked at me perfectly calmly and said, 'Don't worry, Peter. When I go home, to our real forever home, I'll wait for you there. So don't be sad. I'll see you again one day.'

"There was no point in telling her she wasn't going to die, eventually, anyway. So I said, 'I'll be coming.'

"Then . . . she asked me if I'd kissed you. I said not yet. She told me I'd better hurry or somebody else would beat me to it."

Then he leaned over and did just that. His lips were full and soft and somehow he tasted of the wonder of the sea and even of the infinity of this empty glacier lake. Anastasia closed her eyes and lost her mooring, free-falling into the unseen band of the Beloved, whose endless numbers have existed through all time.

Then he looked in her eyes and smiled. "Keep a secret?" he said.

"It's one of my best talents," she answered.

"This is the first time . . . you're the first girl that I've kissed because I wanted to. I mean, who wasn't an actress playing a part, or a local girl who kissed me first, mostly to tell her friends she'd done it."

"You mean, one of the frog girls Alice talked about?"

He rolled his eyes. "It's not that there haven't been opportunities. The problem is . . . I've never really been in love."

"And might you be now?" she asked softly.

"I'm afraid I might. And you?"

In response, she leaned over and kissed him again, full on the lips.

"I've never kissed anyone before, either," she said, then remembered the passionate intensity of her audition with Pierce Hall. "For real," she added.

"It's kind of nice, isn't it?" he breathed, leaning back into her.

It was nice. And very exciting; as strong as the physical excitement was the overpowering thrill of being loved and wanted and chosen above all others, a feeling Anastasia had never known. It was the seasoning to the taste of his lips, and then his mouth. It was the context of joy when they lay beside each other, still fully clothed, but with his hands exploring the curves of her back and waist and then the shape of her breasts, which molded into his palms as the two of them moved together.

"Don't worry, I don't believe in sex outside of marriage," Peter whispered at one point. She told herself it was sweet for him to say that, but in truth, she was relieved and able to enjoy it without tension when they lay close enough that she could feel his hardness through his clothing and her own. It was an oddly intimate feeling; a vulnerability he was sharing with her that he had withheld from all the other girls.

"Oh, Stace, what's happening to us?" he asked, and he smiled down at her.

They returned to Peter's home to find the hours suddenly far too short for every whispered confidence that needed to be shared, for every kiss stolen at the turn of the stairs. Anastasia found herself inexplicably kept awake by the simple knowledge that Peter lay as near as the next room.

The next morning, Thursday, Alice had to give in and be taken to hospital. Peter carried her to the back seat of the car, where they hugged good-bye; she gave him last-minute instructions on how to behave himself and he promised she could visit the set as soon as she was better. She waved at Anastasia and Peter until the car turned out of sight down the street.

As sorry as they were that Alice had to go, Anastasia and Peter reveled in the gift of privacy given them on their last day of freedom. They returned to their secret place by the beck; God smiled and the afternoon was uncommonly sunny and warm. Peter wanted to know every detail of her life, and was fascinated by it. He talked of his dreams for the future; when the question was put to her, Anastasia realized she hadn't dared have any. The present had always been precarious enough. The future seemed a minefield of buried disasters.

Somehow the movie of which they were the stars was the farthest thing from their minds, and they kept it so, even knowing they had to leave early the next morning.

That was tomorrow. Today, she and Peter talked for hours, pausing frequently for tussling and kissing. When they finally drowsed hidden in each other's arms, Anastasia lay confident in the knowledge that, whatever the future held, she would be safe.

CROSSING THE CHANNEL from Dover to Calais was easily Anastasia's most horrific trip since that long-ago journey with Peter up the A1. Walking with Elise to the postbox had been so fraught with danger it was unfathomable that she'd let Leah talk her into accompanying her and Bruce to have lunch with Conan Marcel in France. That she actually boarded a boat. On the water. No way to get off. Anastasia had lasted an entire ten minutes—until they were in open waters—before the panic attack started. No matter how she'd tried to get her breath, she couldn't. It was appalling but true that she was sure she was about to have a heart attack and die, right there, in front of hordes of strangers. Not only that, she wanted to die, to make the terror stop.

Even though Bruce had bundled her down onto the auto deck, and they'd illegally sat in the back seat of someone's Rolls-Royce and sung old Tom Jones songs, the trip was beyond excruciating.

Why was she putting herself through this, after all these years? Hadn't she found a haven and accepted her life there? Fifty years alone in the west wing suddenly didn't sound so bad. Why on earth was she testing the waters when she knew them to be shark infested?

Pierce. Gray. Janie.

That was why. And if she faced facts, she knew she didn't want to be buried alive in Geoff's castle. Not without a fight.

Conan Marcel was an expansive man in every sense of the word. In the decades since Anastasia had last seen him, he had gained considerable girth, but had also grown into his considerable wealth. His sweater, trousers, and jacket were tailored to fit him precisely, and he looked not only stylish but comfortable with himself.

"Children, children!" he roared, throwing his arms open as wide as the door to the three-hundred-year-old farmhouse twenty miles outside Calais. Anastasia couldn't help but smile, remembering that the last time he'd called them that, he'd been much closer to correct. "*Entrez! Entrez! Entrez!*"

His designer clothes lost any attention once the trio had entered his refurbished farmhouse. Every painted surface was either gray or white, but this austerity was offset by the incredible range of French antiques adorning each room. Gilt-leafed mirrors gave an illusion of space; medieval triptychs sat flanked by golden candelabras on an exquisitely carved altar.

"It's marvelous, Conan," drawled Leah in her best haute-L.A. voice. "An Irishman does Calais."

"It is beautiful," Anastasia added, and Bruce chimed in, "Nice work, old man."

The centerpiece of the living room was the grand piano, upon which sat reams of music and notations.

"Is this where you write?" asked Anastasia.

"*Non,*" he said in his jovial Irish-laced French. "My computer's in the other room. Sit, sit, do sit."

They looked apprehensively at the Louis XIV chairs, certain they'd actually come from Versailles, but as Conan had bid them sit, they sat.

"A bit of wine to take the edge off the journey. Luncheon is ready, and we'll eat soon. Have a glass and catch your breath."

Anastasia, Bruce, and Leah exchanged looks that harbored a blend of anxiety and amusement as Conan poured four glasses of white zinfandel and let each select a glass from the silver tray.

"Cheers," he said, and took the first gulp.

Each followed his lead, and breathed a collective sigh of relief when no one pitched over.

"So, my dears, it is intoxicating to see you again. The others will understand if I say especially you, my Isolde."

Somehow the danger of entering Conan's lair was enough to begin to fortify Anastasia's nerves. She smiled. "And you, as well."

Conan sat at his piano and ran his fingers up and down the keyboard in a sweeping gesture before breaking into an epic version of "Isolde's Passion."

Conan had what Anastasia thought of as an Irish complexion: light skin and ruddy cheeks. Now his whole face looked ruddy, however, whether from age or enjoyment of the grape, Anastasia didn't know. His shock of unkempt black hair always looked like an uncombed wig plopped aboard his scalp, but it was way too enthusiastic about the different directions it took to have been manufactured; his eyebrows also looked like they hadn't finished conferring about which way to head. Yet, for a large man, when he sat at the piano, his dexterous fingers led the way to uncharted worlds.

"Ah," he said as the last notes lingered in the air. "Those were the days. Now, if you'll excuse me—I've let the housekeeper off for the day. Let me put the finishing touches on the first course and you can come and tell me your secret reason for calling."

He gave a small bow and turned from the room.

"So what are we going to say?" hissed Bruce.

Leah sipped her wine. "I thought we might as well get straight to it: We're onto you. Turn yourself in and we won't do you any harm."

"He's let the housekeeper off. One less witness, perhaps?" Bruce asked.

"We may as well pretend we're here to persuade him to attend the reunion," Anastasia said. "Get him talking about old times. Introduce certain names to the conversation. See what he does with them."

"I think our best bet is to stay stupid," Bruce said. "No matter what clues he baits us with, to let them fly straight past."

"And why is that?" queried Leah.

"Do you really think the three of us could hold him here if he caught on? At best he'd run. At worst, well, none of us is armed, I assume?"

Both women shook their heads.

"So I say we play stupid, get out, alert the authorities."

"Ladies and gentlemen, I bid you come," rumbled a deep voice from behind them. They each gave an involuntary jump, then smiled at Conan as they filed past him into the arched dining room.

They were seated at a medium-sized refectory table, Conan at the head, Anastasia at the foot, Leah and Bruce opposite each other on the sides. The table was set with thick clay server plates and goblets. Behind them on each of the four walls hung enormous canvases: large grotesque depictions of the Four Horsemen of the Apocalypse as obese Spanish peasants.

The first course, already before them, was a vichyssoise with fresh bread and Gruyère cheese. Conan had provided spoons, but once he had proposed another toast, he attacked his soup as much with his bread as with his utensils.

"Now. To what honor may I ascribe this meeting?" The question was posed to Anastasia.

"Well," she began, again giving him a shy smile. "The three of us seeing each other again . . . it's brought back such memories . . . oh, out with it. We're hoping to talk you into attending the reunion in May. It wouldn't be right without you."

"Darlings, how kind of you. I don't know about my schedule . . ."

"You needn't decide right now," Anastasia said. "Just don't say no. We were also hoping we could get you to reminisce a bit. Leah is writing a retrospective for the film's re-release, and she's trying to find fresh perspectives."

"Yes," Leah leapt in, "what are some of your fondest memories of *T & I?*"

Conan tore off another large section of bread and sopped it in his soup before taking a large soggy bite and masticating thoughtfully.

Anastasia noticed that her companions were playing with their food as much as she was. "Eat!" mouthed Leah, who resolutely scooped a spoonful of soup—and swallowed it. Bruce and Anastasia followed suit.

"The thing I remember most," Conan started, "was the day Pierce brought me to his country home to meet his Isolde. A stolen afternoon. Just the three of us. Do you remember, *chérie?*"

Anastasia smiled at him sweetly, as if they were the only two people in the room. "Of course I do. You played for us. And the other gentlemen who'd come for dinner."

"Ah! You do remember! You were Pierce's inspiration, and mine as well."

"Did you and my father get along?" Leah asked blithely, and all three heads swiveled to look at her.

Conan's startled expression was quickly replaced by a benign wistfulness. "But of course, *ma petite.* Not that we didn't have our differences. Would you ever imagine two geniuses not having an explosive partnership? But we were the closest of friends. He could show me footage and I would know without explanation the exact mood he had created, the precise music to complement what was already there. *Tristan* was our third film. Who would have thought our last? Ah, every time I think of it, it saddens me. The projects we could have done had he not expired so early. The world's loss."

They all murmured into their bowls and sat silently for a moment.

"Ah!" exclaimed Conan. "Life goes on. Let's move to the next course, shall we?"

And he was on his feet, noisily collecting bowls and spoons.

As he disappeared through the swinging door to the kitchen, Leah shrugged and whispered, "Feelings: easy come, easy go."

He swung back through momentarily, his face a deeper scarlet than the thought of Pierce's death had caused. "*Merde*," he said. "I was certain I'd lit the burner to steam the vegetables. But I am not a snob when it comes to eating. If you don't mind, perhaps we'll have the salad next, then the main course will be ready."

"Fine," said Bruce.

"Splendid," said Conan, refilling wine goblets. He swung back into the kitchen and reappeared with two plates of crisp salads, different shades of lettuce topped with wild greens. "And the dressing?" he said. "A secret blend!"

He gave one plate to Leah and one to Anastasia, then swung through again, returning with those for Bruce and himself.

"I'll do what I can for the reunion," Conan said as he served. "Perhaps I could do a new arrangement of several of the major themes. Even if I can't come, I'm certainly willing to do my part to make the *T & I* legacy one that will never, ever be forgotten. I personally promise."

He was halfway into his seat when he remembered something, leapt up, and returned to the kitchen.

"I don't like this legacy business," muttered Leah.

"Never forgotten? Personally promise?" asked Bruce. Wearing a look of pseudo-alarm, Bruce switched his salad plate with Anastasia's. Anastasia switched hers with Leah, who returned hers to Bruce, who switched his with Conan's. They dropped their hands to their laps moments before their host returned with the longest pepper grinder Anastasia had ever seen. Leah and Conan himself were the only two who took fresh pepper.

"So," Conan continued, enthusiastically forking into his

salad, "have you any dramatic ideas for making this film stand out in the memory of the world?"

Leah coughed and Anastasia said, "It's already a classic, don't you think? Why should we have to do something else?"

"My dear girl. Have you no feeling for showmanship? It's undignified, I know. But headline-grabbing never hurt." He took another large bite, which didn't stop him from expounding. "That was the problem with what's-his-name. The producer. Eddington."

"There was a problem with Gray Eddington?" asked Bruce.

"I don't like to . . . speak . . . out of school, as it were," Conan replied. But somehow he was losing his concentration. "Sorry. What was I saying?"

"Gray Eddington?"

He withdrew a large monogrammed handkerchief and mopped his brow. "Yes. Eddington. Total ass. Pardon my French."

Noticing his agitation, Bruce pursued, "Why? What did he do?"

Their host was breathing heavily, his sight focused somewhere on the wall above the opposite Horseman. "The eyes," he said.

"Excuse me?" asked Leah.

"Stop it!" he roared. Gasping, he stood, knocking over his chair. He ran clumsily past them, shaking his arms wildly at the wall behind Anastasia.

She was just as quickly on her feet. "Conan, what is it?"

"The eyes! Close them! Dear God! Close the eyes!"

He lunged for the wall, hands flailing spastically. He knocked into the carved sideboard, scattering candlesticks and plates.

"What's wrong?" Anastasia cried, following behind him, but Leah leapt up and pulled her away.

"It's your fault! Your fault!" the composer was bellowing to the walls, turning from one to the next. "Oh God, the pain!"

He grabbed his chest and fell to one knee. "No!" he screamed, clambering again to his feet.

Anastasia didn't wait to see more. She ran toward the kitchen door. "Where's the telephone? We've got to get help!"

The door continued swinging behind her as she stopped to take stock of the large room. A long wooden farm table stood directly before her; along one wall ran a double sink and professional-quality gas stove.

Her eyes swept past hand-painted tiles to a small eating table below a window overlooking the back terrace and swimming pool. There, on the wall to the side of the table, was a mounted telephone. Anastasia ran to it and dialed the operator. "*Allo?*" said the voice.

As Anastasia responded, trying hard to remember enough grammar school French to convey the source of the emergency, a blur of movement caught her attention as the silhouette of a man ran past the window before her.

She gasped. For a moment she stood torn between dropping the phone and racing outside to investigate, and staying on the line to summon help.

"*Allo?*" repeated the female voice from the earpiece.

"Yes, *oui*," Anastasia said, leaning over to get a clear look outside the window. She thought she saw the form disappear around the corner of the potting shed.

She made a decision and turned her attention to asking the operator for an ambulance. Once she was fairly certain this had been accomplished, she had the presence of mind to turn off the gas below two lit burners and turn off the oven before racing back into the dining room to find Conan sprawled on the floor. Bruce had peeled off their host's jacket and was unbuttoning his shirt.

Leah stood over him, chanting, "Dear God. Dear God. Dear God."

"An ambulance is on the way. Is he still breathing?"

As if in response, there was a rasping from his throat and his chest rose.

"Conan!" Bruce said, slapping his face. "Conan, man, can you hear me?"

A sour wheeze was his only response.

"While I was in the kitchen, I saw someone, a man, I think, running past the window. He disappeared round the potting shed before I could get off the phone."

Another rumbling came from Conan, and they all turned back in time to see the vomit rising from his throat.

"Help me turn him over!" said Bruce. "We don't want him to choke!"

Anastasia knelt beside him and on the count of three they all pushed. Bruce gave him a couple of hard slaps on the back. The smell was not inviting.

His body was twitching, spasming.

"Had either of you tasted your salads?" Anastasia asked.

Both Bruce and Leah shook their heads.

"I hadn't either. Don't touch them. Perhaps they'll find something."

"Dear God!" said Leah.

"Close the fucking eyes!" Conan suddenly roared, managing to flop himself completely over onto his back.

All three of them jumped back, and watched, helpless, as his eyes rolled back into his head and a wide stream of blood ran from the side of his mouth to the floor.

"Oh, no," said Bruce.

"Is he dead?" Anastasia said. And with trembling hand she reached over and closed his eyes.

"Maybe it's not too late," said Leah. "If the ambulance would only get here!"

"I'll go out and help flag it down," Anastasia said, still curious about the intruder she'd seen.

"Wait," Bruce said, as he knelt beside the composer and began CPR. "First we have to decide what we're going to tell them."

"What do you mean?" Anastasia asked. "We tell them the truth."

"Yes. But how much of the truth?"

"Oh," said Anastasia. "You mean, Scotland Yard considers you a suspect . . . and here you are."

"And here I am."

"We could say nothing, and let them surmise it was a heart attack," Leah said.

"But then we might never get to the bottom of it," said Anastasia. "If it is the salad, we might lose key evidence."

"You're right, unfortunately," said Bruce.

"I'm going outside," Anastasia said. "I'm assuming whoever else was here has fled, but I want to take a look."

Of the several sets of footprints in the dirt surrounding the potting shed, one looked to Anastasia to be fresher than the others. But the ground was dusty, and it was hard to tell. From the back of the shed, Conan's property quickly became wooded, which would have added ease to anyone's hasty departure.

The ambulance and police weren't long in arriving. The paramedic detected a faint pulse in Conan Marcel. "Heart attack," he said in French.

"What's the prognosis?" asked the inspector who arrived shortly after they'd administered several shocks, to no effect.

"I can't say it's good. We've got to get him to the hospital, now."

The composer was lifted onto a stretcher and wheeled out into the waiting vehicle.

"What happened?" the inspector asked, turning to the three foreigners. He was nearly as chubby as Conan, but lacking the flair. His uniform hung on him limply.

Anastasia cleared her throat. "We think he was poisoned," she said in English.

One eyebrow rose as pointedly. "Oh? By whom?"

"That's the question," said Leah fluently in French. "We were here because we're investigating a number of suspicious deaths among our . . . circle of friends." She gave her companions a hard look urging them not to mention the *T & I* connection.

"After Conan took ill, I ran to the kitchen to call the ambulance," Anastasia added. "From there, I saw a man run away from the house, toward the shed."

"What did this man look like?"

"I didn't get a very good look at him. If it was a him. Tall and slim, I think. Wearing a black jacket. Perhaps."

"This is of great help," said the inspector dryly, his first words in English.

"You could check the kitchen for fingerprints," Anastasia said. "And check these salads."

"The salads?"

"That's what Conan was eating when he fell over."

"Yes," said Bruce, also in French, "although it could have been something he ate earlier."

The inspector had his pad open and pencil at the ready, but he hadn't been writing down much. "Pardon me, but why would Mr. Marcel serve himself a poisoned salad?"

"There was a man outside!" said Anastasia. "The kitchen door was unlocked. He could have come in and poisoned the salad while we were eating the soup!"

"Also, Conan didn't exactly serve that salad to himself," said Leah.

"What do you mean?" asked the inspector. "If he didn't serve the salad to himself, to whom—or by whom—was it served?"

"Let's see," said Bruce. "I gave mine to Anastasia."

"But I passed it to Leah."

"I gave it back to Bruce."

"But then I switched it with Conan's."

The inspector sat down, shaking his head. "Some strange English tribal ritual?"

"So, whose salad did Conan actually eat?" asked Anastasia.

"It would have been originally served to Bruce," Leah said. "I think we passed around the same salad the whole time."

"Oh, great," said Bruce. And he sat down. They were all thinking the same thing: someone had tried to poison Bruce before.

"So if it was the salad, it could have been meant for Bruce. And Conan is a suspect. If it was something else, it could have been intended for Conan," figured Anastasia.

"Planted by this mystery man," said the inspector.

The ambulance was ready to depart. The inspect sent a deputy to call the chief paramedic back in. "Do you have a tentative diagnosis?" he asked.

"Heart attack," he said, obviously in a rush.

"These folks suspect poison."

"Heart attack. If we've any chance, we've got to go."

The inspector waved him away, then turned to the three friends. "I'd like each of you to give a statement to my deputy. Not what you suspect, not wild theories, but what actually happened. Make sure I have your names and addresses. We'll check into it. Yes, yes, we'll fingerprint the kitchen. We'll call you back if we need any more information."

"I think he wants to get rid of us," whispered Leah.

"Can you blame him?" replied Anastasia.

It didn't take long to give a concise version of the events preceding Conan's attack. After each had separately repeated the story for the record, they were dismissed—shooed, in fact—from the house. Led by Bruce, they trudged slowly down the front steps and around the house to their rented car. Bruce arrived first and had opened the driver's door when he gave a muffled squeak.

"What is it?" asked Anastasia, hurrying to join him.

"Hurry and get in. Both of you."

Bruce held his door open and his seat forward so Anastasia could climb into the back. As she did so, her eyes widened and her jaw dropped. But she sat down without saying anything. Leah had also taken her place in the front passenger's seat.

They pulled out the front gate and headed at a moderate pace down the country road. Once they'd made two more turns and were well out of sight of the farmhouse, Bruce swerved to the side of the road and put on the brakes.

"*What the bloody hell are you doing?*" he demanded.

"Sorry," said Elise from where she crouched next to Anastasia in the back seat.

"Sorry?"

"I wanted . . . that is, I thought . . . I was worried about you. I didn't feel right letting you all march into danger, and I was curious and feeling left out. So I followed you. But as soon as the cab left me off at Marcel's farmhouse, I heard a big commotion, then someone was running and I felt so stupid that I panicked and hid."

"A man almost died in there!"

"Someone almost *died?*" The blood drained from Elise's face.

"Conan Marcel could be dead already! Yes! What if the police had found you skulking about a murder scene? Elise? Bloody hell! It's bad enough they're giving me a hard time!"

"Sorry," she said. "Do you think I could sit up now?"

"Bloody hell!"

"You saw someone run outside?" Anastasia asked.

"I didn't get a good look. I heard a door open and I ducked down behind the car. Someone ran past—but I didn't see him, and I don't think he saw me."

"Do you think it was a man?"

"From what I could see under the car, they looked like men's shoes. Black. Polished. Shiny. Running past. Then a few minutes later, I heard the front door open and Stacy came out. I was about to wave her down when suddenly there were sirens and constables all over the place. So I stayed hidden."

"Bloody hell," said Bruce. "Stay down."

He put the car in gear, stepped on the gas pedal, and accelerated along the road toward the ferry.

Taking no chances, Bruce made Elise get out of the car several blocks from the rental car return and gave her strict instructions not to talk with any of them on the ferry. He didn't want anyone to report that their trio had turned into a quartet.

The car rental agency had a television going; a news crawl across the bottom announced the death of composer Conan Marcel at his home. Anastasia, Bruce, and Leah tried to remain calm as they returned the car and hurried to board the ferry, whose departure was imminent. Leah went in search of coffee, then began a brisk walk around the deck, trying to defuse some of her nervous energy. Anastasia had never seen her so on edge. But then, it wasn't every day you saw someone murdered before your eyes.

Anastasia and Bruce stood by the port rail, chatting of insubstantial things, Bruce scanning the shore until he saw Elise emerge at the last moment from where she'd been waiting to board. Once she was on the gangplank, he relaxed visibly.

"I don't know what she was thinking," he said. Then he turned around and leaned on the rail, this time facing Anastasia. "I'm still shaking," he said. "I don't believe it. We visited Conan Marcel, and he's dead. A man is dead." He exhaled a deep breath. "I've never seen someone actually die before. Have you?"

"No. But we've got to calm down and try to think rationally."

"So was Conan the killer? Was the poison meant for me? Or is the killer someone else? And if so, did we lead him to Calais? Are we responsible?"

"I don't know," admitted Anastasia. "If Conan isn't the killer, is this the real killer's way of showing us that he's onto us? That he knows what we're doing?"

"Bloody hell," Bruce repeated. "There is no way this has turned out to be a good day."

"Either we've inadvertently killed the culprit, or the culprit has killed right in front of us," Anastasia postulated.

"I need a drink," said Bruce. "How are you doing?"

Anastasia was embarrassed to say. She was fine. In contrast to the trip over, she felt strong, invigorated. Facing down murder seemed quite freeing.

"I could use a drink, too," she said. "There's nothing like a real trauma to keep your mind from needing to invent one."

"Now I'm the one who's hyperventilating."

"Who can blame you? What say we change the subject for a while? There'll be time enough to deconstruct everything once we're back at your place."

Bruce turned back around, focusing on the swelling waves around them. "Do you remember on the way over, when I asked if you knew where Peter was?"

"Yes," said Anastasia, warily.

"What I really wanted to know is, what happened? What went wrong between you two?"

"Nothing went wrong," Anastasia answered slowly. "It was one of those things."

"That answer might work for some gossip rag," Bruce said, "but you're talking to me. I was there, Anastasia, I saw what the two of you had. I don't buy it."

"I can't talk about it."

"It's been twenty years!"

"I know. But I can't. It doesn't matter now, anyway."

"Stace, come on. You won't even tell me? I was his best friend. Then suddenly I wasn't. He was changed. Different. Overnight. You know what happened. You must."

"No," said Anastasia.

"No, you don't know? Or no, you won't say?"

"No," said Anastasia. And that was that.

CHAPTER 6

PIERCE HALL'S
TRISTAN AND ISOLDE

THE STORY

"*The Romance of Tristan and Isolde* contains a bit of magic and mystery. But no more than everyday life."

—director Pierce Hall

My lords, If you would hear a high tale of love and death, here is that of Tristan and Queen Isolde; how to their full joy, but to their sorrow also, they loved each other, and how at last they died of that love together upon one day; she by him and he by her.

Long ago, when Mark was king over Cornwall, his nephew, a young warrior named Tristan, saved the land from the ruthless hold of the Morholt.

The king's loyalty to Tristan caused great consternation among the rival knights, especially Tristan's evil cousin, Andret. They threatened to desert Mark should he remain childless, leaving his kingdom to Tristan, and insisted Mark take a wife. Tristan was dispatched to fetch him the fairest wife of all: Isolde of the Golden Hair.

By slaying the monster that ravaged her land, Tristan did indeed win the hand of the Irish princess Isolde. The princess couldn't help her attraction to the magnetic young warrior, even after discovering that he had killed the Morholt, who was her uncle. However, when Isolde discovered Tristan won her only to give her away, her love turned to fury. But sailing to Cornwall, Tristan and Isolde mistakenly drank together of the potion Isolde's mother intended for the wedding night of Isolde and Mark. Thus a white-hot love was born, driving Tristan and Isolde to become the most passionate of lovers.

In Cornwall, King Mark was delighted by Isolde; their marriage celebration was a grand festival. The people of the land were won by their new queen's kindness and healing powers. Even though she was taken with her new husband, Isolde was unable to quench her passion for Tristan. The king's enemies gleefully reported to Mark that his wife and nephew were lovers.

Finally presented with irrefutable evidence, Mark sentenced Tristan and Isolde to be burned at the stake.

After a daring escape, the two lived together as fugitives in the forest. Tristan's love for Isolde finally forced him to wish a better life for her. He persuaded the king to take her back. Following her conscience, she knew she must return.

Andret and his allies convinced the king to bring his queen to trial once more; Tristan, in disguise, saved her from death again. King Mark's love for Isolde, as well as the love of her subjects, sent Andret into hiding, where he finally confronted Tristan and met his demise.

Tristan knew he must leave Isolde for both their sakes; he traveled to a far country where he befriended young Prince Kaherdin and served him so well that he was offered the hand of Kaherdin's sister, Isolde of the White Hands, in marriage. He accepted, but could not bring himself to make love to his lawful wife.

Only once in the intervening years did Tristan manage to see his *beloved Isolde. Disguised as a mad fool, he reappeared at Mark's court. He and Isolde again became lovers for a few bittersweet days.*

After returning to his new home, Tristan again went to war beside Kaherdin. Caught in an ambush, Tristan saved his friend but was mortally wounded himself.

Kaherdin, in debt for his life, hurried to bring Isolde of the Golden Hair to Tristan before he died. Tristan clung to life, hoping to hear news of the white sail Kaherdin would raise as a signal that Isolde had come. But when the ship finally appeared, Tristan's wife, overcome with jealousy, falsely told Tristan the sail was black. He died in despair.

Isolde the Fair, who wasted away in the absence of her true love, had summoned all her strength to come to him. Arriving to find him only an hour dead, she kissed her beloved once more and died in his arms. Tristan and Isolde were together at last, their forbidden love finally pure in the Courts of Heaven.

BY THE TIME PETER and Anastasia arrived at the first location in remote northern Scotland, it was the site of organized frenzy. Here they'd be doing exteriors of Tristan's first appearance in Ireland, when he washes up onto the shore half dead, to be found and nursed back to health by the local queen and her daughter Isolde. Pierce wanted a bleak winter-awaiting-spring feeling for those shots, and the north coast was willing to oblige.

After that, they'd film Tristan's slaying of the monster on his return to claim Isolde as a bride. Those scenes, although in the same locations, were to be ripening spring. Both fake snow and an organic green spray paint, along with hothouse plants, were at the ready.

It struck Anastasia as she looked at the shooting schedule that this was really Tristan's movie. Peter was in nearly every scene. She was in perhaps half the scenes, Pierce in a third of them. King Mark didn't appear in any Irish or French locations, so Pierce had the luxury of concentrating solely on directing for the first three weeks.

Instinctively, Peter and Anastasia chose to keep their relationship low profile, dreading the ribbing of the rest of the cast and the hawk eye of Pierce. The frosty temperatures and near primitive locations in which they were staying went virtually unnoticed by the young stars of the film. Their inexplicable buoyancy and good humor were infectious, and even the crew was better-natured about the cold and damp and strange catered food than anyone had a right to expect.

Anastasia's delicious secret overwhelmed her natural shyness and she became a favorite on the set, conversing enthusiastically with cast and crew. Anastasia was certain that no one had so far guessed the truth. Now that she was chatty with everyone, it was only natural to include Peter. Pierce seemed grateful that she and Peter had reached a truce. As much as Anastasia yearned to get past the exteriors into some more deeply dramatic scenes, she was just as glad they weren't filming anything tragic and intense yet. It would be a challenge to knock the stupid grin off her face for that long. She had never even been close to being in love before, and it was too delectable. The secrecy only added spice. It gave her the time and distance to adore Peter.

And adoring Peter was an incredibly natural thing to do. He had moved from being the vicar's son to carrying the weight of a huge film production with ease. He was a thoughtful and gifted actor. He took his work seriously, but in between scenes or after the day's shoot, it was hard to catch him when his chiseled features weren't animated with laughter. Anastasia realized he'd probably been this open and admired during rehearsals, only she hadn't believed his demeanor was sincere. But it was. It was Peter. And he was hers.

Part of the attraction, of course, was that the young man in question was in love with her. The two couldn't be alone for more than seconds without being pulled irresistibly together, their hands trying to claim every inch of each other. The fact that they never had any real privacy only heightened the ecstasy of the moments they snatched.

Pierce always met with Anastasia and Peter after dinner, and they continued to work through future scenes. The more the three of them worked on the script, the more Anastasia appreciated both the masterful shaping of the story and the flowing, haunting translation. Pierce's knowledge of it was so intimate it was clear he'd shed blood working it over and over with the screenwriter.

Even though they made the best of primitive circumstances, all were glad when it was time to move on to the next location, which promised both more substantial scenes and relative civilization.

Castle Heath on Scotland's rocky west coast was a well-preserved ruin. Its keep and turrets were sound, however, and it would be used for exteriors as the dying Tristan kept watch for the ship bearing Isolde. An interior room that now had only three walls, one with a small window to the sea, would serve as Tristan's bedchamber. There was also a roofless chapel where Isolde would die on the bier alongside her beloved.

It wasn't unusual to shoot the ending of a film first. Peter was again in every scene, although he was dead in several. Anastasia finally had a major scene—the climax in which Isolde arrives to find her recently expired lover and then dies herself.

However, most of the female scenes at this location belonged to Nicola as the other Isolde, Tristan's jealous wife. Anastasia was just as glad to be getting done with Nicola's part early.

Anastasia had no scenes on Monday, only final fittings for her death-scene robes. Afterwards she headed through the misty Scottish dawn to say hello to Jane Whittle, who had joined them to do Isolde's makeup for the rest of the film. It was easier than Anastasia had dreamed for Pierce to okay the hiring of both Jane and Ken McIntosh. Jane had signed on at once. Ken, while grateful for the offer, was committed elsewhere.

Anastasia and Jane had a happy reunion in the caravan where Jane was working on various men-at-arms and castle people. They promised to meet later for a cuppa.

"Oh, Stacy," called Christy McDermott, the unit publicist who caught her as she tried to find something non-sugar-coated on the outdoor catered breakfast table. "Has Pierce told you that we're having press on Wednesday?"

"No," Stacy answered, turning to find Christy dressed in trousers with a man's shirt and suspenders, carrying her clipboard and looking busy and on top of things, their link to world media.

"You're shooting your death scene that day, which means both you and Peter will be in costume. That will be a closed set. Afterwards, before you change, there'll be a still shoot. Then we'll allow some press photogs to get coverage of the scene—as well as some casual shots of you, Peter, Pierce, and Nicola, hanging out. Publicity shots, you know."

"Fine," Anastasia said. As long as she could die without an audience, she didn't care what came after. She was an old pro at photo shoots. She knew it was part of the game. But Christy wasn't finished.

"Then that evening, I've got you scheduled for a couple of print interviews."

"Fine. I'd appreciate knowing who they're with beforehand."

"There's another thing," said the young woman. Now her

eyes were sparkling. "I've arranged a surprise for you. I ran it by Pierce, who thought it was a good idea."

"Can't wait," said the actress.

"If it's all right, we'll let you wait till Wednesday."

Anastasia did some mental figuring. It wasn't near her birthday, so it couldn't be a cake. She couldn't think of what else Christy had in mind. "Fine." She gave a cooperative smile and went to eat her breakfast.

Somehow Peter thought it was only polite to sit with Nicola as well as with Anastasia at the nightly buffet spread for the cast and crew in the restaurant of the Cock and Bull, where Peter and half the others were staying. Richie Riley usually joined them, which made Nicola's company less unbearable. The two young women had never warmed up to each other.

"She really fancies you," Anastasia hissed to Peter on Tuesday night as she waited for a ride back to the Rose and Garter. Call was so early the next morning that they were forgoing their nightly work session with Pierce.

Peter grinned impishly. "Well, she does have a great set of gams, doesn't she?"

"Peter!"

He laughed and his hand brushed Anastasia's waist lightly. "She flirts with everybody above the line, it's just her way. She's a player. My guess is that in Nicola's scheme of things, Pierce would be worth catching if he was interested. Since he doesn't seem to be, I'd make an amusing distraction. But I doubt that to her I'm even worth turning up in a publicity photo with."

"I think you underestimate yourself."

"Hmm. She and I are both staying here. I guess we'll find out."

Anastasia put her hands on her hips in mock outrage.

"Joking! I'm joking!" he protested.

"So, Anastasia. Are you ready to die in the morning?" They turned to find Pierce behind them.

"I regret that I have but one life to give for my director," she said dramatically.

"Oh, I'm certain you'll give three or four at least, so I want you asleep in short order," Pierce said to Anastasia. "If you'll excuse us, Tristan, since Isolde and I are both at the Rose and Garter, I'll escort her back and see she's safely locked into her room."

Anastasia and Richie were the first to report to the principals' makeup caravan the next morning, although they were joined by Peter and Nicola within the quarter hour.

As the first hints of rising sun found foothold in the east, Anastasia thanked her lucky stars that her costume included a heavy robe over her gown. It was freezing. As they did the final rehearsal, it felt to Anastasia that no one existed in the world except her and Pierce and the corpse of Tristan. It was as if White Hands were unimportant, ethereal, a child to be shooed away. She heard the guiding edicts from the director as echoes from her own mind. Her attention was riveted by the death of her beloved Tristan; her deepest desire was to depart a world in which he lived no longer.

Pierce only let her rehearse it once. He wanted to save the rest for the camera.

Then, as the stand-ins appeared for the final lighting adjustments, Nicola grabbed Pierce's attention for work on her motivation. It seemed to Anastasia a ridiculously long and animated discussion for White Hands' thirty-second appearance; in this scene, Nicola didn't even have lines.

Anastasia had been warned repeatedly by hair and costume people not to rumple herself by sitting down, so she went in search of something to lean against. As she did, she heard a low voice from behind in her ear.

"Okay, so you were right."

She glanced back to find that Peter had followed her.

"I did have a visit from our friend last night."

"Seriously?" Anastasia turned around. "From Nicola of the Great Gams?"

"It turns out her gams are nowhere near the whole story."

"No? What is the story? And how do you know it?"

"Shhh." He put his powder-white hand across her lips. "How I know is that she dropped by in a robe ready to drop—which she did before I could stop her. Wow. I wonder how much is natural."

"She threw herself at you naked?"

"Would you expect any less from Nic?" Peter couldn't hide the glint in his eyes.

"What did you do?"

"Hmm," he said, turning away, suddenly fascinated by a thread from the hem of his tunic.

"For pity's sake!" Anastasia hissed.

"I thanked her for her interest, but explained I was committed elsewhere."

"Did you say *where* elsewhere?"

"She wouldn't have believed me if I hadn't. And why shouldn't I, when I have the most luscious—"

"Careful," Anastasia warned, stepping beyond his grasp, "you're covered with powder."

"You can't let little things like the fact I'm dead come between us," he teased.

"So, did it work?"

"You mean, did my manhood remain outside Nicola's domain?"

"Peter!"

"Yes. She finally got the picture. And I escaped unscathed."

"Only after you got the picture."

"Yes. I did quite, didn't I?"

"Wipe that grin off your face. Do you think she's . . . upset?"

"It's hard to tell with her. Once she discovered I was serious, she took it graciously. But it can't be good for one's ego to be naked and rejected. In any case, I thought you'd like to know. You may proceed with the 'I told you so's.'"

"Terrific. Nicola already dislikes me for taking her role. Now I've taken her man as well."

"I was never her man."

"Not for her lack of trying." Anastasia looked thoughtful. "There's only one thing to do," she finally said. "Since I won't give her the part, I guess I've got to offer her you. Go make love to her, quick, before the scene."

Peter's jaw dropped. "Are you serious?"

Anastasia shot him a look and left, shaking her head and stifling a laugh, trying to recapture her concentration.

As she stood alone in a hidden corner of the chapel, she found herself wishing Peter hadn't told her of his encounter with Nicola, at least not until after the day's shoot. She'd never felt completely worthy to have taken "Nicola's role." And although she bet Peter was right, that Nicola was interested in him as a diversion, she had no desire to compete with her. She didn't especially like Nicola, but had no axes to grind. Although Nicola might not say the same about Anastasia.

To make matters worse, Anastasia's one line to Nicola as she mourned by the body of Peter was, "Lady, rise and let me come by him; I have more right to mourn him than have you—believe me. I loved him more."

Great. Just great. Anastasia was starting to get a headache.

She closed her eyes and tried to center herself with the breathing exercises she'd learned in acting class. As she thought about it, the rivalry between her and Nicola had parallels to that of the two Isoldes. Isolde of the White Hands had cause to weep at Tristan's bier, but she had greater cause. Tristan was hers. Her loss was greater.

By the time they were ready to roll, Anastasia felt a resolution of spirit at the same time that her body was trembling, ready to betray her. She blocked out everything else.

As they proceeded with successive takes, however, the part of Anastasia that was the observer noticed an almost imperceptible change occurring between her and Isolde of the White Hands. As they went from coverage in the wide shot to two shots, to close-ups of each woman, it seemed Nicola's reaction was becoming more hostile, while Anastasia's became more possessive of Tristan and more dismissive of the lesser Isolde. Their actions didn't change, but Isolde of the White Hands went from battling guilt to sheer hatred of the "other woman" in her marriage. In response to the flash of steel from her eyes and the imperious set of the chin, Isolde the Fair paid less and less attention to the pitiful woman she knew Tristan didn't love.

Pierce must have noticed it as well, but he didn't stop them. If anything, he seemed intrigued.

Anastasia meant to congratulate Nicola on her good work after they finished their scene together, but the raw hostility she'd read in her eyes—well, the character's eyes—took away that urge. Nicola was dismissed while they shot Isolde's death.

Anastasia cleared her mind of any emotions other than those of being with her dead lover, and having both the strength and the weakness to join him on the other side. She had no room for anything but dying and hitting her marks. She forgot Nicola's existence.

Then somehow it was late afternoon and they were finished with the chapel scenes.

"Cut!" yelled Pierce at the end of the dolly shot that recorded the chapel populated by the bodies of Tristan and Isolde, the grieving forms of Kaherdin and Isolde of the White Hands, and various extras. "And print. That's it. Good work, people!"

The A.D. standing next to him immediately added, "Everyone involved in the still shoot, stay put!"

Peter raised himself on one arm next to Anastasia. "God, I need to kiss you," he said.

Hair and makeup people descended for touch-ups and to remove Peter's death makeup for the still shots. When the setup was complete, the two of them and Nicola were called over to re-create various moments from Isolde's death scene.

The actors then changed clothes and met outside for casual photos with Pierce. Richie joined them, whether by invitation or insinuation, Anastasia didn't know. After a hard day of dying, they were all ready to cut loose, and the five of them took advantage of the remaining daylight to pose rakishly throughout the castle.

Then different photographers grabbed them for distinctive solo, duet, trio, and quartet shots.

"Can I have you three, then?" asked one photographer, motioning Anastasia, Peter, and Nicola together. He posed them with Peter in the middle, the two women flanking him. Just as he began to shoot, Nicola turned toward Peter, ran her thigh up his, and captured his earlobe in her mouth. The photos were snapped, but before anyone had a chance to respond, Richie sauntered into the frame.

"That hardly seems fair," he said to the photographer. "Why don't you take a few more?"

As the gentleman obliged, Richie lowered Anastasia into a swoon and kissed her. Nicola again pressed Peter into service.

So somehow, Anastasia ended up a couple with Richard Riley.

"I think that's enough for the day," said Pierce good-naturedly. "We're all getting a bit punchy."

"We do have a surprise for Stacy, though," Christy piped up.

Anastasia had completely forgotten Christy's cryptic reference to the surprise she'd cooked up. Christy pulled Anastasia forward while the photographers readied their cameras and the other four actors watched from a few steps behind.

"Stacy Day, look who's here." Christy beckoned to a figure waiting behind a rampart wall. Out walked a woman in a clean but shapeless gray dress, her hair up in a bun like a schoolmarm's.

Anastasia gasped, the shock evident on her face. "Mother?"

"It's Beverly Day, our beautiful star's mother!" Christy announced to the staring press. "She's come from London to see her daughter in action."

Beverly walked over and gave Anastasia a brief kiss. The cameras clicked.

"Mom," Anastasia finally whispered, "what on earth are you doing here?"

"Christy invited me," she said. "Which seems to be something you had no intention of doing."

They spoke quietly enough that no one could make out their words, the content of which they continued to hide with weak smiles for the camera. "And I can obviously see why," Beverly said. "You hardly want me to spoil your fun."

"Mom, those photos—we were kidding around."

"That's what you call it nowadays? He is good-looking, I'll give you that," Beverly said, smiling over at Richie, who mistook it for a genuine overture of friendship and smiled back.

"Over here, Mrs. Day. Anastasia!"

"Look this way, please!"

Oddly, the women continued to oblige the photographers,

their arms still laced about each other's waists.

"Mom, I'm not dating Richie. I'm just acting in this movie."

"That's supposed to make it better?"

"Beautiful, Mrs. Day, beautiful."

"Can we try a few over here?"

Incredible, Anastasia thought. *Mother is still capable of reducing me to tears in fewer than five minutes.*

Thankfully, Peter had quickly assessed the situation and came over, seemingly excited. "I'm so pleased to meet you, Mrs. Day. I'm Peter Dalton. Your daughter is very talented. And it's clear now where she gets her beauty—both inner and outer."

Peter turned to the photographers. "You've gotten what you need, surely?"

He turned back to Anastasia's mother. "Have you seen the view of the ocean from the ramparts? It's really something. Stacy, may I borrow your mother for a moment?"

And, miraculously, he glided Beverly through the knot of on-lookers, who dispersed and began to go about their business.

"Stacy," Christy said blithely, "your first interview is with American press. Perhaps your mother might want to join you for part of it?"

But the young woman pushed past Christy—and kept going. "Give her a minute," Pierce instructed. "Go find the reporter and make him comfortable. Tell him I had to confer with Anastasia, but you doubt it will take long."

Pierce found the actress in the chapel, which was now cleared of furnishings, cables, lights, and cameras. She sat alone on the stone steps leading up to where the bier had been. Pierce entered slowly, finally coming to lean against the south wall below where she sat.

"It looks as if our surprise surprised you," he said.

She managed a nod.

"I'm sorry, I did mean to talk to you about it. But with production starting and everything going on, it never made the top of the list."

"You let Christy bring my mother without even consulting me."

"We would have asked you immediately when the idea came up, but you were in the North York Moors with young Dalton."

"Yes, and whose idea was that?" Anastasia shot back. She looked up at him, gathering her fury. "This was—way out of line. You have no right to be in contact with my mother—or any other family member or personal acquaintance—behind my back."

"You're right," said Pierce. Anastasia was still shaking, from which complex mix of emotions, he wasn't sure.

"For God's sake, what were you thinking?" she exploded.

He came and sat beside her on the front step, leaving a comfortable amount of room between them. His long legs easily reached the stone floor of the aisle. "Anastasia. Whether we talk about it or not, you're very young. Sixteen. Carrying an entire feature film. That's extraordinary. The reason you're carrying the movie in the first place is because you can handle it. You have an incredible presence and maturity for any age. But this picture is going to generate a lot of talk. And it can never seem, even in the wildest imagination, like we've taken a delicate young thing and thrown her to the wolves. We're past the age of needing chaperones, thank God—"

Anastasia turned on him violently, but he held up his hands. "But. We thought it wouldn't hurt if there were photos of you and your proud and delighted mum giving her blessings on the set."

"My mother doesn't give blessings," said Anastasia.

"It seems not."

"For your information, she thinks I'm a worthless no-talent and a whore, as well. Probably the only virgin prostitute in the country. I'm surprised she was sober enough to answer the phone when Christy called. That ought to make for some incredibly interesting press interviews."

"I'm sorry. I had no idea. We'll keep her away from the press, of course. I'll have Christy take her back to the Cock and Bull, make sure she has a nice supper and a nice room, and we'll pack her off first thing in the morning."

"I don't know what kind of damage she's done—she's doing even now. I can't control her, you see."

"It's not your job to control her. This is my screwup, and I'm sorry."

Anastasia sighed. "Let me go find her. I need to talk with her before she goes back to the hotel."

"Fair enough," said the director.

They stood to leave, Anastasia preceding Pierce toward the door. She turned as she reached it, emotional storm clouds still billowing. "Mr. Hall, let's get one thing straight. Although I'm in your movie, you have no right to continue to meddle in my personal life. None. You wanted me to make a truce with Peter, and I have. But that's it. That's as far as you go. Is that understood?"

"Understood."

And she swept out the door.

But Anastasia couldn't find Beverly anywhere. She did find Peter, and took him aside.

"Where is she?"

"I don't know. We had a perfectly pleasant time, then she needed to use the loo. I haven't seen her since." He gently pushed Anastasia's hair back from around her face. "She does seem to be on good behavior, however."

"That's a relief, I suppose." She looked up, searching his face. "You do believe me, don't you? About what she's like?"

"Of course, my love. I know well enough that people with

problems like hers can be masters of cover-up when they put their minds to it."

The simple fact that Peter believed her let the tension begin to drain from her shoulders.

They heard a cough behind them and turned to find Christy shuffling nervously.

"Guys?" she said. "The interviewers are waiting."

"I'm ready," said Peter. "I hope they'll understand we're tired, and keep it short."

"I'll give her twenty minutes and come get you," Christy promised.

"Pierce and I feel it would be best if my mother did not speak to the press," Anastasia said, fighting to stay calm.

"He told me," she said, looking stricken. "I am sorry, Stacy."

"It's all right," the actress answered. "You didn't know. Where is my mother now?"

"I saw her down walking the shore with Nicola."

"With Nicola?"

"They struck up a conversation by the catering truck, and next thing I knew, they said they were taking a stroll."

Peter put a gentle hand on Anastasia's arm, pulling her a step away. "Of everything you have that Nicola wants, for God's sake, give her your mother," he murmured. "At least for twenty minutes."

"But who knows what she'll say!"

"Stace, she was perfectly well behaved when she was with me. And frankly, who cares what she says to Nicola? Who really cares?"

"All right," she said, and turned to Christy. "Can those twenty minutes start now?"

After the interview, Anastasia found Beverly had returned and was talking cheerfully with Christy. "Stacy, I'm sorry there were no available rooms at your hotel, but we were able to get your mother a luxury room at the Cock and Bull. We'll be heading over in a minute," the unit publicist explained.

"Can you give us a few minutes before you go?"

"Yes, of course. Come find me when you're done," Christy said with an overzealous smile.

Anastasia guided them toward a dramatic promontory outside the castle walls that gave a sweeping view of the ocean and of the small town reaching out onto the jetty below. The two of them seemed tiny against this gigantic landscape.

"It is good to see you," the daughter began. "Christy didn't tell me she'd called you. If she had, I would have guessed you wouldn't be interested in coming."

"There are a few things I need to discuss with you," Beverly said.

There followed a wary pause.

Anastasia decided to jump in. "You haven't been drinking. Whether you believe it or not, that makes me very happy."

"I'm glad if it makes you glad."

"It mustn't have been easy to stop."

"It wasn't so hard. Once I found my life's true direction."

"Oh. Good."

The two sat, each lost in her own thoughts. Anastasia hardly recognized the woman next to her, her shapeless gray dress barely moving in the breeze, her oft-coiffed hair bobby-pinned up, her nails free of polish. Anastasia was afraid of what her mother might say next, so she barged ahead with the statement she'd long been composing.

"Mom, I've never said this," she started. "But thank you for taking such a chance and bringing us to England. I know it was a big risk. It mustn't have been easy for you to be on your own when I was at Chester. But those years meant a lot to me, and I wouldn't have had them without you."

Her mother stared out at some unknown focal point in the distance. "I know you meant to try to help me, too," she said.

Anastasia felt the blood rising in her cheeks. *Tried to help? Giving up your life at thirteen is only worth a pat for "trying to help"?* She managed a couple of deep breaths. *Finish,* she told herself. *Just finish.*

"I don't know what impression you've gotten of this film shoot, Mother. But the fact is, it's a very good, important film. I'm proud to be in it. It was an honor to be chosen. I wish you could be happy for me."

"Someday you'll understand, I hope, about mothers and daughters. How anything that makes you happy makes me happy as well. But Stacy, dear, all I wish for you is that you find true and lasting happiness. Life is about more than pride in accomplishments. It's about the spirit. That's what it all boils down to, and everything else is just trappings. Trappings which distract us from our true purpose."

"Are you still studying with the Master?"

"He is a very old spirit. He has taught me to find my inner light. When you follow the path, you don't need crutches like alcohol or possessions or worldly knowledge—or organized religion—or even food, really."

Again at a loss, Anastasia gave the ridiculous answer, "That's nice, Mother."

"He never pressures anyone to follow the Way of Enlightenment. If you are one of the called, you recognize his voice and you follow. Stacy, I will only ask you this once. For the sake of your immortal soul, leave with me in the morning. Join me in our compound in India. Walk with me on the Way."

"Mother, it's funny you're bringing this up now. You and I never really talked about anything—spiritual. But I just met Peter's father, who's a vicar, and he and I started talking about God—"

"Didn't you hear what I said about organized religion? Don't be tempted down that bourgeois Western path!"

The hope of reconciliation in Anastasia's heart turned to a ball of lead and dropped heavily into her stomach.

"I can't come with you," was all she said.

"The way of the flesh is never right. I pray you'll see that eventually."

"For God's sake, Mother!" she finally burst out. "Where do you get these idiotic ideas about me and flesh, any flesh? I'm a virgin, Mother. A virgin! I've never even had a boyfriend before. I've been too busy working to make us a living!"

"You are full of anger," said her mother. "I will pray for you. You let people kiss you—as you did this afternoon—and you laugh and think it's a joke. You are photographed for all the world to see wearing so few clothes that it's more provocative than none at all. Selling your body to sell products."

"It's called 'modeling,' Mother. And someone had to support us! I had to do something to make money!"

"You didn't have to whore yourself. You don't have to do it now. Come with me."

"Why can't you accept me, even a little, even if you think I'm messing up—if only because I'm your daughter? Why can't you love me? I love you, Mother. I love you so much."

Beverly stood, smoothing the starched cotton of her dress. "I'll pray for you."

Anastasia's mother turned and walked back across the wind-swept castle lawn to where Christy waited by the auto. She didn't look back.

Anastasia didn't go to dinner. Instead, she shut herself in her room and ran the bathwater full force, so that no one passing would hear her wrenching sobs. Beverly's long-implied rejection of her daughter had become concrete.

As long as the bath was drawn, she climbed into it. When she finally got out and pulled on her nightgown, she sat in a green-and-gold-striped wing chair staring at the unlit fire in the small hearth before her. And she realized she felt a longing, a physical ache for Peter. She so badly needed him to love her.

She sat for long minutes, thinking of him. She loved his mind and his spirit so fully. She loved how he never just accepted what he was told as fact. He investigated, he read, he experienced for himself. Peter was devout in his faith, and he was on this shoot. He didn't think he was damned for doing it. Oh, how she longed for him to be here, to comfort her, to tell her she was not worthless. She was not unlovable. She was not damned.

But when the knock came quietly on the door and she opened it to find Peter, she was speechless.

"I walked over," he said. "I thought you might need some company."

He came in and closed the door softly. When he gathered her to himself, they neither kissed passionately nor discussed theology. Instead, Peter had her ring down for a wake-up call early enough that he could return to his hotel to answer his own call. Then he enfolded her in his arms, and they lay on the bed. He soothed her while she cried. And then he gently cradled her as she fell asleep.

CHAPTER 7

From the film review of Tristan and Isolde *in Daily Variety,
April 15, 1991:*

*Adding bravura performances, hot sexual chemistry, and plenty of
action to a classic story of intrigue and forbidden love, the late Pierce
Hall's final tour de force has the potential for an even bigger box office
harvest than Zeffirelli's* Romeo and Juliet *if Paramount can position
it among the crowded late-summer fare.*

*Indeed, Hall's ability to wed actor to role has produced Oscar-
caliber performances from all three leads. The tautness he brought to
the direction of his thrillers has served to strengthen and simplify this
intergenerational love triangle that originated as an epic bard's tale.*

*In this version, Tristan's birth, banishment, and anonymous up-
bringing happen before the credits. The film opens with his return to
Cornwall and earning his place as the favored warrior in the court of
King Mark before discovering the monarch is his uncle. From there it
moves quickly to Tristan's slaying of, and near-mortal wounding by,
the Morholt, which brings him to the healing hands of the beautiful
Isolde (played with a feisty maturity by newcomer Anastasia Day),*

who is, alas, the niece of the slain warrior.

Peter Dalton makes a magnetic screen hero as the prince who must consequently woo the woman he loves to be his uncle's bride. The experienced young actor comes into his own as Tristan, a man plagued in turns by love and guilt, yet always true to his warrior calling. Dalton easily holds his own on screen with Pierce Hall—no easy feat—who plays Mark lustily. No pining, wronged monarch here. Mark is every inch a king, yet his will and temper are at crucial moments overcome by his love for Queen Isolde. Hall's charismatic performance will leave women easily understanding how Isolde is torn between two strong suitors.

As Isolde, newcomer Anastasia Day shines between these two mega-talents. Her young queen is a strong-willed, trained healer—a modern ruler for an ancient century. Isolde is the member of the triangle most plagued by guilt over her "unholy" relationship with Tristan, and her anguish is genuinely moving.

The political corruption that is meant too clearly to echo modern times would be cumbersome if it were not for the masterful touches of ace villain Garrett Clifton. Yet the moral lessons of ageless politics are always encapsulated between strong action sequences. The tearjerker ending at the deaths of the title characters is bound to leave moviegoers awash in emotion.

Tech credits are tops. Kudos to Brendan Todd's art direction and the cinematography of Milos Atillier. Music by Conan Marcel is certain to garner notice at awards time.

———————•———————

My dear Anastasia,
So sorry you missed dessert. I'm sure there'll
be lovely sweets at the reunion. See you there.
—a friend and admirer

Anastasia let the laser-printed note on the white bond stationery flutter down onto her lap. Things had not gone well since the four of them had returned from Calais the evening before. Now she, Bruce, and Elise sat silently under the glass walls of the conservatory, waiting for the early morning shroud of fog to burn off.

None of them had gotten much sleep. Leah had gone directly back to her hotel upon their return. An hour after the occupants of the Amerman house had retired for the night, they'd been roused by Inspector Irving of Scotland Yard, along with a couple of his cronies, whose insistent knocking would have pulled someone from a coma.

The lanky inspector had gotten word that Bruce once again happened to be involved in an unexpected death.

Irving had a long, drawn, horsey-type face, with a thatch of bushy hair and operatic eyebrows. It was clear he was not there to play games. He'd claimed his business was with Bruce only, but Anastasia and Elise had both insisted on being present in Bruce's small office as the three law officers grilled Bruce about the events of the past day. Anastasia had been outraged by the tone they took, but Bruce had remained calm, and warned her with a look to do the same.

When asked, Anastasia had given her version of the story, speaking calmly but making certain the inspector knew she felt he was harassing the wrong person.

The only time she had been overtly uncomfortable was when Irving asked Elise where she'd been when her husband was in Calais. Bruce had shot his wife an urgent glare that brooked no argument. She'd said simply she'd been home all day, awaiting the return of the others. The inspector had questioned her no further, but Anastasia didn't like the feeling they had anything to hide.

The gentlemen from the Yard had left by one-thirty a.m. She, Bruce, and Elise had dispersed to their rooms shortly thereafter.

Anastasia was certain her hosts hadn't gotten much more sleep than she had.

So she wasn't surprised when, in her early morning wanderings, she was joined first by Elise and then by Bruce. She and Elise were still in nightgowns, with robes pulled over. Bruce, on the other hand, was already dressed in jeans and a cardigan. They didn't speak much. Elise put on the kettle. She went to fetch the morning paper, and came back carrying not only the *Times*, but a white envelope, computer-addressed to Her Grace, the Duchess of Esmonde. She looked wan as she came to where Bruce and Anastasia had settled in the garden room with their English Breakfast tea.

"This was under the front door," she said.

Anastasia made a jagged tear in the envelope in nervous haste. Once she had perused its contents, she passed the sheet over to Bruce.

"So. Ended any meals before dessert lately?" asked Bruce.

"Not since yesterday," said Anastasia. "Meant to peek into Conan's oven, but forgot somehow. Smelled good, though. Cinnamon, I think."

Bruce gestured toward the letter. "It's on a different paper stock than the first note you got, but the days of finding culprits by checking typewriters for the sticking letter 'd' are gone, I'm afraid."

"How can you be so bloody calm?" asked Elise. "The murderer brought this *here*. To our house. Our home!"

Anastasia admitted, "This does mean that someone who knows we were in Calais knows we're now here. You're right, too, that this is a different stock of paper than the first, seemingly from a different printer. Which, given the universal availability of both, means precisely nothing. The only common factors are the signature and the pressing to attend the reunion."

Bruce looked at her over his cup, his face haggard but alert. He said slowly, "I'm afraid it also means you're going to have to attend."

"Yes, right. If anything, it makes me think I'd best be a continent away!"

"Whether this note was written by an uncannily prescient admirer or our killer, it tells me the same thing. As far as the reunion goes, Anastasia, you are the main attraction, the big draw. The bait, as it were."

"Oh, jolly good," she said.

"Don't you see? You've got to announce you're attending. If we haven't found our man by then, I have little doubt we can flush him out that night. And if he—or she, of course, excuse me—is indeed plotting something in the meanwhile, your announcement will make it that much easier to follow the threads."

"Stop pulling your bloody threads!" said Elise. The vehemence in her voice caused them both to look up, surprised. "For God's sake, if you don't stop this, you could very well end up either under arrest or dead. And the whole nightmare we've worked so hard to put behind us will start all over again! But this time, there might be no escaping it. Don't you see? What will my life be if you're spending the rest of yours in prison?"

"It's not going to happen," Bruce said.

"You've already got me lying to Scotland Yard," Elise responded. "I want you to stop pursuing this. Please."

Bruce went to stand before his wife. "Don't *you* see?" he asked. "This is the same nightmare. It never really ended. It won't until someone stops it. And no one has more invested in stopping it than we do."

Down the hall, the door buzzer rang. Elise stood and stalked away to answer it.

Anastasia and Bruce stayed rigid, not daring to look at each other. Was Elise right? Was the ring at the door Inspector Irving returning, this time with handcuffs?

Instead Leah followed Elise into the room. Leah was dressed in one of her signature pantsuits, but the creases hadn't been ironed. The fabric on the left leg was wrinkled. Anastasia had never seen Leah disheveled before. She looked to have gotten less sleep than had those in the Amerman house.

"It's not a game anymore," said Leah.

"Sit down," Anastasia invited, but Leah didn't even hear her.

"I thought when you called, it was some abstract entertainment, a kind of game we were playing to connect dots that don't connect. But people are dying. My father might have been murdered. It isn't a joke. I don't want to be a part of this. I don't know what's going on, but I want out. I have a car waiting. I'm going home."

Anastasia walked over to her friend. "Are you sure?"

"Absolutely certain."

"All right. I understand. I really do. Have a safe trip." The calmness of her answer surprised even her. "I'll miss you."

Neither Bruce nor Elise spoke as Leah turned and fled back down the hall.

"Well. She's a lot of help," Elise finally said.

"She's got a point, actually," Bruce answered his wife. "I want you to go away, too. To your sister's."

"What?"

"It's probably best," Anastasia agreed. "If the killer's onto the fact that we're onto him—which our personalized mail service would seem to prove—then the three of us staying together make a nice fat target."

"You won't have to lie to Scotland Yard if you're not around when they come to call."

The anger had drained from Elise. "No, Bruce, I'm not leaving you. If you're in danger, I'm in danger."

Bruce stood and put a hand on her shoulder. "Then you can understand how I feel. I've already lost one wife to this nightmare. I couldn't stand it if I lost you, as well. Please, please go away. If I'm going to be a target, give me the freedom to be a moving target. If this killer got you, I'd go crazy. It wouldn't matter if they caught him or not."

Silence surrounded them. Finally Elise turned to Anastasia. "What about you?"

"I'll have Reginald send a car. The best thing might be if the killer thinks he's scared us into giving up. We can stay in touch by telephone. Is there somewhere you can ring me from, if you think your wire's tapped, or your mobile might be picked up?"

"There's a fairly private call booth at the local pub. We'll set up a signal so I'll know to call you from there," Bruce said.

"Say I ring twice and hang up, then ring twice and hang up."

"You both still think you're playing spies!" Elise said. She was close to tears. "Scotland Yard is this close to arresting you, and a bloody maniac has been at our front door!"

"Which proves ignoring this is no longer an option."

The fear in Elise's posture caused Bruce's voice to soften. "Darling, I'll be very careful. Now go and pack."

Both women left their china cups on the kitchen counter and went in separate directions to do just that.

———————

ONCE THEY SETTLED INTO the hotels near Ravenswood Studios, life took on a sort of pattern. After six weeks of interiors, the production would move again to do the many forest scenes and other exteriors down south. But for now, the days were easier.

Most of the rest of the cast had joined them. Up north, they'd had only the actors who appeared in the Irish or French scenes. Now they'd moved on to the main thrust of the story, which took place in King Mark's realm in Cornwall. So Nicola was gone, replaced by "the lads." Now that Anastasia and Peter were friends, the other young actors felt free to rally round her as well. Anastasia noticed that even though Peter was four or five years younger than most of the others, he was their natural leader. One day Anastasia laughed out loud at the commissary when she realized she felt like Wendy surrounded by Peter Pan and the Lost Boys. If Nicola was Tinkerbelle, at least she was out of the way.

Their energy, of course, was consumed by the film. Many of the scenes were complex and emotionally demanding. But Anastasia found in Pierce Hall the kind of teacher and mentor that those with rare gifts and good luck occasionally find at university. When she and Pierce worked together, it was as if he could read her mind. He was a hard taskmaster; he pushed his actors, demanding perfection. He often got it. Working with Pierce was not a comfortable, benign fit. In his presence, Anastasia often felt like the lion tamer in the circus cage. It seemed you were in control, but you knew it was due only to the good graces of the powerful animal with which you worked, and the fact that he chose to keep himself in check. There was a power and a danger in Pierce as well. Everyone working on *T & I* knew when he was on the set; they knew when he entered a room. He projected a magnetic aura that kept the actors' blood racing and attention absolutely focused when they worked with him.

When he acted, he drove himself no less hard. Before their first challenging scene together, Anastasia was once again attacked by the worst of her insecurities. But Pierce had no time for Anastasia the nervous teenager; there was far too much he expected from Anastasia the actress, his peer. She was forced to rise to the occasion.

It was after one of Queen Isolde's most dramatic scenes with King Mark—their confrontation after Mark finally arrests his wife for her love of Tristan—that Pierce made an unusual request.

Anastasia was emotionally exhausted. She'd been bound with ropes during the scene, which had only increased the intensity; she hadn't been able to dissipate her anguish by physical movement, it had all stayed centered inside. Isolde did love Mark, and Mark loved both Isolde and Tristan. But in this scene, there was no way beyond his fury. He felt betrayal so complete that, face-to-face with his beloved, he condemned her to death.

It was the first time Isolde had not been able to make any impact on her husband at all. During their meeting, she moved from feeling guilty toward him yet dependent on his mercy to realizing there would be no mercy. Mark decreed there would be no trial, no appeals. She and Tristan were to be publicly burned at the stake the next day. In Pierce she saw the depth of Mark's love become the strength of his hatred as his feelings for his wife turned inside out and hardened. For Anastasia, the arc of the scene charted the death of Isolde's hope.

After the final take, when the prop master moved in to loosen the thick, prickly ropes that bound Anastasia's arms, she found herself trembling. While feeling the satisfaction of a scene gone well, she wanted nothing more than to escape to her dressing room, where she let the costume assistant undress her and whisk the gown away. She pulled on her robe and collapsed onto the small sofa. She needed to be alone to decompress.

She didn't hear the knock on her door, and was startled when it opened and Pierce leaned in. "Hello?"

Her adrenaline surged. She leapt off the couch to face him.

"Good Lord," he said, amused by her stricken look. "I don't really plan to execute you tomorrow."

She managed a weak smile. "No? Or even Tuesday next?"

"I'll have to check my calendar, but I don't think there's anything like that scheduled. Actually, I came to see if you were free for dinner. There's something I'd like to discuss."

Of course she was free for dinner. No one ever dared schedule anything on a heavy shooting day like this, when you had no idea when you'd finish.

"Sure," she said. "What time?"

"I'll stop round in half an hour. And buck up. We can even dispense with the ropes while you're eating."

After Pierce finished his final preparations for the next morning, he drove them to a tony restaurant across town where it was unlikely they'd run into anyone else from the production.

Even as her emotions were quieting, Anastasia was apprehensive—as any cast member was when summoned to a private audience with the director. She remained fairly certain the day's shoot had gone well, and, in fact, Pierce was in good humor. He seemed remarkably relaxed for someone who had the twin pressures of acting and directing. She was still not past the steady current of excitement that emanated from the fact that she, Anastasia Day, was sitting in a restaurant with Pierce Hall.

After they ordered, he leaned back in his chair, savoring his glass of burgundy. As he closed his eyes and expelled a breath, he looked young and virile and satisfied with life and himself.

He opened them to find his companion watching him.

"You know that Gray Eddington and I have worked together in the past," he said. She wasn't sure if that was a question or a statement, but gave a confirming nod.

"When Gray came to find me living the good life—well, the quiet life, anyway—with my wife and children in Provence, he came to talk me out of retirement. He and I make a good team, though of course, he's interested in our collaboration only as long as it's lucrative. So the first thing I did when he came to vacation with our happy family"—his voice was wry at this point, but Anastasia didn't dare any interpretation—"was to show him two scripts I'd written in which he might have some interest." He planted all four chair legs on the floor and leaned in. "Blast, I wish I still smoked. A cigarette is good for dramatic emphasis."

"And Gray was interested, I take it."

"So interested that he was willing to do anything to lure me back. Even if it meant making *Tristan and Isolde.*"

"You mean *T & I* wasn't one of the scripts you showed him?"

"Hell, no. He's a producer, not a patron of the arts. *T & I* was the cost of making the other two. We have a three-picture deal. I made sure this would be the first."

Anastasia found talking about things outside their insular world relaxed her. Her head was clearing and she was becoming more Anastasia and less Isolde. It felt disconcertingly natural to be discussing financing deals with a major director.

"So, what are the other two? If I may be so bold."

"Sophisticated thrillers. Eddington and I have done well with them in the past."

"I saw *At Interval,*" Anastasia said. "It was wonderful."

"Thrillers are a much better financial gamble than are period pieces. I didn't need Gray to tell me that."

"But he saw some potential in *Tristan?*"

"He had to have thought it had equal odds, or we wouldn't be here," Pierce said pragmatically.

The waitress brought their appetizers: consommé for Anastasia, clams for Pierce, who gave the woman a wink and sent her off, flustered.

"I'll come to the point. Gray has already started raising capital for the next picture. That's his department. All of my attention—and 95 percent of his—is still focused on this film, of course. But we're in it together, so it behooves me to do what I can to help with the next."

"Of course."

"Which means I might slip out to London now and again for the odd dinner or meeting."

She found this an interesting education, and was happy to be Pierce's sounding board, but was at a loss as to why he was telling her.

"So. What this is coming around to. I think you'd be well suited for the female lead in the picture. You're physically right for it, a little young, but you're growing older all the time. You'd bring the right depth and dimension to the part. And it might be a savvy career move for you to go from Isolde to a modern role."

Anastasia set her spoon down carefully on the plate beneath the soup bowl. Oh, she hated what she knew was coming next. Her mother had been the champion of it. Offer something stupidly wonderful, then give the impossible conditions in the next breath, and use those conditions to control her. Her stomach knotted.

"And?" she said, staring fixedly at the clear broth before her.

"And I wondered if you might be interested."

"If . . . I were?" She was trying to keep her anger in check.

"If you were, I'd start talking to Gray about it. You'd need to keep it confidential, of course, but I'd also want you to come in to some of the meetings in London, for the purpose of charming various key people off their seats."

"There's . . ."

"What? There's what?" He seemed genuinely puzzled at her hesitance.

"There's no catch?"

He reached across the table, lifting her chin with his fingers.

"Good God, girl, why do you always think good news is bad news in disguise?"

She looked at the surprising gentleness in his eyes. "In my experience, bad news has proven more trustworthy."

"So tell me. Would you be interested?"

She managed a smile, followed by a nod.

"Good heavens. You really are expecting someone to burn you at the stake." He held up a hand to summon the waitress. "We need a bottle of champagne and two glasses over here," he said.

While he ordered, Anastasia sat, consciously dropping her natural defenses to allow a glowing happiness to blanket her body from inside. She knew she would have to relearn her responses to things. It would take time—but in some cases, as she was beginning to see, it would be worth it.

While Anastasia worked most often with Pierce and Peter, the rest of the cast was stimulating as well. Her favorite co-workers were Garrett Clifton and Bruce Amerman. Garrett and Anastasia hit it off from the first. Garrett played Andret, King Mark's other nephew and the villain of the story. As someone well acquainted with brutal, serious put-downs, she recognized his as jest at once and enjoyed paying him back in kind. Besides being a good actor, Garrett had a brilliant and creative mind, and Anastasia was intrigued by his perspective on things. Their mutual admiration made acting opposite each other even more fun. Andret was so darn evil and Isolde was such a paragon of tortured good that it was, as Anastasia's long-ago friends in South Carolina would have said, a hoot.

It was also a relief that there was no sexual tension between them. Garrett wasn't obvious about the fact he was gay, but he didn't hide it, either. His partner, Bill Overton, a well-respected costume designer, discreetly visited once when Garrett had a couple of free days in a row. Anastasia, Peter, and Bruce had joined them for a relaxed and raucous dinner.

Bruce Amerman was Peter's best friend on the set, and Anastasia understood why. Bruce played Dinas of Lidan, who, besides being a nobleman in his own right, was seneschal of Mark's kingdom. In the story, Dinas managed to remain loyal to Mark yet a true friend to Tristan and Isolde.

Bruce himself was a study in contradictions. Fresh-faced, hopeful, and talented, he was also plagued by self-doubt. He worked hard at brooding. His mind was sharp and quick and he enjoyed verbal jousting with Garrett; their friendship had been cemented early on when Garrett called Bruce a cynic. Like his character, Bruce was a stalwart ally to those he liked. It would have galled him to know that both Anastasia and Peter thought of him as a nice guy.

Shortly after their arrival at Ravenswood, Anastasia found another friend: Leah Hall. It seemed strange that the eternally young thirty-eight-year-old director had an eighteen-year-old daughter, especially one who was self-possessed beyond her years.

Leah had been hired to write a book on the making of the film. She seemed a good choice for the assignment. She'd already been published in magazines like *Punch*. Anastasia was certain Pierce had pulled some strings to get Leah the book assignment, partly by offering her unlimited access to the set, a privilege other writers would not have. Leah was a talented writer and a keen observer; she was a forceful enough presence that she was immediately thought of as her own person. Leah already had a signature style in both her dress and her lifestyle that was rare for anyone, let alone a teenager. Anastasia was fascinated by her. Leah loved dressing in period clothing. Since her figure was sleek and boyish, clothes of the 1920s and '30s served her especially well. She mixed and matched decades with ease, however, even showing up some mornings with her long, straight hair caught carefully in a snood.

It was a mystery to Anastasia how anyone developed such self-possession. Was one simply born with it? Did it come from having genes the caliber of Pierce's? In any case, Anastasia hadn't had a real girlfriend since South Carolina, so it was fun to hang out with Leah. Come the end of the day, Leah would often sit in Anastasia's dressing room, light a cigarette, and debrief Anastasia on what she'd observed.

It was Leah who inadvertently started the chain of events that resulted in Anastasia and Peter's relationship being made public.

Two weeks after they began the studio shoot, Peter's most recent film, *Wooden Soldier*, was scheduled to open in London. Since many of the young actors in *T & I* had appeared in the film, arrangements had been made for a car to take them to the city for the premiere. Pierce had scheduled shooting so that Peter, who was a lead in *Wooden Soldier*, could be away for two days doing publicity for the new film. In exchange, Peter promised Pierce he'd mention *Tristan and Isolde* at every opportunity.

Leah overheard this conversation. "There's a foolproof way to guarantee the premiere of *Wooden Soldier* generates publicity for *T & I*, you know," she said casually.

Both men looked up, surprised. "Enlighten us, by all means," Pierce said.

"Have Peter take Anastasia as his date. Let it be Tristan and Isolde's first public appearance."

Pierce, remembering Anastasia's vitriolic reaction to attempted meddling in her personal life, said, "We're a bit past the days of the studios setting up dummy dates for their stars."

"What's the downside? It's natural to take a colleague out for a night on the town. And not only would the interviews mention that Peter was involved in another film, photos of the two leads would appear in virtually every paper the next day."

Much to Pierce's surprise, Peter said, "It wouldn't hurt to ask her. Could you film around her for two days, as well?"

"I think I could do some rescheduling," Pierce said, adding, "Good luck."

"Stace, imagine, two days together in London!" Peter exclaimed, after recounting the conversation in her dressing room.

"Pierce will really let us go?" she asked. "And no one suspects? They think it's a publicity stunt?"

"Unless you've told Leah."

She shook her head.

"Pierce doesn't think I'll be able to persuade you."

At this she grinned and threw her arms around him, inhaling his musky scent. "What fun! I've never been to a premiere. And to go with you! It's too wonderful!"

Looking back later, from the range of years, Anastasia was amazed at the amount of naïveté both she and Peter had all the way through the premiere of *Wooden Soldier*. She thought she understood publicity, but she had no comprehension of the kind of huge, insatiable beast *T & I* would become, how the lives of the participants would be forever changed. The trip to London was the early warning. Unfortunately, that first warning would come too late.

The day before the London excursion was Richie's last scene, save one short exterior for which he'd return several months hence. As much as Anastasia had enjoyed his shy crush, what had started out as puppy-dog devotion had become a nuisance.

He was also increasingly difficult to work with. Compared to the others, Richie acted in fits and starts. He was constantly questioning how to play scenes, even after things had clicked in rehearsal and they'd begun to shoot. Pierce had been patient with him at first, but even the legendary "actor's director" was becoming fed up.

That day's scene took place in the queen's dayroom as Kaherdin brings Isolde the jasper ring and the message that Tristan is dying. The scene was straightforward. They'd had several run-throughs the night before. Pierce had finally called a halt even though Richie wanted to continue working. They were all sympathetic. They knew it was hard to leave a production "family," especially when the family would continue happily without you.

Anastasia and Pierce were already in royal robes when Richie bounded onto the set. He pulled Pierce aside and launched into what Anastasia guessed was yet another motivation for the scene. Isolde couldn't quite hear the redhead's newest stab at subtext, but she did see Pierce smile and shake his head. "Yes, it's interesting," said the director. "But it's also another movie. Let's do it as rehearsed. Places!"

Richie blew his lines the first few takes.

"Richard, we do need to move on. Let's nail it," Pierce said as they each found their marks yet again.

Richie looked to Anastasia, who mustered a warm smile. *You're out of here this morning, no matter how long you drag it out,* she thought with quasi-empathy.

He began the next take with new energy. There was a collective sigh of relief as he hit beat after beat. Then, at the penultimate moment, his character, Kaherdin, was supposed to offer the queen a gold bracelet, and almost nonchalantly place the jasper ring beside it. Recognizing the ring, Isolde was then supposed to look at its bearer with new eyes and beckon him away from the others to the window to inspect his wares in the light—and to hear his message.

But as Isolde recognized the ring, Richie threw himself into her arms and buried his face in her bosom, grabbing her breasts. Caught completely off guard, Anastasia leapt to her feet and pushed him backwards. As "cut" was called, she slapped him—hard—across the face.

"Richie!" Pierce exploded. "What—the hell—was that?"

"I thought if Tristan and Kaherdin, as sworn brothers, loved each other's Isoldes . . ." He stopped, seeing the rage on the director's face.

"I repeat. What the hell was that?"

"I was improvising," said Richie.

Pierce Hall growled, "Leave the improvising to the actors."

At the muffled amusement from the assemblage, Richie turned for support to Anastasia, who had retreated behind her carved chair. She glared at him. What did he expect? He was behaving like an idiot. "Grow up!" she said.

"Five-minute break," Pierce announced. "Then we're doing it for the last time."

To everyone's surprise, Richie walked through the next take, nailing it. Relieved applause followed.

Pierce went to congratulate him, but he walked past.

Unexpectedly, Richie put a restraining hand on Anastasia's arm and led her behind a hand-painted prop screen. He looked down at her. "I'm going to be a world-famous actor, you know," he said. His puppy-dog eyes held a Doberman snarl.

"Good for you," said Anastasia.

He rubbed his cheek ruefully where a small patch of red still betrayed the sting of her hand. "I have been nothing but good to you," he said. "You didn't have to make me look like a fool."

The absence of any softness in his expression threw her off kilter. "You made yourself look like a fool," she said.

Before she knew what was happening, Richie's right hand fell sharply across her own cheek.

He turned and left.

The young actress stayed put for a moment, pulling herself together. The sudden chill in her once-friend's demeanor shook her as much as the slap. Fortunately, everyone was still going about his or her business, and no one had noticed their exchange. She left the set quickly in search of Janie and her magic face powder.

In fact, Jane was the only one to whom Anastasia ever told the truth of Richie Riley's good-bye. The makeup woman was livid, and wanted her to complain at once, but Anastasia didn't want to prolong the incident even that long.

Besides, with Richie gone, her thoughts could turn unhindered to the next day. And turn they did.

Anastasia had never been to a premiere. *Wooden Soldier* wasn't a huge film, but it was big enough to make a splash.

The photo snaps and flashes began the moment she and Peter emerged from the car. The two of them held hands and walked the carpet slowly, pausing to give genuinely happy smiles to the press and fans gathered on either side of the ropes.

I'm going to a movie premiere with one of the stars, Anastasia told herself, silently amazed. *I'm holding Peter Dalton's hand.* And her smile deepened.

The next morning she did a shoot Pierce had set up through a friend at *Vogue*. It was noon before she got a chance to call Peter.

"So, have you seen the papers?" he asked.

"No," she said. "How are the reviews?"

"The reviews are good," he said. "But it seems you and I are the big news. I've seen our photo in three papers already, with varying degrees of speculation about the nature of our relationship."

"That should make Pierce happy."

"I'd say we've done our job," he answered. "It's time to play. I don't know what you have in mind for the afternoon," Peter said, "but the Olivier-Oberon version of *Wuthering Heights* is playing at one of the revival houses. Have you any interest in seeing it again?"

"I've never seen it at all."

"You've never seen it?" he asked. "Cathy and Heathcliff are

the patron saints of anyone who's found love on the moors."

"Anyone else's love on the moors might seem second rate," Anastasia returned, skeptical.

But Anastasia loved *Wuthering Heights*. She allowed herself the indulgence of weeping at Cathy's death, knowing Peter was there to comfort her. As they re-emerged into the white sunlight, Anastasia stopped to study the original poster displayed outside the theater.

"Do you know the difference between Cathy and Heathcliff and us?" whispered Peter beside her.

"What?" she asked.

"Our love is real," he answered.

She turned, gazing up at him, as he embraced her and gave her a real, true kiss in front of the poster of the fictional lovers.

So absorbed were they in each other that they didn't even notice the photographer across the street who'd followed them and was surreptitiously clicking off a roll.

Anastasia was still floating the next morning as she elbowed her way to the breakfast table at the back of the soundstage, to pour herself a cup of coffee.

"Good time in London?" came Pierce's deep voice beside her.

"Yes, thank you," she answered. "I'd never been to a premiere. And I think the *Vogue* shoot went well."

He added milk to his steaming tea and steered her off beyond the crunch. "You and Peter seemed to do a good job of generating publicity."

"We tried. I hoped you'd be happy. When duty calls. God save the Queen and all."

They now stood by themselves in the unlit shadows in the back of the cavernous room. "Anastasia, I know you think this is a joke, but there are still over three months left to go on the shoot. Remember your promise."

"What? I go on a public date with Peter for the good of the production, and next thing everyone thinks I'm ready to surrender my maidenhead."

"You must admit the photo does go beyond the call of duty."

"Which photo?"

Pierce unfolded the London morning paper he'd been holding under his arm and offered it to her. There, in two columns, black-and-white, was a photo of Peter Dalton in a clinch with Anastasia Day below the poster for *Wuthering Heights*. "The Next Generation?" read the bold lead to the cutline.

"Well, you asked me to make up with him," Anastasia said weakly.

"Remember the movie has to come first," Pierce said, crushing the newspaper into her hands. "Now, you're supposed to be in makeup."

Anastasia could tell Peter had arrived by the sudden plethora of raucous remarks.

"Way to go, Pete!"

"Give her one for me, old boy!"

"Say no more, say no more—nudge, nudge, wink, wink!"

"What on earth are they talking about?" Peter asked, joining Anastasia as he munched a pastry. She silently handed him the newspaper.

"Well, well," he said.

"That's it?"

"Pretty good picture. No wonder everyone's talking about ravishing you."

"Peter!"

"Well, it's a little late to do anything about it. Might as well look at the silver lining. No more skulking. And the caption could have said 'Pretenders to the Throne' or something. 'The Next Generation' is actually quite kind."

"Let me see that," she said, snatching it back. She looked

at the photo in a more considered manner. "You do look dash-ing," she admitted. "But now Pierce is going to be watching us every second."

"Since when have we ever been less than professional?" Pe-ter asked. "See you in makeup." He gave her a brief kiss. "This might not be such a terrible development. The only thing I'm worried about . . ."

"What?" She was curious.

He sighed. "After a couple of pints one night during the *Sol-dier* shoot, I confided to Garrett that I was a virgin. I'm afraid that admission is returning to haunt me."

"You confided that to *Garrett*? Quiet, demure Garrett?"

"Mistake, huh?"

"I'm sure you explained the spiritual and ethical reasons for your decision. And I'm sure he respects them," she said, her voice laced with irony.

"At the time, I wasn't feeling virtuous. I was feeling randy."

"So the downside of our relationship being out in the open is that everybody gets to speculate about the status of our sex lives. It's seems our only recourse . . ."

"Yes?"

"Is to be quiet and grin a lot."

"Come here," Peter said, pulling her onto his lap. "You're making me want to grin right now."

Within a couple of weeks, the fact that Peter and Anasta-sia were an item was accepted as the warp and woof of life on the set. They were discreet about public displays of affection, but did nothing to hide the delight they found in each other. Christy, the unit publicist, began leaking items about them to the press, and Dale, the still photographer, snapped candid shots.

But everyone's preoccupation was the shoot, especially as the early honeymoon period of excitement wore off and the physical and emotional exhaustion of long hours and of their pursuit of perfection set in.

One morning two weeks after the London excursion, Anastasia arrived on the soundstage to hear an anguished cry. She and Leah and two gaffers were the first to find the source: the bird trainer. He stood before his wood-and-wire cages; there were six, stacked in pairs. In the center of each lay a white rock dove, its neck wrung, its head skewed at an impossible angle. The keening of the birds was silenced; only that of the trainer pierced the day.

Anastasia's hand flew to her mouth, the other reached out for the trainer's shoulder.

"Who'd have done such a thing?" stammered one of the electricians.

"I'm sure they're covered by the production's insurance," Leah said, searching for comforting words. "I mean, we can certainly have them replaced."

As the production manager arrived to take charge, Anastasia turned hurriedly away, pulling Leah with her. "Who would do such a thing?" she asked. But the horrific sight, the precise way each bird was laid out, centered on its towel in the exact middle of each crate, was burned into her memory and would haunt the fringes of her mind for months to come.

Anastasia didn't know when she began to realize that her initial buoyancy, born of winning the part and finding Peter, was beginning to wear thin. Perhaps it was after a long shooting day, when at the completion of her scene Pierce said, "All right, fine," instead of "Great! We've got it." To further complicate things, she and Peter had a small spat about who made whom fifteen minutes late back to the set after lunch.

She knew Garrett was still teasing Peter, which made Peter irritable, which made Anastasia irritable. Part of it was that she was tired and wanted a few days off. A few days to sleep in, and be somewhere—anywhere—else. She was tired of seeing the same faces every day. She was tired of being surrounded by men, tired of playing Wendy.

She was just tired. And they were only two months into the shoot.

That night, instead of eating supper with the gang, she went back to her hotel and went to bed.

Somehow the extra hours of sleep didn't help as much as she'd hoped. The next morning, she flubbed her lines in two successive takes. It wasn't that Pierce said anything. He just shook his head and said, "Let's try it again."

The third time, she got it, but worried she'd spent her energy on the lines rather than the emotions of the scene. It wasn't a big scene, and there were a dozen actors in it; she was far from the focal point. Pierce stood for a moment after "cut" was called, as everyone turned to him to see if there would be another take.

"Oh, all right," he said. "Let's move on."

Anastasia's confidence plummeted. "Oh, all right," wasn't good enough. And it was her fault.

Not that anyone said anything. In rehearsals, even one-on-one, Pierce was his old, charming, demanding self. Even Peter, also the perfectionist, didn't seem to act any differently toward her. But she had the dreadful feeling they were trying to cajole her out of a slump. She didn't want to burden Peter with her loss of self-confidence; somehow it would take them off even footing.

So one afternoon in the dressing room, she spoke to Leah. If any of the actors asked Pierce to let them watch dailies, he said yes. Anastasia had never asked. Neither had Peter. Peter said it would ruin his concentration. Anastasia was too terrified. But Leah went every night.

"Leah, you watch the dailies," she started. "Are they all right?"

"You don't think you'd have heard if they weren't?"

"That's not the answer I was hoping for."

"You've seen the sets and the costumes. You know the cinematographer and the actors. You've worked with the director. What would you expect?" Getting no answer, Leah said, "They're bloody brilliant. Is that what you're looking for?"

"Am I all right?"

"Ah, now we're getting to it." She blew three perfect smoke rings in a row. "Confidence crisis, is it?"

Anastasia looked at her.

"You don't think Pierce would let you know if you're not? He's not exactly the retiring type. You're perfectly fine, that I've noticed."

From Leah, this was as high praise as she was going to get. It would have to do.

Virtually all the actors in residence at Ravenswood played members of King Mark's court, so the whole lot of them moved south together into the long summer days of Somerset.

While they'd been cooped up for twelve-hour days inside studio walls, the chilly spring had given way to the deepened hues and thickly fragrant air of July. Anastasia had been relieved when they'd arrived at the civilization of life at Ravenswood; she was now almost giddy to be released from metal walls and artificial light into the freedom of deep forest and sweeping hills.

Scoffield, the town that would serve as their headquarters, had one large, rambling hotel. The Red Lion was over three hundred years old. It had strange halls leading off in all directions, and one ancient cage lift that virtually everyone ignored in favor of the sturdier-looking stairs. Unfortunately, it didn't have space for the entire cast and crew of the film. For the first time, they were separated into tiers—not of importance, the location manager insisted, but by frequency of being needed on the set. Crew members and actors who worked every day were ensconced at the Red Lion; those whose schedules were more flexible were divided between two smaller hotels five miles away in the neighboring town of Sweetwater.

For the first time, Peter and Anastasia were staying in the same hotel. Up a winding dark wooden staircase covered with old, thick burgundy carpet was an odd length of hall that boasted the five best rooms in the hotel. In contrast to the corridor, the rooms were spacious and airy; they had private baths. One room was inhabited by a permanent guest; the one next to this gentleman was the largest, and consequently assigned to Gray Eddington as both his quarters and the makeshift production office.

The three rooms across the hall were allocated to Anastasia Day, Pierce Hall, and Peter Dalton, in that configuration. Anastasia knew it would create more trouble than it was worth to try to talk the powers that be into giving her and Peter the adjacent, adjoining rooms. Even though Pierce was frantically busy and seemed not to notice where he slept or what he ate, she wouldn't have been surprised to find he'd purposely taken the center room, designating himself hall monitor for the sake of the film.

Frankly, it might be for the best that she and Peter weren't sharing a suite. There would have been added pressure, no question.

Still, their lack of privacy continued to chafe. Peter had returned his mother's car on their way to Ravenswood, which took away their mobility. Consequently, their only real chances to be alone were in their caravans, where one never knew when there'd be a knock at the door.

Late in July, they had two night shoots in a row. The first night was Tristan and Isolde's first secret meeting in the garden behind the castle. The second was yet another assignation between the two; this time, King Mark has been tipped off, and is hiding in a tree above their rendezvous point. But Tristan sees Mark's reflection in the brook, and instead of trysting, he and Isolde discuss their love for the king.

"Anastasia, I've really got to see an abrupt change in your demeanor in that one instant. You're expecting a night of lovemaking, and instead you're suddenly trying to save your neck."

It was odd to have Pierce directing from a tree.

Anastasia thought she'd manifested an abrupt change. She'd try harder.

"Now you're mugging," Pierce growled after the next take. "It has to be small, very small for the camera. Yet pronounced."

She tried small yet pronounced.

In fact, she tried it five times.

"You're not getting it," Pierce said. Anastasia turned to Peter in despair. Pierce climbed out of the tree.

"Pierce, old man," Peter started. "I think—that is, *I'm* getting it."

"Let's take a brief moment, then try it again," Pierce said. The director beckoned the actress away from the others. Tall grasses sighed around their feet under the blue-filtered light that assisted the moonlight.

Pierce leaned against a large, gnarled oak trunk. "Listen, I don't think it's working out for you to stay at the Red Lion," he said. "I'm having Maureen move your things to Sweetwater tonight while we're working."

Anastasia stared at him, processing what he'd said, momentarily stunned. Before she opened her mouth to see what would come out, he said, "Yes. That's it, exactly. There was barely an expression on your face. But what was going on behind your eyes was enormous."

"But—what—"

"Remember how you felt just now. Turmoil. Slightly off

balance, yet knowing your reaction would be important." He turned and walked back toward the waiting crew.

"You mean, you didn't? Maureen's not—?"

"Of course not," he said over his shoulder.

"Damn you," she muttered under her breath.

They did another take. This time, Pierce said, "Now, that was close. All right, let's move on."

"I'm going to kill him," Anastasia said matter-of-factly to Peter.

"Don't let it get to you," the young man said, and he goosed her. "You can't let directors mess with your head. Concentrate on the fact that I'm going to take you out for breakfast. Although when I think of staying out all night with you, this isn't exactly what I have in mind. We're only in two more setups. Think you can make it?"

"Yeah," she sighed. "At least I don't have to climb the darn tree."

The final shots of the night were relatively simple and had no dialogue. By the time Pierce called the final "cut," the eastern sky had melted from black to gray and the quilt of stars had turned to an emerging pattern of clouds. There was another big scene to go, but it was the dawn confrontation between Mark and Dinas, in which Dinas pleads for the life of Tristan and Isolde. It was one of Bruce's biggest scenes in the film. Anastasia and Peter were done.

"Did you say breakfast?" Anastasia asked Peter, her adrenaline subsiding.

"Yes. And not at the catering truck. Let's slip away. But first—what time's call today? I don't remember."

"You don't remember because you don't have any call today," said Pierce, suddenly behind them. They both turned, Peter expectantly, Anastasia warily.

"Seriously?"

"They're doing the final dressing on the ship down in Dunmore Harbor. We'll be shooting there for the next three days. Which is what I wanted to discuss with you. Be sure to get rested up today. We'll need to jump in at first light tomorrow. We'll spend the day on the love scene. *Au naturel.* I know you've both been looking forward to it. So let's get it out of the way."

"Tomorrow?" Anastasia asked weakly.

"So we're really going to be naked?" Peter asked.

"You know that. We have rehearsed. Full-body makeup. It'll be a closed set, though. I know you've been dying to have some fun," he smirked. "So think of it as finally being undressed together. Like I said, go get some rest."

Bruce, in costume and makeup, interrupted to talk to Pierce. Anastasia was tired and furious. "You can't let directors mess with your head," Peter had said. Yet that's what Pierce Hall did deliberately at every turn. There was no reason to taunt them as he had. Anastasia had come to this picture a non-swearer. "Damn smug bastard," she said.

"Sorry," Pierce said, turning back to her. "Didn't quite catch that, luv."

But she knew he had.

"Pierce," Bruce was saying, "I've gone over the dialogue. And the part here that we're having some trouble with—well, I've tried some rewrites. I think it'll play better with a few changes."

"Rewrites?" Pierce said. "Do you know how many hours Tyler and I have spent poring over this bloody script? Now, if you'll excuse me, I'm attempting to finish a conversation with Anastasia."

And he threw the pages back at Bruce. The young actor's face flushed, and he turned away, leaving the pages on the ground where they'd fallen.

"Might I have a word?" Pierce asked Anastasia.

The actress knew that Pierce was truly angry. She had never seen him treat one of his actors the way he'd treated Bruce. More than other directors, he was willing to work with his actors, to incorporate their ideas.

Anastasia looked the director in the eye—and stooped to collect Bruce's pages. When she stood again, she was hoping he'd say something, anything, vaguely demeaning. She was ready to blast him with both barrels.

"Anastasia. This hasn't come at the best time. But I trust you recall a certain conversation back at Ravenswood about my next film. Tonight is one of those dinners I mentioned. Bad timing, as I said, but no way out. Gray will have my head if we don't go. We've got you a suitable dress, and I've asked your friend Jane to help you do your hair and makeup. It's a two-hour trip to London. The car will come for us at five-thirty. I'll expect to find you downstairs at the hotel. Good night—er, morning." And he stalked away.

How did he do it? How did he continually leave her aghast?

"Wait," she demanded, and he stopped and turned back to her. She could see the tension in his shoulders. "If you're mad at me, don't bloody well take it out on other people," she said. "Read Bruce's rewrites. It's an important scene."

Anastasia extended the sheets until he came back and took them from her. Then she turned and walked away.

She wanted to scream. If he was so disappointed in her, if he had such an immense personal dislike for her, surely he wasn't still planning to drag her into his next picture. It must be that he'd told Eddington months ago, and Eddington had talked her up to whomever, and now they were expecting her. But if she wasn't going to star in his next film—and for the first time she felt the terrible disappointment and great relief of consciously knowing she wasn't—why should she have to suffer through a dinner? She was sure that any backers, any studio, would breathe a sigh of relief if Pierce announced he'd changed his mind and was going with a "name" in the lead. Pierce was already gone, but she'd find him this afternoon and tell him not to waste either of their time with this awkward pretense.

Peter had come over to collect her. "Let's go," he said tersely.

The young man didn't speak in the company car. He'd persuaded the driver to take them to a pub in town that served full breakfast. In fact, he seemed as on edge as she.

"What's the matter?" she asked when they'd been seated together at an old, rather unstable wooden table in the corner. There wasn't much room between them and the next patrons, so they had to speak quietly.

"You can't tell me you're looking forward to tomorrow?" he asked.

"Of course not. I'm dreading it. Frankly, when we rehearsed it back at the manor house, I thought it was clear you'd had much more experience with love scenes than I have. I didn't think you'd mind so much."

"Love scenes with actresses I didn't care a fig about," he said. "Not with you. Not with everyone giggling, saying, 'Oh, they've wanted to be naked, but we haven't let them until we're all here to get a gander.'"

"We've been up all night," she said. "We're both tired."

"Damn. I feel like it's 1984 and Big Brother is ruining our lives. Doesn't it make you want to—" He stood abruptly and stalked back to the call box behind the noisy room. He made his connection, and when he returned to the table, he had a new look of determination.

"Who'd you ring up?"

"I left a message for Bruce. I'm going to ask him to help us find a car. Don't care where or how dear. Let's eat and get some sleep. It's five o'clock. I'll pick you up in front of the chemist's at noon."

"Where are we going?

"Wherever we damn well please. Just the two of us. Alone."

Bruce had gotten them a car. It wasn't even a rental; he seemed to have some pull with a young woman from wardrobe who had a sturdy, though not flashy, runabout.

When Anastasia climbed in opposite Peter, she felt like a foreign spy. They both wore sunglasses, as if any member of the cast or crew couldn't spot their signature heads of hair from across town. Just looking at Peter, tight jeans and T-shirt defining his well-sculpted body, she had to force herself to return to normal breathing. She was sitting beside the much-sought-after Prince Tristan, but it was 1991, not 991, and he was wearing sneakers and driving a stick shift. More to the point, he was the most desirable young actor in the world, and he was smitten with her. The thrill bumbled through her like a bee, leaving a thin, shivery trail of wonder in its wake.

Oh, she loved him.

And she loved loving him. It was enough to make her forget her upcoming miserable evening, to forget Janie, who was coming to her room at four-thirty to help her dress; even to take her mind off where she and Peter were heading now, and what she knew they would do when they got there.

He drove along country lanes through the majestic rolling hills of Somerset. Since they were working constantly, they didn't know their way around very well. It wasn't long before Anastasia realized they were in fact returning to the location they'd used for the castle gardens. It looked oddly vacant; the crew had done a good job of cleaning and restoring the acreage to its original pristine beauty.

Peter urged the small car from the dirt road and across the

rutted fields into the trees. Once out of sight, he stopped the motor, then leaned over and kissed the girl beside him. "Ah," he said, breathing deeply. "We can almost pretend we're back on the moors."

The setting was different; this breadth of nature with its copse of trees and long grasses felt much closer to civilization. Yet it was the same in that it enabled them to feel as if they were the only two people in the world.

Once outside the car, Peter took her hand. They walked the field together until they found a flat, even stretch of land hidden by tall grasses and protected on two sides by a towering stand of trees. There, Peter spread out the two lap blankets he'd found in the auto, took off his shoes, and sat down, opening his arms to welcome her.

"Oh, this feels so good," Anastasia finally said, "to get away, to clear our heads. I wish we could do it more often. I bet it would help our work."

Yet she wasn't completely relaxed. Back on the North Moors, they'd had no unspoken agenda. Here they did.

The day was overcast but comparatively warm. Gray clouds filtered the sun like netting. Even though it was July, Anastasia wished she were wearing long sleeves. As she thought purposefully irrelevant thoughts, she felt Peter tensing beside her. Finally, he turned her shoulders to him and kissed her for a very long time. His tongue explored her mouth; his embrace brought her to him. When he stopped, he looked at her searchingly.

"Was that all right?" he asked. "I mean, I'm nervous as hell. Should I go on?"

"I guess that's why we're here, when we know Pierce is going to skin us alive."

His fingers fumbled at the buttons of her shirt. She laughed and took her blouse all the way off, and sat still as he leaned behind her. She felt him undo the clasp of her white cotton bra and she let it fall free.

"Oh, Stace," he said again, lying beside her and kissing her breasts.

"Bloody hell," he whispered suddenly, tears obvious in his eyes. "I don't want to do the scene tomorrow. I really don't. I don't want the whole world to see your breasts. I don't want them to know what we look like when we kiss. That should be ours, ours alone."

"But—we have to. It was made clear it was part of the job before I took the part."

"I know, I know. But I didn't love you then."

Anastasia grabbed two handfuls of his thick sandy hair and pulled his head down to her bosom. Together they lay quietly in the shadowy afternoon. Peter loved her, and that was enough. She was filled with contentment.

But that wasn't what they'd come for, and they both knew it.

When he finally roused himself, leaning on his elbows looking down at her, she thought his face seemed streaked with regret.

"We don't have to do this," she said, "if we don't believe it's right."

"It's not the unforgiveable sin, that I've heard," he said, "and we'll be doing it tomorrow." He punctuated this with a movie kiss, deep and energetic.

"But not really. We won't really be doing it."

"Stace, I love you," he said. "And I'm tired of Pierce and Garrett and the virgin jokes."

Promise me you won't bonk Peter Dalton. She could hear Pierce's words as loud as thunder in her mind.

Fuck you, Pierce Hall, she thought. And she helped Peter take off his shirt and his blue jeans as he helped her remove hers.

They lay together in the midst of the outdoors, he in his Jockey shorts, she in her panties.

The hard lines straining his shorts gave the unmistakable message. "Yeah," he laughed, following her gaze. "The joys of youth. On call, twenty-four hours a day."

She didn't protest as he removed her underwear, then his own. She'd never seen a man totally naked, not like that, anyway, but she had little time to look before he was on top of her, urging her thighs apart with his right hand. She felt a stab or two between her legs before his sword found its sheath. She bit her lip to keep from crying out as he thrust and thrust again. Finally, his face tightened and he let out a cry of fulfillment, then collapsed upon her chest.

So we've done it, she thought.

And then he was off her, lying beside her on the grasses, where they'd rolled, completely off the prickly blankets.

"Is there . . . anything you want me to do?" he asked.

"No," she whispered. "I'm good."

They lay silent for a while, each thinking private thoughts. Peter sat up first. He let his eyes travel up and down her body, but they paused at her thighs.

He reached over tenderly, dipping his fingers between her legs. When he held them up, they were stained with blood.

At first she thought in a panic that she must have gotten her period, but quickly realized that couldn't be. He'd known what it was before she had.

"I love you, Anastasia," he said. Tears now spilled from his eyes and traced down his cheeks. "I really do."

CHAPTER 8

THE SETTING

Director Pierce Hall and production designer Brendan Todd scoured the British countryside to find settings that would provide the perfect backdrop for their tale of forbidden love.

Due to the political climate, the Irish locations were filmed in northern Scotland, and Scotland also provided Castle Heath as a stand-in for the castle of Isolde of the White Hands in Brittany. The cast and crew enjoyed their weeks in these remote locations, soaking in local color and scouting out the best in local pubs.

"Although I prefer the manners and morals of an earlier setting of the Tristan and Isolde myth, it's virtually impossible to find any workable castles dating from before the thirteenth century," notes director Hall. "Both Castle Heath and Castle Dunmore in Somerset have a large portion of their original design still intact. It was of great help to be able to exist in the atmosphere of a different time."

Castle Dunmore, which was used as King Mark's fortress, has been the home of the Dukes of Esmonde since the sixteenth century. Although the family continues in residence in the more modern additions—from the fifteenth and sixteenth centuries—they did stop *by to chat with production personnel from time to time.*

"There's something eerily evocative about buildings that have existed for eight hundred years," says Peter Dalton. "It's as if the shape and density of the stones themselves have soaked up a record of those earlier times. It's fun to lose yourself in an ancient time—but to know that at the end of the day you get to return to a hotel with running hot and cold water."

———•———

SHORTLY AFTER HER GRACE the Duchess of Esmonde returned to the castle, her stepson Geoff appeared in person to invite her to lunch with himself and his wife.

Cathy was wearing a linen skirt and pleated blouse ringed by a triple strand of small, perfect pearls. Fresh-cut flowers from the local florist brought splashes of color to both the luncheon and serving tables. The luncheon plates were Coalport, the salads made with endive and wilted greens.

She really is much better at this duchess thing than I ever was, Anastasia admitted to herself, taking the already set place between husband and wife.

Finally Geoff finished his soup, dabbed unnecessarily at the corners of his mouth with a napkin, and said, "Catherine and I are about as far from the Hollywood crowd as we can be. But it seems there's excitement surrounding the re-release of *Tristan and Isolde.*"

The dowager duchess nodded. She couldn't imagine why they would possibly care, unless they were afraid she'd do something to embarrass the house of Huntington.

Geoff glanced at Cathy and plowed on. "Quite so. Seems there's a gentleman there from the studio, name of Enright. He's been in touch."

"Oh dear. Is he expecting me to call?"

"No, no. Rang for me—for us."

Now Anastasia was really puzzled. "I hope no one's been bothering you. If they have, I can—"

"No, no bother. Mr. Enright asked if . . . well, they seemed to be looking for a suitable site for the reunion and the festivities surrounding it. Something that would play well on the telly, you know. He asked if they might hold the reunion here, in the castle, since it was used in the film. And now it's your home. Would look good on the press releases, that sort of thing. I told him we hadn't a Great Hall. He said the armory would suit. And he offered a fair sum. They'd take care of everything, he said. All we'd have to do is stay out of the way. Until the party. Of course, we're invited to the party."

"Dear God," Anastasia said, hardly realizing she'd spoken aloud. If she wouldn't come to the party, the party, it seemed, would stalk her. At the thought of attending a party—of simply being in the armory when it was filled with people—her heart began to accelerate. She wasn't going, never said she would. How could Geoff have agreed? Yes, Neville had let them film at the castle. Upkeep was tremendously expensive and had to be met somehow. Now they were offering a tidy sum to Geoff. But to make your home—and your stepmother—yourselves—things to be gawked at . . .

"Do you think Bruce Amerman might be there? Or Richard Riley?" Cathy was asking, her eagerness seeping through her decorum.

"It makes no sense, though, does it?" Anastasia asked finally. "The gala is to be after a big screening, and we're hours from London. They'll never get everyone here for a party."

"Oh, had you left before we got the news?" Geoff replied. "There's an anonymous benefactor—a friend of yours, it seems.

This person is building a cinema here in the village."

"A friend . . . of mine?"

"A lovely theater it will be, too. Rocking seats. Cup holders. Humongous screen. Surround sound. Three-D projection capabilities!" added Cathy.

"But the reunion is next month. There's no way they could finish—"

"They're well into it," Cathy said proudly. "The aldermen had a special meeting. Plan approved. It'll be done, and early, mark my words."

"Wouldn't it be an eyesore? The village is so quaint . . ." Anastasia was grasping at straws.

"To the contrary," Geoff reported happily. "They're designing it to match Market Hall. The locals are quite ecstatic about not having to travel to see a film."

"Who is the benefactor, Geoff? Even if he wants his identity to remain secret, someone's writing the checks."

"We've tried to find out. The drafts have been written by an attorney, who claims he himself doesn't know who's ultimately behind it. The account is in the name of the Dunmore Cinema Corporation, and has been wired through a series of banks."

Life had once again broken loose from Anastasia's grasp, and was careening out of control. Blood pounded in her ears. Her breath was coming in spurts when it came at all.

"Thank you for the luncheon," she said. "I'm suddenly very tired from my trip."

And she fled from the table.

———————•———————

PIERCE DID NOT SPEAK to her once during the trip home from London. Instead, he smoked cigarette after cigarette until the confines of the back of the limousine were almost unbearable.

Anastasia didn't dare say a thing.

She and Peter hadn't returned to the Red Lion until five o'clock, by which time Jane had worn a path in the carpet by the front window. Peter parked purposefully in front of the hotel, and put his arm around Anastasia's waist as they entered.

Jane was upon her the moment she passed through the portal, saying, "Dearie, we've only half an hour."

Peter gave her a quick kiss and went to join the *T & I*ers who were gathered for a pre-dinner drink in the pub to the left of the entrance. As Anastasia was hurried to the stairs, she glanced back into the pub in time to see Peter toss the car keys to Bruce. The smile on his face, she knew, would convey the message of their afternoon's activities faster than a public broadcast system.

"Is Pierce upset?" Anastasia whispered.

"He's not happy," Jane replied.

But Jane worked her magic, and Anastasia descended the stairs in evening attire at half past five to the minute. Pierce was already waiting. To Anastasia's immense relief, Gray Eddington was waiting as well. Both men wore evening clothes, jackets and trousers well tailored for them. Both sipped Scotch and looked at ease in their clothes. Yet somehow Pierce, white silk scarf stylishly draped around his neck, had a cunning to his appearance that the more rotund gentleman could not match. One wielded power purposefully, because he commanded it; the other offhandedly, because he simply exuded it. The latter created a powerful magnetism; the actress again felt sympathy for the women caught in Pierce's wake.

Her own dress was from a well-known designer. The lines were simple and elegant. Yet she felt that her companions were dressed for dinner while she was wearing a costume.

To Anastasia's further relief, the Lost Boys were gone from

the bar. Pierce barely looked at her as he put down his glass of Scotch and stalked to the waiting car.

"You look lovely, my dear," said Gray, who had the courtesy to escort her outside.

Once on the road, Pierce and Gray leaned together in conversation, to which the actress was clearly not meant to be party. Left to her own thoughts, Anastasia settled against her window and watched the countryside roll by.

As they reached the outskirts of London, Pierce put away the papers the men had been perusing and with no warning began talking to Anastasia, giving her a pithy rundown on who would be at the dinner, his or her professional background and relationship to the upcoming film.

"And my part in all this?" she finally asked.

Gray smiled broadly. "Simply to be your lovely, intelligent self. Leave the work to the pros."

They rolled to a stop outside the Eddington's townhouse on Wilton Crescent in Belgravia—a lovely part of town quite far from the London of Anastasia and Beverly's world. Gray offered her an arm and walked her up the front steps.

The dinner was small and elegant, only twelve guests in all, including an interesting Italian countess who had been invited to make up numbers. Gray's wife, Diana, was a consummate hostess. It was her duty to put the guests at ease, and she did this magnificently. The servants were so well trained (how many were the Eddingtons' and how many were brought in for the night, Anastasia had no idea) that drinks and dinner seemed to serve themselves.

She was aware that one of the gentlemen was the president of Heather Hill, Ltd., the film production company with which Eddington, and often Pierce, worked, and which was going to be producing their next thriller. Another gentleman was from a large Hollywood studio that was planning the American distribution. Two others were successful businessmen with access to outside funding. Their wives knew Diana Eddington, and all seemed to be having a lovely time.

Anastasia thought several times during dinner how nervous she might be had things been different. If she was actually going to appear in Pierce's next film, for example. Dining with the heads of production companies was certainly a plum activity for a young actress. Too bad it would count for naught.

Pierce Hall spent the evening making the men salivate at the prospect of working with him, and charming their wives. It was natural for him. He never had to work at it. He was nothing but adoring when he introduced Anastasia to their fellow diners. Playing her part, she proceeded to act the captivating young woman. Only she could sense the steel barrier between her and the onetime mentor who'd brought her here.

It would have been difficult enough to live through the evening knowing she had become a professional disappointment to Pierce. But the unfortunate timing of her and Peter's act of willful emancipation had been meant partly as a personal affront, and had been received as one. Yet she and Pierce had been working together for weeks while at odds. They continued to do so through dinner. Anastasia thought of it as an evening-length improvisation: an enchanting actress is introduced. It was a cinch for Lily. Like a comfortable reunion with an old friend.

Anastasia and Pierce were the first to leave. Everyone understood they had early call. Gray was staying over in London, so it was just the two of them heading out into the muggy evening.

As soon as they re-entered the limousine, the Cinderella spell was broken. Lily was gone. The chill descended. Pierce turned on the small reading light beside him, pulled out script pages and notations, and lit up a cigarette.

Without a word or a glance, his companion was dismissed.

It was after midnight when they returned to the Red Lion. The lobby was empty except for a lone clerk trying to stay awake at the desk.

Pierce took the left hall in long, brisk steps. Anastasia had given up hoping to talk to him. She made her way slowly, letting him disappear in front of her up the winding stairs. Tears crowded her eyes. If he hated her so much, why didn't he replace her? This was torture. How was she ever going to face the cameras—and him—in the morning?

When she rounded the final turn to her floor, she found Pierce there, waiting, in the black evening jacket with his white silk scarf now dangling from one hand.

"All right," he said. "We need to talk."

He turned and walked to his room, unlocked his door, and invited her in with a sweep of his hand. She entered a few feet and he closed the door for privacy, leaning against it.

"So. Let's get down to it. You and Peter had sex, isn't that right?"

His voice was not at all angry; in fact, it was absolutely flat, like a teacher giving a test that's required by law.

"Yes," she said. "That's right."

"You used protection?"

It was exactly like he was her professor, doing his duty, giving her "the speech." He had no emotional connection to his words whatsoever.

"No," she said. "We didn't."

"Fuck," he answered. "Well. I hope you at least enjoyed it."

"Actually, it hurt," she said.

He walked over to his toiletry bag, unzipped it, and rummaged around. He found what he was looking for, and threw her a square foil package containing a condom.

"Next time, don't take such stupid chances," he said. "Now go on, get out of here. Go to bed."

But she couldn't go. She stood rooted to the spot.

"What?" he asked. "What is it? We've both got early call."

"Why," she started, and the tears finally overflowed.

"Why what?"

"Why do you hate me so much?"

"I don't hate you," he said.

"You don't talk to me! You don't care about a blasted thing I say or do! I do the one thing you told me not to, and you send me off to bed like—like a pet dog! And I try so hard for you. I give you everything I have! But nothing's ever right. Nothing's ever enough! Why don't you just fire me?"

Pierce sank onto the end of his bed, his head in his hands. "I don't hate you," he said.

"Then talk to me! Yell at me. Something! I can't stand this!" She rushed at him, her fists raised in fury. She beat against him half a dozen strikes before he clamped his hands over her wrists.

"Why don't you even like me?" she asked, sobbing now against his chest.

"Hush up," he said.

"Why?" she repeated.

"Hush, I said." And he planted his mouth firmly over hers. The kiss was probing and deep and he pulled himself away.

"Oh God," he said. "Anastasia, you're killing me."

She looked up at him, lost in the confusion of her emotions.

"You tell me Peter made love to you—what can I do? You tell me he hurt you, and all I wonder is, did he kiss you like this—"

And he was kissing her throat and her ears, and her body lit up like a Chinese firecracker. He laid her on her back on the bed. "Did he caress you, did he claim you by giving himself in exchange?" And his large, gentle hands were under her dress and against her skin, and they were both naked, and she was kissing him, and he was kissing her, and stroking her until she was incoherent, a mass of Christmas tree lights running up and down her body, never stopping, until she lost all sense of time and space. Somehow she felt him between her legs when he wasn't even close, but then he did go down, and vanish between her thighs with his fingers and his tongue. She didn't feel him for a moment, and opened her eyes to see him, Pierce Hall, opening the very condom he'd thrown her earlier.

"Put it on me," he said, and he guided her hands until it was in place. Then his mouth was at her breasts, and his hands were under her buttocks, and just as she was ready to scream for him to take her, he crashed into her, but she was wet and waiting, and ready to the point that his pounding triggered an explosion and she cried out into the pillow as her body shuddered and shuddered and shuddered again.

She held him then as he came, moaning into the pillow next to hers.

Afterwards, he held her for a long time. She lay there, floating, willing herself not to think.

Finally Pierce kissed her forehead to rouse her, and gently stoked her hair.

"Anastasia," he said softly, "talk to me."

She forced her eyes open and looked at him, studying his strong face, the irregularity where his nose had been broken. How could she have not noticed before?

"I'm in love with Peter," she said.

"I know."

"So," she asked, "was this—am I the newest notation for your book of conquests?"

"My reputation has been a bit . . . enhanced in the telling," he said. "But no, my love. I know Peter has prior claim, and I have no right. Quite against my will and common sense, I've fallen completely, helplessly in love with you."

He leaned upon one elbow and traced her nose with his finger. "Ah, fate," he sighed. "I've waited so long to feel like this, and when I finally do, you're newly turned seventeen and have an age-appropriate boyfriend." He sat up. "It's karma, I suppose; all the misery I've caused come back to haunt me. Well, come on, now, you've got to go back to your room. I promise I won't intrude in the future."

Anastasia watched him silently as he pulled on his briefs and gathered her clothes. She put on her panties and the frock, which he zipped for her, then rolled the rest into a small bundle. Their rooms had adjoining doors, but the second would be locked from her side.

She ran a hand through the tangle of her hair. They faced each other in the soft light from the desk lamp. All she could think as he stood there nearly naked was that he was so tall. Yes, his chest was firm and wide, his thigh muscles taut and lean, but he was so . . . tall. He could engulf a person. He had engulfed her. The thing that frightened her was that she thought he had engulfed her long ago, long before that night.

"Come here," he said, and he captured her in a final embrace. He kissed her, a kiss of undisguised longing. Then he stepped away.

"I promise not to intrude again unless the time comes that you ask me to." Pierce walked her to the door. "I do hope for one thing," he whispered, and she studied his face, still trying to decipher the truth there. "That you'll try not to regret this."

He opened the door to the silent hall, and beckoned her out, watching until she'd entered her own room and bolted the lock.

Inside, she dropped numbly onto the end of the bed, forbidding the haze in her mind to clear. She managed to unzip the dress and drape it across a nearby chair before climbing beneath the covers.

And as she drifted off, she couldn't help but think that twelve hours earlier, she'd been a virgin.

BY THE TIME ANASTASIA joined the bleary-eyed crew members in the lobby at four forty-five the next morning, Pierce had already gone with an earlier contingent to Dunmore Harbor. Peter came down moments after she did, as the production cars pulled up in front. They climbed into the back of one car together, and he cheerfully put his arm around her.

"Ready?" he asked.

"As I'll ever be," she answered.

The drive was only twenty minutes. The town of Dunmore, where they'd also be filming the castle scenes, was charming in the early summer morning. The castle itself sat perched on a promontory overlooking the town, which was built around a market hall, which had also survived the centuries. Citizens were beginning to move out and about, and Anastasia watched them, fascinated, feeling strangely alive and connected to all of life.

When they arrived at the new production setup, she was surprised to find she was famished. Jane greeted her with a cheery "Good morning," and said the makeup crew was ready any time. But Anastasia, who'd planned on fasting the whole day in hopes of looking suitably lithe, found herself planted in front of the catering table socking away food like she hadn't a care in the world. Peter joined her, also oddly ebullient.

The kicker was that Pierce was in fine fettle, greeting everyone warmly and joshing with the unit drivers.

"Fine day for a classic love scene," he said, finding his actors in the midst of the food. He chuckled at Anastasia, who was hungrily finishing both the banger and pastry left on her paper plate.

"Trying to add a final inch to the bust, eh?" he teased.

She made a face at him.

"Think we'll have some heat today?" Peter asked, quoting the weather forecast they'd heard on the radio in the car.

"Should be pleasant down here on the water," the director said. "Especially, of course, for those not wearing any clothes."

"Pierce, old man, what's the cause of your jolly mood this morning?" Peter grinned.

Pierce shrugged good-naturedly. "Probably the same thing that's causing yours."

Anastasia choked on her bit of roll. Both men pounded on her back.

"Now come on, to makeup with you. We'll be ready for the first setup as soon as we've got full light." And Pierce turned again to the various production people awaiting his attention.

The whole day of filming the Great Love Scene seemed hallucinogenic to Anastasia. A great part of it was her lack of sleep. Another was her unwillingness to consciously deal with the last twenty-four hours of her life. It felt much safer to submerge her body into Isolde's. There was simply no other way to deal with the fact that Pierce Hall was directing her lovemaking with Peter Dalton; that she and Peter were as good as naked while Pierce was fully clothed and in charge.

The oddest thing was that Peter didn't mind. She knew he'd been dreading this as much as she, but today he and Pierce were joshing and working together. It was a closed set—the crew was minimal, and all of them were very professional. She knew Milos, the cinematographer, was a master at painting portraits with the lens, and that he was looking out for the actors as much as the director was. That made it easier for Anastasia to do her job.

She didn't talk much to either Pierce or Peter between shots, when she and Peter were robed, waiting for lights or props to be reset. She sat quietly, inside herself, while the two men palled around.

Yet when cameras rolled, she found it unexpectedly easy to come alive as Isolde, to respond to the gentle pitch of the sea (the great boat was moored), as well as to the fervor and warmth of Tristan the beloved beside her.

The day's shoot went quickly and well. The content and composition of the shots thrilled the cinematographer; the energy and emotion thrilled the director. General exhaustion and the thrill of triumph blended when the final "cut" of the day was called.

"Hurry and get dressed," Pierce instructed Tristan and Isolde as the lights were being struck. "I'm taking you and Milos out for the most incredible dinner."

The four of them went to a seaside restaurant framed with twinkling fairy lights, where food and champagne abounded. Milos was obsessive about his work, as was Pierce, but when they went off duty, they went off duty. Peter, delighted to be once again in the bosom of Pierce's good graces, joined in. Finally, Anastasia began giggling with the rest.

Back at the Red Lion, Pierce dropped Peter and Anastasia off, then went to confer with Milos about the next day's shoot. Peter put his arm protectively around Anastasia and paused with her in a hidden alcove by the final turn of the stairs.

"You come through all right?" he asked.

"Yes," she said.

"It seems all we needed to do was stand up to Pierce, all along."

"Umm," she said.

"I love you, Stace," he said, and kissed her warmly.

"Love you, too," she said.

"You look exhausted."

"I am. Aren't you?"

"And then some. I'll say sweet good night, then."

He walked Anastasia to her door and kissed her again under its portal. "Good night," he whispered.

She walked alone into her room. She fell facedown onto the bed and began to sob into the pillow.

The next morning she awoke long before the phone by the bed shrilled to life.

What on earth had she done? Never before had she so blatantly meant to do one thing and done something else. She loved Peter. And she'd had Pierce. Not only had him; wanted him. Been consumed with wanting him. And now his private looks, his private scents, would forever live as repertory among her memories.

What to do? What expiation? And there must be expiation. For Peter was hers, was loyal and true. And Pierce was . . . well, who knew what Pierce was? He was experienced, that was certain. He'd said all the right things: *I've finally found you, I've waited so long to feel this way.* But face it, a successful ladies' man doesn't say, "*Chérie,* won't you be the next in my long line of lovers?" No. He says, "You're it. You're the one. I've finally found you." What makes him successful is how he can say it each time with such sincerity, such conviction, that intelligent, wary women are willing to believe.

She had been impressed by his conviction.

As the hours, then the days passed, and Anastasia ran this conundrum around in her mind, she finally concluded there was no point in confessing all to Peter. It wouldn't help and could do much harm. The best thing she owed Peter was herself. She would let Pierce see that she'd considered her options and chosen elsewhere.

Peter, past the anxiety of the Great Love Scene, was as relaxed and cheerful as ever. He'd proven his point sexually and was content to return to his moral beliefs, which Anastasia was happy to adopt as her own. They now felt free to spend lost hours in his hotel room in new intimacy, finding many delightful ways of pleasing and satisfying each other that included everything but actual intercourse.

Anastasia once again loved talking with him. She loved hearing him discuss great books and philosophies. She loved reading the daily papers and sharing the heartbreak of children dying of hunger and AIDS, and a world on the brink of destruction. They discussed what they could do to help, both in the present and in the future.

Peter told her he'd been accepted at Cambridge, and they discussed his quandary about whether to take time off from his career or to continue to ride the momentum of his success. Anastasia had told him before the London trip that Pierce had talked to her about a part in his next film. She had never discussed future plans before. She'd never had a future to discuss. It was heady stuff.

True to his pledge, Pierce did not intrude. As a matter of fact, after Pierce had attended a benefit in London, there were photos of him and Nicola Neve in the papers the next day.

"Nic, I'll be darned. Worked your old black magic after all," Peter chuckled.

Anastasia rolled her eyes and hurried past to the next page. When Peter left the room, she violently chucked the paper into the dustbin.

FOUR DAYS LATER, on Wednesday, April 25, Anastasia rang off the phone from her check-in with Bruce. He'd received no more visits from Scotland Yard, nor any more unposted letters. He reported that Elise was eager to come home.

Anastasia had passed along the news of the reunion being held there at the castle, and of the "anonymous admirer" who was going to the trouble and expense of building a cinema in Dunmore. Bruce found this as odd as Anastasia had, and agreed that someone's insistence on bringing the reunion onto Anastasia's home turf was a worrisome development. Bruce again urged her to announce she would attend. She hadn't been able to bring herself to do so—not because she was hesitant to become knowing bait for a murderer, but because the idea of being in a large, open room filled with people was enough to send her entire pulmonary-circulatory system spinning out of control.

After arranging their next telephone rendezvous, Anastasia settled into the curved back of the chair at the carved desk in her drawing room. She was cocooning again, and she knew it. She wondered how she'd ever had the audacity to leave her rooms, let alone the castle. Now someone was trying to bring a stampede of publicity crashing into her own home. This was her sanctuary. Why would someone go to such trouble and expense to rob her of this?

The telephone trilled in the hallway outside the drawing room, and Reginald gave a soft knock.

"The post, Your Grace." He set down the silver tray that framed one benign-looking brown envelope. Then he continued, "There is a telephone call as well. Miss Leah. And, if you'll permit me to say, she sounds a bit off-center."

Anastasia hadn't heard from Leah since her abrupt departure. As soon as the door closed, she took up the receiver.

"Leah?" she said. "Wait—it's ten in the morning here—it must be the middle of the night in L.A.!"

"Anastasia, he was here!"

"Who? What are you talking about?"

"Him! The killer! Whoever the hell's been following us!"

"Where are you? Are you safe?"

"Yes. The police have come and gone. I'm at some friends' house now." She was trying to sound controlled, but a tincture of panic still colored her voice.

"What happened?"

"I came in late from a party—well, early for me, actually. Everything seemed fine at home, the alarm was still set, everything. I puttered around, went to bed. Maybe an hour later, I woke up because I was chilly. Something told me to stay still. I lay there, pretending to still be asleep, and I felt a draft on my arm. I realized my bathroom window was open. And I knew it hadn't been when I went to bed."

"Dear God, Leah . . ."

"From where I was lying, I couldn't see anything. So, still pretending to sleep, I rolled over and looked, and *he was there*, standing in the shadows in a corner of the room. Watching me."

"Who was it? Who?"

"I couldn't tell. He was wearing a black ski mask, and a black duster-like coat . . . and black leather gloves. And he was *watching me*."

"So *what happened?*"

"There's a panic button wired into the alarm by my headboard. I pushed the button that sets off the million-decibel screech horn, grabbed my revolver out of the nightstand, and ran out the bedroom door on the opposite side of the bed from him, like, all in one motion. It turns out the bastard had cut the phone lines, so the alarm didn't go through to the police station, but it sure as hell startled him and woke all the neighbors. I made it outside, where, thanks to my air raid siren, we were having an impromptu block party. It might amaze you to know how many of my neighbors carry cell phones in their pajamas. The police came, and everyone went back to bed. Except me."

Anastasia gave an involuntary shudder. "You're all right?" she asked again.

"He knew I was home. He knew how to disarm my alarm. He knew where I slept and how to get in. He was *in my bedroom*. If I hadn't woken up . . ."

"Had he taken anything? I mean, was he trying to make it look like a robbery?"

"No, not yet. He probably would have killed me first, wouldn't you think? There were no prints, either."

"Did you tell the police?"

"The whole story? No. That would have been tomorrow's headlines. The reunion would have been blown out of the water."

And that would be so bad? Anastasia wanted to ask. "So, what are you going to do?"

"I'm staying here with Callie and Ed tonight. Then, I'm not sure. I might come back over to England. I'm afraid you and Bruce are right. Pretending this guy doesn't exist isn't going to make him go away."

Anastasia reluctantly agreed. "It's time to go back on the of- fensive. Leah, please come back. If you're up to it."

"I don't know. I can't think clearly right now. But Stace—be careful. This guy gets around. He could be at LAX even now."

"You're sure it was a guy?"

"Am I sure? No. He was wearing guy clothes, but no, I'm not positive. I couldn't even really tell how tall he was, because I was in bed."

"I'm so glad you're all right. Let me know if you're coming back."

"I will. And Stace, take my advice. Don't stay alone."

"Talk to you soon," Anastasia replied. She carefully replaced the receiver, and glanced again at the small padded envelope.

As her world had become ominous, the package had as well. Anastasia picked it up and looked at the typed address. And holding it, she knew.

This time the postmark was intact: London. She hesitated to open it, but it was very thin and small and she couldn't imagine a bomb fitting inside. Bombs didn't seem the modus operandi, especially if the killer was obsessing on a face-to-face rendezvous. And anthrax would need only a letter-sized envelope.

The brown padded mailer opened easily, as did the small white box therein. Out slid a slim black case, three inches square and less than an inch deep. She unclasped it gingerly, holding only the edges to keep from smearing any fingerprints—although she knew the killer was far beyond carelessly leaving prints.

Open, the right-hand side had a small digital time display, with buttons up the side: Hour, Minute, Record, Play. Across from it, a photo had been inserted—a still from the movie, of King Mark and Queen Isolde. Pierce Hall and her. A jagged X had been slashed through Pierce.

The record and play buttons indicated there was a digital memory chip: the sender could record his own greeting. Anastasia took a deep breath and hit Play. The voice that spoke wasn't human, but synthesized.

"I told you you were playing with fire," it said.

"Damn," she said. "Oh, damn."

She leaned back, recalling the last time she'd heard those words.

It was the afternoon after the fire in the queen's chamber. She'd been at a meeting in the production caravan. Pierce had seemed quiet and distracted. Afterwards, Anastasia had waited outside for everyone else to leave, then she returned. The director alone remained. He rang off a call, then turned to her.

"It's a go with Brangien in the morning," he told her.

"All right," she said, then, "What are you thinking about the fire?"

"Faulty wiring. Official cause."

"Is that good?"

"Means insurance kicks in."

His thoughts were still far away. She tried to guess her way in.

"You're not sure, though."

"What's that?"

"You think someone started it deliberately."

He sat contemplating a moment, made a decision, drew a typed note from his pocket. "You're playing with Fire," it said.

"Good Lord! Did you report this?"

"The fire marshal thinks someone left it this morning, after the fact, to take advantage of the situation. Truth is, they're bending over backwards to keep the production—and the production pounds—rolling here in Dunmore."

"Who?" She was more incredulous than angry.

"I have no proof."

"What if they do it again?"

"That, I'm not worried about," he said. "The shoot is almost over. And I think the point's been made." The discussion was ended.

Now, twenty years belatedly, she wished to God she'd pressed Pierce further.

Anastasia held on to the slim alarm clock, trying to think clearly. This tied the murderer directly to the production. And it showed the perpetrator knew where she was. She turned the envelope over to look at the date. April 22. It wouldn't have been difficult to post it and hop on a plane to visit Leah a continent away.

It was obviously time to go on the offensive. But how?

She opened the clock again and ran her fingers over the rough X slashed over Pierce in the photo, then couldn't help looking at where her own smiling visage remained, as yet, unmarked.

"Damn," she muttered eloquently. "Oh, damn."

ANASTASIA FOUND HERSELF once again in a car with Pierce Hall and Gray Eddington. This time it felt much different. They had wrapped the day's shoot at 2 p.m. on that July Tuesday and would resume at noon the next day, beginning the lush exteriors. Ten minutes after the day's final take, Anastasia had cleaned off her makeup and pulled on her jeans. Her dinner clothes—not formal this time, thank heavens—were already in the auto the production assistant had brought round. Pierce and Gray met her there.

It was Pierce's car, a red Mercedes convertible, though thankfully with the top on. Gray got into the passenger seat and Anastasia climbed in back. Pierce leaned in, ostensibly to throw his shoulder bag in back for the trip.

"How are you with reading on the road?"

"I'm fine," she said.

He pulled a film script from his bag and set it on her lap. "Your character is Julia," he said. He put the seat back, closed the door, got into the driver's seat, and off they set.

As before, Pierce and Gray began talking business immediately, Gray's lap full of files, papers, and legal pads. Pierce had put a cassette of Mozart sonatas into the car's stereo system. The music wasn't loud, but the rear speakers effectively screened out the conversation in the front seat.

Anastasia spent a few minutes studying the title page: "*Beggar's Moon*, by Pierce Hall."

So even though she had chosen Peter, he still wanted her to act in his next film. A delicious icy thrill ran through her. She settled back and began to read.

From time to time, Pierce would turn around and ask her something, or remark on some point of interest as they passed. Whenever he did, she would jump, pulled from inside the taut, suspenseful world of the story that surrounded her. No wonder Eddington had pounced on this script and had been willing to facilitate *T & I* to be sure it got made. It was every bit as tightly woven and harrowing as any of Pierce's earlier thrillers, which had done smashing business worldwide.

And he wanted her to play the female lead. To play Julia.

She read the script slowly and carefully, trying to pick up as much subtext as possible. She was allowing herself to become excited, which was against both her better judgment and her lifelong policy of trained pessimism.

"This is it. We're here," Pierce announced as the auto made a turn onto a graveled lane.

Anastasia checked her watch, shocked to find that while she'd been engrossed, two hours had somehow gone by. She was two pages from the end. She read them quickly, then squinted to clear her vision from the printed page and look out the window.

"This isn't London," she said.

"London?" asked Gray. "No, dear girl. Denbighshire. Dinner tonight's at Cambry Hall."

As he spoke the name, the auto pulled clear from the patch of woods and they could see the house on the small rise before them. It was Georgian, and while it was considerably smaller than her grandparents' Wilton Glen, it was much friendlier. The front lawns were green, and several of the windows lining the two-story square front were thrown open to catch the sultry July breeze.

Pierce turned into the circular drive and parked in front of the four cement steps to the walkway up to the front door.

"Finally!" Gray exhaled, his door open before the engine died. "Two hours without a phone is well past my limit."

"Someday, they'll install a receiver in your head," Pierce

answered drolly to the receding form of his friend.

Pierce opened Anastasia's door and offered a hand to help her out. His casual kindness was catching her quite off guard. On the set, while usually in good humor, he was still the ultimate perfectionist.

"Thank you for letting me see the script," she said. "I had time to read the whole thing."

"Think there's anything there?"

"Pierce, it's wonderful."

A small smile crept across his face. "Perhaps we'll have a few minutes to discuss it later," he said. "Now you might fancy a rest before dinner." He picked up both his bag and hers and followed her up the walk.

The actress was dwelling in a state of constant exhaustion. Rest sounded sweeter than ambrosia. "It won't be rude?" she asked. "I mean, to arrive and disappear? You're sure our hosts will understand?"

Pierced laughed his rumbling, sexy half-Irish laugh. "I'm your host," he said. "and I insist."

"This is . . ."

"Cambry Hall is my house—miraculously, even after the divorce. Too small and square for Alana, thank the good Lord. She never lived here. But I've hardly lived here myself."

"It's lovely," she stammered.

"Thank you. I'll make certain you have a tour before we leave in the morning."

They were met at the door by Nell Duffy, the housekeeper. She was wiry and tall, and cheerfully accommodating.

"Nell, see Miss Day settled in her room, would you?" he said. "Shall I leave my bag here for your husband?"

"Ach, you're always the one to be teasin', " said the stalwart woman, picking it up. "It'll be no problem for me."

"Conan Marcel, the composer, will be here by five to play me some music," Pierce said to Anastasia. "Come down whenever you're ready. He's eager to meet you in person. Our other dinner guest will be Art Mendoza, one of the co-chairmen of Heather Hill, Ltd., who wasn't able to be at the London gathering. We're going to hammer out the final details on *Beggar's Moon* before it gets the green light and is placed in the hands of our various agents and solicitors. He's also looking forward to meeting you."

"What am I to say, to talk about?" she asked, suddenly frightened of inadvertently blowing the deal.

"Relax and be yourself," Pierce answered. "That's your entire script for the evening."

And he headed down the main hall.

Anastasia followed Mrs. Duffy up the center staircase, looking around in amazement. This was Pierce's house. The many windows made it sunny and light. It wasn't overly furnished, and the pieces were authentic and well chosen. It was an interesting blend of antique and modern. It felt comfortable but not exactly lived in.

She'd been averaging five hours of sleep a night, as had the other crew and principals on the shoot, so the minute Mrs. Duffy finished hanging her frock in the closet of the corner guest room, she collapsed onto the bed and into a deep sleep.

Anastasia awakened in the gentle light of early evening. She freshened up and dressed for company in a simple cream-colored sheath. She pulled a brush through her red-gold hair and lured some recalcitrant curls back on either side with combs. "Well," she shrugged into the mirror, "Pierce said to be myself."

One other car had joined Pierce's in the drive. Since it was too early for dinner, she followed the cascading sweep of piano music downstairs to find Gray and Pierce in deep reverie in a large drawing room. They each held drinks and were listening to a short man coax amazing sounds from the pianoforte, the likes of which she'd never heard from the instrument before. The piece he played as she entered had flourish and fanfare. It was obviously music for the court of a king. She stood quietly inside the door until the musician finished. The two men nodded appreciatively.

Anastasia couldn't help herself. She applauded.

The gentleman spun on the bench. "Ah," he said, sighting Anastasia. "Ah."

Pierce stepped forward. "Conan Marcel, may I introduce—"

"No need. It is she. It is Isolde."

The energetic composer with the wild hair and flashing eyes bounced across the room, made a deep bow, and pressed his lips to the back of Anastasia's right hand.

"It is a delight to meet my muse in person."

She smiled shyly and followed him back into the room.

"All right, you blasted Irishman, she's here now. So play the love theme."

"If that meets with your approval?" Conan proposed to Anastasia.

"I'd love to hear it."

Conan Marcel sat down and for the first time played the haunting melody that captured the passion, longing, and heart-break of Tristan and Isolde's love. The dissonance made the listener want to laugh and weep, fall in love, embrace the mysteries of life and protest the finality of death, all at the same time. Long before it was finished, Anastasia was winded. She made her way to sit down in a brocade wing chair.

Gray Eddington was the first to find his voice. "I think you've caught it, Marcel, old man."

"Yes," said Pierce. "I think you have."

Afterwards, Mr. Duffy informed them that Mr. Mendoza had arrived and dinner would be served within the half hour. Gray retired to a guest room for his coat and tie and Anastasia returned to her room to freshen up. As she chose her lipstick, she wondered if she should send Lily down to dinner or if she was up to attending herself.

"Relax and be yourself," Pierce had said. Perhaps she'd give it a go.

She returned downstairs to find one of the tall, thin doors opening to the main hall from the drawing room was slightly ajar. Anastasia could hear the voices of Pierce and another man, whom she presumed to be Mr. Mendoza, coming from within.

As she paused to collect herself, she heard them already in earnest conversation.

"There's no way we can persuade you to take the male lead?" came the thin but intense voice of the businessman. "You know, of course, it would make it easier to make certain other casting concessions."

"Not on this one, Art. I want to focus all my attention on directing."

"And we want you to direct, of course. But you realize that means we'll need a name."

"I have several ideas for the male lead. And yes, I understand you'll want someone with marquee value. But let me assure you, by then you'll have a 'name' as the female lead. It'll be the smartest thing we could do, to sign Anastasia now—and quickly—before *T & I* makes her an international star."

"I have no doubt that you're right. My only concern is her age. *Beggar's Moon* is not about a teenager. Be honest with me, Pierce. How old does she read?"

There was a pause. Anastasia closed her eyes in a vain attempt to regain a normal pulse.

"Art, I understand your concern," Pierce answered seriously. "But Anastasia Day has a rare quality that is ageless. How old was Audrey Hepburn when she appeared? How old were the characters she played? Who knew? Who cared? She just was. She sprang into the world fully formed, at the beautiful age. Like Venus on the half shell. Half a dozen actresses in the world have done that. You're about to meet one."

Anastasia moved silently away from the door. She suddenly needed to use the loo.

Fortunately, on her return she met Gray in the hall. Lily took his arm and together they joined their companions for dinner.

Conan Marcel had been caught in the undertow of the incoming tide of inspiration. He made a hasty exit the moment the dessert plates were removed. Lily joined the remaining gentlemen in the parlor, where the men had cigars and after-dinner drinks. She had found Art Mendoza an enjoyable conversationalist. When he'd brought up Pierce's new script, she'd been ready to dissect what made Julia such a complex heroine. Art enjoyed her analysis. Pierce was pleasantly surprised.

Gray was catching a ride into London with Art. When Gray went to collect his things, Anastasia said her good-nights and excused herself also, leaving Pierce and Mendoza alone for any final words. It also gave her the opportunity to escape to her bedroom before any potentially awkward leave-taking from her host. Although, in truth, other than his thoughtful actions toward her and his extravagant words to Mendoza, Pierce had shown no personal interest in her whatsoever.

Anastasia was too wound up to head straight upstairs. The drawing room now sat dark and empty. She let herself in, following the path of bleached moonlight across the Oriental carpet. It led to four tall windows that reached halfway to the ceiling. The house had not been closed for the night, and one of the windows was open, its sheer white curtain doing a gentle dance. She drew it aside and was pleased to find that the two end windows had small balconies wide enough that one could step fully outside.

Which she did. To her right, lights illuminated the walk to the front drive. From there, within minutes, she heard male good-byes and the start-up of an automobile. The motor hummed round the drive and receded, leaving the night undisturbed.

Anastasia drank deeply of the country air. The half-moon hung at a tilt above her, sending friendly light to the lawns as they sloped down to centuries-old trees whose leaves swayed in the murmured music of the night.

It struck Anastasia then—for Lily was gone, and Anastasia alone remained—that she, the daughter of an alcoholic Southern hairdresser, once an uneducated and nearly destitute seam-stress, was standing in a dinner frock on the balcony of Cambry Hall, the guest of a great director. The guest of Pierce Hall, who, the first time she'd realized who he was, had nearly caused her to toss her cookies. Now he had caught her off guard once again—this time by his kindness. He was a surprising man. And he could still scare her to death.

"Look. Down the rise. See the deer?"

Damn the man. Didn't he realize he was daunting enough without sneaking up on a person? She hadn't even known he was in the room before he'd spoken softly from behind her.

She looked where he pointed. Sure enough, a doe and a fawn had silently wandered out of the woods, peacefully grazing.

"I took you by surprise," he said, his deep voice quietly melo-dious. "What were you thinking?"

She didn't turn to look at him. "I was remembering the girl I was three years ago. Wondering how I got here."

"Ah," he said, "but the secret is that you're exactly the same person you were then. Your circumstances have changed, that's all. We're alike in some ways, you and I. When one comes from an impoverished background, it's sometimes hard to believe your good luck—even when you've worked so hard to create it. But we're scrappers, we two."

She realized she'd been fooled by the Venus on the Half Shell Syndrome herself. She'd assumed Pierce Hall had been born a great talent, arriving in the world attending important dinners, having an estate or two peppered about the countryside.

The scent of him so close was scrambling her thoughts. She spoke quickly.

"You come from hardship, too?"

"I wasn't a street urchin, but we hadn't much. Mum was a housewife, Da a merchant seaman, never home. Lucky for me, our priest had a love for Shakespeare—not the text, the sword fights. I didn't know Shakespeare had words till I was ten. That's when me da died and we moved to me mum's sister's in Brighton." He chuckled. "Yes, I've fought my way up, and so have you. I recognized it in you the first day we met. But you're different from many who have struggled. Somehow through all those years, through all your battles, you've protected your pilgrim soul. It's still there, gentle and intact, under everything. That's the most miraculous thing about you."

The young woman stood, dumbfounded, not daring to lift her gaze from the doe, the moonlight, the painting of the night. She knew if she did she would cry.

But when Pierce laid his large hand on her shoulder, she gave a shiver and pulled away.

Fortunately, he laughed.

"Don't worry, Anastasia. I'm not going to attack you like some wolf in the night. I have no interest in being your lover. Well, now, that's not exactly true. I have a great interest in being your lover. But not only your lover. You have the kind of soul that blends the whole self together—body, mind, and spirit. With you, it's all or nothing. I know that. I would like all." He sighed.

"But a pilgrim soul can't be taken. It can only be given. And it's yours to give."

"Good night," he said. He gave a quick kiss to the top of her head. "We'll leave just after breakfast."

And he was gone.

On the ride back, she asked nonchalantly if his talk with Mr. Mendoza had produced the desired outcome. He said it had. They fell back into discussing the new script. After an hour's back-and-forth, Anastasia was even more exhilarated about its potential than she had been before.

Pierce was buoyed by the talk as well. He took a deep breath, ran a hand through his thick hair, and roared, "It's great to be back!"

Anastasia asked why, if work was such an integral part of him, he'd taken such a long hiatus. He said that his ex-wife hated the movie business, had a great dislike for the performing arts in general, and had given him an ultimatum. Her or filmmaking. She'd given him this ultimatum several times during their eighteen-year marriage, which had resulted in lengthy separations. But this last time, he'd been exhausted from doing four projects back-to-back. A farm in Provence sounded like a welcome break.

And so it had been, for almost a year. Then he began to get antsy, and finally to go crackers. He realized that, no matter how wonderful and smart and rich Alana was, if he couldn't be married to her and be himself, there was little point. He should have seen that long ago. But she was a great gourmet cook.

Anastasia, emboldened by his frankness, asked if his wife hadn't minded his reputation with the ladies.

"Ay," he said. "The shadow of the Great Lady-Killer which stalks me wherever I go!" He looked honestly chagrined. "It is the most cumbersome baggage. Truth be told, I've had very few intense relationships in my life. Three. There have been three. The first was Alana, whom I married when I was nineteen and still in school and she was twenty-two and expecting Leah. Since then—over nearly two *decades*, mind you, during our times of separation—when she threw me out with the rubbish for doing the very work that supported our family—in twenty years, I've had two serious relationships. Everyone knows who with. That's the problem with being an actor as well as a director. Somehow your life becomes public fodder. The other women with whom I've been photographed over the years have basically been partners in press."

"Not lovers?" Anastasia asked.

"And what, may I ask, gives you the right to expect an answer to such a question?"

"I'd like to know the company I keep."

He grimaced. "Touché." But his tone had changed. "Anastasia," he said softly, "I want you to know that what happened . . . between us has nothing to do with . . . Lord, with anything that's come before.

"Why should you believe me?" He laughed a self-deprecating laugh. "I have nothing to say in my own defense. Except that it's the truth. Here is my answer to your question: no, I do not deserve my reputation, while yes, I am human."

"Have you slept with Nicola Neve?"

"Excuse me, when is it my turn?"

"I've made love with Peter Dalton and Pierce Hall. End of not-so-thrilling conversation." Although, to tell the truth, she thought wryly, to many women that might be a particularly thrilling conversation.

"Not that it's a topic I normally discuss, but no, I've never bedded Ms. Neve. As a matter of fact, last time I saw her in London, she was changed. Can't put my finger on it. She went through the motions of being interested, but she was sort of . . . glazed. As if she was on drugs, but I don't think she was. Strange thing, really. I've wondered about it. Mostly I was glad she's already done her scenes for *T & I*."

Anastasia found the information about Nicola puzzling as well. But the mention of their current film, along with their ever-increasing proximity to the set, turned their thoughts again to the project at hand. During the next minutes, their conversation curved subtly until they were again director and actor preparing for the day's shoot. They arrived back ready to get to work.

But things were never to be the same.

For over the next hours, days, and weeks, Anastasia found herself, against her will, falling in love with Pierce Hall. With his talent, his commanding nature, the respect he earned from everyone with whom he worked; his height, his flashing eyes, once-broken nose, his strength and gentleness. And yes, his pilgrim soul.

The only problem was, she wasn't falling out of love with Peter or with his exuberance, his wit, his faith and philosophy, his questioning, his virility, his kindness.

It was torture.

She tried to compensate by throwing herself wholeheartedly into her relationship with Peter, attempting to spend every minute by his side. Their spirits were high. They laughed often and made out with abandon.

And every night, alone in her room, she cried herself to sleep. While she fought to keep her body, and even her thoughts, true to Peter Dalton, her willful heart, while completely his, belonged to Pierce as well.

Whoever invented the myth that a person can't be in love with two people at the same time was lacking crucial data. The problem that she confronted again and again in the heat of every dark night was that they were the two most wonderful men on earth. If she had met only one of them, life would be perfect. She would be completely happy with either. Completely.

She could not tolerate loving both.

She prayed, given the flagrance of her relationship with Peter, that Pierce would turn his affection elsewhere. But he remained engulfed by the film. No one ever saw as much as a production assistant or an extra leaving his room in the early morning hours. He simply had no time or interest.

And Anastasia wondered, in the long shadows of the night, if Pierce didn't sense the desperation driving her public infatuation with Peter and suspect its cause.

Anastasia's passion and anguish drove her to take new risks in her acting. The knowledge that they were doing great work brought a current of elation to both cast and crew. They were working now in the castle, which had wisely been abandoned to the film crew by its occupants.

The day they shot the scene of King Mark and Queen Isolde's private reconciliation—the scene Anastasia had done with Pierce in her audition—was hell. By this time, her guilt was a two-edged sword. Guilt toward Peter for loving Pierce; guilt toward Pierce for making such a public denial of her feelings for him.

The scene between the reunited king and queen took place the night of her return, in the king's bedchamber.

Pierce elected to interpret it according to Anastasia's suggestion: it is Isolde who reaches out to Mark, knowing he has the right to reject her. Knowing, too, that if he does, she will live the rest of her life in isolation.

But Mark can't help himself. He burns with consuming love for Isolde. And she, in turn, offers the powerful love born of memory and gratitude to him.

Anastasia was frankly terrified of filming the scene. King Mark might be kissing her, but he was using Pierce Hall's mouth, and arms, and intensity. She countered her feelings by ignoring them, by pretending there was nothing to it. Pierce himself was the most nonchalant he'd ever been before acting in a scene. He had, however, left it to the last shot of the day.

Then, as cameras rolled, in a room filled with two dozen people, Pierce looked at her with eyes exposing naked love, which he then denied, tearing himself in half, because he knew he could not ask it in return. He turned away. But she did love him. It was her now reaching out for him, knowing he had every reason, every right, to ignore her, to reject her for all time.

And he did.

But then he forced himself to risk the agony and pain of exposing his love once again. He turned back to her, opening himself to accept her again as half himself.

As they embraced, they kissed a kiss so full of agony and passion and ecstasy and longing and hate and love that it left them both in tears.

Anastasia might possibly have survived, had that been the end.

But they had to do it twice more, for coverage.

And every time he looked at her, every time he touched her, her whole world rocked with the magnitude of an earthquake.

By their final kiss on the third take, it seemed everyone in the room was flattened by the intensity of the emotion and desire playing out before them. No one moved. No one breathed.

Pierce finally disengaged, called "Cut," and looked up. "Milos, how did that look?"

"Fucking great," the cinematographer answered. Anastasia had never heard him talk like that, let alone while working.

"Fine," said Pierce. "We're done for the day."

And he walked off the set.

Anastasia stood dazed for a moment, then wandered out of the glare of the lights into the shadows to catch her breath before heading to her caravan. She hadn't known Peter had stayed to watch the scene. When he came up to her, she began to tremble.

"You're in love with him," Peter said. His voice was stained with disbelief and betrayal.

"Peter, I—"

"You what?"

"I love you, too," she answered.

When she looked up, he was gone.

Anastasia had no dinner that night. Instead she sat alone in her room, not bothering to turn on any lights.

Somehow she knew Pierce was in the next room, as silent and vulnerable as she.

The passage of time went unnoticed. All she knew was that it was in thick darkness that she finally went to unlock and open her side of the door that adjoined Pierce's room. Her mind was still in a fog as she knocked on the inner door.

Then it opened, and her fog was gone, and in its place was life, and love, and every sensation known to humankind, and Pierce had gathered her so completely to himself that even fully clothed she could not tell where she ended and he began.

CHAPTER 9

From the Daily Variety column "Have You Heard?" May 3:

Saw mega-agent Dave Dial at the Moonglow Foundation fundraiser last night. He says the bidding's been hot and heavy for the new action thriller script from Bruce Amerman. Amerman's attached to this one as director. . . .

Bruce stood over her with the bottle of Chivas. It had been nearly full at the beginning of the evening. They'd made impressive progress.

Two days earlier, she'd been certain she'd never again leave her rooms at the castle. All it took was the call from Leah, the knowledge her whereabouts were known, and one night of lying awake, waiting for the shadows in the corner of her bedroom to coalesce into a phantom figure, and she'd ordered the car the next day. She decided the castle was simply too large to be guarded by a sleep-in staff of five who spent the nights, after all, sleeping.

If Leah's advice about not staying alone was sound, Bruce was twice the sitting duck she was. And she needed to talk to him, to speak her thoughts out loud—although, for some reason, she hadn't told him about her recently acquired digital clock. They'd decided to rendezvous and come up with a plan of action.

Bruce had pulled his car into the garage early in the day. Then, late afternoon, he'd left his house on foot. His third stop was the local pub. There Anastasia joined him, making certain Benton had dropped her after dark—and that Bruce was waiting so she didn't have to enter the confined, crowded room. To her mind, the pub held as many terrors as the open sea.

As soon as Benton pulled away, they'd left on foot, heading the opposite direction of Bruce's house. They took a serpentine path through back streets and alleys until they were certain they weren't being followed, and eventually trespassed alongside the house of the neighbors whose back garden abutted the Amermans'. Anastasia wore jeans and a dark jacket for the occasion. She felt the thrill of the game as Bruce cupped his hand to give her a boost to the top of the garden wall. He looked quite dashing in the role of action hero. Or antihero. Cynical yet courageous. At least becoming a serious "player" hadn't necessitated the shearing of his thick hair. As long as he had the hair and the dimples, he'd still be Bruce.

He was also in distressingly good physical shape. Once she was over the wall, he'd effortlessly scaled it. Together they'd kept to the shadows until they'd let themselves into the Amermans' house through a hidden side door.

They turned on no lights. Instead, Bruce got the revolver he kept hidden in the hall closet, two shot glasses, his favorite Scotch, and they'd settled themselves into the shadows of the conservatory.

"I wonder if I shouldn't go out again and come in through the front door," Bruce said. "Perhaps I'm better bait than an empty house."

"Bait? I thought our elaborate exercise was so that any random killers in the neighborhood would think no one was home, and therefore *not* try to kill us." The idea that a killer could know her whereabouts that very second gave her a chill.

"I'm ready to find out who's been plaguing my life for the last two decades and do away with him. I'm bloody tired of this."

"That would look good to Scotland Yard, wouldn't it?" Anastasia asked. "Another corpse, and you holding the smoking gun. 'But the corpse was the killer, Inspector!' we cry. 'He killed everyone else, so we offed him in self-defense. He wasn't Bruce's next victim, we promise!' That would tidy things up right away."

"And Elise accused *me* of looking on the dark side of things."

"Sorry. But come on, you're the psychological genius around here. Since it wasn't Conan, who are our suspects? And whose whereabouts are in question the night Leah had her visitor?"

"Do go on, Ms. Holmes. Perhaps you're thinking more clearly than I. Who is currently on your Favorite Suspects list?"

Anastasia sat forward on the loveseat, trying to bring Bruce's face into focus across the expanse of gray light. "Assuming Conan was murdered, it is possible that whoever ran past the window in Calais is our killer, the same one who recently woke Leah."

"If you're going to be thorough, everyone at the scene of Conan's death is suspect, including you and me."

"True. But we were both in England—and on the phone with each other, in fact—at the exact time Leah's intruder paid his call. Supposing the killer was in both Calais and California, that rules us out."

"Leah was in both places. I wouldn't put it past her to fake her own nocturnal attack."

"Except that she's been my friend for years. She doesn't freak out easily, and this whole thing has her genuinely panicked. Whereas the perpetrator has had twenty years to get used to it." Anastasia hesitated before proceeding. "If we're going to be thorough, how about Elise?"

Bruce snorted. "I do love the woman," he said, "but I don't think she could be hiding *this* much gumption from me." He took another draught of liquid fire. "If she has been, she'll have more to answer for than a dozen-odd corpses."

"Bruce, honestly."

"Well, a person needs a bit of passion in his life, wouldn't you say?"

This time it was Anastasia's turn to drain her glass. "Passion has caused me nothing but severe pain," she said. "If I never feel passion again as long as I live, I will die a happy woman."

"Spoken a bit . . . passionately," he commented.

"Let's stay on the original subject, wot?" she said.

"Well. So, besides those visibly present in Calais, who might be considered on the list? Perhaps those we know are involved with the reunion?" As he thought this over, his gray eyes looked troubled. "Stacy, think. There's hardly anybody left! Who would we most want to see? Peter. Garrett. Conan. Pierce. Gray. All gone. Shit."

A shiver edged through her, and she looked for a bright spot. "We don't know that Peter's dead. Or Nicola." Anastasia took a deep breath and entered dangerous waters. "And we have to look at motive. I know for a fact that Nicola Neve unsuccessfully propositioned both Peter Dalton and Pierce Hall."

"I know for a fact that Richie Riley unsuccessfully propositioned *you*."

"He didn't proposition me, exactly," Anastasia protested. "Though I admit we didn't part on the best of terms. Still, let's not forget that Leah stole your girlfriend."

"I never said I wouldn't be willing to kill Leah," Bruce answered. "Still, none of this seems motive for murder. At least not for the murders of nine people." He picked up the bottle from where it sat at his feet. "You want another shot?"

"Yes. I do."

"All of this has opened a can of worms in your life, hasn't it?"

"Yes," she said softly. "A big one. Has it for you?"

"Yes," he said. "Fairly tall. I think it has to do with the passion thing. During *T & I*, we were living life so on the edge. Taking risks. Loving. Hating. I thought that intensity of feeling was a given, would always be available for the taking."

"I'm as glad to live without it."

"So you say. But are you?"

"Yes. I've found a quiet, centered life."

"It appears you've spent the last ten years hiding."

"Hiding? For pity's sake, I married a good man. A duke. I have my own damn castle. That's something of an accomplishment."

"Stacy, face facts. His Grace was a geezer. And you're one of the few phobics I know who has been able to literally surround herself with a moat."

"Look who's talking! The world's paragon of happiness!"

"Ah, but I've never pretended not to be wounded."

"That's true," said Anastasia. "You've grown into it. You were miserable when you weren't miserable. At least now you can take some pride in your achievement."

Bruce didn't take umbrage. "I think we're more alike than either of us might wish," he said quietly. "I think at some point in the distant past, we each decided we would never be like other people. Happiness wasn't something we would ever have. And instead of fighting the decision, we knew inside ourselves we were unworthy of happiness, so we accepted our solitary fates and got on with things."

The duchess stared at him. But she didn't argue.

He picked up the bottle of spirits, but set it down again without pouring any.

"The thing is," he said, "I think we're beginning to fight back. I look at you and this is what I see. When you're safe, you allow yourself to collapse. When you're facing things head-on —even if it means danger, or murder, for God's sake—you come alive. I certainly can't throw stones. I've felt pretty much the same way myself."

"I've never heard that dealing with murder was a cure for acute panic disorder."

"Cure? No. Certainly not. But perhaps it is the thing that will make . . . us . . . feel that a better life is worth fighting for."

Anastasia thought again of how strangely unselfconscious she'd felt following Bruce through alleys and over walls.

"Let me ask you a question. When did you decide if you never felt passion again, it would be for the best?"

Anastasia knew exactly when it was, to the second. She walked over and picked up the bottle of Scotch, pouring her own.

Bruce took this as an invitation to go on. "My guess is that it had something to do with the ending of the world of *T & I*. Whenever that was, and whatever that world meant to you. Because that's when it was for me."

"Yeah?" she asked. "When was it for you?"

"The night of the premiere. Probably the night the rest of the world assumed was the highlight of our lives."

Anastasia had been mostly dead inside before that night. But whatever had been left, that night had finished off.

"Why?" she asked gently. "What happened on that night for you?"

"I realized I'd lost Peter. For good. His thriller, *Domino*, was opening the next week. It was already getting great press, especially for him. Playing a modern-day murderer was the perfect counterpoint to Tristan. He was already shooting his first Hollywood feature. He'd flown back to London for our premiere. I'd fooled myself into thinking that I'd been wrong, that he was still his old self. My best friend. But the night of the premiere it was clear he'd left me behind with the other mediocres. In the middle where I belonged."

Anastasia didn't know how to answer him.

"You knew it, too, didn't you?" he pushed. "You knew by then our Peter was lost."

"Yeah," she said. "I did."

"What happened?" he asked, rhetorically.

There was silence.

"You know, I never did thank you for getting us that car," she finally spoke.

"I never thanked you for standing up to Pierce about my rewrites. You saved the scene."

"Pierce even called you in to help with other rewrites, didn't he? They must have been good."

"It made me think I might have a future as a writer," Bruce admitted. "You and Peter put the car to good use, I hope."

"We did."

They were both drunk, and for the first time, Anastasia wished they weren't. She wished she were in complete control of her emotions. This was getting dangerous.

"I loved him," Bruce said in the dark. "Peter. I don't mean physical love. I mean I wanted to be him. I wanted to laugh like him. I wanted to have his talent. I wanted to have his looks." He added softly, "You loved him, didn't you?"

The Duchess of Esmonde nodded. "You know I did. Very much."

"The last time I saw him, it was awful. I was in L.A., writing some damn movie. His last film was coming out. I turned on the telly, and there he was, on *Entertainment Tonight*, stoned out of his mind. His eyes didn't even focus. It tore me up."

"But Bruce. Your future wasn't bound up with his. You were a success. You were in Hollywood, working, and you weren't stoned."

He didn't even hear what she said.

"After the premiere, I knew my life wouldn't work out. I knew I hated acting. And I married a card-carrying bitch."

"You certainly can't blame Peter for that," she said, trying to snap him out of his self-pity. "As a matter of fact, if she was such a bitch, why *did* you marry her?"

"See if you can guess," he said.

Bruce left the room. She heard him go into his study. A drawer slid open and thunked closed. He walked back into the conservatory and handed her a photo in a scalloped-edged frame. He sat beside her on the loveseat and snapped on the flashlight he'd brought so that the beam fell onto the picture. "That's Claudine," was all he said.

Anastasia looked at the portrait in her hands. And she gasped.

"Beautiful, wasn't she?"

"Well, I—good Lord."

"Doesn't take a Freudian to figure this one out. I married Peter's girlfriend. Or a second-rate copy." He snapped off the torch.

"Good Lord."

"Weren't aware you had a clone? Kind of frightening. I mean, her hair was different. Straight and brown. She colored it. And she had that little button nose."

"It's the nose I always wanted."

"Don't be silly. She looked like a Barbie doll. You're an original. Would you believe I didn't even see what I was doing till it was too late?"

They sat together, overwhelmed by the past and the present.

Finally Bruce laughed. "If I thought I could've told all this to a shrink, I'd have been in therapy years ago."

"The thing I don't understand," Anastasia started, "is . . . you were never a second-rate Peter. You were always a first-rate Bruce, and we all loved you for it. Peter, and Garrett, and Pierce—Pierce hired you for all his films, for pity's sake!"

"How about you?"

"Me?"

"Umm. You loved me, too?"

"How can you even ask such a thing?"

"Don't know. I've been scared to for twenty years."

He'd gotten her to smile. She looked at the hands in her lap. "You've always been special to me. Since the day of the first read-through when you told me that everyone else was as terrified as I was. When I said I didn't know anyone and you said, 'You know me.' I loved you from that instant."

"You were grateful."

"You were virile. I noticed."

"Yeah, well, I noticed, too." Bruce Amerman leaned over and kissed her. A serious, grown-up, passionate kiss. And she not only let him, she kissed him back.

"Dear God," he said when they finally broke apart. "If I'd done that twenty years ago, it would have saved me an entire first marriage."

"Bruce, you're married now."

"I know. I also know you're not in love with me. But there are some things you don't want to die without having done."

"Yeah?" she laughed. "How was it? Must have been a letdown after all these years."

"Well, no. In fact, definitely not!" He laughed as well.

"I haven't kissed anyone like that for a long time," Anastasia said. "I thought I never would again. Thanks."

He put his arm around her and she laid her head on his shoulder. They sat quietly together like friends who have known each other for a long, long time.

And Anastasia began to come up with a plan.

It wasn't until the next morning that they found outside the conservatory garden door, three yards from where they sat, a white rock dove, its neck broken in a clean snap.

———————————————

TO HER DISMAY, PETER refused to speak to Anastasia outside of their scenes together. As Tristan, he looked at her with new depths of searing love and passion. But as soon as "cut" was called, the steel curtain descended behind his eyes, and he was gone. If he'd meant this to torture her, it worked. Now she was in agony over her lost love for Peter.

The horrid part was he seemed to be in agony, too. But he wouldn't let her close.

Everyone on the set noticed they'd had a quarrel, but since they were both throwing themselves into the work, life—and art—continued as usual.

After a week, the company had completed most of the castle scenes, and had moved to the forest exteriors.

The day they shot the scene where Tristan and Isolde are discovered by Mark, sleeping together with Tristan's sword between them, Anastasia could stand it no longer.

The scene had a small cast—Pierce, Peter, and her—and relatively small crew. When the camera stopped and Pierce and Milos decided they'd gotten what they needed, Peter turned and immediately stalked toward his caravan.

Anastasia didn't care who saw. She grabbed his arm and forcibly pulled him off the path, away from prying eyes.

"Please, Peter, at least talk to me!"

He sneezed. For the past few days, he'd been battling the beginnings of a nasty summer cold.

"Peter, it's me, Stacy."

"I thought I knew a Stacy once."

"You're not being fair."

"Okay," he said, grabbing her arm and pulling her to him. His fingers dug into flesh. "Okay, you want to talk, here's what I have to ask you: have you fucked him?"

"What are you talking about?"

"You know damn well. Let me spell it out. Have you done the deed with Pierce? Have you coupled? Shagged? Tupped? Has he impaled you?"

"Peter!" she cried. "I love you!"

"You're the one who wanted to talk. This is a yes/no question. Has Pierce Hall thrust his penis into your vagina?"

She looked away. "I don't know you when you're like this."

"Just tell me no."

She began to cry.

His nails dug deeper as he stepped closer to her. His face was kissing distance from hers as he said, "I guess I don't know you, either."

He flung her away and left her there. She followed slowly. She heard him sneeze as he walked back through the set.

"I want you to stop by the infirmary before lunch," Pierce said to Peter as he passed.

"Yes, boss," Peter answered, his voice dripping acid. "Your wish is my command. Then I'll be in my caravan reading my Bible—the story of David and Uriah. You see, I, too, had but the one lamb."

Unexpectedly, Anastasia found herself angry. She left the set and went to find her one confidante: Jane. She poured her heart

out to her friend, fully expecting to confess, be roundly casti-
gated, and feel anguished contrition.

Instead, Janie listened carefully and gave her a hug.

"Darlin', I know it's hard. But life is never fair, and sucks
Scotch eggs more often than it rewards with sconcs and tea. It's
not first come, first served in love. It's who you love most, and
who is willing to love you the most in return."

Jane's practical terms put things in a different light. For while
Peter was ignoring her, Pierce was not. Even on the days she'd
felt most wretched about Peter, she hadn't been able to temper
her joy in Pierce's company.

She loved working with him on the set. She loved watching
him work with others. She loved his brilliant ideas, the even keel
he kept the production on, his ready laughter, and even the dark
temper that could remedy things some claimed unfixable.

But she also loved the little things, like watching him walk
through doorways. He was so tall—almost six foot four—that
his form filled the doorframe. Her mind loved his genius; her
body couldn't get over the fact that this great handsome bear of
a man, the very model of masculine virility, had chosen her.

They kept their relationship strictly low profile. They let their
guard down only at night when they met in one of their hotel
rooms. Pierce and Gray worked into the night so often they'd
long had their dinners sent up; Anastasia started having hers
sent up as well. Gray, Peter, and Jane were the only ones who
knew Pierce and Anastasia were in love.

One night after she'd left Pierce's room so he and the producer could continue their meeting, she overheard Gray warning
Pierce about letting news of their relationship get out. The gist of
his argument was Anastasia's age. Yes, he, Gray, understood how
mature Anastasia was, but it would take a lot of explaining to the
outside world. He urged circumspection. Frankly, Anastasia and

Pierce were happy to comply.

The bond between them flourished. At night, they'd discuss the day's work. Pierce's observations always made her laugh. He would talk through script problems with her, or shooting dilemmas, and often she would say something that would help redirect his thinking. If he was working late, Anastasia would crawl into her own bed and go to sleep, knowing Pierce would join her when he could, putting a protective arm around her, nuzzling her neck, giving a deep sigh of satisfaction before he, too, succumbed to his exhaustion.

The day she had her confrontation with Peter, Pierce held her. He told her she had to make a final decision between them, and once she had, she couldn't look back. It wasn't fair to either man. He understood her guilt, he said, but she had to get past it. She was the joy of his life. He had no intention of letting her go because of the rocky timing of the beginning of their love.

"I've learned what a rare and special thing it is to feel about someone the way I feel about you," he said. "And by God, I'm ready to fight for it."

Those were heady, powerful words from a man like Pierce Hall. And they would have been even if Peter had not made a complete surrender.

As July gave way to August, they entered what Pierce called "hell weeks" as they came to some of the most complex scenes of the film. These included scenes where Isolde is brought to be burned at the stake, where she is welcomed back as queen by the people of Cornwall, where Tristan slays the Morholt and is hailed as a hero, and where, with Tristan at her side in disguise, Isolde faces the Ordeal by Fire before King Arthur.

There were suddenly hundreds of extras around, all in period costume. It gave a different energy to the set, and brought a high level of excitement.

It felt as if they were working around the clock. The logistics of hundreds of people and dozens of horses kept Pierce up late doing a last check to be certain every detail was in place for the next day's shoot, before meeting until the wee hours with Milos and the assistant director. Even when he couldn't come to her bed, he'd awaken her the next morning with a kiss and a hot cup of tea.

All of it was leading up to the Ordeal by Fire, which was the longest and most complex series of scenes of the hell weeks. In it, Isolde has to prove her innocence by carrying a hot iron from the fire in the presence of King Mark, King Arthur, and knights and people of the realm. Tristan meets her there, disguised as a beggarly pilgrim, and is pressed into service to carry the queen from boat to land, stumbling as he does. This allows Isolde to truthfully swear before the kings, "By all the holy things of earth, I swear that no man born of woman has held me in his arms, saving King Mark, my lord, and that poor pilgrim who only now took a fall."

Two days before that sequence of scenes, the production manager changed the shooting schedule. The scenes in which Tristan appeared as the pilgrim would be shot first. Schedule changes were not unusual. No one gave it any thought.

The scenes went well. Peter treated Anastasia with professional courtesy. In return, she skipped lunch as a token gesture to make herself a bit lighter to carry.

When the scenes were completed, Gray and Pierce approached Peter together and asked if they could have a word with him in private after he'd changed. Anastasia overheard this and watched as Peter returned in jeans and T-shirt to the caravan that housed Pierce's office and dressing room. The director signaled the producer that he wanted to talk to Peter alone, and Gray nodded his assent.

Anastasia's confusion only increased when, less than five minutes later, Peter exited the caravan, head hung, looking up only to locate the driver of a dark blue sedan whom Pierce motioned over. The driver followed Peter back to his caravan. After less than five minutes gone again, Peter exited and wordlessly handed the driver his shoulder bag. They walked together to the car and drove away.

Anastasia knocked on the door of Pierce's caravan, determined to catch him before anyone else demanded his attention. She found him sitting inside at the table, a cluster of handwritten notes around him. He had no time to shilly-shally when he was working, so she got straight to the point.

"What was that about?"

He stopped what he was doing and turned his full attention to her. "Bad news, I'm afraid. Peter's sister died."

"Oh, dear God," she breathed. "Not Alice!"

"Yes," said Pierce. "I'm afraid so."

Anastasia stumbled back onto the built-in vinyl bench opposite Pierce's table. "Dear God. Dear God," she kept repeating. It broke her heart that Alice had died, and Peter had been left alone when by rights he should have been able to come to her. She should have been able to comfort him. They should have wept together. They should have gone together to the funeral.

Instead, she had abandoned him in his hour of need.

And Alice was dead. Cheerful, original Alice. Anastasia had loved her. Yet she and Peter were each facing her death alone.

"So, Peter's gone?" she asked. "He's already left for the funeral?"

"He's gone for a couple of days," said Pierce.

"When did she die?" Anastasia asked.

"Tuesday."

"And when is the funeral?" She planned to go, even if it meant missing a day of filming.

Pierce stretched out his long legs and studied his shoes sadly. "The funeral was this morning."

She stared at him, uncomprehending. "The funeral was this morning, and no one called till now?"

"Peter's father called the day she died," Pierce answered. "But he understood Peter was working."

Anastasia leapt to her feet. "You knew? You've known for three days? And you didn't say anything?"

"Peter's father hoped they could hold off the service until Saturday. But something about the bishop's schedule . . . I told them about the complex scenes we were shooting. I offered to tell Peter if they wanted me to. They finally left it up to me. It was a difficult decision," he said softly.

"You purposefully didn't tell Peter? And you didn't tell me? I thought we were honest with each other. I thought we trusted each other. I trusted you! And you kept something like this from me. Who do you think you are, God? Or do you think I'm such a child—Peter's such a child—that you have to edit the world for us?"

"Alice's death is a very sad thing. I understand that you're upset. I know you were very fond of her."

"Yes, I'm upset!" she yelled, eyes blazing. "Yes, I loved Alice. But I'm talking about betrayal of trust. Even someone with an ego as big as yours doesn't get to go around treating people like this! Dear God! His sister's funeral!"

She stormed out of the caravan, banging the door closed behind her. She knew she was causing a scene, but she didn't care. She was furious.

She was also done for the day. Even if she hadn't been, she would have gone straight back to the hotel and locked herself into her room. There, she wept tears of sorrow for Alice, for Peter, for his parents. She wept tears of outrage that her relationship with Pierce Hall had ended so badly. He'd certainly shown his true colors—unfortunately, after she'd chosen the wrong man. Her punishment for this was severe: not being with Peter during the hardest time of his life.

She had never been so sad or so sorry—or so angry.

In rebellion, after her five o'clock wake-up call the next morning, she rolled over and went back to sleep.

She didn't awaken until a panicked production manager rang her room saying they were all on the set, ready to go, where was she?

"Sorry," she said laconically, "I must have overslept."

"But everything's set up! Everyone's waiting!" the hapless woman repeated.

"Then send a car back," Anastasia said calmly, and hung up. She rang the restaurant downstairs and asked them to send up tea and biscuits. Then she showered at a leisurely pace.

That morning's scene was the smallest of the sequences. It was the medium shots of the immediate group surrounding Isolde during the Ordeal by Fire: King Mark, King Arthur, Gawain, Kay, Andret. Pierce had brought in important actors to play the Arthurian crowd. Actors of a caliber such that in ordinary times Anastasia would have gone out of her way to make certain they would think her a consummate pro. But today she didn't care. In fact, she hoped they'd ask someone why Anastasia Day was so angry with Pierce Hall. Certainly they'd understand her moral outrage.

She made the driver of the unit car wait as she took her sweet time getting dressed. Once on the set, she added as much time as she could with hair and makeup. It only amused her as Jane and the others raced about. As she walked to her own caravan to put on her costume, she did feel a pang for the crew who had been set up for so long waiting for her. She considered many of them friends and would ordinarily never have caused them grief. To her mind, they were innocent victims in this war of wills.

She fought all attempts by her dresser to hurry her along. By the time Leah came to plead with her to come to the set, she'd kept everyone waiting nearly two hours.

She'd never acted like a prima donna before, and considered this not bad for a beginner.

As she walked onto the set she felt the chilly silence surrounding both cast and crew.

"All right, everyone, let's go," said the assistant director.

Camera, sound, and lighting people slowly swung into action. Makeup people checked the actors who'd been sitting on canvas chairs talking or doing crossword puzzles. The famous actors who were in for the day re-emerged from their caravans.

And Pierce, in costume as King Mark, walked across the island set in front of the newly created forge and the dolly tracks toward Stacy where she stood, a defiant stare awaiting him.

He grabbed her right arm with his left hand and in the other scooped up a canvas stool without breaking his stride. He was so much larger than she that she felt she would have been pulled along by his wake even if he didn't have her in a vise grip. She had to trot alongside him to keep her arm from being wrenched from its socket. Well, he was never one for the slow boil. They might as well have it out now.

Activity hadn't stopped, but she was aware that all eyes were on them as he pulled around the back of a production truck. Once out of sight of the others, Pierce set the stool down firmly and yanked her close enough that he could speak in a quiet voice, colored by controlled rage.

"By God," he said, "if you're going to act like a child, you're going to be treated like one."

Before she could protest, he sat down on the stool and pulled her firmly facedown over his lap. Her outrage struggled with her pride as she fought to free herself without making noise that could be heard on the other side of the truck. For she knew that everyone's attention was focused their way. She was furious, and she was mortified.

He deftly tossed her queen's robe over her shoulder and folded her gown up, leaving her covered only by the light sleeveless shift in which she would play most of the scene.

Then he gave her the first spanking of her life. His hand was so large and strong, the blows so stinging, it was all she could humanly do not to cry out. She knew that even if the waiting assembly couldn't see what was happening, they could wager a pretty good guess. That hurt more than each deliberate smack on her bottom. Pierce stopped at ten. He'd made his point.

Not daring to let her go, he stood her up, took her by the wrist, and led her back. Business resumed at once.

"Hair!" Pierce called. "Makeup!" and he sat Anastasia in her chair, causing a grimace she couldn't help. The requested people were quickly around her, and Pierce headed off, calling, "Places for run-through!"

There was an outbreak of chatter as everything moved into final position. The crew was avoiding eye contact with each other, attempting to keep straight faces. But their anger was gone, and spirits were lighter. Anastasia sat, jaw locked, wishing she could melt into the ground.

But the morning's drama wasn't over. The fire was restoked under the two crosses: the real one of iron, which glowed red-hot, which Isolde would supposedly carry to Arthur in her bare hands; and the prop cross of plastic tucked on a hidden ledge well away from the flame, which the blacksmith would actually pick up with his tongs and hand her.

The setup was simple. She was to accept the cross from the forger, carry it nine steps toward King Mark, fling it away, hold up her unblemished hands for all to see, and kneel at the feet of her husband—although kneeling in humility before Pierce was going to take all the acting ability she had.

The first take started well. A trained blacksmith was playing the forger. Whatever he lacked in swarth had been supplied by the makeup department. But as he grimly offered the dignified queen her cross, a loud "No!" tore across the set.

Anastasia, trained to stop at no voice but the director's, extended her hands.

"Stop!" the voice cried. Anastasia looked up to see Richie Riley, in civilian clothes, rushing into the shot.

"Cut," called Pierce.

Richie stepped between Anastasia and the forger and said simply, "It's the iron cross. He's got the real one!"

"No, I took it from the ledge, as we rehearsed!" the blacksmith protested. As proof, he pulled the tongs back and grabbed the cross himself.

"Bloody hell!" he yelped, dropping the tongs and waving his fingers gingerly.

Pierce, the blacksmith, Anastasia, and Richie were the first to reach the stone kiln. There, still glowing hot on the embers, was the iron cross, where the camera had caught it moments ago.

It took only seconds for them to realize there were two iron crosses. Someone had removed the safe cross from the shelf and replaced it with one of iron that had been very recently removed from the fire.

"Here—" said Richie, and he stooped down into the tall grass to pick up the missing false cross.

Pierce lowered his voice and asked the blacksmith, "Who was near the kiln before the take?"

The man stammered, "No one. Everyone. I don't know. I didn't see anything."

"All right," Pierce said. "Are your fingers badly burned?"

"No," said the day player. "That's one thing to be said for my line of work. I'm well calloused."

"Then we've lost enough time. Props, let's reset. Places, everyone!"

He didn't even look at Anastasia, who was more shaken than she cared to admit. She opened and closed her smooth palms several times, trying not to imagine the agonizing consequences of the switched props. She never thought she'd be glad for Richie's return, but she was.

However, after the scene was completed, she had to look hard to find him. She wondered with embarrassment if he'd witnessed her earlier comeuppance.

Anastasia found the American sitting on the back steps of the wardrobe caravan, where he'd been fitted for Kaherdin's costume for the next day's arrival at King Mark's court. He looked older than she remembered.

"Hi," said Anastasia, purposefully slipping back into her American accent. She stood in front of him. He looked up at her, squinting at the sun, which cascaded from behind her shoulders.

"I wanted to say thanks," she said, unconsciously rubbing her hands together. "How could you tell the blacksmith had an iron cross?"

"I saw it steaming," he said.

"Oh. Well. Thanks again."

Richie didn't reply, and feeling a foolish teenager, she turned away. She'd only taken a couple of steps when he said, "Stacy."

She turned back.

"You could have told me."

"Told you?"

"That you were seeing Peter."

"Oh. We didn't tell anybody at first. It wasn't only you."

"It was only me making a spectacle of myself pursuing you."

"Sorry," she said, "I never meant . . ."

"I know," he said.

"Okay." That ended the awkward exchange and she started away.

"I'm sorry," he said, stopping her again.

"What?" she asked.

He waited for a gaggle of extras to pass by.

"I'm sorry I slapped you. Never slapped anyone before. Never threw myself at anyone's bosom before, either."

"Forgiven."

"Friends?" Richie asked.

She nodded.

"So. Are you and Peter still . . . ?"

"No."

"Oh. Sorry. No, actually, I'm not."

She smiled.

"Dinner, then?" he asked.

She looked at him. He looked like a normal, albeit extremely handsome, university chap. There was no trace of the frightening malevolence she'd seen the last time they'd spoken.

Then Richie smiled, and his eyes twinkled. "Come on," he urged. "It seems a fitting token for saving your virgin hands from burns, blisters, pus, the stench of searing skin . . ."

"All right, all right," Anastasia laughed. "But please stop!"

"I'll find you after the day's shoot. Which might, unfortunately, go long. I've heard there was a late start."

Heat prickled Anastasia's cheeks. She might never live this down.

Oh, how she hated Pierce Hall.

She got through the rest of the day, and even enjoyed working with the Arthurian actors. The unit was able to pick up time and complete the afternoon's schedule, which included scores of extras.

Garrett, as the villainous Andret, was in virtually all the

shots. Anastasia stayed close to him between takes. He teased her mercilessly about the morning's events, then let the subject drop and treated her normally—for Garrett. On his and Bruce's suggestion, the cast and crew took up a collection to send as a contribution in Alice's honor to the charity of the Daltons' choice. Anastasia was touched by the generous outpouring of love and giving by virtually everyone. She hoped Peter would be, too.

After the final scene of the day, she pulled herself up to the third-floor landing of the hotel, visualizing nothing but the imminence of warm bathwater encasing her. She was startled when the door to Pierce's room opened and Gray Eddington looked out.

"Ah, Anastasia," he said, and beckoned her inside. If it had been Pierce, she would have kept walking, but she did not have the wherewithal to be impudent to the producer. A cold ball of dread dropped inside her, and she hoped she wasn't about to face the disapproval of both men together.

But once she stepped into Pierce's room, Gray nodded to her, then to Pierce. "Night, then. See you in the morning."

And he was out the door.

Pierce was in jeans and a denim shirt, papers spread out where he and Gray had been working. Pierce was perhaps the most direct person she'd ever met. No one went through life with unresolved issues between himself or herself and Pierce. They might resolve to mutual dislike, but not for lack of having it out.

All right, she thought. *If he can face up to this right now, so can I.*

He stacked his papers and stood, taking a step closer to her. He didn't seem combative, but he did seem concerned.

"I understand you're angry," he said. "But you'd kept all those people waiting, and they needed to feel like the score was settled. At least I took you behind the truck. It hurt your pride more than your bum. But it improved everyone else's mood considerably."

She hadn't expected an explanation. It didn't wash as an apology, if that's what it was supposed to be.

"Do you really think that's the main reason I'm angry with you?"

"If not, perhaps you'll enlighten me."

"Alice died!" Anastasia screamed. "She died, and you didn't have the decency to let Peter know!"

"That's it, isn't it?" Pierce sighed. "It was a hard decision to make."

"You know how much Peter loved her!"

"Yes. But she was already dead when their father called. It wasn't as if I kept him from a final good-bye."

The clouds didn't lift from her face.

"Stacy, think. Think about what we were filming for the last week. How many actors, extras, and sets were involved. Do you think Peter could have done what he did if he knew about Alice? Would it have been fair to even ask it of him?

"Rescheduling this particular week of shooting would have cost hundreds of thousands of pounds. And, when Peter comes back, would he have been up to doing these very emotional scenes in front of hundreds of extras? Getting those scenes in the can now means he'll have a much gentler re-entry when he returns."

"You have the nerve to tell me you didn't tell Peter about his sister's funeral for his own sake? At least be honest. Admit that all you think about is your blasted movie!"

Pierce strode across the room to her, but she turned away. He grabbed her shoulders and turned her to face him. "Listen to me. Listen. There are millions of pounds entrusted to me. And the careers of dozens of people. If this film goes over budget, if they close us down, it's on my head. No. I don't think you do understand. If I'd told Peter and he'd gone to the funeral, and he'd lost it, and we'd lost him, we'd be in serious trouble—and Alice Dalton would still be dead. That's the bottom line. I didn't kill her, Anastasia. She's dead no matter what."

"You're a coldhearted beast."

He stared at her, trying to read her thoughts, to find some way in. "All right," he said. "I can see that you're angry, and I admit that it's partially justified. What I did was calculated, even hurtful. I take responsibility for it. I don't say I wouldn't do it again, but I admit you've a right to be angry. Just not in an open-ended, long-suffering manner. If you're mad at me, punish me and have done with it."

She stood, arms crossed, watching him.

He took off his belt, folded it, and offered it to her.

"Are you serious?" she asked.

"Fair's fair," he said.

"I'm just mad enough to do it," she hissed.

He flicked his wrist, offering her the belt one more time.

She stepped forward and took it. "Take down your jeans," she said. She cracked the leather against her opposite hand, to get the feel for it. Pierce unzipped his denims and pushed them from the confines of his hips.

"Turn around," she said. "And drop your briefs as well."

"Blimey, the girl's serious," he muttered, sounding fairly alarmed. But he did as he was told.

"Bend over."

He bent over the bed, steadying himself with his palms on the mattress.

And Anastasia proceeded to whale the tar out of Pierce Hall.

"Anastasia, please!" he finally cried. "Don't you think—aah!—that's enough?"

"I wasn't sure until just now that you—" she threw her arm

back, stepped forward, and delivered the three hardest strokes yet, "were really sorry."

"I'm sorry," he said. "I'm really sorry!"

And he collapsed, breathing hard, eyes watering, onto the bed. He lay there for a few minutes, waiting for his senses to stop reeling. When he'd recovered enough to turn his head, he saw her collapsed onto his overstuffed chair, belt on the floor beneath her hand.

"I didn't know I'd hurt you that much," he said.

"The last three were for Peter."

He lay for a few minutes before standing carefully and gingerly pulling his briefs back around his hips. "Blimey." He stood for a moment, his chest still rising and falling as he attempted to regulate his breathing. "Feel better?" he asked.

"Actually, yes. A bit."

"Look," he said then. "I know you feel bad for Peter about his sister. I do, too. But don't waste your time pitying him because he's lost the only girlfriend he'll ever have. I have it on good authority that he's been having a jolly time of it schtupping the nurse."

Her jaw dropped. "Nurse Robbins?"

"I wouldn't make this up."

Was the world nothing like she'd imagined it?

"Do you have anything to drink?" she asked.

"MAY I WARM YOU?" the willowy woman asked, china teapot poised above Anastasia's cup.

She smiled in return but put her hand over the mouth of the cup. "No, but thank you. It's lovely. And so kind of you to see me after all these years."

"We're only sorry it's been so long," responded her husband.

Anastasia was sitting in the impeccably appointed parlor of the vicarage of Andrew and Sarah Dalton. It was twenty kilometers from their former home, in a larger, more well-to-do parish. Sarah had taken great care in the decorating: the carpets, wallpapers, and furniture were chosen just so. Still, Anastasia would call it "careful" rather than "cozy." The kind of elegance-on-a-budget one crafted when one had no children mucking about.

It hadn't been difficult to locate the Daltons. One call to the office of their former parish had accomplished it. She'd then rung the new office of the Reverend Dalton and been invited to come straightaway.

Bruce had helped her with auto hire, and she'd driven alone all the way from London. Anastasia found she actually enjoyed car travel; it was as though she were anonymous, in her own little bubble. During the trip, she'd turned off her mind to the present, filtering out everything but memories and the knowledge that a murderer needed to be caught.

Yet the scene that kept replaying in her mind as she drove was one she hadn't reported to Bruce. After the horror of finding the dead dove, the murderer's calling card, only feet from where they'd slept, Anastasia retreated to the Huntington family flat in London. From there, she'd rung Scotland Yard. It was astonishing how quickly Inspector Irving came round. A short, square fellow, introduced as Inspector Raymond, accompanied him.

Her Grace showed them the talking clock, which Irving confiscated. She told him of the bird. She described both the dove incident and the fire on the set of *Tristan and Isolde*. Irving had asked her previously about her relationships with the decedents, and had been happy with specific versions of *I made a movie with them*. She expected more questions along the same lines. So she was taken aback when he leaned forward in his chair and asked, "How well do you know Mr. Amerman?"

"Good heavens. You're not still flogging that theory, surely?" she exploded.

"Excuse me, Your Grace, but according to your own statement, he was last seen sleeping within feet of this dead bird. He was present on the film set where all this started. His work takes him frequently to Los Angeles. He recently took a fatal outing to France, and he felicitously lost a hostile wife who was suing him for a large settlement. We'd be foolish not to notice such a string of coincidences, wouldn't you say?"

The Duchess of Esmonde picked up her orange drink, clutching the cut crystal of the glass forcefully. "I've told you that the murderer recently intruded on Leah Hall in California at the same time that I was talking to Bruce on the telephone. He was clearly thousands of miles from the scene of the attack."

"Who rang who during this conversation, Your Grace?"

"Sorry?"

"Did you ring Mr. Amerman, or the other way round?"

"Why—he rang me."

"And how do you know he was calling from London, not Los Angeles?"

"He told me."

"Ah. And you believed him."

"Of course! And—he was home when I rang him."

"When was that? That you rang him?"

"The next day."

"Just so. Not quite out of the woods yet, are we?"

The tall, thin man sat so calmly in one of Neville's carved chairs, twisting things so perversely that she wanted to scream. His crony Raymond sat silent as death.

"And his wife, Elise Amerman. When was the last time you saw her?"

"Elise? She's at her sister's. Has been since last time you were at the Amermans'."

"You haven't seen her since?"

"No. I'm sure her sister can vouch—"

"No doubt."

"What are you suggesting? That they're acting in collusion?" Her voice was rising. She was sure the London housekeeper would be reporting this particular meeting to Geoff. The unsavory drama that comes with letting an actress marry into the family!

"I'm not suggesting anything at this time. Your Grace, I realize where your loyalties lie in this situation. But please, answer me this. Has Mr. Amerman ever said anything that would lead you to suspect he had any grudges—or strong emotions of any stripe—for the decedents? Or against the missing Nicola Neve, or Peter Dalton? Would he have any reason to want to take extreme measures to get someone's attention?"

"No!" she answered. "No! We were all friends, good friends. You're wasting valuable time! Can't you see that?" She was starting to panic. This was the opposite of what she'd thought would happen.

Irving stood, his hat in his hand. "I see that I'm upsetting you. Is there any other information you have? Anything else you think might be of help?"

Anastasia stood as well, stretching to her full duchess-height. "No, Inspector. But I implore you to investigate all avenues open. A great many lives may depend on it. If I was ever sure of anything, I'm sure that Bruce Amerman is not a killer."

"Just so. In that case, my final question is this. Why did you call me here without telling Mr. Amerman you were doing so? And why didn't you show him the clock?"

Anastasia should have anticipated the question, should have had a ready answer. Instead she stood, momentarily adrift.

"Just so," said Irving. He bowed. "Thank you for your time."

That meeting and her attendant fury had compelled her to find the Daltons, then propelled her into an auto—and headed back toward the moors.

She hadn't let herself stop, except once for petrol, and then she didn't dare get out of the car. The open road and the unknown people were too much for her. She was terrified she was going to be overcome at any moment with no one to help her and no safe place to hide. So she'd driven, urging her car to fly straight to the Daltons. She was determined to find out what had become of Peter; determined to discover if he had any information that might help them stop this ghastly rampage.

After the Daltons had welcomed her and they'd taken tea in the parlor, Sarah stood. "I'm sorry to run off, but I'm the head of the Ladies' Guild and we've been planning our auction all year," she said. "But if you'll be staying the night—and I'm sure Andrew will insist—we shall have more time to visit this evening. Please excuse me," Sarah said.

"Of course," replied Anastasia. Sarah had aged. Her hair was a soft silver. Andrew Dalton still had the high cheekbones—even more pronounced since he'd shaved his beard—and large, round eyes that had been the trademarks of the movie star Peter Dalton. His face was thinner now, his thick hair also streaked with white. But they were still a very handsome couple.

"She seems . . . almost serene," Anastasia said as Sarah exited the kitchen door and appeared rounding the house on the path to the street.

"Yes," said Andrew. "The combination of a life of faith—and having nothing left to lose."

The guest was again surprised by his candor.

"I seem to recall that in our last parish, you enjoyed strolling the churchyard," he went on. "I think you might find this one lovely as well. Care to join me for a walk?"

That was all it took. The great cloud that had chased her from London took control, taunting her as it began to engulf her.

The vicar offered a hand. How could he not hear the rasping of her breath? Her chest was constricting, and the pain shot out in all directions. How foolish she'd been! Thinking she could drive up here like a normal person. And now she was going to die here. Embarrassing, but poetic justice.

Andrew had gotten her up and was guiding her by the elbow toward the front door. She knew she would be dead, actually dead, if she set foot out that door. The enormity of the vortex outside, the sucking whirlwind it created, caused her to cry out. She was no longer aware of who was with her. She collapsed onto the mat on the inside of the door, holding her chest, great sobs wrenching from the center of her being.

She was completely humiliated. She didn't want to die here, like this. The hot pains in her chest intensified as she fought to pull life-sustaining air into her lungs. It wouldn't come.

Anastasia gave herself over to the engulfing darkness.

Finally, little by little, the world began to come into focus, an inch at a time. She found herself on a single bed. She let her fingers explore the cool sheets beneath her. They were decorated with small sprigs of flowers. Thank God. That meant she wasn't in hospital.

She closed her eyes briefly, and opened them again to find Andrew Dalton sitting in a chair beside her bed. He'd taken off his jacket and undone his clerical collar. His comforting demeanor was now one of father rather than priest.

He reached over and gently turned the cold compress that lay across her forehead.

"How long since I fell?" she asked wearily.

"Only about twenty minutes. How long have you been having panic attacks?" he asked in return.

"Years," she whispered. "Decades."

"Dear child," he responded. There was genuine sympathy in his voice.

"I'm very sorry," said Anastasia. "Mortified, actually."

"No need," he answered. "In fact, you mustn't be. It only increases their hold on you."

"What?" she asked, pulling herself up to sit against the white iron headboard.

"That's the irony. Panic attacks are much worse if they cause you to panic. You feel one coming on, and you panic, and that feeds it. There's a gentleman in my church who suffers from the syndrome, so I've been doing some research."

"How on earth do you not panic?"

"That's the rub. When the symptoms start—say, shortness of breath, nausea, chest pains, instead of thinking, 'I'm out of control' or even 'I'm dying,' you take control of your inner dialogue. You tell yourself, 'I'm having a panic attack, and while it's unpleasant, I've had them before. I know it will last about twenty minutes, and it's not going to do me any lasting harm. I've ridden them out before, I can do it again."

"Really? Does it work?"

"Over time. It's not an easy thing to train yourself to do."

"But the attacks are so . . . mortifying. And you never know when it's going to hit you. With my luck, it's in public. Or with someone I want to think well of me."

"And your defense is to think, 'So what?' Who cares who sees you? Who cares what they think? First of all, most people are understanding of weakness in others, as we've all got some thorn in our flesh. Secondly, what other people think doesn't matter. It can't govern your life."

"That's easy to say," Stacy answered.

"Exactly," the Reverend Dalton said. "And very difficult to do. Which is why you need to get help in how to do it. And Stacy, you do need to get help. There's no reason to go on living like this. You don't deserve it. Nobody does. Now, I'm going to be the vicar for a minute, so bear with me. First, you see a medical doctor, to rule out any physical problems. Then you find someone who specializes in acute panic disorder, and you work through it. You probably feel like you're alone in this, but it's actually very common. And so are its causes. We know you grew up in an environment which gave you an acute need to be in control to survive. Agoraphobia is actually an elaborate coping device—but a pretty shitty one. Pardon my French."

"It's shitty, all right. I've never thought I was strong enough to fight it."

"You can," he said. "God doesn't mean for any of his children to be emotionally crippled. He'll help you past it. I guarantee it. Vicar's word."

She gave a wry smile. "I feel so foolish."

"I know all about coping techniques, believe me," he said. "Last time you visited, we had two children. Now we have none."

"Oh, Reverend Dalton," she cried, "I am so very sorry! And I'm sorry I haven't visited before now."

"Am I correct in guessing that you're carrying some baggage about Alice's death, or about Peter? If that's true, let's mutually have out with it, shall we?"

"I've always felt bad I wasn't able to comfort Peter," Anastasia blurted. "That he wasn't able to go to the funeral. We'd broken up before she died, and I've felt so guilty."

"I've got you beat on this one," Andrew said. "You see, if I'd admitted to myself what was happening during Alice's final illness, I could have called Peter home to see her while she was still alive. But I kept telling myself she'd been that bad before and had lived through it. I denied my little girl was dying until she was gone. I let her go without seeing her brother again. After that, it didn't seem to matter much if Peter was at her funeral or not. I told Mr. Hall to use his own best judgment. Alice wouldn't be at her funeral, after all, so what was the point?"

Anastasia digested this information. "So it wasn't that Pierce refused to tell him?"

"No, no. He was very sympathetic. Rang us every night till Peter came home, to see if I'd changed my mind."

"Have you regretted not insisting that Peter be home for the funeral?"

"I wondered if I would. But no. I haven't. It finally seemed foolish to me. Yes, it's nice to have neat endings, but Peter and Alice knew full well what they meant to each other. They had Alice's lifetime of loving each other. The fact that Peter was away when she died couldn't diminish that. Or at any rate, there was no reason it needed to."

"Reverend Dalton—"

"Andrew."

"Andrew, I have to ask. Do you know where Peter is?"

He shook his head. "No. We don't. And I'll tell you confidentially, before Sarah gets home, that leaves an open wound that aches far more than the fact of Alice's death. We've never been able to grieve for our son and move on, you see."

"Many people feel that way about him," Anastasia replied.

"I know," he said.

He turned to look out one of the two windows that fit into the rounded wall that formed the front of the vicarage. Old-fashioned beige venetian blinds hung in each. It was twilight. Sarah would be home soon to start supper.

For the first time, Anastasia knew she had to entertain the

possibility that Peter was dead. It was impossible not to remember his passion for goodness. No matter what kind of trouble he'd gotten himself into, he was a kind soul. She didn't believe he would let his parents suffer like this if he could help it.

Andrew had pulled his focus back into the room. "You and I tend to get to the point with each other," he said. "So tell me, how is your mother?"

"She's dead," the young woman answered simply. "I got a telegram five years ago saying she'd died of malaria in India. She'd joined a sect and moved over there. I never saw her again. I guess that's made it hard for me to accept that she's really gone. To close that door and move on."

"I'm sorry. That's very sad." He took her hand. "And you were married?"

"Yes," Anastasia answered. "My husband died last year. October."

"Dear child," he said. "It's amazing you've held up as well as you have. You have my profound admiration."

"Oh, no," Anastasia protested. "I've not done half so well as you. You're still so kind. And hopeful."

"If I am, it's because I've prayed to be able to recognize the grace in my life. Tragedy is common, but the grace that comes with it is always so much wider and deeper."

"Do you really believe that?" she asked.

"Absolutely," he responded. "I've lived it."

"Andrew? Are you home? Is Stacy still here?" They heard the door open downstairs, and Sarah's tread across the foyer.

"Yes, dear. She's resting. Let me come and help with dinner," the vicar replied.

"Let me wash up," Anastasia said. "I'd like to help, too."

"Lovely," said Andrew. "Whenever you're ready. It'll be nice to have an old friend in the kitchen." He gave a wink and headed out the door.

FRAGRANT PINK BUDS STOOD in relief to the light blue sky above their heads. It had been a muted afternoon, but little wonder. Their picnic had taken place in the cemetery in Helmsley, at Alice's grave.

When they'd told her today was Alice's birthday, Anastasia had stayed to join their annual pilgrimage. The Daltons treated her as if she were a daughter. She suspected they all wondered what it might have been like if life had taken a different path. She never mentioned the murders to them. It seemed an unnecessarily cruel coda to the losses they'd already suffered.

"So we'll be packing up, then," Sarah said. "Thank you for coming. It made this year special."

"It was an honor," their guest replied.

"Do you want to walk out with us?" Sarah asked. Anastasia had followed the Daltons to Helmsley in her rental car so she could head back to Bruce's from there.

"If you don't mind, I'll sit a minute, get myself centered for the trip."

The three hugged, and the Daltons turned together toward the cemetery gate in the distance.

Anastasia leaned back against Alice's tombstone. The top was carved into the shape of a benevolent angel, which looked over a picture of Alice etched into the stone. Anastasia was glad they'd included the photo. Much of Alice's beauty and some of her vitality came through in the portrait. She still clearly remembered how matter-of-factly Alice had reported that she'd be buried here. Somehow she'd been able to accept her own death, while it had caused no end of grief and trouble in the lives of so many others.

The cemetery closed at six o'clock. It must be nearing that now. Much of her drive would be made in the dark, but that was preferable. It would seem like her auto was traveling in its own little box.

She stood up—and as she did, a man's scream rent the air behind her.

She spun around to find a short, thin, bespectacled man standing not a meter away. He looked as if he'd seen a ghost.

"Ho!" he said. "I had no idea—that is, I didn't think anyone else was here!"

"Sorry to startle you," Anastasia said.

"My," he said, leaning the rose plant he carried against the gravestone. "My, my."

"Will you be all right?" she asked.

"In a moment. I've got to pull myself together. They're waiting for me to come out to close the gates."

The gentleman was in his fifties, with thinning hair rimming a bald crescent topside.

"It's a beautiful plant," Anastasia said. "Is it for Alice Dalton's grave?"

"Yes. That's right. Every year the same order—a plant of yellow tea roses. We don't usually carry them, but since it happens every year, I know to order them. And a lovely specimen this year."

"Someone sends them every year? How thoughtful."

"Yes. Always with the instructions that they're to be delivered at closing time. Doesn't want anyone to know, is my guess. A private thing."

"May I see the card?" Anastasia asked, snatching it before the florist could object.

For my Angel-Beans, was all it said.

"Someone comes into your shop every year to order this?" she asked, forcing herself to remain calm.

"No, no. Comes over the wire. Quite anonymous. Same every year."

Dear God, thank you. Thank you, thank you, she thought.

"It's a beautiful plant," she said enthusiastically. "I'm sorry, what's the name of your shop? I'd certainly like to know where to get such quality in the future."

It worked. The little man blossomed like the tea roses.

Anastasia took his arm as they headed together for the exit.

CHAPTER 10

From the London Tatler, August 4, 1990:

Word comes to us that there's quite a bit of real-life lust on the set of Pierce Hall's new film, Tristan and Isolde. The cat's out of the bag about the passion between Peter Dalton and Anastasia Day, the young lovers who play the young lovers. It seems Dalton stole Day's affections from an American actor, Richard Riley (early photo shoots show a blissful Riley and Day). But wags on the set say Dalton, too, should watch his back . . . Seems when Peter's working, the lovely Anastasia's been spending a lot of time in the company of Garrett Clifton, who plays the villain.

Does the hero always win? Stay tuned. . . .

The sun was so strong that it shone white-bright even through her closed eyelids. Anastasia smiled in mock annoyance and turned over onto her stomach, her hair swinging over her ears in braids, to let the warmth radiate across her back.

Life was just the damnedest thing.

She'd thought that the final day of principal photography for *Tristan and Isolde* would be the saddest of her life. Sure, she'd see various members of the cast and crew now and again in the studio for looping, or on other projects. But it wouldn't be the same.

The night before the final morning's shoot had been downright maudlin. They'd taken over the best restaurant in town, which happened to be the Lion's Head right there in the Red Lion. Almost everyone had gotten completely snockered—the exceptions being Pierce, Gray, and the assistant director, responsible to the end.

Yet even they were affected by the speeches, anecdotes, and ribald songs and sketches, coordinated, of course, by Garrett. Somehow in hindsight, the recent fire, Anastasia's late morning, and even the unfortunate doves were comic material. Peter participated fully, as raucous as anyone.

The only obvious absentee was Richie. Anastasia had asked the unit manager, who said Richie had been invited to the wrap party, but was in L.A., and hadn't even bothered to respond.

"What can you do?" asked the chap. "Richie's going to be famous, you know. Has to get on about it, I suppose."

Yet guilt did nag at her—as did the memory of his last stint on the set. The evening she and Pierce had reached their unexpected truce, Pierce had invited her to dinner with him and the revered actors who'd come in for the Arthurian scenes, gentlemen so famous even Anastasia had heard of them. The only thing that had rescued her from her acute embarrassment at those actors' witnessing of her prima donna–ism and its aftermath was the difficulty—that only she noticed—Pierce himself had sitting down.

It had been a lovely, memorable meal. By bedtime, Pierce had recovered enough to seal their reconciliation.

The next morning, the director was gone long before she'd awakened. She'd showered and dressed in her own room. When she opened the hall door to leave, softly humming one of Conan's pieces, half of a folded script page dropped to the carpet below.

She picked it up and turned it over.

Came to pick you up for dinner. Waited. Guess you had other plans.

The memory of it still caused the young woman to grimace. Richie purposefully avoided her that day. He did his scene and left.

And that was the last anyone had seen of Richie Riley.

The festivities ended before midnight as they did have a morning's shoot ahead of them.

Anastasia sat with Leah at the party. Peter had joined the Lost Boys' table, much to everyone's surprise. He'd returned from his visit home a changed person. For one thing, he'd stopped spending time with the boys. He disappeared as soon as he was dismissed from the set. No one knew where he went or what he did. He was friendly to his co-workers, but in an acquaintance kind of way rather than that of a comrade. He made it clear he would not welcome questions, and no one asked him any.

It was not unusual after his return to hear him being paged to the phone. His agent was obviously wheeling and dealing on his behalf. Whereas before he had been plain old Peter, they were now well aware that he was the rising star among them.

They all felt the loss, but none wished him ill.

Anastasia felt she'd lost Peter long ago. So she was surprised when he caught her in the hotel hallway as they were leaving the party.

"May I talk with you?" he asked.

They slipped down a deserted hall to the outside courtyard in the back of the hotel. It was quaint, paved with brick, a now stagnant fountain in the middle. It was late and the courtyard lights had long since been extinguished. Peter led her to a white concrete bench and they sat together side by side. Just the act of doing so made her melancholy.

"Where are you off to tomorrow?" he asked, and the unfamiliarity of his tone put her at ease. This wasn't her Peter. This was someone with whom she'd worked, being polite.

"Back to my flat, to try to put my life in order," she said. "How about you?"

"A day in London to meet with my agents. Then off to the States. Hollywood finally called loudly enough that I had to answer."

"Congratulations."

"Thanks. I'm a bit apprehensive. Don't know anyone in La-La Land. But I didn't used to know anyone outside of Hawnby. Have to make the leap sometime. Or so my agent tells me."

"I hope things go well for you," she said sincerely.

"And for you," he said.

She swallowed hard and gathered her courage. She didn't know when she'd see him again. "I'm—sorry if I've done anything to hurt you. It was never my intention."

"No, no," he said. "You haven't."

The lightness in his tone told her that whatever had existed between them was gone. As if it had never been.

And yet he surprised her in the next moment by bringing out a small box tied by piece of white ribbon.

"I wanted you to have this," he said simply.

The smallest tug untied the bow. The top of the gray box was hinged. And inside was a ring.

At first she thought of the ring of green jasper that Isolde gives Tristan as a seal of her love, so that anytime the ring is returned to her she knows its bearer is authentic and she will do his bidding.

But then she looked more closely in the darkened courtyard, and saw that it was an intricate Victorian design. It was jet jewelry, the kind they'd seen in Whitby. She looked up at Peter with brimming eyes.

"I thought you might like to have this," he said quietly. "To remember Alice by."

"Oh, I do wish to have it," she said. "Thank you very much!"

She'd been about to burst into tears then, in mourning for everything that was lost. But in that moment he leaned over and kissed her. It was a deep, hungry kiss, but it alarmed her. It wasn't a passionate Peter kiss born of sincere emotion, but the recreational kiss of a heady, handsome young man who enjoyed a conquest.

It sobered her immediately and she pushed him away. He looked at her with amusement.

"Good-bye, then," he said.

"Good-bye," she replied.

She let him leave first. "Alice," she said, clutching the ring box to her chest, "I don't know what's happened to your brother."

Anastasia was still melancholy as she climbed the stairs to her hotel room. She opened the door to find the lights ablaze and strains of a waltz coloring the air.

"Dance with me," said Pierce in his deep baritone voice.

"Dance with you?" she asked, but had no time to protest as he swept her into his arms and guided her across the floor, neatly skirting furniture as if they were weaving through a room full of other couples. He spun her and dipped her—*the wonderful things actors have to learn!* she thought. Following his lead required all her concentration, and she quickly forgot everything that had gone before in the emotional evening.

"It's hard to believe the shoot is finished—or will be in the morning," he said.

"Are you pleased with it?"

"How could I not be?" he asked, a large grin on his face. "It's a bloody masterpiece. If we don't screw it up in post. Which we won't."

His excitement was contagious and she tilted her head to look up at him.

"What I find hardest to believe," he said, "is how deeply I've fallen in love with you. Totally, helplessly in love."

"I bet you say that to all the girls," she protested.

"Nope," he said, happily. "You're the first. And, God willing, the last. Not to mention I could eat you up like you were a Black Forest torte."

As if to prove the point, he scooped her up and carried her to the bed, laying her down and kneeling over her, unbuttoning her blouse, kissing and caressing the skin of her neck, her sternum, her breasts.

"You know, I've been thinking," he said, lying lengthwise on his side next to her. "About how you're not sure it's right to make love when you're not married." He ran a light finger over her exposed flesh. "I've been causing you all sorts of guilt."

"I've—never been very good at what the rules are," she said. "No one ever explained them to me. Peter seemed to think—"

He put a hand over her mouth. "You don't know because you love it," he said.

"You've chosen an odd time to initiate a discussion of ethics," she answered.

"Here's the point," he said. "I want to make you happy, not guilty. Yet I certainly don't want to give up nights—and afternoons, and mornings—of wild, tumultuous lovemaking with you. So I was thinking. I'm taking two entire weeks off before we start post-production. If you have no plans, I thought perhaps a Greek island might be nice. And I thought as long as we were on a honeymoon, as it were, we might as well get married. That way I get you, you get a clear conscience, and we both get as much incredibly passionate sex as our bodies can stand."

She sat up so quickly that they bumped foreheads with an impressive whack, but she didn't even notice.

"What?" she said. "Did you just ask me to marry you?"

"Yes," he confirmed. "I have offered to make an honest woman of you. I love you, Anastasia. It would be a small ceremony at first. But at whatever time it seems appropriate to take our relationship public, we could have another—do the church, the gown, the horse-drawn carriage. Whatever you'd like."

"We've already done the huge throne-room wedding," she said, teasing. Then, "You've checked this out? We can be legally married in Greece?"

He threw back his head and laughed. "She's always the practical one. Yes, I've had the elves check it out. It would be totally legal."

Anastasia stared at him. She was overwhelmed. She was not used to making plans more than a day or a week ahead. This shoot was the longest commitment she'd ever made. And no one had ever made a commitment to her. Her father had died, her grandparents' support had come with strings attached, and her own mother, who'd never promised to be there for her, certainly wasn't. She hadn't dared to think about a relationship with anyone, even Pierce, beyond the blissful present.

"Here's the most important question," he said. "Do you love me?"

Did she love him? He'd brought her the most wonderful, the most unwavering relationship she'd ever known. Did she love him? Yes. Completely.

Did that mean she had any clue as to how to make a lifelong commitment?

She wanted to.

Could she do it?

"Why don't we go to Greece," she said, "and take it from there?"

He smiled at her. "Oh, such poetic justice. Of all the women who have longed to capture me, the only one I want wants to 'take it from there.'"

Anastasia smiled back at him. She knew it wasn't a statement of ego, but a statement of fact. "Is that enough?" she asked.

"If you honestly mean we'll take it from there, and not flat-out no, let me borrow your papers—birth certificate, declaration that you're an emancipated minor, etceteras. I'll have a friend of mine at the consulate have them translated into Greek. It doesn't commit you to anything. It only keeps our options open."

Anastasia laughed. One legacy of her mother's was that she always traveled with her important papers.

"Does that frighten you too much?" Pierce asked.

She shook her head. "Translate them into Zulu if you'd like."

He went over to the far side of the easy chair, and she heard the crunch of ice as he picked up the champagne bottle. "A life with you is my dream," he said. "Two weeks with you, I am content."

He set down the flutes and expertly worked the cork from the bottle. "To Greece," he said, raising his glass to meet hers.

"To Greece," she echoed.

"And to tonight," he said softly, "my fair one. My love."

The next morning, filming the final scene, they'd worked together well as always. Afterwards, amidst hugs and tears, they'd taken leave of cast and crew, and each other, actress to director.

Good work. A pleasure working with you. See you soon. An hour later she was leaving the Red Lion with all her bags packed, sharing a car hire to London with Garrett and Bruce. She was dropped at her empty flat. Two hours later another driver rang and she came out, bags repacked, and left for Heathrow, where she didn't meet up with Pierce until she was seated beside him in the almost-empty first-class cabin of the Olympic Airlines jet.

Pierce was ebullient; she was radiant herself. Her happiness was too good to be true, but she decided to go with it while it lasted.

"I don't know about this," she said as they taxied into position for takeoff.

"Why?" he asked, his tone suddenly sober.

"I've heard from a very knowledgeable source that affairs on film sets burn brightly and end badly."

"Never listen to know-it-all directors," he answered. "There are always exceptions that prove the rule."

That had been three days ago. Anastasia lay now, stretched luxuriously in the sunshine on the back terrace of their secluded villa in Aperi, on Karpathos. She adored what she'd seen of Greece. It still amazed her to realize how wide the world was. She wanted to see it all.

The villa came with a cook who served them breakfast on the terrace every morning and provided lunch and dinner as required. The first two days, Pierce had declared a moratorium on mentioning the film industry, but they soon found they delighted in sipping colas during long afternoons discussing both *T & I* and upcoming projects. Pierce couldn't get over the fact that Anastasia not only didn't mind talking about work, she reveled in it. It gave him a new sense of freedom in his natural creative processes. He had several ideas beginning to percolate.

Last night, they'd gone out dancing down in the more populous Pigadia. Neither of them were crowd-type people, but the freedom of their anonymity and the primal response of the roomful of bodies to the driving rock pulse was a giddy release. Pierce was easily the tallest person there, but he danced with a fluidity and grace that helped them blend in. Anastasia couldn't take her eyes off him all evening.

Anastasia added a love of watching Pierce sleep and think and shave to watching him walk through doorways. But her favorite was watching him smile. She was so used to seeing him in intense concentration, serious about his acting and about being at the helm of a very large ship. The smiles he'd most often shown on the set were those of quiet satisfaction. But here, in the long warm days, free from pressure, Pierce's face would explode into a grin. It would capture all his features, changing the shape of his eyes, raising his cheekbones. It gave him a vulnerability, and when she saw his unaffected elation, she could picture how he must have looked as a boy.

Now it was mid-morning. They'd gone for a swim in the sweet azure sea as day broke. After returning for breakfast, Pierce had gone inside to shower, and thus far hadn't returned. She began to wonder where he was.

Anastasia stood and looked up the three whitewashed steps that led to the master bedroom. She thought she could see the outline of a shadow inside. She grabbed her sarong and wrapped it over the bottom of her turquoise two-piece swimsuit.

The sliding glass door to their room was open, a sultry breeze teasing the curtains. Pierce had brought a chair to the door, and had been sitting there, quietly watching her.

When she came inside, he gave a soft smile and held out a hand. She took it and fit into his lap. She studied him, amazed, and with a finger wiped the silent tears of wonder from his cheek.

"Let's get married," she said.

They took their Greek documents that afternoon to apply for a license. "Fine," said the clerk. "Come back in seven days."

Anastasia was enchanted by the look of their names in Greek

when the notice ran in the local newspaper. They were a bit apprehensive that someone in the press would pick it up, but it wasn't a major tourist island, and their names were, after all, in Greek.

The wedding was simple. The mayor came to their villa and married them on the terrace overlooking the Aegean Sea. The cook and gardener served as witnesses. They went out for a wedding dinner. Afterwards they found themselves at a festival and were soon in the midst of hundreds of locals, dancing in the streets.

That night they sat outside, sipping champagne, watching the swaying colored lights below them in the village. They talked about the first time they'd met, when Pierce thought he already had his Isolde and Anastasia thought he was a casting assistant. How they'd shared a warm bottle of Coke. Pierce remembered how he'd been staggered by her beauty but won over by her self-possession. She admitted thinking he was old but handsome, and potentially dangerous.

Guilty on all counts, he said.

When they finally retired to their marriage bed they made love gently and sweetly, and fell asleep holding each other possessively, to be certain the other was still there.

Anastasia thought she couldn't be happier than she was in Greece. She was wrong. The real world was even better. Pierce had rented a two-story flat in London as his home base during the months of post-production. He'd had a decorator pick out the furniture—happily, in a style Anastasia felt was cheery and comfortable. But the decorator hadn't done the kitchen. So it was that Anastasia got to fulfill the one true dream of her life. She returned in triumph to the French country kitchen shops she had passed not so long ago, now in a position to purchase whatever she liked. Decorating that eat-in kitchen for herself and her secret husband would stand forever as one of the highlights of her life.

The day after their return, Gray Eddington was amusingly perplexed to find Anastasia at Pierce's home, opening the front door to greet him, and offering to make tea for the two men.

Pierce hung up the telephone and bounded into the foyer to join them. "Good to see you, Eddington," he proclaimed, slapping his staid partner on the back. "Of course, you know my wife."

If Pierce had played the scene for dramatic effect, he'd been successful. Gray went ashen, and stuttered for perhaps the first time in his life.

"Y-y-y-you're joking, of course," he said.

In response, Pierce held up his left hand, newly graced with a simple gold band. He grasped his bride's hand, where her fourth finger was encircled by the matching ring.

Anastasia gave Gray credit: he was able to assess, process, and respond to the situation within seconds.

"My heartiest congratulations," he said to his hostess with a small bow.

Then he stalked ahead of Pierce into the office off the entrance hall.

Pierce gave her a wink. "Tea would be lovely," he said.

Gray barely waited for the door to be closed.

"For the love of Christ!" he exploded to his partner. "What have you done?"

Outside, Anastasia began to tremble. Pierce didn't answer, choosing to let Gray have his say. "You're a bloody genius. I've said it before and I don't doubt it now. But if you continue to think with your . . . you can ruin everything! In fact, you probably have! Do what you will with your life, it's no concern of mine. You know I've never said anything about whom you've chosen to bed. Never. But, by God, if you sink your career—and this film—you owe me seven million pounds. And I'll take every last one of them out of your hide, I swear it! A schoolgirl! Bloody hell! Does the press know?"

Anastasia stood rooted to the marble beneath her feet. Was Gray right? Had she ruined Pierce's career and, by extension, the film?

But when her husband spoke, she could almost hear the smile he was fighting.

"Sit down, ya jealous prick," he said. "No one knows. And she's no schoolgirl, she's a woman, and I dare you to prove otherwise. She'll be eighteen before this film opens—"

"*Eighteen!*"

"I'd think you'd be happy for me. You've been pestering me to remarry for years. As you pointed out, you've never been moved to give me dating advice before. Schoolgirls are quite out of my line. So I must be in love. Nice thought, that."

"Eighteen," groaned Gray.

"We've already decided not to announce it. We wear the rings only here at home," Pierce said. "In fact, we're planning a public wedding after the opening of *Beggar's Moon*. She'll be nineteen by then."

"Nineteen," Gray repeated numbly.

"We've proven we can be discreet. I believe you—and young Dalton—are the only ones who had an inkling during the entirety of the shoot. Admit it. She's tremendously circumspect, as am I. I'm assuming we can count on your discretion as well."

"After all these years, you had to choose—"

"Enough about my wife, old chap. Yours is well, I hope? How old will Diana be next birthday?"

"What? She's fine, of course, fine. She'll be—dunno, forty-six."

"And a damn attractive woman," Pierce said. "Enough about

the wives, eh? We've got a mountain of work before us. Jealous prick," Pierce finished good-naturedly.

At that, Anastasia freed herself to put on the kettle.

Once they settled in, Pierce was in the editing studios from sunup to sundown most days. That was fine with his wife. Her days were busy as well. She'd signed her contract for *Beggar's Moon*, and began reading the scripts Mayfair was getting for her consideration on the strength of the word of mouth about her performance in *T & I*. She also accepted the rare modeling assignment, if the product was tony enough. Her rate was astronomically high.

Pierce took as great an interest in her career as he did in his own. If she liked a script, he would stay up reading it, and they'd discuss it the next night. He felt she would be better served at one of the prestigious agencies that handled major acting talents; he let slip to his own agent that he'd heard Anastasia Day might be ripe for "stealing." She saw Pierce's point, and knew she'd give in and sign with her sooner or later. In the meantime, she signed for one film after *Beggar's Moon*, a literate modern romance called *Firefly*, to be directed by an American with whom her husband was much impressed.

The flat she'd shared with her mother held such difficult memories that Pierce urged her to give it up, which she did. He introduced her to his financial advisor, who helped her develop investment strategies.

However, Pierce also made a strange suggestion: he wanted her to buy her own little house, a retreat that would belong only to her. Something she would own outright and always have. At first she worried that this meant he wanted to keep his own bachelor pad somewhere, but he convinced her this was not the case. He was older than she, he said, and the business was capricious. He wanted to make certain she would always have somewhere to go if he was not around to protect her. He also insisted she get her driver's license as soon as she turned eighteen. He let her pick out a car for her birthday.

She dragged her feet about taking his advice. She broke down about the driving lessons first. There were so many times she needed to get somewhere—Cambry Hall, for example—on a different schedule than Pierce's that she finally got her license.

Not long afterwards, on her way back from driving herself to a modeling shoot, she got hopelessly lost in Somerset and ended up in one of the quaintest villages she'd ever encountered. Instead of working herself further into a lather, she decided to stop, have tea, and collect herself. As she was leaving the tea shop, she found herself staring straight across the market square at the office of an estate agent and decided on a lark to stop in.

The lone woman holding down the fort was pleased with an unexpected prospect and more than happy to show her some available properties.

One was a secluded stone cottage down its own winding lane, complete with vines and gardens and latticework windows. Anastasia fell immediately in love. It was small, two bedrooms, with a friendly kitchen, an airy living room with dining room attached, and a workroom in back. She asked the price, haggled briefly, and told the startled but delighted woman that as soon as she could get an engineer's report she'd close the deal.

The engineer's report was satisfactory. She bought the cottage, and began spending those weekends that Pierce had to work decorating and making it her own. She named it Lilliput Lane, partly as an homage to her old alter ego, whose earnings had put it within her grasp.

But the focus of her days was still her life with Pierce. Keeping their marriage secret was no great hardship. She had her own phone line in their flat. Pierce was working nonstop, and they had very little time for entertaining. Pierce did occasionally have small dinners for close friends, many of whom were well known in theater and film circles, but they were all discreet—valuing their own privacy, perhaps. Also, they never announced even to these friends that they were actually husband and wife; in fact, both showed proper British restraint with displays of affection. Pierce quit smoking again, this time, he promised, for good.

While they enjoyed their hectic lives in London, they treasured their stolen days at Cambry Hall. Pierce trusted the Duffys completely; he introduced Anastasia as his bride immediately upon their return. The Duffys were delighted, embracing Anastasia as mistress of Cambry Hall at once.

It was during one blissful weekend in the country that Pierce received a call from Buckingham Palace asking if he would accept a knighthood. Pierce and Anastasia discussed it for approximately thirty seconds before he accepted. She claimed she'd always thought of him as "Sir."

She loved listening as he talked through what was happening on post-production of T & I; she found the problems and challenges as interesting as the smooth sailing. She occasionally visited the suites where Pierce and the editor were working. She had to admit it looked great.

The largest problem Pierce was facing was one he hadn't counted on: Conan Marcel, the composer with whom he'd collaborated happily before, was drinking heavily. Always a man of extreme highs and lows of emotion, when Conan was drunk he seemed unable to be creative. Instead Pierce felt he gave himself over to recycling themes and songs he'd already written.

As they got closer and closer to the sound mix when all the music had to be ready, Pierce's concern grew. He finally asked Conan to join him for dinner in the country. It was there that

Anastasia had unintentionally overheard the argument between the two men, the upshot of which was that Conan would be paid and given credit for the acceptable work he'd done, and someone else would be brought in to finish the score.

It was not a happy situation, but Anastasia was proud of how her husband handled it.

Toward spring, he began balancing final work on *T & I* with pre-production on *Beggar's Moon*. Anastasia was excited about returning to acting work. The window between her two films with Pierce had not been wide enough for her to accept other films in the meantime, and she'd missed it.

However, it had been the best winter and spring of her life, and of Pierce's, too. Pierce wasn't used to being able to work the hours he needed to without being consistently nagged and having to apologize to his wife. Anastasia was used to being on her own during her days; it was a wonderful surprise and revelation each night when she came home to a husband who adored her.

One night, Gray and Pierce returned in glowing spirits. They'd shown a cut of *Tristan and Isolde* to the honchos at Heather Hill, who had reacted ecstatically. "Well," Pierce admitted, "'ecstatic' is perhaps too heady a word to use for studio execs . . . but they were pleased, weren't they?"

"For studio execs, they were ecstatic," Gray said.

"Pierce, I'm so happy!" Anastasia said, giving him a hug.

"And that's not all," Gray went on. "Tell her about *Beggar's Moon*."

"What about it?"

"An offer went out to a male lead," Pierce said. "To our first choice, Daniel Green."

"And he snatched at it! His agent could hardly wipe the drool off the contracts!" the older man burst forth. Gray looked like he might pop a few buttons off the waistcoat of his suit.

"I'm not surprised that anyone would jump at the part. It's magnificent," she said. But she herself was thrilled about the idea of working with the American actor. He was one of the few box office stars who was also an actor's actor.

"You work hard enough, long enough, and it begins to pay off," Gray said.

"And we've been working too hard for too long without a celebration. What say tomorrow night the four of us hit the town. Get that wife of yours dolled up, Eddington. She deserves some fresh air. So does my wife."

"All right, you're on," the producer agreed, smiling. "I'll say good night, and see you bright and early."

Pierce and Anastasia saw him to the door. Then Pierce grabbed his wife and spun her around laughing, then carried her toward the bedroom. "You work your whole life for that elusive time that everything will come together, but you think it never will."

"It has," agreed Anastasia.

"It has," he said. He bounced her onto their bed, flung himself down, and laughed as she climbed on top of him, growling.

"We've scared the bad times off," she said. "Our time has come."

"Finally," he answered. "I'm more than ready." And he growled back.

The next morning, Pierce called the Eddingtons to say he had booked the four of them at a special restaurant an hour outside London. He wouldn't say where, but he told Gray and Diana to dress up. Then he headed in to work.

Anastasia had a shoot that day. During her hiatus, she had accepted a lucrative contract to be the spokesmodel for a new perfume by a major cosmetics firm. It was called Constellation: "Like fire in the sky, white diamonds against black velvet . . ."

She, Pierce, and Mayfair had decided the product was classy and the fee high enough that she signed an exclusive perfume contract with them. There would be major campaigns in both Britain and the United States.

She kissed her husband good-bye in the kitchen as he left, promising to meet him early enough that they could change into dinner clothes and pick up the Eddingtons by seven. She set down the pot where she was pouring herself a second cup of tea and melted into his embrace. As he kissed her, he said, "I love you so much." Looking up, he laughed. "And I love that damned rooster."

Anastasia turned to look at the hand-painted cock she'd bought at one of her kitchen shops. "I'm glad," she said. "And I'm so very proud of you."

Her shoot went well. Perhaps because modeling was no longer her life's work, the few bookings she did felt less confining. Afterwards, she hopped into her convertible and headed home, grateful to be finished before the nightly rush.

She pulled into her parking space a little after four, and to her surprise, found Gray Eddington pulling his Mercedes turbo in beside her. He came over and opened her door, helping her out. He was still lighthearted: Anastasia guessed that his being jocular two days in a row might be some kind of record.

"Pierce left the mix early to come make a few changes on *Beggar's Moon* before the final script gets flown to Hollywood," Gray said. "I thought I'd drop off the tapes of the music by the new composer. You can both take a listen. I think they're rather good."

"Great," said Anastasia. "I'm sure Pierce will be pleased. Shall I take them up?"

"There are a few things I need to explain about them," Gray said. So they turned together up the walkway, and up the stairs to the townhouse.

Anastasia opened the door and was met by Pura, the maid who came in twice a week.

"Help!" the woman said wildly in English laced with an Indian accent. "I now arrived. Now arrived. Help! Help!" Her eyes were wide with fear, and her whole body shook. She grabbed Gray's hand—it was her impulse to defer to the man.

"What is it?" Anastasia asked. "What's wrong? Where's Mr. Hall?"

"You come. You help!" she cried.

The maid turned and ran toward the kitchen, but stopped outside the door.

Gray, fearing the worst, tried to hold Anastasia back, but she pushed in behind him.

And there lay Pierce, not moving, on the kitchen floor.

Anastasia screamed and dropped to her knees beside him. "Pierce! Dear God, Pierce!" She slapped his face lightly and recoiled in horror. It was cold, and the skin felt like wax.

"No!" she screamed. "No, no, no!"

Gray knelt beside him and tried to locate a pulse at this neck.

"Dear Jesus God," he said. "Jesus, Mary, and Joseph." He crossed himself.

Anastasia would not, could not, believe what she was seeing. She threw herself on top of her husband's chest, banging on him and pleading with him to get up.

Gray sat back on his haunches. "He's dead," he whispered. "He has been for a while. There's nothing anyone can do."

"No!" she cried, and she stretched on top of him, holding him, trying to kiss warmth back into his blue lips.

"Pierce. Love, I need you. Please come back. Don't leave me!" she whispered to him urgently. He wasn't dead; this was a joke, a trick, played, if not by Pierce, then by fate. Fate, who had never offered her much, who had given her this one thing, this one—and she had been grateful. Every day she had been grateful.

Gray was talking to Pura, but he and his world had ceased to exist. Anastasia was touching Pierce's soft, full hair, running her fingers through it.

"It's so beautiful," she whispered. " I love your hair so much. I love your eyes, I first fell in love with your flashing dark eyes."

But even as she memorized them, Gray reached forward and closed the lids.

"No!" she cried. "Please. Please!" And she fell on top of the body of her husband once more.

"Anastasia," Gray said, "it's too late. It's too late."

But she wouldn't move. All strength was gone from her muscles; she couldn't have moved if she'd wanted to. And then she felt it, an alarming constriction in her own chest. *Yes,* she willed herself then, *I want to die. I want to go with him. Please let me go.* The pain intensified; she found herself shaking uncontrollably, her lungs aching for air they couldn't find. *Yes,* she thought in relief. *Pierce, wait for me, please, take me with you.*

Instead, she felt herself being picked up, forcibly, and carried. She tried to grab onto Pierce, to hold on, to force him to take her with him before it was too late, but she was wrenched free. Tears crowded her eyes, and her breath came in great gasps.

"It's all right, you're in shock, it'll be all right," a voice said from a long way away.

She opened her eyes to find herself in a strange bedroom. Gray Eddington sat beside her. A man she'd never seen before sat at her side. It was he who spoke to her.

"Where's Pierce?" she asked. "I have to go to him! Please!"

"I'm sorry. You can't. It'll be all right."

"I have to go to him! He needs me!" she screamed. With superhuman strength she tried to lurch off the bed, past her captors. Gray caught her, and lowered her back down, holding her arms tightly at her sides.

"You'll be all right. You're in shock, like the doctor says," he said, trying to soothe her, but she struggled to break free.

The doctor had disappeared around to the other side of the bed.

"Stacy, look at me," Gray said. "I want to help you. We'll get you through this."

As he spoke she felt a corner of her dress lifted, her panties scooted down, and the strong smell of alcohol cut through her fog.

"No!" she pleaded, but it was too late. She felt the prick of the needle as it slid into her hip.

"It'll be all right," Gray said again. But even as she lost consciousness, she knew he was lying.

In years to come, Anastasia would wonder often how her life might have been different if Gray hadn't been with her when she found Pierce dead on the kitchen floor. But he had been, and he had quickly taken charge.

She never knew whether he paid Pura to lie or simply to vanish. She did know that by the time the ambulance was called, all of her clothing and belongings had been removed from the flat.

The bedroom in which Anastasia had initially awakened was a guest room in the Eddingtons' townhouse. She awoke the second day to find all of her personal effects sorted in neat piles around her. Gray and his wife said she could stay as long as she needed to.

Gray explained that it would be best not to go public with her marriage to Pierce. He said he was convinced that if the public knew that the thirty-eight-year-old director had robbed the cradle and married his seventeen-year-old co-star, they would be shocked and horrified. It would cast a pall over the triumph of

Pierce Hall's last film. Even though at the time of his death, she was eighteen and he thirty-nine, Gray harped on the fact Pierce was still twice her age; even his knighthood, now to be bestowed posthumously, could be withdrawn, his memory forever tinged with shame.

Gray also claimed he was looking after Anastasia's best interests, but she knew that was a lie. He was looking out after the financial interests of *Tristan and Isolde*. Left as it was, people could feel they were doing a final honor to one of the great talents of their generation by purchasing a ticket. "Let's let this film be a blockbuster out of our love for him," he'd said.

Anastasia, deep under the seas of loss, was left without any coherent answer. Even then she knew he was twisting the facts to control the situation, and her, but the shroud of her grief was so heavy that she couldn't get out of bed, let alone take on a man like Gray Eddington.

The third day, the day before the funeral, Gray came to find her. "We might as well look at this head-on," he said. "Pierce had not had time to file a new will. You, as his wife, have a legal claim, of course. But rather than make it public, take it to court, why don't you and I work out what it is you want, and we can negotiate privately with the estate."

Anastasia stared at him. "I want Pierce," she said.

"Of course, dear girl. But . . ."

"I didn't marry him for his money! For God's sake! I've got enough of my own."

"We'll talk again," Gray said. "In the meantime, is there anything you want from his flat before it's inventoried? I think I could bring out a few things."

"*Our* flat!" she cried. "It was *our* flat!"

"Yes, yes," he said, "so I meant. What would you like?"

She sat breathing hard, wondering if she had to go along with this. She just wanted to get out, get out, get out—of the prison of the Eddingtons' house, of the brutal pain of her life without Pierce.

"I want the goddamned rooster," she said.

The funeral was hell. It was in St. Paul's Cathedral, and it was packed with mourners. The theme of the day was disbelief and shock that Pierce Hall was gone—dead of a heart attack at thirty-nine. The entire British theater establishment turned out, as did many members of Parliament and representatives from the royal family. Anastasia was cognizant of very little of this. She was deeply aware that Alana sat dignified in the front family pew, weeping photogenically into her embroidered hanky. She was flanked by her and Pierce's children, Leah, Rufus, and Jeremy. While Anastasia, whose heart was broken, whose life was shattered, sat a dozen rows back with the Eddingtons. Next to finding Pierce's body, it was the most traumatic thing she'd ever had to face. In her life, that was saying something.

It was at Pierce's funeral that she had her second full-blown panic attack. Only this time, unlike when she'd been alone with Pierce's corpse, she was certain that all eyes were on her. Everyone was watching, smirking, tut-tutting. She only knew that if she didn't die right there at the cathedral, she would die if she had to stay one more second under the control of the Eddingtons.

During the last hymn, she fled from her pew down the aisle, not stopping for breath until she collapsed, heaving with sobs, on the cold tile floor of the cathedral gift shop. When the alarmed clerks asked if they should call for an ambulance, she pointed to Garrett Clifton, where he sat with Bill Overton. The younger shopgirl returned with him before the end of the hymn. Anastasia grabbed onto Garrett for dear life. "You've got to help me," she gasped.

And so, while Sir Pierce Hall's ex-wife, Gray Eddington, and various other dignitaries were photographed leaving in the limo behind the hearse, Garrett and Bill whisked Anastasia back to the Eddingtons' townhouse, where she gathered her possessions. Garrett dropped Bill off at their flat, then drove Anastasia in her own car to Somerset, to Lilliput Lane, where he helped her unload the remnants of her life before helping her get drunker than she'd ever been.

She poured out her story to her friend because she knew she could trust him. They wept together. Garrett stayed with her, sleeping on the floor in the guest room—which didn't yet have a bed—for three days, until he was sure she would be all right.

"I loved him," she said. "My life is over."

"You loved him," Garrett corrected, "his life is over. Yours is only beginning."

"I don't believe you," Anastasia said.

"I know," answered Garrett. "And you won't for a while."

It would be longer than either of them could possibly imagine.

ANASTASIA SAT ON A WHITE wooden bench in the small town square feeling like the female version of Forrest Gump. It was the tenth of May, and she was breathing American air for the first time in twenty-five years. The breeze was warm in Rolling Rock, Kentucky: temperature in the low seventies. And here she sat, having made the trip from England to Kentucky all by herself. No one knew she was here: not Bruce, not Leah, not Reginald. No one.

Anastasia intended to contact one of the counselors Andrew had located for her after the reunion, assuming she was still alive.

Until then, Neville's doctor had given her a prescription for Valium. She was not proud of the fact that she had taken some to get herself through Heathrow and onto the transatlantic flight. On the other hand, here she was in Kentucky, doggone it, something she never would have dreamed of attempting only weeks ago.

Of course, there was every chance this Herculean achievement was in vain.

She surveyed the neat little square. It was a block of land, complete with Civil War cannon and flagpole. The burnished brick courthouse with attached city hall and jail fronted Taft. Lining the other three streets were a diner, a five-and-dime, an antiques store, a Minit Mart, a fabric store, a general store, and a florist.

The florist claimed he had inherited the standing yearly order to send a plant of yellow tea roses to somewhere in England. There was still over three thousand dollars on the account for future bushes. Even if he did know who had given his predecessor the order, he wouldn't go around giving out privileged information. It wouldn't be good business.

She had a sinking feeling that either the order had been placed by a stranger on his way through town twenty years ago, or that she was an outsider who would never breach the wall of protection the locals threw wide around their own.

From there, she'd gone into the fabric store, on the hunch it would be nearly empty on a weekday morning. She'd been right. However, neither of the women clerks admitted recognizing the young man in the photo. She'd gone to great lengths to find a snapshot rather than a published picture.

She'd shown the photo to the two people who'd joined her on the park bench. One had been a lanky black man, the other a matronly white woman. Neither took a second in shaking their heads. Never seen him.

There were no Daltons in the Rolling Rock phone directory; she'd tried that back at the B&B. Nor were there any in the surrounding towns between there and Lexington.

She might have to chalk this trip up to experience.

And then a gangly ten-year-old wearing jeans, a horizontally striped red and blue shirt, and black-framed glasses nearly ran over her feet with his skateboard.

"Sorry," he said carelessly.

"Hey," she said, "come here."

"I said sorry," he remarked, looking at the ground. But he'd been taught enough manners that a command from one of his elders had the power to draw him like a magnet. "What?" he said suspiciously. "You want to get me in trouble 'cause I'm playing hooky?"

"Don't make me no never mind," Anastasia replied, falling back into her native Southern.

"What, then?"

"Do you know this guy?" she asked, fishing out her now-thumb-smudged photo. "He'd look older now."

The boy took the picture and held it up.

"Oh, that's Maggie's dad," he said, and handed it back.

Anastasia sat up straight. "Maggie Dalton?" she asked.

"No," he said in his best don't-you-know-anything voice. "Maggie Thompson. It's Mr. Thompson."

"Where do they live?" she asked. "Where do the Thompsons live?"

"You know, the signs," the boy said, throwing his skateboard back onto the sidewalk with a crash, planting one foot atop it, and using the other to crank himself away.

Anastasia sat flummoxed. This was the best—the only—lead she'd gotten so far. And it could be the answer to one mystery. But the boy could also have been mistaken.

The actress was thankful that she hadn't tipped her hand this morning at the B&B. This gave her the freedom to see what she could learn from Mrs. Barefoot, the proprietor. She walked back to the stately white Southern home, complete with Tara-esque pillars and second-floor balcony. It was only three blocks from the square. Of course, so was most everything in Rolling Rock.

A rainbow of hyacinths perfumed the air as Anastasia climbed the steps. She paused inside the center hall. With her eyes closed, she could imagine herself back in South Carolina, her mother laughing on the telephone in the other room, the breeze flirting with the saffron-colored kitchen curtains.

"Ha-loo," said her hostess, appearing from the back of the house. She smiled to see Anastasia. "Did you have a nice walk, Mrs. Huntington?"

"Yes, what fortunate weather you've arranged for me," her guest returned. "I suppose I should stop in and see my friends before I move on. Perhaps you can help me with directions?"

"I'll do my best," said Mrs. Barefoot, the pilot light in her eyes igniting with curiosity.

"The Thompsons? I'm afraid all I remember of the directions is something about 'the signs.' Does that make any sense to you?"

"A friend of the Thompsons, are you?" she asked, interested.

"Actually, I'm a friend of Maggie's aunt Alice. Unfortunately deceased."

"Dear me, I didn't know."

"You can guide me, perhaps?"

"They're near five miles out of town," Mrs. Worthington Barefoot said. "Take Taft to Clove, turn right and keep going. . . ."

The directions were fairly simple. Anastasia made notes to be safe.

"If you're here on Sunday, you can hear what wonders Mr.

Thompson has worked with the choir over at the Presbyterian Church. They used to be a lost cause, though of course we never said so then. But now, their Easter and Christmas oratorios are famous in three counties."

Anastasia was desperate for some sort of confirmation that Maggie Thompson's father could in fact be the former Peter Dalton.

"Has Maggie as good a voice as her father?" she asked.

"She has a sweet, child's voice. But Peter Thompson does have the voice of the Archangel Michael himself, doesn't he? Although he seldom sings except with the choir. Can I get you a cup of coffee? I was about to go out to the Women's League."

"Oh, no, thank you. Shall I lock up when I go?"

"No need. Just pull the front door closed behind you."

So Mr. Thompson's first name was Peter, and he sang like an angel. It sounded like her search was nearing its conclusion.

But did she want it to?

The last time she'd seen Peter, she hadn't even liked him very much. *Tristan and Isolde* had opened first in the United States, and three months later in Britain. Peter had attended each premiere with a starlet on his arm. Both occasions had required Anastasia and Peter to be photographed together ad nauseam; as far as the media was concerned, Peter Dalton had no other date. But Peter hadn't spoken to her during either premiere, or during press conferences in New York or London. He'd been forthcoming and cooperative with the press, but had appeared and disappeared just before and just after.

He hadn't been at Pierce's funeral. True, he'd been working. But he could have sent Anastasia a card. It would have been decent of him not to ignore her completely.

He had paid for it. His life, at least his public life, had been a hard one by the end. The first five or six years had been the Hollywood dream fulfilled.

She could go and spy on Peter Thompson. See if it really was Peter Dalton, then leave.

But that was hardly the point. Suppose the Presbyterian choir director took frequent business trips, leaving a trail of bodies in his wake?

She didn't believe that for a minute. But the reason for the trip was to talk to him. To make certain he had alibis. To see if he had clues. She'd come all this way. Mrs. Thompson, and Maggie and any other progeny, would have to understand.

It was late afternoon before she was once again in the blue compact rental car she'd picked up at the Lexington airport, following Mrs. Barefoot's directions out of town. This was horse country, and long, luxurious pastures crisscrossed the landscape, beautiful specimens of horseflesh walking the turf, grazing contentedly.

And there, on the left-hand side of the two-lane road, was the marker: a large carved and painted wooden sign that read, *Signs: Sealed and Delivered*. On the bottom was an arrow indicating that interested parties should make the turn onto the gravel road, which Anastasia did.

The lane wound slowly through dogwood and forsythia. She rounded one last turn to find that it continued through an opening in a split-rail fence. On impulse, she edged the car off on the left-hand side and parked. She decided to walk the rest of the way.

The Thompson compound was delightful. Not far inside the fence on the left was a one-story workshop. Sample signs hung from its eaves. *Never Enough Thyme*, read one. They were all beautifully painted and handcrafted, some in the shapes of pigs or moons, stars or watering cans. If these were the wrong

Thompsons, she'd make up for disturbing them by making a purchase.

The workshop was closed at present. She could see, up ahead in a stand of trees, a Kentucky log cabin, made of whole logs. It had a wooden porch with two rocking chairs, a hand-stitched quilt of blues, yellows, and reds thrown over one. There was even a tree stump out front with an ax head buried in it, waiting for chore time.

And then, as she looked down, she was startled to see a child standing almost at her elbow, looking up at her with unabashed curiosity.

"Hi," Anastasia said.

"Hi," said the girl. Her hair was auburn, worn in braids. A blanket of freckles had been spread over her nose and settled on both cheeks. Her eyes were small and almond, both in shape and color. She showed neither friendliness nor hostility. She stood patiently waiting to find out what business this stranger had.

"Are you Maggie?" Anastasia asked. She judged the girl to be ten or eleven.

The head bobbed.

"Is your father home?"

The bob again. "You want me to call him?"

"No," Anastasia. She slid the Victorian ring off her right hand. "Would you please take this to him?"

Maggie nodded slowly, then walked toward the house and disappeared inside.

The Duchess of Esmonde moved quickly from the drive into the shadow of an old maple tree. She wanted the advantage of a first look. She wondered if her course of action had been too dramatic. What if it wasn't the right Peter? How would she explain?

But then the front door of the cabin opened, and a man appeared. She couldn't quite make out his features in the shadows of the porch, but as he reached sunlight at the top of the steps and stood surveying the yard, she gasped and dug her fingernails into the maple bark.

There was no mistaking. It was Peter Dalton.

He had been a handsome boy, but it was as if he'd been born to be forty. He stood muscular and lean in jeans and a green plaid work shirt; his hair, now chestnut with golden highlights, was full and curly, cut above his collar.

He looked so much like the old Peter that she wanted to run. She had counted on it being the wrong Peter. Or a mean, chunky, or dissipated Peter.

His eyes searched the grounds again, and she stepped away from the tree and out of the shadows.

He came down the porch steps and met her in the middle of the yard.

"My God," he said simply. He opened his hand, offering her the ring. "Stacy."

The best answer she could muster was a trembling smile.

He took both her hands and stepped backwards, surveying her up and down. Anastasia was glad she'd chosen the casual look: the blue jeans and sky blue sweater recently purchased for her by Elise Amerman. "Wow. You look terrific."

"Thanks. You're pretty well preserved yourself."

Peter turned then, to where his daughter hovered just inside the cabin's screen door. "Maggie, put on a kettle, kiddo, will you? I think we have company for tea."

The girl disappeared.

"You will come in? I mean, you'd better. If nothing else to explain what you're doing here, how you found me." A cloud of worry settled over him. "Is it out now? Common knowledge?"

"Where you are?" Anastasia asked. "No. No one else knows."

"Then come on. Let me show you around."

He led her up through the porch into the house. It was decorated in country rustic; the coffee table hewn from logs, the electric lights wired through polished oil lamps. Quilts brought splashes of color to the walls.

"Peter, it's lovely," she said.

"It's bigger than it looks. Three bedrooms—one's upstairs, which affords Maggie a bit of privacy."

The sharp whistle of a teakettle came from behind them. The spacious kitchen was open to the living room/dining room, the space divided by a breakfast bar. In a moment, two cups of tea were presented on the breakfast bar, with a pitcher of cream and a bowl of sugar.

"Anastasia, this is Maggie. She knows how to make a proper cuppa," Peter said proudly. "It comes from being stuck with an Englishman for a father."

"Nobody knows you're English," the girl protested. "They all think you're normal."

"Thank you so much. Don't you have some homework?"

"May I have a can of soda?"

"You may."

She raided the fridge and headed past them. "Nice to meet you," she said politely.

"Yes, you too."

Her footsteps soon receded up the burnished wooden stairs.

The man and woman stood cradling their hot cups, looking straight ahead.

"Come sit on the sofa," he said.

Maggie was right. He did sound "normal." But then, he had effectively acquired an American accent by his second film after *Tristan.*

They settled in and fell silent again, so much yet unspoken that there didn't seem a good way in.

"Maggie's your only child?" she finally asked.

"Yes," he said. "Debbie was unable to have any others by the time I met her."

"So Maggie's—"

"My stepdaughter. But I've legally adopted her."

"And what does Debbie do?"

"She was a nurse. Her family had this sign-carving business, which we took over when her brother wanted to move to Florida. It's quite lucrative. We ship all over the world."

"The signs are great," Anastasia agreed. "Do you help make them, or are you the businessman?"

"I make them. And I'm the businessman. I . . . lost her. I'm a widower."

Anastasia set her cup down on the coffee table. "I'm sorry. I didn't know."

"Four years ago."

"If you don't mind my asking—what happened?"

He gave a long sigh. It was obviously a road he didn't relish traveling.

"Debbie was a nurse I met when I was in rehab. When you first saw her, she seemed small, but we all discovered she had a backbone of steel, as no-nonsense as she could be. She didn't fall for anything. She probably saved my life.

"I eventually got her to promise that if I saw the program all the way through, when I was released she'd have a cup of coffee with me. So it wasn't till she'd spent six months saving my sorry ass that I discovered what she was up against. She'd found out three years before that she had multiple sclerosis. She didn't know how fast her case would degenerate, but she was scared as hell. She was a single mother—Maggie was three at the time, and once Debbie was wheelchair-bound she had no idea how she would support them, or what would become of Mags.

"It took a year to persuade her to marry me. She knew we loved each other, but she didn't want me to have to care for her. She didn't know that was exactly what I wanted to do."

"Peter, I'm so sorry," Anastasia said again.

"Yeah," he said. "Debbie thought maybe I was doing penance for not being able to save Alice. But that wasn't it. I really loved Debbie. Took her last name when we married, which made everything a lot easier.

"Although nothing was easy. Her MS degenerated much more quickly than we hoped, than anyone expected. To tell you the truth, maybe caring for her did help me come to terms with losing Alice. But it wasn't the reason I did it. It was a way of working out my salvation from what—and who—I'd become."

"It looks like you've made a good life."

"Yeah. How about you?" he asked then, his azure eyes suddenly searching.

Anastasia wasn't ready to jump in on the current status of her life, so she sidestepped. "I'm a widow myself. Twice over, actually. My husband died six months ago."

"My turn to be sorry. He was a good man, I hope."

"He was nice to me. He was a duke. As a matter of fact, you remember the castle at Dunmore?"

"Good Lord. I thought that fellow was rather old. Ah, but he had a son, as I recall."

"No, I married Neville—the father. And not for the castle." She laughed in spite of her herself. "For the moat. At least, that's Bruce's theory."

"Bruce—?"

"Amerman."

"You're still in touch with Bruce? How is he?"

"Glad you asked. That brings me to the crux of why I'm here." She took a breath. "Before I start, I should ask—you don't take a lot of business trips, by any chance? To California? England? Europe?"

This time Peter laughed. "I feel like I'm in the Witness Protection Program. I have a good thing going. I haven't left Kentucky for years. Practically since we moved here from Minnesota five years ago. You can check with the church where I work every Sunday. Or Maggie's school. I'm a class parent on Wednesdays."

She took a sip of tea and launched into the chilling details of what had brought her to Bruce's, and ultimately to Kentucky.

When she finished describing the alarming number of *T & I* alums who were gone, including Conan's demise and the intruder at Leah's, he sat silent, his face drawn.

"Dear God," he breathed. "Who would do such a thing?"

"That's what we're trying to find out. As a matter of fact, it's become urgent. The reunion and re-release are only nine days away, on May 19."

"Reunion? Re-release?"

"Of *T & I*. Don't tell me you haven't heard. You *are* buried out here!"

"Yes, and it hasn't been easy to manage."

She surveyed the living room, and realized there was no television and no sign of a computer. The magazines before them were *Country Living* and *Woodcarver's Digest*. But who was she to talk? She had buried herself as well. Her Achilles' heel had been that her agent had known where to find her.

She described the festivities planned around the theatrical re-release of *Tristan and Isolde*, and her fear that the murderer would see this gathering as a golden opportunity.

Peter attempted to process what she'd said. "It's so hard to believe. So far outside the sphere of possibility in my world. I hardly even remember my life in Hollywood. It seems like it all happened to another person. So you came here—"

"Mostly to see if it was really you. And if you somehow knew anything that could give us a clue as to why."

He shook his head. "Absolutely nothing comes to mind. *Tristan* did well by me, but I thought it did pretty well by everybody."

"I guess it didn't do very well by you . . . as far as we were concerned."

Peter put down his cup. He faced her, looking into her eyes, trying to read what was written there. "No, he said. "It didn't do well by us."

She said, "I've often wondered if you'd forgiven me."

He reached forward and touched her face lightly. "Long ago," he said. Then he stood and reached down to her. "Let's go for a walk," he said. "Beautiful day. And you know what they say about little pitchers."

They strolled together into the late afternoon along a footpath that started out back and headed up a gentle slope. Walking with him brought a familiar feeling. She remembered her best times with Peter as being outdoors.

They were out of sight of the house before he spoke again. "After my anger died, I realized I never asked to hear your side of what happened. Have you forgiven me for that?"

He'd come to stop at the top of the rise, a beautiful crazy-quilt of emerald and turquoise pastureland spread out before them. He sat down and motioned for her to do the same.

"It took me a while," Anastasia admitted. "You never . . . fought for me. I so desperately wanted you to want me back.

"Oh, I know our breakup wasn't your fault," she said quickly. "Mine. Entirely. But I've always wondered what might have happened if you'd given me an ultimatum, or stood up to Pierce. Had a duel at dawn . . . or something."

"Yeah, I've wondered, too," he said. "So, tell me. What possessed you to sleep with Pierce?"

She looked down at her hands, and laced them, parted them, laced them again. "I loved him," she said. "But no more than I loved you. I know it doesn't sound excusable, and it wasn't. It was a pretty agonizing situation. Until you found out and handed me over to him."

"You've got to understand," Peter said. "I was eighteen. I'd never had a serious girlfriend. I wasn't exactly Mr. Self-Assured when it came to the opposite sex. Whereas I perceived Pierce as the master. He was twice my age and quadruple my . . . self-confidence. There was no way I could hope to compete. So rather than get bloodied in battle and crawl away, humiliated, I didn't even try.

"Pierce Hall was great. I still have an enormous respect and admiration for him. Although, in a way, it was when he sent me to the nurse . . . well, it turned out she was interested in doing more than curing my cold. She was ready to party with me anytime because I was Tristan. I was the star. This had never hit me before. But once I started picking up the signals, I realized Louise wasn't the only one sending them out. In fact, the whole set was like a smorgasbord of females. It was fairly mind-boggling.

"And I fell for it. Actually, not until after Alice died. I'd only been with Louise and you until Alice died. Then I thought, what the hell? And I sold my soul. For all the money I could make, all the women I could screw, all the drugs I could trip out on.

"It was bloody awful. You'd think someone with my upbringing would have been smarter than that. You would have thought."

"Peter, it killed me when Alice died. The worst part was that I couldn't get near you. I wanted so desperately to hold you, to comfort you. It was one of the saddest times of my life."

"God, Stace," he said. "If you only knew."

"If I only knew what?" she asked gently.

Tears were crowding his eyes, and he was trying to gain control of his wavering voice before he spoke again. "It was so awful. Not only was Alice gone—completely gone, with no warning, no good-bye—but I felt utterly betrayed. By everyone. You. Pierce. My parents. Alice. God. Everyone.

"It was enough to send me spinning out of control, to make me keep myself anesthetized for ten years so I didn't have to deal with it. It was enough to make me want to die."

"I'm so, so sorry."

"I've had a lot of time to come to terms with things. Debbie was a lot of help, knowing me in rehab . . . knowing all of it. She helped me forgive you, forgive my parents. But I guess I've never had the ability to forgive myself. I'm still embarrassed at the things I did. At how my parents must have watched me self-destruct in the media. Their son's stupidity in pictures and headlines, for all the world to see."

He put his head down on his knees, a portrait of sorrow.

"That's why you haven't spoken with them?"

A nod.

"Peter, your parents think they're childless. It was hard for them to lose Alice, but it's hell for them every single day, not knowing about you. You've got to find the courage to call them. You must!"

"You've seen them?"

"A week ago. I went looking for you. Please call them. Or let me."

It took him a few minutes to speak. "Give me time," he said.

The sun was well past its overhead peak, following its descent into the west. Anastasia was suddenly aware she was sitting outside, unprotected, in the midst of miles of terrifyingly empty space. But she was with Peter. Peter, who needed her. And she was safe.

"So. As long as we're having a spill-our-guts fest, let me ask the question that's kept me burning with curiosity all these years. How long did your fling with Pierce last? Was he really as smooth as everybody said? Did he leave you 'sad, but loving him'?" More than a hint of bitterness had crept into Peter's voice.

She was unprepared for the tidal wave of emotion that swept over her. She'd been leaning on her hands; her grip involuntarily tightened and she pulled up a fistful of grass.

"Yes," she whispered. "He left me sad but loving him."

Peter looked at her, surprised by the enormity of what was happening inside her. It was her turn to try to find the strength to use her voice.

"We were married ten days after the shoot ended. The next spring I came home to find him dead on the kitchen floor."

"God, Stacy, I hadn't a clue."

"You know the bit about throwing yourself on your beloved's corpse and willing yourself to die? Doesn't work in real life."

"Why did no one tell me?"

"No one knew. Gray made sure all traces of our marriage were erased, and I was in such shock that I let him do it. He convinced me it was what Pierce would want, what would be best for the film. So I let him expunge a whole half of me like it had never been. Because of that, no one knows to this day—except Gray and Garrett—and they're both dead. Gone. And there's a chance Pierce didn't die of a heart attack after all. That he was murdered. It's—I haven't—I can't—"

She fell weeping into Peter's arms. He pulled her to his chest, holding her fiercely. And he began to weep, as well.

PART THREE:

REUNION

CHAPTER 11

From the Daily Variety *column* "*Have You Heard?*" *May 18:*

Celia Demetrius, agent for Anastasia Day, the actress who charmed the world as "Isolde" twenty years ago, has confirmed that her client will attend the T & I reunion festivities this week, which will be held in the castle she calls home. Celia hints that this may signal the formerly reclusive actress's return to acting after the death of her husband, a duke. Apparently Evan Masterson is wooing Day for his new series.

—*Ricardo Rivera*

"Why do I feel like I've just rushed through the line to buy tickets for a pleasant outing on the *Hindenburg?*" Anastasia asked, sinking into her favorite comfy chair.

The two women had returned from a scouting trip through the once-quiet village of Dunmore. Camera crews were staking out the normally serene village; vans loaded with satellite hookups prowled the ancient streets. Leaving town, they'd passed the harbor, where an entertainment reporter was filing a report. But most incredible was the new cinema. As promised, it was octagonal to match the architecture of the town's old market hall.

Now it boasted a pair of giant klieg lights in front and a wide red outdoor carpet leading to the glass doors.

"Definitely down the rabbit hole," Anastasia managed to say as they drove past.

"And through the looking glass as well," Leah had agreed.

The castle was the scene of considerably more havoc than the town. Anastasia had absented herself as far as possible; she and Leah were secreted away in Lilliput Lane.

The cottage had been lovingly tended through the years by Mrs. Nell Duffy, who'd retired from housekeeping shortly after the death of her husband, and Alana's sale of Cambry Hall. There was a small house in the back acre of the cottage, which Anastasia had refurbished and Nell had decorated. The older woman had friends nearby, and even in her seventies she still enjoyed bicycling into town to join them for daily tea. She'd been thrilled to open the cottage for Anastasia and Leah.

"You realize I'm not at all certain I'm going to be able to attend this hoopla tomorrow," Anastasia said thoughtfully. "The idea of a huge room teeming with bodies is more than I can stand to contemplate. It may be mentally—and physically—beyond me."

"You've done a big part by simply announcing you'll attend," Leah pointed out. "My advice is, don't think about it. We'll worry about tomorrow tomorrow. In the meantime, let me mention again my incredulity that you've had this perfectly lovely abode for all these years. And no one, including His Grace, knew you had it, or that you paid for Mrs. Duffy's upkeep?"

"I did it with my own money, why should anyone have to know? It was an arrangement Nell and I had before I married Neville. As for anyone else knowing—Garrett was the only one. I still miss him so much."

"Think how different the world would be without AIDS. At

least Garrett died without being murdered," Leah finally said.

But that simple statement had brought Anastasia crashing back to the sobering reality of what they were up against the next day.

"Don't worry," Leah said, reading her thoughts. "Bruce and I will be with you. The place will be swarming with security. If the murderer's there, let's hope he does try something."

Anastasia shivered. "You want to know what frightens me most when I envision tomorrow? I mean, murderers aside."

"Seeing Richie Riley again."

"I admit, for all our joking about him, I do dread seeing him. But something looms even greater than that."

"What?"

"Watching *Tristan and Isolde*. I haven't seen it for twenty years. Even then I couldn't bear to look at the screen."

"I hate to be the one to break it to you, but you get naked. Dad could handle it, though."

"Excuse me?"

"On film. He knew how to handle love scenes on film."

"Now I really can't wait for the screening. Thanks so much."

The slim shape of Nell Duffy appeared from the kitchen. "Pardon me, Your Grace. But there's a call for you. It sounds urgent—Bruce, he said."

Anastasia had never had a telephone installed in the cottage, and there was no local cell phone coverage. The two friends exchanged apprehensive looks and quickly followed the older woman through the kitchen and out the back door, down the path to her own small house.

Anastasia snatched the handset. "Bruce?" she asked without pleasantries.

"Someone was here," he responded. "Elise saw him skulking through the back garden. We had all the lights off, and we watched him from the kitchen until he came over to try the conservatory door. When he did, we turned on the outside lights. That prompted him to hightail it out of here."

"Did you get a look at him?"

"Afraid not. That's the problem with sitting about in the dark. It was a man, though."

"What are you going to do? Have you called Scotland Yard?"

"What are the odds of me doing that? No. I think whoever it was is gone for the night. But Elise and I are checking into a hotel to be safe. I thought you and Leah should know. It seems our murderer's arrived in the British Isles."

"Be careful, will you?"

"Elise and I will meet you at the castle early, then?"

"Yes, come round the private entrance. Reginald will be expecting you."

"Cheerio."

Anastasia and Leah thanked Nell for the use of her telephone and wished her good night. They crossed the lawn slowly.

"Why on earth would he risk an attempt on Bruce tonight?" the actress wondered.

"I have to say I'm surprised," Leah answered.

"Of course, if he'd succeeded, it would have been a chilling opening to the festivities."

"Who knows we're here at the cottage?" Leah asked.

"No one but Nell and Bruce. Even Bruce only knows the telephone number. So I think we're safe for tonight, at least."

"I hope to God you're right," Leah said. "I pray that you are."

CHAPTER 12

It's unbelievable to me that twenty years have passed since the release of Tristan and Isolde. *In retrospect, the making of the film was a golden era for all involved. Those were heady days, when an unparalleled group of master craftsmen worked together to produce what has become a classic film. That time was also, for many of us, the end of innocence. I am pleased at the reissue of this book in softcover. It brings back many memories. I dedicate it to the memory of my father, Pierce Hall, to a time that will never come again, and to everything that might have been.*

> —Leah Hall, *in the introduction to the reissue of*
> Love Will Find a Way: The Making of Tristan and Isolde

It was an unusually balmy and sunny day, even for mid-May. The front road up to the castle was jammed with media vans and catering trucks. Anastasia directed her friend around the back of the castle hill to the private entrance. Leah had packed her belongings when they'd left Lilliput Lane, where they'd secretly been staying, that morning. Leah was planning to use her hotel reservations in London that night and head back to the States, where work beckoned, the next day.

Both women had spent the morning pretending this was a perfectly logical plan; that somehow, by nightfall, life would once again be normal.

Bruce and Elise arrived at Dunmore shortly after noon, and the dowager duchess had lunch sent up to her sitting room for the four of them. There, they'd gone over what they saw as possible dangers, as well as the perpetrator's possible modus operandi in such a large group. Anastasia realized midway through lunch that the electric currents that overcame her and receded at intervals were a mixture of terror of the crowd and the thrill of the hunt. She had no idea how long she would last, but knew she must serve as bait as long as she possibly could.

They'd agreed to keep a discreet distance from each other. Each would remain open to advances by any interested parties, but none would leave the crowd with another person without alerting the others. If one of them decided it might behoove them to go with a possible suspect, the others would be close behind.

The screening of *Tristan and Isolde* was at five; the gala would be in full swing by eight. The four of them dispersed by two o'clock to change into their party attire.

As Anastasia watched her comrades leave in their respective cars, she closed her eyes and whispered the short prayer Andrew Dalton had taught her: "Lord, ease the pounding of my heart by the quieting of my mind." Then she added to herself, "I don't give a fig what these people think of me. If I have a panic attack in front of all of them, including the television cameras, so what? Everyone's life will go on."

She then took a deep breath and added, "Please, God, let everyone's life go on. Let us stop the murders."

Once Anastasia had told Celia she'd attend the reunion, the Great Cogs of Showbiz had rolled into motion. Anastasia had agreed to do interviews before the screening. She realized with a start that she had less than an hour before she'd promised to present herself, camera-ready.

As she descended the front stairs from the family wing, she was met by Geoff, in both a tuxedo and a state of high agitation. "Stacy, at last! Everyone's been out of their minds trying to find you! I'll admit you've had me going a bit myself. You haven't even been home in the last week! What were Cathy and I to think?"

"Hullo, Geoff," she said with a sweet, placid smile. "As you've said, here I am. Where do I go?"

"Stacy! You're here!" came from Cathy as she rounded the corner. She wore a dramatic pink gown with a white portrait collar and a cinched waist.

For a moment, the actress thought this was going to be easier than she'd imagined. She was getting a good bit of enjoyment out of seeing everyone else in a total tizzy.

"You could have let us know where you were," Geoff said, trying to sound offhand. "Oscar Moore, the director, is close to panic. And they have paid us a good bit. Also, I have some short matters of business to talk to you about as well."

"I said I'd be here ready for interviews by three, and it's only past two," she said calmly as she began walking the dimly lit passageway to the armory, the site of the night's celebration. "And surely any business we have can wait till after all this?"

"Yes, well—" said the Duke of Esmonde as they rounded a final corner and found themselves facing the sudden daylight of the large stone room.

The director saw them and raced over.

"Oscar Moore, may I present Anastasia Huntington, Duchess of Esmonde," said her stepson.

"Stacy," the dowager duchess added, extending her hand to shake Oscar's. He gave a small bow and kissed it instead.

"It is a great joy—and relief—to meet you, Your Grace," the director said. He was American, of medium build, with dark brown hair and beard. He was in his forties, but worked out with the idea of seeming thirty-something, and managed it.

"I hear we'd best get about it," Anastasia said, smiling.

"Follow me. I'll take you to your dressing room," Oscar said.

Anastasia couldn't help but gawk as they walked through the armory. Natural light flooded in from the high windows, but large television lights were being readied for night use. Large, colorful banners of family crests were draped about the walls; she had no idea if those belonged to the Huntingtons or to Hollywood. There must have been fifty people—caterers, camera and lighting technicians, decorators—buzzing purposefully about.

Pierce, you'd get such a kick out of this, she thought.

"We're set up to do the interviews over here," Oscar said, gesturing toward a roped-off area, inside which had been installed a dais, upon which sat the prop thrones used in the original film.

"Good heavens," she said, then suggested hopefully, "Knowing all the coverage the formal event will get tonight, wouldn't it be more visually interesting for me to do the pre-interview in casual clothes? That would give the cutaways a different look."

"Hmm. Nice idea. But I think our audience would like to see you in your gown." He stepped back and looked at her. "Your hair," he started. "Will you wear it down?"

She realized it was pinned up in a purposefully nondescript way. "It's rather much," she said, loosening a half-dozen pins so that it fell below her waist in a thick tumble.

"Stunning," Oscar said. "Wear it down. Definitely."

They're going to put me in a gown on a throne and I'm going to look like Rapunzel, she thought suddenly.

"Stacy! After all these years!" The actress turned to find a tall, lanky, obscenely handsome man marching toward them.

His burnished hair was thick and cut slightly long; his hazel eyes were large and expressive; his nose was strong enough to give him a masculine profile. He wore a light base of camera makeup.

"Richie," she said, extending both hands, which he grasped, leaning forward to kiss her cheek.

"Of course you remember Her Grace, the Duchess of Esmonde," Oscar said with a verbal nudge.

"'Stacy' is fine," she protested.

"We do go way back," Richard said, then turned again to her. "Where the hell have you been? I've been trying to reach you for weeks."

"I've been attending to some business," she answered.

"No one could find you anywhere," he said, and she caught the trace of true annoyance in his tone. Richard Riley, megastar, was apparently not used to being thwarted in getting what he wanted.

"Yes, we're all glad to have her here now," said Oscar the peacemaker. "She's on her way to the dressing room. It looks as if you're ready to get started? Good, good. We'll do your interview first, then Her Grace's, then the two of you together."

"Fine. I'll escort her to the dressing room. Back in five." Richie smiled and put his hand lightly on Anastasia's elbow.

"It's magnificent to see you, at any rate," he whispered in her ear as he guided her away from the cameras in front of the thrones. "I don't know if they've told you—we'll ride to the premiere together. If that's all right with you." It wasn't meant as a question. "Seriously, Stacy, it's great to see you. You look stunning. I love your hair."

"Thanks," she said,

They exited a side door into the sunlight and her companion led her to a caravan with a cardboard sign reading *Hair/Makeup* in the front window.

"They've brought in Clarissa from London," he said. "I'm sure she'll agree that it will be fabulous to have your hair down," Richie said, reaching a hand around to the back of her neck, then running it down, comblike, through the cascade of thick strawberry blonde curls.

"Let me guess. You're also one of the producers of the documentary," Anastasia said.

"Executive producer," he said. "It was the least I could do to get to see you again after so long."

Then he realized she'd had a note of irony in her voice. "I'm sorry. This isn't how I'd planned our first meeting would go. I have been trying to find you so that we could have dinner— something—before all this started. Now you're right. I'm acting like a producer. Forgive me."

"Of course," she said. "I guess I'd better go in. See you after."

"You do look stunning," he said. He leaned over to kiss her again, this time on the lips. In parting he gave her one of his trademark winks.

She gave him one of her trademark smiles. Then she turned the handle and stepped up into the caravan, pulling the door firmly closed behind her.

"She's here!" trumpeted an assistant.

A chorus of "Your Grace!'s" went up. A British crew.

"Hair first," said a woman near the front.

Should worst come to worst tonight, I'll end up a beautifully presented corpse, Anastasia thought.

A woman with assessing eyes and impeccable carriage parted the others and stood before her. Clarissa, no doubt. She had a small frame and serious cheekbones. To Anastasia's relief, a sparkle of mischief lurked behind her professional demeanor.

Anastasia followed her to the swivel chair facing the lighted mirror in the back of the caravan, and sat as Clarissa turned her subject's head from side to side.

"The director and executive producer would like my hair worn down long. But I think . . . it's time to lop it off." Anastasia said. "Rapunzel has had her day."

"I couldn't agree more," spoke the hairdresser.

And the conspirators went to work.

Clarissa left her curls slightly below shoulder length. Anastasia's dress was short and pearl blue with simple lines; she wore a necklace of sapphires given to her by Neville. Low-heeled pumps were her one concession to the fact she might need to run.

It had been so long since she had been in the midst of this lunacy, which seemed trivial in light of what was really at stake, that she ended up a bit punchy.

Both Richie and Oscar looked stricken when she returned.

"Stacy, what did you do?" Richie asked.

"You're right—Clarissa is amazing," she answered.

"Your beautiful hair . . . not that it's not still beautiful . . ."

"Is it less regal?" she asked. "Shall I get one of my tiaras?"

"Do you have one?" Richie asked hopefully.

Anastasia laughed. "Buck up. We'll pull it off."

"Let's move along," Oscar said. "You're up next, Your Grace. You'll use the queen's throne on the right. Let me introduce you to our interviewer, Luke Martin."

She chatted with Luke while they set the lights. Just before the cameras rolled, the interviewer asked nonchalantly, "What do you think about the reporter who claimed in *News of the Week* that he saw Peter Dalton at Heathrow earlier this week?"

Anastasia caught her breath but hoped her moment's pause seemed somehow nonchalant. "Was Peter supposedly seen with Elvis, or Raoul Wallenberg?"

Luke laughed and it wasn't mentioned during the half hour's taping. Oscar finally cut them off so that Luke could talk to Anastasia and Richard together.

As Richard got situated and Anastasia stood to stretch for a moment, a tall young woman staggered by carrying a huge flower arrangement. She set it down for a moment and turned to Anastasia. "This arrived for you, Your Grace."

"Wow. It looks… heavy," she said. It also looked more funereal than congratulatory. "May I see the card?"

Anastasia turned subtly for privacy and tore the miniature envelope quickly. She hoped her eyes didn't reveal too much as she perused its contents. In an awkward scrawl, perhaps written by the author's nondominant hand, it read, *Since you all have to die, you may as well know why: YOU'RE A SLUT.*

She realized all eyes were on her. "How sweet," she said, then turned to the girl. "I need you to do me a very important favor," she said, and led her a couple of paces away. "The phone number of the florist is on the outside of this envelope. I need you to ring him right away and find out who sent these flowers. I assume whoever it was came into the shop in person and handwrote the card. I need to know if it was a man or woman, what the person looked like, how he or she paid. This is truly important," Anastasia said.

"Yes, Your Grace."

"It's also private. I'm counting on you not to tell anyone."

"Of course not."

"Thanks. Let me know what you find out."

"Your Grace? We're ready for you," Luke the interviewer was saying.

Anastasia climbed the steps to sit on the throne beside Richard. Her mind raced. This was a bald-faced threat, there was no way around it. Should she alert Scotland Yard? If she did, what could they do? Actually, she and Bruce had gone out of their way to apprise Scotland Yard, and they hadn't done a darn thing thus far.

She wondered if she could count on their perpetrator to wait to make his move until they were back at the castle after the screening. It seemed likely. There would be no cameras inside the cinema. If the murderer was after a grand finale, a final drawing of the public's attention to the offing of the *T & Iers*, she believed he'd wait for the reception, where the horror would be captured for posterity on tape. She would show the note to Leah and Bruce at the screening and see if they thought it called for any change of plans.

She took a deep breath, smiled, and turned her attention to Luke and Richard.

As they wound up, she found the assistant waiting for her. "Sorry, ma'am, but the florist was closed for the rest of the day. Everything in the village is. They've all taken a holiday to see the goings-on."

"No one was there?"

"No one at all. They had a recorded message saying they'd be open again in the morning."

Anastasia tried to keep her disappointment from showing. "Thanks. I appreciate your trying."

The young woman bobbed her head and moved off.

"Stacy," Richard said, "they think it would be most dramatic if our limo was the last to arrive at the theater. That gives us half an hour before we need to leave. I thought we might want to freshen up in the trailer. We could relax and chat till it was time."

She could think of no excuse. "Thanks," she said. "That would be nice."

Once in the trailer, Richard popped some champagne and settled back, talking about the film he was about to start and telling anecdotes from the sets of some of his other well-known movies. Anastasia half listened while trying to make a mental list of who might think of her as a slut. She didn't think she actually qualified as one, so it had to be someone with his own agenda. She'd hoped this particular line of accusation had died with her mother. Furthermore, if the flowers had come from the murderer, it raised the savage implication that he held Anastasia to blame for the years of carnage. This was not good news.

"Excuse me?" she said, sitting up with a jolt as Richie touched her knee.

"I said, our limo's ready," he repeated, offering a hand.

A serious limousine it was, too. It was white and stretched on for days. Anastasia wondered how it would possibly negotiate the narrow lanes of Dunmore.

Once on their way, Richard uncorked another bottle of Veuve Clicquot, even though they'd barely made a dent in the expensive one they'd left behind.

He took two glasses from the bar and poured them full enough that they spilled over with happy abandon. "Anastasia," he said, "I met you twenty years ago, at the first read-through of *Tristan and Isolde*. My life has never been the same. The film was magic; it launched my career. But our friendship was something special, as well. Two Americans lost in British myth and history.

"But through everything these last twenty years, through all the movies, the success, the fame, I've had one dream I've never had the chance to pursue. To see you again."

"I thought you were married," Anastasia said.

"I was. We've been separated now for six months."

"Oh. Sorry."

"Don't be. The marriage has been over for years. And I was sorry to hear about your husband, of course. But somehow, it might all fit together. I want to do things for you, Anastasia. I didn't know quite where to start, but I thought, you being a duchess and all . . . if your town needed a cinema, perhaps that would make you happy as well."

"You built the cinema?" But even as she said it, it made sense. Who else would have that kind of money to throw around, and would care so much about this reunion?

"Richie, I don't know what to say."

"'Thanks' is a start."

"Thanks," she said, and she drained her glass in a gulp as the driver pulled up in front of the very building they'd been discussing. The streets and pavements were packed with people.

As the limousine purred to a stop, Richie finished his champagne. Then he kissed Anastasia, hard.

She managed to break free before a uniformed gentleman opened the back door, and the pops of hundreds of flashes crackled like fireworks. Richie exited, turned, and waved to the spectators, who gave a crowd-like whoop, then he turned back to the car, gave her a wink, and offered her his hand.

As she stepped out of the car, the cheers swelled. Richie took her hand firmly in his own and led her slowly up the red carpet. They were accosted by nonstop flashes, and they made half a dozen stops to talk to interviewers for various news and entertainment organizations. It was all a bit much.

Perhaps Peter had made the wisest decision, after all.

Once inside the lobby, which was thick with carpets and glowing with chandeliers, Anastasia spotted Leah and signaled they needed to talk. Leah made her way over.

"Excuse me," Anastasia said to the Lord Mayor of Dunmore and the president of Paramount, with whom she'd been speaking. "Leah Hall! How have you been!" she declared, and stepped out of their circle and threw her arms around her friend. Leah's bobbed hair looked jet black against her royal blue jacket and trousers. Her lipstick was bright red; she wore classic flapper pearls and smoked an ultra-thin cigarette through a long cigarette holder. She looked like she was enjoying herself.

"Read this, but give it back to me," Anastasia whispered to her. "It came with a funeral arrangement."

"It's so good to see you, darling!" Leah effused, while sneaking the card from Anastasia's hand and looking down to read it. Her eyes grew huge.

"Damn!" she whispered. "Who on earth . . . ?"

"Florist was closed," was the answer. "Tell Bruce. Keep your eyes open. And be careful." They were moved in opposite directions into the theater, where the screening was about to start.

Once the lights were turned down, the audience was welcomed to the new cinema by the Lord Mayor. Mercifully, the only other people who spoke were the head of Paramount and Richard Riley, who got lengthy applause. He asked all the original participants to stand; Anastasia imagined they might as well have bull's-eyes painted on their evening clothes. She herself tried to quickly see who was in attendance, but didn't have much luck before the lights went out.

It was hard to concentrate on the film. Anastasia had hoped to have her first out-of-body experience and miss it altogether, but she was not so lucky. The cinema was dark, Richard Riley was tickling her palm, and on the screen, fifty feet tall, was Peter. And Pierce. And all the hundreds of little movements and mannerisms and voice inflections that she had managed to forget.

Peter had been so young, so idealistic.

Pierce had been so alive.

Maybe somehow, in the midst of all the prides and passions of that time, she had done something that did deserve punishment. Maybe, somehow, she deserved to die.

But even as she thought that, she knew it was untrue. She had perhaps loved too much. But she had loved. And that wasn't a crime.

After the screening, she and Richard made their way once more to the stretch limo. "Great film," the actor pronounced, grinning. "It's a classic. Really holds up. Did you enjoy it?"

"Truthfully, I found it exhausting."

His laugh was merry and deep, the kind that enthralled moviegoers the world over. "I can understand that."

She wondered momentarily if she wasn't putting up unnecessary defenses against the man beside her. Perhaps, if she weren't so on edge about the threat back at the castle, she might attempt to enjoy his company.

The driver pulled the limousine away from the theater, then, out of sight of the crowds, made an unexpected turn away from the castle route.

Anastasia was jolted out of her reverie as they continued through deserted back streets of town.

"Where are we going?" she asked, but her companion's only response was to pop yet another bottle of champagne.

"Richie, what's going on?" she asked. He handed her another fizzing flute.

"No, thank you," she protested. The glass partition between the back of the car and the driver was closed and tinted, so that the driver couldn't see what was happening behind him. The limo was passing the southern outskirts of town now, beginning the drive along the ocean cliffs, where long stretches went by without any illumination.

Anastasia did her best not to panic. "Where are we going?" she demanded, attempting to sound firm and in control.

"All things will become clear in due time," said Richard.

"This is due time," she said. "This is as good as it gets."

As she spoke the car made a wide turn and the engine died. Anastasia couldn't believe she'd been such a trusting fool.

Richie leaned over and opened his door. They were on an overlook of the harbor; below them, empty fishing boats bobbed in the waves. Occasional sprinkles of light could be seen along the shoreline off in the distance. In front of them was a low wall, behind which was a sheer drop of a hundred feet or more straight down to the rocky ocean below.

Richie seated himself on the carpeted floor against the open door. "Come sit by me," he commanded.

"I'm fine," she replied. "Please tell me why we're here."

"You are a nervous one," he said, and she wanted to punch him.

"Look," she said. "I'm sorry about dinner. Truly I am."

"Dinner?"

"On the shoot. When you asked me out and I forgot. It was beastly of me. I felt terrible, even back then, but there wasn't a chance—"

"You were rather cavalier," he said.

"There was so much going on, you see—"

"And all of it obviously more important than me." An unmistakable edge now sharpened his tone.

"No. Of course not. I said it was beastly."

"As a matter of fact," he said, "you were fairly beastly to me during the whole shoot. I wonder if that's why I've never gotten past this obsession."

The word shot into her like a poisoned arrow. "Obsession?"

She wondered what would happen if she pounded on the dividing window. Or was the driver completely in Richie's employ?

"Yes. In a way, I have to thank you for that."

"Oh?"

"It drove me. Mercilessly. To become successful. To become so damn successful that I could come back and claim you—and you'd have to pay attention."

"You know," she said, fighting to keep her voice steady, "I have things I need to do at the party. There are people who are expecting me, who will come looking if I don't arrive immediately."

"For God's sake, give me a minute," he said. "I just told you I've been planning twenty years for this. Now. Come here. Sit by me."

"I said no."

A flash of undisguised annoyance crossed his features, but was quickly and consciously replaced by good-natured head-shaking. He was a man not used to being crossed.

"You're not an easy woman to surprise, Anastasia," he said. And he moved back up onto the leather seat to sit by her.

"Look," he said, "I know all of this is overwhelming. And none of it's gone quite as planned. I hoped you felt the same way about me that I do about you. That it was only a matter of me asking."

"You've been a star too long," she said.

He grinned, then shrugged. "Maybe I have. At any rate, if you will forgive all my brash behavior, perhaps the best thing would be to get to know each other. To do what we both do best. Work together. Make a movie."

He picked up her left hand and touched the fingers, one by one. "I've bought the rights to a brilliant script. I bought it be-cause I knew the female lead was perfect for you. It will be your comeback, will make you a player again. And the shoot will give us time to see how we like being together."

Anastasia's emotions were ricocheting. Was this offer as in-nocent as it seemed? Or was he really still furious because she'd spurned his advances twenty years ago? If so, what would happen if she refused? The sound of crashing waves served as an effective backdrop. If he really did think she was a slut and had arranged this party to cause harm to a great many people, if something catastrophic was happening back at the castle even now, it might be days before she was even discovered missing.

He had spent years trying to force her to pay attention. Perhaps the best thing to do was oblige. Her tone became conciliatory.

"Richie—Richard—that's very kind, it really is. If I can just make it through tonight, we can talk about it."

"Aren't you even curious about the movie?" he asked.

"Of course. But tonight is really—"

He reached forward and opened a door beneath the bar. From inside he withdrew a bound script. The title had been printed in gold on the black cover.

With a grand gesture, Richie put it on her lap.

It read, "*Beggar's Moon.* By Pierce Hall."

Richie didn't even note her response before excitedly chattering on. "I know you were set to star in it when Pierce died. It's one hell of a script; it's a tragedy it never got made. But what luck for us that I was able to secure the rights. Actually, you were a bit young for Julia back then. Now you're the perfect age."

Her heart was pounding. Her lungs began to constrict.

Lord, ease the pounding of my heart by the quieting of my mind, she pleaded, then added to herself, *Murder. I've got to solve the murders.* She leaned back against the seat and closed her eyes.

This has happened before. While it's unpleasant, it's not going to kill me. Be quiet. Simply be quiet.

And she said, in her sturdiest voice, "Richie, I must go back to the castle. Right now."

"But—what do you say to doing the film? We can announce it tonight. Think of the publicity. Say yes."

You are not having a heart attack. You are having a panic attack. You will live through it. You will be fine.

"Right now," she said.

Ease the pounding of my heart by the quieting of my mind. Ease the pounding of my heart by the quieting of my mind, she prayed over and over. Somewhere in the distance, she heard the car door shut and the engine rev to life.

Miraculously, instead of intensifying, her palpitations began to decrease as they drove. Her breathing regulated. She felt an ounce of victory, like she'd taken the tiniest bit of control.

She kept her eyes closed, staving off conversation, until she felt the limousine begin the climb up the steep incline to the castle parking lot. Simply entering the familiar parking lot still in one piece made her want to collapse in relief. When the car came to a stop, idling, she opened her eyes and found that they had paused in side shadows.

Richard Riley was studying her intently.

"Stacy," he asked, "are you all right?"

She gave a weak smile. "I will be," she said.

"I know this is my ego talking," he said. "But please tell me this isn't about me. Tell me there's something else going on tonight that's bothering you."

She did feel sympathy for him. He had put himself out—executive producing this extravaganza, financing a star-making role for her, building a bleeding cinema, for crying out loud.

"I am sorry. There is something else going on."

"That's a relief. So, if everything goes all right tonight, can we talk again, soon?"

"Yes," she said. "We can talk."

They got out together, and like the consummate professionals they were, they smiled sincere, happy smiles for the cameras.

Their drive had taken longer than Anastasia guessed. The party was already in full swing; the armory, crowded with people, each of whom had surrendered a coveted pass at the door. This meant that if the murderer was inside, he had been invited. He was one of them.

Anastasia thought briefly of fleeing to her rooms to score some Valium. She thought less briefly about fleeing to her rooms and staying there.

"Anastasia Day! How are you? What happened to your hair? And where the hell have you been?" Anastasia turned to find Bruce, elegant in a tux, beside her. Elise stood behind him, clutching a white wine spritzer. "Don't you remember our agreement not to disappear by yourself?" he asked in a hiss. "I thought we'd lost you before things got started!"

"Sorry," she said. "I'll explain later. It involved our friend Richie."

"Yes? Any indication he's the culprit?"

"I don't think so. I think he's still Richie."

"Leah told me about the card. May I see it?"

Anastasia rummaged through her purse, pulled out a Kleenex for herself, and palmed the card off to her compatriot.

"As for my hair, I cut it," she said cheerfully. "What do you think?" But Bruce's attention had been arrested by the back-slanted handwriting she'd shown him.

"Good heavens," he said, handing the card back. "It looks like it'll be an exciting party. And guess who's here."

"Who?"

"Our mystery guest. The talk of the town."

Anastasia gave an impatient stomp of the foot.

"Nicola."

"Oh dear," the actress breathed.

"What?"

"I stole her part. We know she put the moves on Peter, who told her flat out he preferred me to her. If anyone could have come away from the shoot thinking I was a slut, as the card so poetically states, she'd be my first guess."

Bruce smiled. "Good. We've got ourselves a suspect. Go say hello." Then, at normal volume, he added, "Well, you're looking great. Good to see you. We'll do lunch."

He gave her a wink and disappeared with his wife into the crowd.

Anastasia desperately needed five minutes to sit and collect herself. She remembered that there were a series of alcoves behind the arches along the corridor that ran the length of the back wall. The alcoves had once served as dressing and armor-fitting rooms for the knights.

But before she could steal away, she was accosted by Oscar the director. "You have the worst way of disappearing," he said, "and there's a shot we've got to get immediately. The two Isoldes, together again. It'll be great! A clip from your meeting over the body of Tristan, then the two of you, lovely women, twenty years later. Perfect. Fabulous."

"Yes, that would be great. Give me five minutes to freshen up."

"No need. Joe, fetch Miss Neve."

Ease the pounding of my heart by the quieting of my mind, she breathed silently.

Then Joe arrived before her, leading Nicola Neve.

In Anastasia's mind, it was as if the room were suddenly emptied of everyone else. The silence between her and Nicola was deafening. The two women locked eyes, questioning. Searching. Nicola Neve was still a very attractive woman, but the twenty years intervening were clearly etched in story lines on her face. Her hair was still coal black, and she wore it short. Her dress was velvet, a dark midnight blue, nicely styled, but nothing to stand out in a crowd. She was rail thin. Too thin.

Anastasia was certain she was being similarly assessed and similarly found wanting.

Beside them, Oscar's mouth was moving, but neither heard a sound.

"Hello, Nicola," Anastasia finally said. "I've thought of you in past years and wondered where you were. I hoped you were happy and doing well."

"I was. You married money, I hear."

The dowager duchess was a bit taken aback. "Not really," she said.

"A title, at least."

"Yes. I suppose so."

"Wonderful, ladies," Oscar broke in, a hand on each of their shoulders as he guided them to where the cameras had been hastily set up. "Let's get some footage of the two of you together."

"Gladly," said Nicola, giving Oscar a flirtatious smile. To Anastasia's genuine surprise, Nicola spoke of her acting days with intelligence, and made some illuminating comments about the part of Isolde of the White Hands.

On tape, at least, there was no sign of enmity between the two women.

"Miss Neve, would you please clear up for us the mystery of where you've been for the past twenty years? Since the filming of *Tristan and Isolde?*"

"Please forgive me if I keep my private life private, Luke," she said. "I realized the toll that living in the public eye had taken on me, and knew, if I was to find peace, I needed to move on. So I did."

"You've been concentrating on your private life? Have you found happiness, then?"

"Yes," she answered. "Enough said."

"You've a family? Children? Have you any interest in getting back into show business?"

"Enough said," she responded again, leaving the air rife with mystery.

"Cut," said Oscar, obviously delighted. "Thank you both."

Anastasia realized how canny Nicola was being. By simply showing up, then remaining sphinxlike, she was becoming the talk of the reunion.

Nicola unexpectedly leaned forward and gave Anastasia a hug. "Perhaps we can talk later. Privately," she said.

Trying to muffle her astonishment, Anastasia said, "Sure."

As Nicola melted into the crowd, the Duchess of Esmonde decided to once again make a break for it.

"Such a lovely dress," she heard from beside her, and turned to see Cathy and Geoff glowing, in their element. Geoff even wore his red sash, which marked him as a member of the Knights of the Order of the Garter.

"Thank you," Anastasia replied to Cathy. "You both look fetching, as well. Are you doing all right?"

"Oh, yes," Cathy returned, happily. "There are so many interesting people here to meet."

"Yes, there are. Be sure to introduce yourselves to Richard Riley. Tell him I said you should."

"Oh, we've already met. He's been such a help with all the planning. Such a nice man."

Geoff had been studying Anastasia curiously, a frown of consternation on his face.

"It's your hair," he finally said. "You've cut it off."

"Yes," she admitted, a bit defensive. "I thought it was time. That is, I don't think your father would mind."

She knew from her panic at Geoff's simple hair question that she was becoming overwhelmed. She had to disappear for a moment, to collect herself. It was imperative.

Besides, she needed to think. There was something about the content of the note that was nagging at her.

Anastasia slid through the crowd, purposefully looking past anyone who might catch her eye and stop her. She made it to the arched walkway at the back of the armory and ducked under a medieval hunt tapestry into the closest alcove.

She let the tapestry fall into place behind her and sighed audibly with relief. She was about to collapse onto an uncomfortable-looking leather sofa, when she saw that someone else was already lying on it, having a smoke.

"Sorry," Anastasia said automatically.

"Not at all," answered Elise, sitting up. "It's your sofa."

"Elise! What a relief. May I join you? I need to collect myself. What a night."

"It's only begun."

There was a hard edge to Elise's voice that made Anastasia turn and study her. Not only was she smoking, which her friend had never seen her do, she had been drinking. A lot. A tall tumbler of Scotch dangled from her hand even as they spoke.

"So, why did you cut your hair?" the Scotswoman asked.

"People were making too much of it," Anastasia answered. "It was time for a change. You started it, really. Getting me into jeans and sweaters again."

"Ah. So I helped Sleeping Beauty awaken. And, in doing so, cooked my own goose."

"I'm afraid I don't follow."

"Oh, come now," Elise said, her words slightly slurred. "We're a bit past the politeness stage, wouldn't you say? When women have shared as much as we have."

"I really don't understand what you're getting at."

"I know you're having an affair with my husband. There. Is that plain enough for you? And I was even kind enough to trot off out of the way."

Anastasia stared at her, incredulous. Maybe she should have gotten herself a drink, after all. "No. You're wrong. You're very wrong. I would never do that to you. Ever," she protested.

"I know my husband. I'd have to be blind not to see the way he looks at you."

"We're good friends. As you and I are. Bruce and I are only trying to clear up this terrible situation."

"You're willing to look me in the eye and tell me that Bruce has never laid a hand—let alone his lips—on you."

Anastasia wanted to scream and tear at her hair. Her overwhelming emotion was that she didn't have time for this now. She decided the truth was probably the safest and easiest way out.

"He kissed me once. But it wasn't about us. It was about old times. Everything we'd been through. Everyone we'd lost."

"So you admit you've smooched. That's a start. For auld lang syne, why not. That explains it all. Why Bruce stares after you the way he does. Why he comes alive when you're together. For old times' sake. Ha! I like that!"

"Elise, we all come alive when we're together. It's adrenaline. We're trying to catch a murderer! I thought you were with us on this!"

"That would be the best part, wouldn't it?" she asked. "The loyal little wifey helping at their side. At least I might stay alive—which is more than can be said for Claudine, poor bitch. Your friend Bruce might be capable of more than you imagine. You both think you're so smart. You think you know all there is to know. Well, fuck that. And fuck you!"

Elise stood unsteadily and chucked the contents of her glass at Anastasia's face. Then she stalked out of the room.

Fortunately, she was so drunk that most of the Scotch missed Anastasia by a good margin, splattering the sofa instead. Enough hit her hair to make several curls sticky. She knew she'd smell of alcohol until she washed it out.

"Oh, damn," she said. "Damn."

Her worst regret was losing a valuable friend and ally.

She sat for a moment, eyes closed, calming herself. She needed to check in with Bruce and Leah. She didn't care that they shouldn't be seen together; they needed to compare notes.

The Duchess of Esmonde pulled herself up, did her best to shake out her hair, and headed back toward the armory.

Waiters in formal attire buzzed about the long dinner tables, filling water goblets, setting down baskets of rolls and round silver plates of butter pats. They were getting close to dinner.

Anastasia decided to check out the seating arrangement at the long head table, both to find her own place and to see if there were any surprises among those seated there. At each setting was propped a menu card—gazpacho garnished with garlic croutons was the first course—and a place card. She walked along, reading the expected names of the attending *T & I*ers. She found her seat next to Richie's. But there was something unexpected. On her plate was an envelope, her name written across the front in short, brisk letters.

She surveyed the room, but saw no one watching her. Most of the crowd was still in the back half of the hall, where the libations continued to flow and a jazz trio brightened the mood.

Anastasia picked up the envelope and moved into the privacy of the arched hallway. As she turned it over, she noted with surprise the Esmonde crest. The handwriting inside matched that on the front. In a script that looked formal and vaguely familiar, it said, *I have something for you from your mother. Meet me on the Moorish balcony before dinner.*

She fell back against the cool stone of the archway. The stationery taunted her. Someone had gained access to the family quarters, possibly even her own sitting room, and was using family stationery. She looked again at the text. For God's sake, her mother was dead. Couldn't this night evolve without invoking her? Whoever this was had, in one letter, violated her home and her heart. It didn't take much to edge her fear into fury.

Anastasia peered around the corner back into the crowd. She was able to spot Bruce and signal him to join her before stepping back out of sight.

"Anything to report?" he asked.

"Only this," she said, handing him the envelope.

He read it, and looked up, perplexed. "What does it mean?"

"I have no idea."

"I thought your mother was dead."

"That's my understanding as well. But I guess I'd better go."

"I'll follow you, of course. The Moorish balcony—where's that?"

"It's off the south side of the armory. Someone did their homework to find out about it."

"How do you reach it?"

"You go upstairs here, and back through the hallway above this one." Anastasia looked again at the message in her hands.

"You have a bad feeling about this, don't you?" her partner asked.

"I'd feel better if you brought a security man with you."

Bruce bit the inside of his lip. It was clear he was still apprehensive of involving the authorities.

"Here," Anastasia said, "take the note. Show it to one of them. Tell him we think it's a stalker. That's all you need to do."

"All right," Bruce reluctantly agreed. "You want to wait here?"

"No," Anastasia said. "I'll head upstairs. It has to look like I'm going alone."

"I won't be far behind you. Whatever you do, do not go outside onto that balcony before you see me behind you."

"I promise," she said. "Oh, by the way, your wife thinks we're having an affair. See you in a minute."

Anastasia went back toward the stone steps that hugged the inside wall of the back hallway and climbed carefully.

Once she reached the second floor, instead of starting down the old passages, she walked around to where vaulted archways of the upper floor completed the pillars of the first floor, and watched the partyers below.

Bruce was conferring with a burly, crop-haired security guard, who seemed to be taking him seriously. Straight below her, the waitstaff was setting the table with the cold soup of the first course. Anastasia was certain the castle kitchens hadn't seen this much activity since Geoff's investiture. She was impressed that Richie, and whomever he'd worked with to arrange this extravaganza, had gone to the trouble and expense of renting real crystal and china for the three hundred diners. From above, the circular gold and blue bands on the plates and bowls looked elegant framing the ruby red of the gazpacho with contrasting croutons and greens.

When she scanned the room again, she saw no trace of Bruce or the security man; she assumed they were heading up.

She turned and started toward the back passageway.

The upper hallways of the armory were seldom used and therefore had never been very well lit. Low-wattage electric bulbs dotted the ceiling every few meters, casting long shadows, coloring everything a foreboding gray. Someone had gone out of his way to discover the balcony. Unless the letter was from someone who already knew there was one—and what it was called.

But who? And why?

Anastasia rounded a final curve into the hallway that led another forty meters to the small outside balcony. Its rounded wooden door, usually bolted shut from inside, now stood partially open.

Anastasia ducked back around the corner into the long hall from which she'd just come, looking quickly for her reinforcements. No one yet. She pressed herself against the wall opposite an old storeroom, trying to occupy as small a space as possible.

Oh, Mother, she thought, *what on earth have you got to do with this? You disappeared. Then you died. That was horrible enough. Can't you stay gone?*

She couldn't stand knowing who was waiting on the other side of that balcony door. But she couldn't stand not knowing, either.

As she waited her mind raged with a tumult of swirling thoughts. From them, suddenly, the answer to one of the night's riddles emerged with complete clarity.

Within moments, she heard soft footfalls approaching from the direction of the party.

"Bruce!" she whispered. "Over here."

But the form that rounded the corner was not Bruce. It was Nicola Neve.

"Nicola," Anastasia said, quietly. "You surprised me."

Nicola shrugged. "I saw you come up. And, as I said earlier, we need the opportunity to talk together privately."

"Yes, we do. Could it be later?"

"I don't think so. I'm in the mood now. And I'd think you'd be curious to hear the message your mother sent you."

"*You* have a message from my mother?"

"Yes. And frankly, time is of the essence."

Nicola floated across the hall and tried the handle of the square wooden door that led into the storage room.

"It will only take a minute. You'll thank me, I guarantee it." She went in.

Anastasia looked down the corridor, hoping to catch sight of Bruce. No luck. She didn't have much time, if her new suspicion was correct. She had promised not to go anywhere alone with anyone. Still. Nicola might be loony tunes, but she was small. Anastasia was fairly sure she could take her on in a fight, if it came to that. And whatever information she had might be important.

Anastasia crossed to the storeroom and went inside, leaving the door open.

Her eyes didn't adjust to the low light very quickly. This

seemed to be the final resting place for crates and pieces of old furniture. Nicola found a long crate and perched upon it.

"What do you have from my mother?" Anastasia asked.

"I have the story of her last years. I have her final will and testament," Nicola said.

"What are you talking about?"

"The day your mother came to the set changed my life," the former actress said. "We went for a walk, and we talked. She told me about her past, how empty she'd felt, the problems she'd had with alcohol. And she told me about the answers she'd found. What she said made a lot of sense to me. I eventually went with her to meet the Master. What he said made sense as well.

"As you know, I had it all. Money. Fame. Men. I was past needing those things. Your mother saw you still chasing after them, and it broke her heart."

"What?" Anastasia asked. "I never—"

"When your mother became a full member of the Family of Truth, she took the name Star—actually, the Indian equivalent. I became her spiritual daughter. Together we moved to the Family's compound in the Kashmir Valley in the Indian Himalayas."

"You became my mother's spiritual daughter?" Anastasia asked. She knew her mother had never been emotionally sound, had never seen her own daughter in the best possible light. She hadn't known a final rejection could still hurt so deeply.

"Yes. We lived together with the Family for many happy years. I got to see firsthand what the Master taught was Truth.

"But then . . . something happened. Something I thought could never happen. Mother fell into heresy. She became an apostate."

"My mother? An apostate? What's that?"

"She fell away from the truth. She left the Family. But she was punished."

Anastasia stood over Nicola, hands on her shoulders. "Who punished her? What did they do?"

When Nicola looked up, she was still serene. "God punished her. As he punishes all the wicked. She was free to leave the Family, of course. But she died of malaria before she could even get out of the valley."

"Did anyone help her?"

"We had barely enough medicine for the chosen, let alone the heretics."

"You mean the Family knew she was sick and let her die?" The horror clogged Anastasia's throat.

"Death is best for infidels, you see. Then they may appeal to God's own mercy."

"Nicola! Listen to what you're saying! How can any group that claims to seek God, to seek the truth, be so cruel?"

"It only seems cruel. It's ultimately kind."

"Killing people is ultimately kind?"

Nicola sighed. "There's no way that someone who has not received the Enlightening can understand. Anyway, it wasn't long after that that the Master went on to his own Deification. We were happy for him, of course. But we were all left as orphans, to do as we'd been taught. It was time for us to move out into the world. With him still guiding us spiritually, of course."

Anastasia tried to continue to sound calm. "So you're saying that the Master is still guiding you since his death. And he teaches that the kindliest thing for . . . infidels . . . is death."

"Yes," she said sincerely. "Yet people fight so hard against it."

It took Anastasia only three bounds to get to the door, but Nicola had the head start. The brunette caught Anastasia inside the storeroom, throwing all her weight against her so that the door boomed shut. She had the younger woman pinned inside. And then Anastasia felt something sharp pushing at her, against her breastbone.

"There are easier ways to kill people," Nicola explained carefully. "But if I kill you with a clean plunge to the heart, you'll go directly to the Courts of Judgment, instead of having to serve time simply to get there. Say a prayer, Anastasia."

"Nicola, for God's sake!" Anastasia said. In the dimness, she could barely see the glint of the blade pressing into her flesh.

"You aren't paying attention," the woman hissed. "This *is* for God's sake! Will you beg his mercy, or not?"

Anastasia brought her knee up sharply into Nicola's abdomen, at the same time screaming at the top of her lungs. Nicola grabbed her stomach, surprised. Then both women were on the floor, feeling over the dark stones at their feet for the dropped dagger.

Anastasia found it first and grabbed it. But Nicola had been trained for her mission. She swung around in a practiced movement, bringing the force of her elbow sharply into Anastasia's solar plexus. As Anastasia doubled forward, Nicola wrenched the dagger back and drew it up quickly to Anastasia's throat.

But as she did, the door banged open, leaving both women blinded just long enough for the intruder to grab Nicola from behind, disarming her in the process.

Anastasia put her hands to her throat and whirled around.

"Bruce! For God's sake! What took you so long?"

But as she spoke, Bruce and the guard came running up to the open door.

She turned again and found Geoff kicking the dagger far from Nicola's reach, then lifting her off her feet, her arms pinned beside her.

"I was on the balcony and I heard you scream," Geoff said.

"Geoff," Anastasia interrupted, "explain what happened, and have Nicola arrested immediately. I've got to get downstairs before everyone's killed!"

And the dowager duchess tore from the room, running as fast

as she possibly could through the dim corridors and headlong down the stairs.

As she reached the ground floor, she heard the announcement for everyone to find their places at the tables. Without a moment's pause, she careened down yet another hallway toward the main buildings of the castle. Waiters with trays scattered on either side of her.

She skidded sharply as she banged through double doors into the serving room off the kitchen. In it sat tall, multi-tiered carts holding the shrimp cocktails for the next course.

Anastasia continued through, bursting through the doors into the kitchen, nearly upsetting two carts that were coming through.

"Where is the chef?" she hollered. "Who made the gazpacho?"

There was chatter and movement among the pots, pans, and workers before a rotund gentleman in chef's whites appeared before her.

"I am François, the chef," he said. "Any complaints come to me." His tone implied frankly what would happen to anyone who dared make a derogatory comment.

"No complaints," Anastasia said, "But this is urgent. Describe to me the garnish on the soup."

"What?" he exploded. "I am serving three hundred twenty-two people for five courses and you want to discuss garnish?"

Anastasia drew herself up every bit as tall. "I am Her Grace, the Duchess of Esmonde, not to mention the star of this damn movie. I'm sure your soup is wonderful, but this is a matter of life and death. *What garnish is on the soup?*"

"Why, the homemade croutons. Seasoned with garlic and Romano cheese—"

"And the greens used as garnish. What are they?"

He looked confused. "There is none."

"Who garnished the soup? Whose job was it to add the croutons?"

"I don't know. One of the assistants—"

"Quickly!" Anastasia called out. "Who garnished the soup? Please! I need your help!"

"I did," said a female assistant. "Clive helped as well."

"What greens did you add?" Anastasia asked.

The woman pointed to a round wooden bowl. Some of the remaining greens were thin and flat like sweet grasses; others were rounded like stalks. "I was told to spread these first, then top them with four croutons per bowl."

Her Grace turned to François. "These are not your greens?"

He shook his head, perplexed.

"Who instructed you?" Anastasia asked the assistant evenly.

"I don't know. There were so many people around. Someone from the kitchen—"

"A woman? Wearing whites over her clothes?"

The assistant nodded.

"Was she thin? With short dark hair?"

The young woman's face lit up. "Yes. Yes, she was!"

"No one touch these!" Anastasia said, pointing to the barrel. "Guard them for the authorities. They're poison. And quickly! We've got to stop everyone from eating the first course!"

She turned on her heel and ran, François close behind her. *At least she was going to send me straight to the Courts of Judgment*, Anastasia thought.

They arrived in the armory to find everyone seated and chatting. When Richard Riley saw her, his whole body sighed in relief. "Anastasia!" he said. "We were going to have to start without you."

"Richard, I can't explain right now, but there's been a sudden change of menu. No one is to touch the gazpacho. It's very embarrassing, but it turns out that the kitchen dog . . . has urinated on the greens."

A look of incredulity passed over Richard's face.

"The kitchen staff will replace the soup with the next course within moments. Please make the announcement, then we can start."

He looked at her, amazed. Then he looked at the man in the tall chef's hat behind her, who had not heard exactly what she said, but was nodding in agreement.

Richard went to the microphone. "Good evening, ladies and gentlemen," he said. "And welcome, a thousand times welcome. We've already had a memorable evening, and I promise you there is much more to come.

"But first, I'm told there's been a slight change of menu. The kitchen will be removing your soup, replacing it with . . . something much better. I'm told you'll be happier when all is said and done if you let the kitchen remove the soup without tasting it."

A murmur arose, then scattered laughter.

Waiters were already emptying soup bowls into a large tureen and stacking the empty bowls, while others appeared behind them with the carts of shrimp cocktail.

"We've asked the local vicar to bless us—and then, on with the festivities!"

This was met with applause. Anastasia had innocently taken her chair next to Richie. The young local vicar stood to say the blessing, speaking into the microphone to be heard over the clatter of the dish exchange. At the conclusion, a string quartet struck the chords of Conan Marcel's "Theme of Love Forbidden." And everyone began to eat.

Anastasia gave a monstrous sigh and felt her muscles go limp.

In the back corridor, she saw the flash of a uniform. "I'm sorry, Richie, you must excuse me," she said. "There's someone waiting to speak to me outside. I'll explain everything later, I promise."

And she slipped away from the table.

Nicola had already been handcuffed and put into the constable's van outside the kitchen exit from the castle.

To Anastasia's surprise, this was all being overseen by Bruce's old nemesis, Inspector Irving from Scotland Yard. Bruce and the security man were there, answering questions. The chef had followed Anastasia outside, and not long after, Leah arrived at a fast clip.

Irving had already gotten the basic information about the attack in the storeroom from Geoff, who'd been dismissed to go to dinner, and from Bruce. Anastasia, aided by François, quickly outlined the massive murder plot that had been thwarted only minutes from its successful completion.

François promised that he and his assistants would stay as long after the dinner as needed to give full statements. Two men were dispatched to confiscate the deadly greens.

As the chef returned to the kitchen, Inspector Irving saw Nicola safely squared away, and the van rolled out. To Anastasia's surprise, the inspector motioned Bruce into private conference. Anastasia and Leah exchanged glances and invited themselves to follow.

Looking at the three gathered expectantly, the inspector said, "The suspect talks quite freely of her intentions to do in Her Grace," he said. "We'll be able to book her straightaway. She claims not to know anything about poison, or about any other murders—says she only recently left India—but once we have the evidence in hand, we shouldn't have a hard time changing her story."

This information conveyed, the horse-faced inspector looked suddenly sheepish.

"I'm afraid I owe Mr. Amerman an apology," he said. "All of

you, perhaps. It seems that Detective Raymond, one of the chaps assigned to this case full-time, took his assignment a bit too seriously. Overstepped his bounds. He has been disciplined."

"Yes, Inspector?" asked Bruce. "Could you be a bit more specific?"

The tall man cleared his throat uncomfortably. "He exceeded his jurisdiction. Followed you to Calais, I'm afraid. No jurisdiction in France, none at all. And the other night, though assigned to watch your house, he had no call to go wandering your garden, let alone go peering into windows. Quite against policy. But no harm's been done, I hope, and as I said, he is being disciplined."

"So it was a detective I saw run past the window at Conan's farmhouse?" Anastasia asked. "And the feeling I got that someone was watching Bruce's house?"

"What? Oh, hmm, possibly. Could have been."

"And it was your man who frightened my wife and me out of our skins last night?"

"He knows better now."

The three friends looked at each other incredulously.

"You know, Inspector," Anastasia started, "things like this don't look so good for Scotland Yard, do they?"

The inspector didn't answer.

"I was thinking. If, perhaps, someone in your position could use his influence to keep this story from exploding all over the press, well, it would help keep these other embarrassing details from coming to light. Wouldn't it?"

"Humph. Yes. Well, I suppose so."

"In other words, we might be able to downplay the more . . . sensational aspects of this case?

"I said I would see what could be done," he said. "Now, I would ask that neither you, Mr. Amerman, nor you, Your Grace, leave the country without notifying me first. There will be depositions and so forth."

Both nodded their agreement. The inspector moved off, looking relieved that the encounter had been concluded.

"So," said Leah to Anastasia, "tell, tell! How did you figure out about the soup?"

"Nicola's card said that everyone had to die. So there had to be some way of mass destruction. As we noted, the killer has never been a mad bomber, or otherwise called attention to herself. She's been more subtle than that. We knew there had been poisonings. Conveniently, that was the one activity that all of us would be involved in tonight—eating. It wasn't hard to put together great masses of people, food, and poisoning. And the menu cards were so specific, down to the flavoring of the croutons, it seemed odd not to mention the type of greens, or at least that there were some. It seemed unlikely someone could sneak in and actually alter ingredients, but fairly quick and simple to sprinkle something on top.

"When I remembered that Conan had died after eating only his soup and some salad, it seemed worth checking out. Fortunately, I was right."

"How about the rest of the courses?" Leah asked suspiciously. "I assume they're all right. Nicola didn't expect us to live past the soup."

"Wow," Leah said. "In that case, I admit I'm famished. Though I'll make sure everyone survives the shrimp before I eat mine. You two coming?"

As Anastasia began to follow her, Bruce put a restraining hand on her arm. "Stace," he said, "I owe you an apology. I got the guard, as agreed, and we were on our way to follow you when Elise lit into me like a banshee. She was snockered, out of her head. It was all I could do to wrestle her out of sight, then it took both me and the guard to get her off me and quiet her down. By the time we got free, and got upstairs, I couldn't find you any-where. When we did—well, needless to say, if it hadn't been for Geoff we'd have been too late."

Bruce looked chagrined. "I'm sorry. It was unforgivable. I'm sure that when Elise comes to her senses, she'll be mortified."

Anastasia said, "The important thing is, everything worked out. You've been there every step of the way. It wasn't your fault, and Elise couldn't have known. I hope we can convince her that she has no reason to worry about us."

"That's my department," said Bruce. "Now that this whole mess is behind us, I think she and I have earned a holiday."

"I think so." His friend smiled.

Not caring who saw, they joined hands, and headed back in.

But before they made it back around to the door, another male voice surprised them.

"If I may interrupt?"

The friends whirled to find Geoff, the Duke of Esmonde, be-hind them.

"If I may have a word with Her Grace?" he asked.

"Of course, Geoff," Anastasia said. "Especially as I owe you a considerable debt of gratitude."

Especially as I was suspecting you of terrible things on my way to the Moorish balcony, she thought guiltily.

Bruce gave a quick smile, motioning that he'd see her inside.

"I didn't mean to be quite so mysterious," Geoff began. "Send-ing you a note to meet me on the Moorish balcony and all that. It did seem it might afford us a bit of privacy."

"The note was from you."

"Yes," he said sheepishly. "As I said earlier, I'd been want-ing to talk to you before the event tonight. I suppose I got a bit caught up in all the dramatics of the evening."

"Lucky for me that you did. So you were there waiting—"

"On the balcony, yes. When you never arrived, I came out to have a look-see. That's when I heard you scream."

"Thank you. You put yourself in harm's way for me, and I'm grateful."

"You'll perhaps give me a fuller explanation of all of this later?"

"Gladly."

Geoff nodded, satisfied. "Then, back to my original purpose. Going through some of Father's personal things, I recently found a small package he must have received only the day before he died. Upon examining its contents, it seemed clear it was for you. From your mother. It wasn't exactly addressed correctly—it said something like 'to Anastasia the Duchess, at the Castle, Somerset.' It had been misdelivered at least twice before Lord Greenley put two and two together and forwarded it to Father. Unfortunately, he died before it reached you . . . so finally . . ."

And he handed her a small wrapped box. "Sorry for the delay." Geoff gave a small bow and turned to go back inside.

Anastasia stood, holding the package. She finally pulled on the bow, untying it, and opened the lid. A folded piece of paper from a yellow legal pad sat on top. She opened it with trembling fingers. There, for the first time in decades, she saw her name written in her mother's flowing script.

"Stacy," it said. "I am not well, and I only hope I can get this posted before it's too late.

"I enclose the only thing of value I never turned over to the Family. It is not made of precious stones, its value is purely personal. It's a necklace and earrings that belonged to my own mother, Myrtle Preston, back in Virginia where I grew up. They were her favorites. She gave them to me the day I left home. I can see now that she must have loved me as much as I love you.

"Forgive me. Remember the good times. We did have some good times."

The handwriting had grown weak and spidery. The closing, which seemed to have come more quickly than the writer intended, was light on the page, and shaky. "Love, Mother," was all it said.

Trembling, Anastasia picked up the rhinestone heart on the silver chain. She easily unclasped the cluster of sapphires from around her neck and dropped them into the box, replacing them with the shiny necklace she held in her hands. She replaced her earrings as well.

Then she turned and walked back into the party.

CHAPTER 13

Yes, readers, I'm back moments ago from the Soiree of the Year—the Tristan and Isolde reunion held in the very castle where the classic film was shot. The fete was hosted by Richard Riley and Anastasia Day, now, of course, the Dowager Duchess of Esmonde. Such food! Such drink! Such gossip! Everything went off without a hitch, and now the reunion is history as well. Join the party in our exclusive four-page spread this Sunday.
—Wendy Coburn, London Daily News website

In the small hours before dawn, Anastasia opened her eyes to the feel of cold steel against her temple.

"I am sorry you figured out about the gazpacho," she heard a flat, hard voice say as she pulled herself awake. "Although, truth to tell, there weren't even that many true *T & I*ers at the banquet. I would have enjoyed seeing Bruce Amerman writhe. His annoying wife, too, of course. And who wouldn't have gotten a kick from watching the death throes of Richie Riley? We could have witnessed the final minutes of one of the world's great egos.

"But the biggest disappointment was not getting to kill you.

It would have been great. All those cameras recording it for posterity.

"Oh well," the voice continued with a verbal shrug, "easy enough to finish the job now."

Anastasia stretched as if slowly ascending from sleep, and languidly reached an arm under her pillow. Silently, she pressed the record button on the small tape recorder hidden there.

"Leah?" she asked, seemingly groggy. Anastasia sat up, withdrawing her hand from behind the pillow as she did so, and pointing the revolver she had also hidden there toward her friend who now sat next to her on the bed. She used the split second of surprise to disengage the safety.

"I wasn't quite sure when to expect you. I guessed tomorrow at lunch, a sort of perfect symmetry, bookending the last lunch you shared with your father."

The two friends sat in the darkness, weapons pointed at each other. It took an enormous amount of control for Anastasia to keep her breathing normal. After Nicola's arrest, when the pieces still didn't fit, Anastasia had redone the puzzle in her mind again and again. This was the only way it all made sense. She had prepared for it, planned her defense.

But she still didn't want to believe it was so.

"You must have been quite amused when Scotland Yard carted off Nicola," Anastasia said, using all of her willpower to keep her voice light.

Leah laughed. "Nicola is a poor sick puppy. Delusional, even, with all her charming talk about infidels and death for everyone. But dangerous? Come on. She couldn't even take down one unarmed opponent. What are the chances she could plot and execute a string of undetected murders over a span of twenty years?"

Anastasia grimaced in agreement, then said, "Leah, come on,

you're giving me the creeps. Put down the gun."

In response, the woman beside her smacked her with the revolver, hard, on the side of the head. "You don't have time to pretend you don't get it. When I mean to kill, I do. And you're minutes from dead."

Anastasia's head throbbed; it was all she could do to keep her own gun pointed at the woman she'd known as her friend. She grasped it hard, as if it were welded to her fingers. "It did take a brilliant mind to kill all those people over such a long time without anyone realizing. And when someone finally saw what was happening . . . you must have enjoyed putting Bruce and me through our paces."

"It was amusing. For a while."

Anastasia observed with some surprise that even though her adrenaline was pumping, her nerves were perfectly calm. It was almost as if the two old friends were having a heart-to-heart, exactly as they would have if Anastasia had accepted Evan Masterson's offer and was trying to decide where to live and whom to date in Los Angeles.

Yet, this woman had slowly, methodically brought great pain to her life. And now she planned to end it.

"So, who was first? Your father?" Anastasia asked.

"He was first, and could have been last. But it was such a kick to watch him die. His pain was delicious. Both physical and emotional. To be killed by your own daughter. Imagine. So lovely it gives me shivers even now. But then, so was watching your anguish. Father's death nearly did you in, didn't it?

"It all became rather addicting. I hadn't known T & I was so close to being finished; that it could go on to bring his name to future generations. I had to kill his legacy, as well. So that when people remember T & I in years to come, it will be with horror rather than respect."

Anastasia realized that the tone of voice in which Leah spoke was the most chilling thing. It was gravelly, almost unrecognizable. Demonic.

Anastasia tried to regulate her breathing. "What did you mean when you said your father's death nearly did me in?"

"You know, Stace, the only way you consistently disappoint me is when I expect you to be smarter than you actually are. Although I've got to say I didn't expect *this*." She nodded toward Anastasia's gun. "Bully for you. But did you really think I didn't know that you had seduced my father? That you and he were living together when he died? For God's sake! It was obvious, even during the damn shoot.

"For one thing, my father never spanked his children. Only his lovers. The day he thrashed you on the set was final proof."

"Ah. The day of the switched crosses at the forge. That was you?"

"I was a little pissed off when he spanked you and I realized he was at it again. Philandering."

"I don't understand. Why is it a bad thing that I loved your father?"

"You tell me. If there was nothing wrong with it, why keep it such a big secret?"

"That was a mistake. It was Gray's idea, not ours."

"Don't you understand anything?" The voice had turned to a snarl.

"I guess not."

"My father was a very weak man. He claimed to love us—my mother, and us kids—but he was very weak. Until Mother got him to come and live with us, away from everything, on our farm in France. We were all happy. So very happy.

"Then Eddington turned up. Lucifer himself, to tempt my father away from his true self, his true family. And it worked!"

Leah leaned forward, her eyes flaming with fury. "I knew Father would see what a mistake he'd made. He'd see, and he'd come back. He'd be ours again.

"Then he met you. Jezebel. The seductress. And, weak man that he was, he fell under your spell. It wasn't like I didn't warn him that he was playing with fire, as it were."

"But your parents were already divorced when *T & I* started shooting."

"They were constantly breaking up and getting back together. That's what they did."

In an attempt to make her friend see reason, Anastasia softened her voice and said, "Leah, your father was a genius. He loved theater and filmmaking. He was a brilliant director and actor. While he was living with your family in France, he wrote three scripts! It's who he was. You couldn't have been surprised to realize that!"

"He only made plans for his next film because you'd seduced him. He did it for you. What were your tricks? I can understand Peter Dalton falling for them. He was young and naive, and certainly capable of making foolish decisions, as the world found out. But Father? How did you do it?" Leah cocked the gun, not wanting an answer. "You know he would have gotten tired of you, and quickly. That was his pattern, too."

Leah was obviously somewhere in her own little world. Anastasia felt she had ceased to exist, except as the next victim.

"My father promised me he'd do that one film and see how it went. But damn him, by the time it was wrapped, he'd already committed to two other films. He told me it was over with my mother. He was never coming back to us. To any of us."

"Leah, he loved you completely. He got you a job on the set."

"He got me a job writing a fluff book!"

"You were a teenager! I'm sure he would have found more creative things for you to do as you got older."

"You were a teenager, too, Lily. How many creative things did he think of for you to do? At any rate, he wasn't ever going to hire me again. He made that clear after the doves."

"You killed the doves? Pierce knew you killed the doves?"

"A person's got to have a way to release anger. And birds are easy yet satisfying. We had a dovecote in Provence. I'd done it before. My strangling them made Father furious, of course. But it got his attention."

Anastasia didn't want to fathom it. "So you murdered him."

"I thought he'd gotten the message after the fire. I thought you were just another on-set tootsie. Until I got to London to crash with Daddy Dearest. I let myself in with a key I'd nicked when he first rented the flat, and tiptoed to his bedroom to see if he was already asleep. And so he was . . . but not alone. And not, I might add, under the covers. I walked the streets that night, and came up with a sweet little calling card for the next day. So he was the first, and you, slut, will be the last."

Anastasia closed her eyes as the emotions washed over her. She remembered the last night she spent with Pierce. The joy they'd shared, the utter contentment she'd felt in his embrace.

"You're right about one thing," she said. "His death did nearly do me in. I had no interest in stealing him from anyone. But I did love him, so very much. It wasn't a passing fling. Yes, I was living with him when he died. He was my husband.

"Leah, listen to me. All my life I've lost whatever meant the most to me. My father, my chance at school, my mother. But losing my husband was the worst. Especially since Gray covered up the whole thing. By negating the biggest part of who I was, he negated me. I wasn't worthy to have a relationship with Pierce, therefore I simply ceased to exist.

"As you put it, it nearly did me in. I'd made it through everything else. But losing Pierce—it was the end. That's when I began to have panic attacks."

"Shall I start humming 'Hearts and Flowers'? As good friends as we are, it seems there's a final level on which we haven't been completely honest with each other, wouldn't you say, Stepmom?

"Here, slut, this is for you." Leah tossed a book onto Anastasia's bed. "Daddy had signed this for you the day I stopped in for our fateful lunch."

Anastasia casually leaned to pick it up; it was a book of Romantic poetry. Then, equally as casually, she swung her legs around and began to get out of bed.

A shatteringly loud gunshot blasted past her, just over her head. The noise was deafening. Anastasia fell immediately back onto the bed, waiting for the ringing in her ears to quiet, hoping her hearing wouldn't be permanently compromised. Even if permanently was only the next few minutes. "For God's sake, Leah!"

"Don't make me angry, Stacy. I am so enjoying our little *tête-à-tête* here in your secret cottage that you personally led me to last night. Don't be stupid enough to try to outfox me. I'm in charge here, and you know I'm in charge. Your gun is a desperate attempt, while mine is an old friend.

"But do tell how you knew to expect me, even if you thought we had a luncheon date. I am pleased with your progress, little slut. How did you know?"

"Well, it did occur to me that Nicola was incapable of enough planning to buy a dozen bagels, let alone surreptitiously kill nine people over twenty years. And if she thought she was getting points for an infidel head count, why not admit it? Not to mention, I think that a check of her passport will confirm that she didn't leave India until her Master died a few years ago, as she claimed.

"That left a vacuum. It also left the question of the kitchen assistant's description: a thin woman with short black hair. And I had to start asking some hard questions. How did you know to put in your book that the fire in the queen's chamber started on the bed? Why had Pierce not been willing to discuss his suspicions about the arsonist, even with me? Finally, I had to admit that you had access to everywhere a murder had occurred. Not only that, everyone would have let you into their house, or picked you up in their car.

"And . . . Pierce had been eating by himself in the kitchen when he died. If he'd admitted a guest, surely he would have either met with him in the parlor or offered him some food. It seemed likely, therefore, if there was a murderer, it was someone with whom Pierce was casually intimate."

"So you didn't figure it out till last night?"

"No."

"And you were going to use yourself as bait, one last time, to lure me here to lunch. With Scotland Yard waiting, perhaps. Sorry I dropped in early and ruined your plan.

"Live with this, for the last few minutes of your life: you were responsible for all those deaths. Some of them were quite gruesome, especially the poisonings. Compliments of the seductress Lily. You gave me the idea. Did you know that lily-of-the-valley is extremely toxic? A bite of a stalk or even a sip of the water in which they've been standing is enough to kill. Common garden flower. Free poison, no bothersome receipts. Easy to transport. Ghoulish hallucinations. Excruciating pain. Then heart failure. Oooh. I'd have to say your friend Janie was one of the best. Although Bruce's first wife was pretty good as well. At first I was sorry that Bruce had left and she received the order of gourmet takeout. But when her father discovered she'd been poisoned and blamed Bruce—that *was* good for a few jollies.

"Who'd suspect that pretty little lilies are such bad news? That pretty little Lily caused all those people to die. You were right earlier this evening. Guns are such an uncouth, American way to go. Oh well."

Leah Hall had obviously come to the end of what she felt she needed to say.

Anastasia said, "Leah, I'm your friend. Doesn't that count for something in this stalemate?"

"Stalemate? You don't have it in you to kill anyone. Even though it *is* a thrill, it's one you'll never know." Leah turned so she was fully facing Anastasia, and raised her gun squarely to Anastasia's eye level, compelling her intended victim to do the same with her own gun. "You were obviously friends with a Leah who doesn't exist," she said. "Good-bye, Stace."

"Don't do it." The powerful voice came from the door to the hall.

During the split second that Leah turned to look, Anastasia grabbed the book Leah had thrown and backed off the other side of the bed, weapon still pointed.

"Well, well, well. So the reunion goes on, after all," Leah said. "Peter Dalton, as I live and breathe. I've been so hoping to find you, to make you part of our cozy little circle. And here you are, perfectly accessorized for the occasion."

It was true. Peter held Neville's hunting gun, and from his stance, the way he had the gun cocked and positioned, it was clear he knew what he was doing.

"Come on, Leah. Fun's over. You can look back with pride at the havoc you've wreaked and the lives you've wrecked. But I've called the constables; they should be here any second. It's time to stop."

"Oh, all right," Leah said. "I'll turn myself in. 'I've killed nine—oops, now eleven—people, but I'm really sorry, Your Honor. Won't do it again.'"

Anastasia began to silently slide into the space at the head of her bed, putting as much distance as possible between herself and Peter. At least Leah would have to make a choice.

"Leah, please," Peter said firmly. "We'll testify in court to your insanity. I think there are some rather nice mental health wards out there. With luck, you can write a bestselling book."

Anastasia almost smiled. Bless Peter's heart. It was nonsense, but it was keeping Leah's attention away from her own movements.

"You know what gives me the clear advantage in this situation?" Leah asked, as if she hadn't heard. "I'm willing to use my gun."

At that, Anastasia lunged for Leah's chair from behind—and a second loud gun report rocked the room.

Suddenly, there was blood everywhere.

"Oh, dear God. Dear God, dear God," Anastasia said.

And then, Peter had his arm around her and was herding her from the room. She saw then that the blood had come from Leah, who had shot herself in the head.

Peter led Anastasia into the living room and sat her down in an armchair. He turned on the overhead light, then went to the kitchen and got a wet towel. He gently began wiping as much blood off her as possible.

She reached out a trembling hand, and he clasped it between his own.

"It *was* Leah," she whispered in disbelief. "Leah killed Pierce. Leah killed Janie." She turned and looked Peter square in the eyes. "How can this be?"

"I don't know," he said. "But I'm so sorry I doubted you."

"Leah is dead," she said.

He held her gaze.

"If you hadn't been here, *I* would be dead."

"I'm so sorry," he said again. "If I'd really thought Leah

could . . . I never would have let you use yourself as bait to draw her here. Never."

"I knew it had to be Leah, but I didn't really believe it. Thought she'd come tomorrow. Still somehow thought it was a game."

The survivors clung to each other, Leah's blood staining them both.

"I was so disappointed I couldn't talk you into attending the reunion. But supposing you had? What if she'd known you were meeting me here afterwards? We might both be dead."

"I think she probably planned to kill herself after she killed you," Peter said. "It was over. And after killing so much . . . what is there to live for?"

Anastasia had no answer.

"Now, are you all right?" He ran a gentle finger around the periphery of her face. "Because if you are, I'll go out and meet the police."

Anastasia nodded. "But if you do, your anonymous days are over. If you'd like, you can leave. I'll handle it."

There was no mistaking that the boy she'd known had become a man as he stood tall before her. "Thanks for the offer," he said. "But if I've learned anything from my visit with my parents, it's that I can't hide anymore. I have to take responsibility for my life. My whole life.

"Not to mention, they know I'm here. I made the call. Besides," he said, more gently now, "there's no way I'm going to let you go through this alone."

"Thanks," Anastasia said.

He stood and walked resolutely toward the back door.

Anastasia sat for a minute in the sudden silence of the early dawn. Her mind understood what had happened there tonight, but her heart was far from beginning to comprehend.

Much to her surprise, when she looked down at her lap, she found that she was still holding the book that Leah had thrown onto her bed, the one that Pierce had inscribed to her on the day of his death. It was a collection of sonnets and love poems from Shakespeare through the Romantic poets.

She ran her hand carefully over the textured cover. Then she opened it.

Sure enough, there was script in Pierce's firm, magical hand: a poem by W. B. Yeats, which he'd inscribed for her. In those quiet moments she read:

> *When you are old and grey and full of sleep,*
> *And nodding by the fire, take down this book*
> *And slowly read, and dream of the soft look*
> *Your eyes had once, and of their shadows deep;*
>
> *How many loved your moments of glad grace,*
> *And loved your beauty with love false or true,*
> *But one man loved the pilgrim soul in you,*
> *And loved the sorrows of your changing face;*
>
> *And bending down beside the glowing bars,*
> *Murmur, a little sadly, how Love fled*
> *And paced upon the mountains overhead*
> *And hid his face amid a crowd of stars.*

Anastasia closed the book gently and sat, knowing that she could face the cacophony of the coming dawn.

Watch for the next
Movie Mystery:

GRACES TO THE GRAVE

"Lady, you are the cruell'st she alive
if you would lead these graces to the grave…"
Twelfth Night

SHARON LINNÉA's most recent novels are the Eden Thrillers—*Chasing Eden, Beyond Eden,* and *Treasure of Eden,* written with Chaplain (Col.) B.K. Sherer, her best friend since 6th grade.

For the writing of this novel, she owes much to a youthful stint living in a vicarage in Sussex, England, to all of her friends still there, and to years of consorting with known actors.

Sharon lives outside New York City with her husband, son, daughter, quarter horse, Siberian huskies, poochon, and two pairs of cats.

She still hopes someday to have a French country kitchen.

Visit her at SharonLinnea.com